MILLIONAIRE UNDER THE MISTLETOE

MILLIONAIRE UNDER THE MISTLETOE

KIM LAWRENCE
JANICE MAYNARD
LINDA THOMAS-SUNDSTROM

HarperCollins
PUBLISHERS
Since 1817

First Published in Great Britain 2017
By Mills & Boon, an imprint of HarperCollins*Publishers*
1 London Bridge Street, London, SE1 9GF

ISBN: 978-0-263-93174-7

24-1117

Our policy is to use papers that are natural, renewable and recyclable products and made from wood grown in sustainable forests.
The logging and manufacturing processes conform to the legal environmental regulations of the country of origin.

Printed and bound in Spain
by CPI, Barcelona

THE PLAYBOY'S MISTRESS

KIM LAWRENCE

Kim Lawrence lives on a farm in Anglesey with her university lecturer husband, assorted pets who arrived as strays and never left, and sometimes one or both of her boomerang sons. When she's not writing she loves to be outdoors gardening, or walking on one of the beaches for which the island is famous – along with being the place where Prince William and Catherine made their first home!

CHAPTER ONE

DARCY slid her pink feet—the bath had been *very* hot—into a pair of slippers and padded through the quiet flat to the phone. It was nice to have the flat to herself for once. Jennifer was a great flatmate, but she thought silence was something you filled with noise—preferably the loud, throbbing variety! Music-wise the two were not compatible.

Propping the phone against her ear, Darcy hitched the towel wrapped sarong-style, around her slender body a little tighter and waited for someone to pick up. She was just about to hang up when Jack Alexander answered the phone.

'Hi, Dad,' she called cheerfully down the line. 'Is Mum around?' She eased her bottom onto the table-top, anticipating a nice long natter.

'I'm afraid you can't speak to your mother, Darcy…she…she isn't here…'

It wasn't the news that her hyperactive mother wasn't at home that struck Darcy as strange—her community-minded parent was on more village committees than she had fingers to count them on—it was the peculiar note that bordered on panic in her phlegmatic stepfather's voice.

Her post-warm-bath, pre-glass-of-wine, mellow holiday mood evaporated. Darcy wasn't psychic, but she did know Jack, and she had the nasty suspicion that the icy fingers tap-dancing up her spine knew what they were about.

Her heart was thudding as she lightly asked, 'What is it tonight? Practice for the carol concert or the church roof committee…?'

Jack would tell her what was up in his own good time—he wasn't the sort of man who could be hurried. An affectionate smile briefly curved her lips as her thoughts rested on the man who had married her mother—Darcy loved him to bits.

Darcy had been five and her elder brother, Nick, seven when Jack entered their lives. After a couple of years Clare had come along and then, much to everyone's surprise, the unplanned but much loved twins. The Alexanders were a tight-knit family.

'Neither,' came back the strangled response.

The line between Darcy's straight, well-defined, darkish eyebrows deepened; Jack sounded perilously close to tears. This, she reminded herself, is the man who delivered his own grandchild in the back of a Land Rover without breaking sweat. She immediately ditched tactful reticence in favour of the upfront approach.

'What's up, Dad?' she asked bluntly.

'It's your mother...'

Anxiety grabbed Darcy's quivering tummy muscles in an icy fist; eyes wide in alarm, she shot upright from her perch on the console table. All sorts of awful scenarios ran through her head and with some trepidation she put the most alarming of these into words.

'Is Mum *ill*...?'

'No...no, nothing like that; she's...she's...'

A noisy sigh of relief expelled, Darcy slid to the floor.

'She's gone away.'

'Away as in...?'

'She's spending Christmas in a...a *retreat* in Cornwall.'

'But that's the other end of the country!' Darcy heard herself exclaim stupidly—as if the *where* mattered! It was the how and why that were infinitely more important. Her spinning head struggled to make sense of what she was hearing and failed miserably. No matter what else was wrong in her life, there had always been a solid, reliable, constant...Mum... No, this just didn't make sense—no sense at all!

'It wouldn't matter if it was down the road; they don't even have a phone,' her stepfather came back in a heavy, doom-laden tone. 'I don't know what I'm going to do! Everyone's asking after her. She's making the costumes for the school Nativity play, the WI want two-hundred mince pies by Thursday... How do you make mince pies, Darcy...?' he asked pathetically.

'We've got more important things than mince pies to worry about.' As if he needed reminding of that! 'Have you any idea at all why has she done this, Dad? Did you have a row or something?'

'No, nothing like that; she'd been a bit quiet lately...but you're right; it must be my fault.'

'Nonsense!' Darcy meant it. The day she found a man who was half as marvellous as Jack Alexander she was going to stick to him like superglue!

'Apparently she needs time alone. Are you still there...? Darcy...Darcy...?'

'Sorry, Dad, I dropped the phone.' There was a distinctly surreal feel about the entire situation. People like Cathy Alexander didn't suffer from identity crises, they didn't walk out on their family with no proper explanation!

'God, Darcy, what am I going to do...?' She could hear the escalating panic in her stepfather's gruff voice. 'Sam, Beth and the children arrive from the States on Friday. It's too late to put them off.'

'No, you mustn't do that!' Darcy replied swiftly. Since Jack's daughter from his first marriage had moved to the States the opportunities for Jack to see her and his only grandchild were few and far between.

'Nick rang to say to expect him at the end of the week, and no doubt Clare will show up some time.'

Darcy permitted herself a wry smile—it was so like Clare not to commit herself to a date.

'Your grandmother is likely to drop in on us at any moment. Can you imagine what she's going to make of this…? At the last count we were doing Christmas dinner for fifteen people that I know of, and the Aga's gone out and I can't light it! I never did have the knack with the darned thing like your mother has…'

Darcy could hear him gulp down the line. She took a deep breath; desperate circumstances required drastic solutions.

'Don't panic,' she instructed her harassed stepfather with shameless hypocrisy. 'If I pack now I should be there about… There shouldn't be too much traffic at this time of night, should there…?'

'Your skiing holiday, Darcy!'

Darcy recognised a token protest when she heard it.

'I know how much you've been looking forward to it…'

Darcy allowed herself a final indulgent moment to wistfully visualise crisp snow-covered slopes, twinkling mountain villages and the hunky outdoor type she had been destined to meet amidst the après-ski *gluwein* before she squared her slight shoulders.

'With my luck I'd probably have come back with several limbs in plaster.' You had to be philosophical about these things.

Did her cancellation insurance cover family crises caused by the parent of the policy-holder unexpectedly needing to find herself…? Somehow Darcy didn't think so.

'You can't cancel,' Jennifer insisted a little later that evening as she sat on Darcy's bed. Darcy smiled and continued to replace the skiing gear in her suitcase with clothes more suited to Christmas in a remote corner of the Yorkshire

Dales. 'You've been looking forward to it all year. I don't see why it has to be you; why can't Clare go home to help?'

Darcy laughed. 'I don't think domesticity is really Clare's scene,' she responded wryly. Her beautiful, talented and slightly spoilt half-sister had a heart of gold, but she needed therapy to recover from a broken fingernail.

'And it's yours...?'

Darcy couldn't deny this. 'I'll have to learn, won't I?'

Jennifer, seeing her friend wasn't to be dissuaded, sighed. 'Well, I think you're being a fool.'

Darcy shrugged. 'So what's new?'

Jennifer's expression darkened. '*That*,' she said angrily, 'wasn't your fault!'

'Tell that to Michael's wife and children.'

This year Reece Erskine wasn't taking any chances. He was going to lose himself in the wilds of deepest, darkest Yorkshire until the so-called *festive* season was well and truly over!

So he didn't like Christmas... Why was it considered a crime when a man refused to participate in the manic few weeks that culminated in several days of gluttony in the company of people you avoided for the rest of the year?

Of course, the most insupportable part was the fact that everyone was so *understanding*. He refused to put on a paper party hat and suddenly he was failing to come to terms with his loss. He'd had it with pop psychology, no matter how well-intentioned!

After the debacle last year, when the girlfriend—and he used the term in the loosest possible sense—of the moment, armed with champagne, sympathy and a criminally sexy nightie, had tracked him down to the hotel he'd holed up in, he wasn't leaving any clues. She'd proved to be a scarily tenacious woman! She'd had her revenge, though; she'd sold the story of their so-called 'stormy relationship' to a tabloid.

Whether he would have been quite so keen to avail himself of Greg's hospitality if he'd known that the renovations of the big Victorian pile had been at such an early stage was questionable, but that was academic now he was here.

'God, man, you're getting soft,' he told himself in disgust. His deep voice sounded eerily loud in the empty lofty-ceilinged room. 'What's a rat or two between friends...? A bit of good old-fashioned frontier spirit is what's called for here. Who wants to call Room Service when he could pump up the old Primus stove?' His tone lacked conviction even to his own ears.

Having unrolled his sleeping bag, he made his way into the overgrown garden that stretched down towards what sounded like a river in full spate. He tightened the collar of his leather jacket around his neck; it was almost as cold out here as inside.

From the bone-chilling temperature in the old place even after he'd lit that smoky fire in the cavernous grate, he suspected he'd need to invest in a few thick blankets to supplement his state-of-the-art bedding, which might well live up to its press and be able to withstand a night in the North Pole, but the Yorkshire Dales in December—forget it!

He looked around in distaste at the bleak landscape. God, the place was so *grey*—grey and extremely wet! It was baffling when you considered how many people waxed lyrical about the area.

The periphery of his vision picked on something that broke the dismal grey monotony. Something suspiciously like a human voice raised in song drifted across from the general direction of that fleeting glimpse of scarlet. Reece immediately felt indignant. Greg had sworn on his very alive grandmother's grave that Reece wouldn't see another human being unless he wanted to—and even then it wouldn't be easy!

Reece had come away with the distinct and very welcome impression that the natives were hostile to strangers.

Eager to defend his solitude against intruders, Reece followed the melody to its source, wrecking his shiny new boots in the process. He discovered the clear, pure sounds actually came from just beyond the boundary of the sprawling grounds. He could no longer eject the songbird, but his curiosity was piqued.

His days as a choirboy enabled him to correctly identify the number as *The Coventry Carol*. How very seasonal; how very corny, he thought, his lip curling.

Acting on impulse—which wasn't something he made a habit of—Reece swung himself up onto the lower bare branch of a convenient oak tree. The identity of the owner of the bell-like tones was going to bug him unless he satisfied his curiosity. Besides, if he was going to be carolled on a regular basis it was as well to be forewarned.

From his lofty vantage point he could now see into what must be the garden of the sprawling stone-grey house that sat at the bottom of the lane that led up to Greg's investment.

In the summer the green-painted summer-house was a magical place, where wisteria tumbled with vigorous old-fashioned roses up the clapboarded walls and over the roof. In Darcy's childhood it had been the place her knight in shining armour was going to propose. However, the romance was purely a seasonal thing; in the winter it became a cold, unfriendly place her childish imagination had peopled with ghouls and similar nasties—it was still private, though, hence the bit of impromptu choir practice.

Her voice, never in her view solo material at the best of times, was every bit as rusty as she'd expected.

'I can't do it!' she groaned.

That new vicar, she decided darkly, was a dangerous man, who had shamelessly used his spaniel eyes and a judicious amount of moral blackmail until she had almost been falling over herself to volunteer to stand in for her musical mother and perform the solo in the Christmas carol concert.

It wasn't until she'd been halfway down the lane from the church that the full horror of what she'd done had hit Darcy. She'd suffered from terminal stage fright since that awful occasion in infants' school when, after she'd been given the linchpin role of the donkey in the nativity play, the strain had proved too much! She'd frozen and had held up proceedings until she had been carried bodily off the makeshift stage.

What's the worst that could happen…? What's a bit of public humiliation between friends…?

A loud noise like a pistol shot interrupted her gloomy contemplation of her future as a figure of fun. If she hadn't automatically taken a startled step backwards the large individual who along with a piece of rotten branch had fallen at her feet would have landed directly on top of her.

As it was, the summer-house didn't escape so lightly—the jagged end of the branch penetrated the roof, ripping off several tiles, and travelled downwards, gouging a nasty big hole in the side of the structure. But at that moment Darcy's concerns were reserved for the man lying in a crumpled heap at her feet.

She dropped down on her knees beside him; phrases like 'recovery position' and 'clear airway' were running through her head. Despite the first aid course she'd completed early that year, she felt completely unprepared to cope with an actual emergency now that one had fallen at her feet.

'Please, please, don't be dead,' she whispered, pressing her fingers to the pulse spot on his neck. To her immense relief, she immediately felt a steady, reassuringly strong beat.

Grunting with effort, Reece rolled onto his back. For only the third time in his life he was literally seeing stars. He ruthlessly gathered his drifting senses, the halo vanished and he realised he wasn't seeing an angel but a golden-headed schoolboy. Given the clear soprano of his singing voice, the lad had a surprisingly low, pleasing speaking voice.

'I'll do my level best,' the leather-clad figure promised, much to Darcy's relief.

'I live just over there.' The scarf she wore wrapped twice around her neck prevented her turning her head to indicate the overgrown path behind them. 'I'll go and get help.'

Darcy froze with shock when a large hand curled firmly around her forearm.

'No, don't do that.' He hadn't figured out the extent of his injuries yet, and if the boy disappeared who knew if he'd ever come back or get help? The kid looked scared half to death.

'Give me a hand to get up.'

He seemed determined to get up with or without her help, so Darcy shrugged philosophically and helpfully slid her arm under the shoulders of the tall, dark-headed figure.

It wasn't as easy as she'd expected; he might be lean, but her unexpected visitor was endowed with a generous share of muscle and there wasn't a single useful roll of excess flesh or fat to grab onto.

'Ahh...!'

The involuntary grunt of pain that escaped his firmly clamped lips made Darcy jerk back with a squeamish squeak.

'Did I hurt you...? I...I'm *so* sorry.'

If all he'd done was bust his shoulder he'd got off pretty lightly. Reece supported his injured arm with his healthy arm and hauled himself upright, ignoring the sharp, burning pain in his shoulder as best he could. Nostrils flared, he spared the hovering boy a brief glance. The kid had a soft round face, snub nose and big blue eyes, and he looked as if he was going to throw up—which made two of them.

'Not your fault,' he gritted. The knowledge that he couldn't blame anyone but himself for his present situation wasn't doing anything to improve Reece's frayed temper.

'Should you be doing that?' Darcy wondered fretfully, watching the tall figure get slowly to his feet.

The stranger ignored her query. 'Listen, I think I might have hurt my shoulder.'

From where Darcy was standing there didn't seem much 'might' about it. It was obvious he was in pain; it was also obvious he was more good-looking than any man had a right to be.

Her slightly awed gaze was tinged with vague resentment as she took in the impressive overall effect of the combination of square jaw, sharp high cheekbones, wide, firm mouth and straight, strong, patrician nose. Even if you took that rich, thick dark hair complete with auburn highlights and those stunning, thickly lashed green eyes out of the equation, he was knockout material; with them he became almost *too* handsome.

Those spectacular eyes were at that moment slightly dazed as he looked around, obviously trying to get his bearings.

'I've got a phone in my pocket.' Lifting his arm gingerly from his chest, Reece nodded towards the breast pocket of his leather jacket. 'Could you fish it out for me...?'

The kid was looking at him as if he had two heads, which, given the cautionary tales that were drummed into the youth of today about strangers, was hardly surprising. He attempted a strained smile.

'I'm quite harmless.' He used the tone he normally reserved for frightened animals—perhaps it would work on kids too?

Darcy almost laughed at this preposterous claim—no man with a mouth like his could be classed as harmless! She withdrew her gaze from the said mouth with some difficulty—it was, after all, rude to stare.

She took a deep breath; she felt oddly reluctant to touch him, which was strange because she usually had to repress her naturally tactile nature—men especially could take a spontaneous hug the wrong way, as she'd learnt to her cost!

'Inside pocket.'

Darcy swallowed and for some reason got a lot clumsier. Her nostrils twitched, and her tummy muscles went all quivery, her twitching nose detected a faint whiff of expensive masculine cologne, but most of all she got a noseful of freshly scrubbed *male*. He felt warm, and despite the sub-zero temperatures she suddenly felt uncomfortably hot; she averted her flushed face as her fingers skated lightly over the surface of a broad, solid chest.

The sad thing was this was the closest she'd been to a male since Michael—*How sad is that?* Perhaps I'll be reduced to tripping up sexy strangers so I can grope them, she reflected with an angry self-derisive sniff.

It was a relief when she finally retrieved the phone and held it up for his inspection. They could both see straight away that the mangled mess was never going to work again.

The stranger swore; considering the circumstances, Darcy thought he was quite restrained. She had no inkling that he was restraining himself in deference to the presence of an impressionable youth.

'You must have fallen on it,' she said sympathetically.

He turned his head stiffly, his green eyes gazing directly down into her face. 'Brilliant deduction,' he observed nastily.

Darcy coloured angrily; so what if it hadn't been the

most intelligent thing in the world to say? *She* wasn't the one who'd been stupid enough to climb up a rotten tree. Which reminded her. Why had he been climbing a tree…? His clothes, which she had noticed straight off were extremely expensive-looking, were not what she'd call accepted tree-climbing gear.

Some people never lost touch with the inner child, but somehow she didn't think this man was one of them—in fact, it was hard to imagine that he'd *ever* been a child. He gave the impression of having emerged into this world complete with cynicism and raw sex appeal.

Reece bit back the blighting retort that hovered on the tip of his tongue and forced himself to smile placatingly at the boy.

'Are there any grown-ups around, lad…? Your parents…?'

Lad! Darcy blinked incredulously. 'What did you…?'

She'd be the first to admit that she was no raving beauty, but although she'd never brought traffic to a halt, or reduced a crowded room to awed appreciative silence like Clare, she had turned a head or two in her time. *Lad…!* Nobody had ever implied she was butch before!

True, she hadn't put on any make-up this morning, and add to that the fact the yellow cagoule she wore was a cast-off from one of the twins and was thickly padded enough to disguise her unchildlike curves completely, then just *maybe* his mistake was understandable; especially if he'd fallen on his head.

Her lips pursed; for a moment she couldn't actually decide whether or not she was insulted, then her ready sense of humour came to her rescue.

I've always said I don't want concessions made for my sex, that I don't want to be treated as a sex object—well, now's my chance!

Having three brothers, she'd learnt at an early age it was better to laugh at herself before they had the chance.

'My dad's at home.' She couldn't resist the naughty impulse to raise her normal husky tone to her approximation of a reedy boyish treble.

She gestured towards the path half-hidden by a massive holly bush smothered with red berries. 'It's not far; can you manage?' she wondered, her eyes travelling with an increasingly doubtful frown up and down his tall frame; underneath that naturally olive skin-tone he didn't look a good colour.

'You'll be the first to know if I can't,' came the dry response.

'But your head's bleeding.'

'It's nothing.'

Darcy shrugged; if he wanted to play the macho hard man it was nothing to her.

'Be careful of the...' Darcy waited like a worried little mother hen as her unlikely charge avoided the motley collection of dirty boots, Wellingtons and trainers which always seemed to breed in the back porch. 'Dad!' she yelled lustily, preceding him into the rustic surroundings of the kitchen.

If he hadn't been clutching his arm Reece would have clutched his head—the kid's piercing tone had increased the throb in his head to the point where he found it difficult to focus.

Her three brothers were already in the kitchen, and her yell brought Jack in matter of seconds.

'Good God, what's happened...?' her stepfather gasped, staring in horror at the blood smeared all over her jacket.

'Don't worry, it's not mine,' Darcy assured him.

The stranger swayed gently; it was a development that alarmed Darcy. 'It's his,' she explained, placing a supportive hand beneath the tall man's elbow. 'Part of that oak tree next door fell through the roof of the summer-house.' She gently led her white-faced charge properly inside.

Reece bided his time, waiting for the tidal waves of nausea to pass.

'I've been telling the new owner's agent since the summer that thing was dangerous!' Jack exclaimed. 'Are you sure you're all right, Darcy?' He scrutinised her healthy-looking, pink-cheeked face worriedly. 'Hurt anywhere?'

'I'm fine.' Darcy unwrapped the looped scarf from around her throat.

'And you, Mr…?'

The dazed-looking stranger with blood running down the side of his face closed his eyes and leaned heavily against the wall. An anxious Jack looked to Darcy to supply the information.

Her shoulders lifted. 'Don't ask me—I've no idea who he is.'

'How come you were in the summer-house with a guy and you don't know his name?' Nick wondered, regarding the stranger with a suspicious light in his hostile blue eyes.

'I wasn't in the summer-house; I was outside.' Darcy kept her impatience in check—Nick always chose all the wrong moments to play the protective big brother; he was the most infuriatingly inconsistent person she knew.

'Doing what?' Nick persisted doggedly.

Darcy rolled her eyes in exasperation before returning her attention to the man beside her. 'You should sit down,' she said in soft aside to the object of her brother's suspicions.

'Give me a minute,' the stranger responded tersely, resisting her efforts to point him in the right direction. Darcy was a strong girl but she knew right away that moving this man against his will was beyond her capabilities.

'Harry, Charlie, could you give me a hand?' she called to her younger brothers.

The twins shook their identical heads in unison.

'We'd like to, but…' Harry began.

'There's blood…' Charlie completed with a shudder of disgust.

Darcy, in no mood on this occasion to see the amusing side of a pair of strapping, beefy specimens who came over 'funny' at the sight of blood, gave a snort of exasperation. 'You're hopeless, the pair of you!'

'Wimps,' Charlie agreed cheerfully.

Harry nodded his agreement. 'Maybe he's one of those contractors working on the Hall.'

'Nah! They've all gone home for the holiday,' his identical twin pointed out. 'Besides, does he look like a builder to you…? He's obviously loaded.'

Darcy was inclined to agree with Charlie, but she couldn't help but reflect that the injured stranger looked more than physically capable of the odd bit of manual labour. Her mind drifted back to the way the hard, muscular contours of his lean torso and broad chest had felt— With a muffled snort of dismay she brought her reflections to an abrupt halt mid-drool.

The tiny sound drew Jack's concerned attention.

She flushed uncomfortably, shook her head and silently mouthed 'I'm fine', which she was, if you discounted the fact she was sleazing over a total stranger who was bleeding on their kitchen floor. She grabbed a clean tea towel from the dresser drawer to stem the flow.

'Maybe he's the bloke that bought the place,' Darcy heard Harry suggest.

Reece, who was feeling less awful, noticed a little hazily that the notion seemed to afford amusement all round.

'My God, mate, but you've been done,' the instigator of the theory sniggered, digging his twin in the ribs.

Darcy gave a long-suffering sigh. 'I hardly think now is the right time for a cross-examination,' she told them repressively.

At first it had felt as if the room was full of a lot of people. On closer examination Reece now realised there were actually only four besides himself and the choirboy, all male. The two youngest, despite being almost his own height, were scarcely more than boys, and either they were identical twins or he was seeing double.

'Shut up!' With enviable lung power the diminutive figure beside him silenced the assembly. 'Let's not get side-tracked here; it doesn't matter who he is—he's had an accident. Charlie, go get the First Aid kit.'

'I don't know…'

Darcy, wise to male helplessness ploys, was ahead of him. 'First shelf down in the bathroom.' She turned to the younger—by five minutes—of her twin brothers. 'Harry, get the dogs out of here.' With a lot of noisy encouragement the dogs eventually removed themselves from the chairs.

Reece remained mildly disorientated while his youthful rescuer continued to throw out a steady stream of orders as if they were going out of fashion to everyone, including himself. The hell of it was he found himself obeying the kid and meekly sitting down in the larger of the two armchairs. The small figure was arguing with the dark-haired male around his own age.

'How should I know why he was up a tree? Maybe he's a tree surgeon…?' Her elder brother had a very suspicious nature and seemed to have jumped to the deeply embarrassing and bizarre conclusion that she was trying to cover up some sort of secret assignation.

Darcy couldn't help but wistfully wonder what life was like with a few secret assignations—alas, unless she could rid herself of her wholesome image and get herself a bit of glamour it seemed unlikely that she would ever find out!

'My name's Reece Erskine.' So much for anonymity.

Nobody started in recognition at the sound of his name—Maybe I'm not as famous as I think, he wondered. A self-deprecating little smile made his mobile lips quiver as he relaxed a little.

'I don't need to trouble you; if I could just use your phone…' His firm words only elicited a few fleeting glances of benevolent dismissal.

Reece wasn't used to having his opinion dismissed and he found the novel experience irritating. It was even more irritating that he didn't have enough functioning brain cells to demonstrate to them how very much in control he really was.

'Shouldn't we call an ambulance?' a worried Jack Alexander appealed to his eldest stepchildren.

'Was he out long?' Nick asked his sister.

'I'm not sure…'

'I wasn't unconscious at all.' Reece's jaw tightened; he might just as well have spoken to the brick wall beside him for the notice anyone was taking.

'It would probably be quicker to take him to Casualty ourselves.' Darcy held out her hand expectantly as young Charlie returned conspicuously empty-handed.

'I can't find it.'

She gave a sigh of exasperation and glared up at her tall young brother. 'Do I have to do everything myself?' she wondered witheringly.

To Reece's amazement, the big guy shifted uncomfortably and looked sheepish before he joined his twin at the far end of the room. He was finding the family dynamics of this noisy household deeply confusing. Maybe it's me…? Maybe I'm concussed, he thought. He closed his eyes and the room continued to spin.

Darcy took the stairs at the far end of the room two steps at a time. She tore along the narrow upper hallway, shedding her layers as she went—the First Aid kit was exactly where she'd said it would be. Why couldn't men find something when it was right under their noses…?

'Learnt helplessness,' she snorted in knowledgeable disgust, and Mum let them get away with it, she thought disapprovingly as she rapidly retraced her steps. Her respect for what her mother accomplished on the home front had increased by leaps and bounds since she'd arrived home.

She ripped the scrunchy thing that had slid down to the slippery end of her shiny pony-tail free and shoved it in her pocket before she gave her head a little shake and lifted her fine hair free of the collar of her ribbed polo-necked sweater.

'I'll just clean up this head wound first.' He endured her cleaning the small but deep head wound with stoicism. 'I think it might be your collar-bone.' Darcy bent over the chair, bringing her face almost on a level with his.

He didn't know where she'd come from but he wasn't complaining; she was a major improvement on all the brawn. He watched her narrow, slender hands as she set about her task. They were nice hands, and it was an even nicer face. A roundish face with a pointy little chin, a hint of sultriness about the full lower lip…? No more than a hint, he decided, revising his original estimate as she raised the big blue kitten eyes to his face and murmured… 'Sorry. I broke mine once,' she continued in a slightly husky, oddly familiar voice. 'I know how much it hurts. I think it'll be less painful if it's supported, but if I hurt you too much, yell.'

'I will.'

Darcy's eyes lifted; under the scrutiny of those wide-spaced blue eyes, Reece got that strange feeling of familiarity again as she gave an unconvinced little smile.

'A fine little nurse our Darcy is,' the fatherly-looking figure remarked fondly.

Darcy; where had he heard that before…?

'They'll want to X-ray you in the hospital, I expect.'

She was halfway through tying the supportive sling gently around his neck before a stunned Reece saw what had been blindingly obvious all along.

The schoolboy and the slender, but very obviously *feminine* blonde were one and the same person!

'You're a girl!' he blurted out unthinkingly.

The note of resentment in the shocked cry made Darcy's lips twitch and her stepfather's expression grow concerned.

'Perhaps I ought to call that ambulance.'

Darcy put the final twitch to the knot around his neck and straightened up, brushing her hands down the gentle curve of her thighs.

'I'm Darcy.'

'Reece,' he gulped, not meeting her eyes. Since discovering the gender of his rescuer Reece seemed unable to stop looking at her breasts; they were full, rounded and at that moment strained against the tight sweater she wore.

She bent a little closer. '34 C,' she whispered.

His head came up with a jerk; predictably she was smiling.

In someone more fair-skinned the deepening of colour beneath that even olive tone of his skin would have been a full-scale blush.

'Mr Erskine thought I was a boy,' she explained solemnly to her family. Having been the victim of this mortifying case of mistaken identity, she didn't feel inclined to spare her patient's embarrassment.

After a startled pause, this announcement was greeted

with predictable hilarity. The twins cracked up; even Jack looked amused.

'Now, there's a novelty.' Nick lost his habitual sardonic sneer as he grinned in malicious delight at his sister.

Not wanting to come over as someone totally without humour, Reece smiled—it wasn't the easiest thing he'd ever done.

Darcy wasn't a vindictive girl—she'd made her point, and she had no wish to see him squirm excessively. She decided to take the spotlight off his mistake.

'Wasn't it you, Nick who gave up your seat on the train to the pregnant lady who *wasn't*…?'

Nick winced. 'Don't remind me.'

Reece's eyes did another unscheduled detour—this time in the direction of her flat midriff. There was no possibility that anyone would make that particular mistake in her case. Her jeans were cinched in around an impossibly narrow waist by a wide leather belt, and the blue denim clung to a nicely rounded bottom and slender thighs… The more details he took in, the more he felt inclined to think he really was concussed—nothing else could explain the fact he'd mistaken her for a boy!

'I'll take him to the hospital.'

'That's all right, Darce, I'll do it,' Nick offered.

Darcy reached up and ruffled his hair affectionately. 'No, you've just had a long drive—I'll do it. Always supposing you two filled up my car last night after you used it.'

The blond-haired seventeen-year-olds looked innocently hurt that she'd raised the possibility they might have found a better use for her twenty quid.

'As if we would.'

The three older members of their family snorted.

'It's really not necessary…' Reece began, getting to his feet. 'I've no wish to impose.'

The pocket-sized blonde looked amused by his attempt to regain a bit of dignity. 'You've already imposed, Mr Erskine,' she responded bluntly. 'So you might as well get your money's worth.'

CHAPTER TWO

REECE levered himself into the cramped front seat of the Beetle. He rapidly discovered there was a soggy patch in the worn upholstery. A quick survey revealed the half-open window was the most likely culprit. He tried to close it, but it seemed as though the ventilation was permanent.

Reece, who liked his cars the same way he liked his women—sleek, racy and maintenance-free—gritted his teeth and settled back to make the best of it.

'I'll be with you in a minute,' the diminutive blonde promised, bending down to peer with concern at him through the window.

Reece saw she'd discarded the yellow cagoule thing in favour of more feminine garb—a dark ankle-length trench coat that billowed as she ran off down the steep path towards the grim-faced big brother, who, it seemed to Reece, was the only one of the family with enough common sense to view him, a total stranger, with even a hint of suspicion.

A heated conversation ensued and, thanks to the broken window and prevailing icy wind, Reece could hear snatches of what they were saying.

'Give me the keys, Darcy.'

'Don't be stupid, Nicky, you're shattered.'

'And you're not?'

A blustery gust snatched away the next section of the conversation but it involved a considerable amount of gesticulation—it seemed to Reece that his colourful neighbours favoured extravagant body language.

'What if he's a homicidal psychopath…or a sex maniac? Or worse?'

Reece's muzzy, throbbing head didn't immediately make the connection between the sinister character they were discussing and himself until the brother continued in a suspicious growl, '...And I'm sure I've seen his face somewhere before. Erskine...Erskine...why does that sound familiar...? Don't laugh, Darce, I'm serious. Your trouble is you're too damned trusting.'

Under the circumstances, it seemed more than legitimate to eavesdrop. Reece leant casually towards the open window but unfortunately a large dog chose that particular moment to poke his nose through the gap and lick him affectionately on the forehead. He withdrew swiftly to avoid any more displays of overt affection.

'See!' he heard the girl cry triumphantly. 'Wally likes him.'

He assumed the canine approval finally swung it because a few moments later the blonde came jogging energetically down the path towards the car. She fended off the affections of the dog, who bounded over as he saw her coming, and only clicked her tongue in irritation as she brushed off the large muddy paw-prints on her coat.

'No, Wally, you can't come today.'

Reece didn't think he'd miss the large, slobbering dog.

'Sorry I was so long.' Darcy's smile faded as her eyes collided with the large stranger's green eyes and their gazes meshed. His stare had a heady, narcotic quality, and for a moment Darcy was physically incapable of looking away.

A breathless, confusing moment later she was free of that mesmeric gaze, and other than a heart that was still thudding too fast and loud and a dryness in her throat there were no lasting side-effects. It all happened so fast she wasn't really sure in retrospect if anything unusual had happened—he certainly wasn't acting as if it had.

Naturally she was relieved to see that the clouded vagueness had gone from his eyes, but she didn't consider the cool, analytical detachment that had replaced it to be an unqualified improvement!

'I'm not in any position to complain...?' The fleeting smile might have softened his hard eyes but Darcy was making a point of not looking—she didn't want a repeat performance of that silliness! The little shudder that chased its chilly pathway up her slender spine had nothing to do with the weather.

'Darcy.' For a fleeting, selfish moment she almost regretted not letting Nick, even in his exhausted condition, drive him.

'Of course...*Darcy*. I'm in your debt, Darcy.'

Darcy could almost hear him thinking, Outlandish name...outlandish family. She had a strong suspicion that had this man not considered himself in her debt he would have had no qualms about complaining; he didn't give her the impression of someone who had a particularly high patience quotient. She just couldn't see him suffering in silence.

'I'm not keeping score.' She decided to make allowances for his attitude. I probably wouldn't want to smile either if I'd just bashed my head and bust my arm, she reasoned.

'You're just being neighbourly, I suppose?'

This time it was impossible to misinterpret the acerbic scepticism in his voice. She twisted the excess moisture from the ends of her wet hair as she slid in beside him. With a wet splat the hair was casually flicked over her shoulder. There was a faint puzzled line between her feathery eyebrows as she turned in her seat and levelled her thoughtful gaze at him.

'Is that so unusual?' she asked, unable to keep the edge from her voice.

'Only slightly less so than an honest politician.'

Reece had noticed straight off that at some point during the last few minutes she'd paused to anoint those wide lips with a covering of glossy lipstick, and the soft colour clung stubbornly to the damp outline. This evidence of female vanity amused Reece; it also drew his attention to the soft lushness of her mouth.

Through the miasma of dull pain he felt his libido drowsily stir. It was the sort of mouth it was a crime not to kiss. Reece shifted uncomfortably as she gazed trustingly over at him. That was definitely one for the modern-man-is-a-myth school.

'Well, it looks like your cynicism has survived the crack on the skull intact—congratulations.'

'You sound disapproving…?'

Darcy shrugged; she didn't fight with people who were in urgent need of medical attention—even if they were misguided.

'In my experience people rarely do anything for nothing,' he announced, authoritatively doling out some more of his homespun cynicism.

This was a man who had very definite opinions, she decided, and a strong belief in his own infallibility. Darcy was beginning to suspect it might be mixed blessings that Reece Erskine had recovered his wits—he was one seriously joyless individual. In a different situation she might have been tempted to put up a strong argument against this jaundiced slant on life, but under the circumstances she contented herself with a gentle, 'I promise you, I have no hidden motives.'

Despite her assurance, his silent response—this man could do things with an eyebrow that defied belief!—made it abundantly clear that he wouldn't have taken her words at face value if she'd had her hand on a stack of Bibles.

She found it increasingly hard to hide her growing antipathy as she carefully scraped a clear area in the condensation on the windscreen in a businesslike manner.

Reece couldn't decide if he was being reprimanded or

not. However, there was nothing ambiguous about her disapproval—the stuff was emanating from her in waves! He caught the full force of it almost as clearly as the light perfume that pervaded her smallish person—his nostrils twitched; it was light, flowery and vaguely distracting, but it made a pleasant change from the wet-dog smell that wafted every so often from the direction of the old blanket flung over the back seat.

He watched as she wiped the excess moisture from her face with the back of her hand; her skin was remarkably clear, creamy pale and very lightly freckled.

'She doesn't like wet weather,' Darcy explained defensively as the engine spluttered and fizzled on the first three attempts.

'Who doesn't…?'

'Bingo!' Darcy gave a gentle sigh of relief when the engine eventually came to life. 'She's temperamental sometimes,' she explained, banging the dashboard affectionately.

Reece wasn't really surprised that she endowed the rusty pile of metal with human characteristics—it was entirely in keeping with the sentimental, mawkish traits this girl had displayed so far.

'The heater will warm up in a minute,' she promised with another trusting beam in his direction—she wasn't the type to hold a grudge, it seemed. 'I'll take the back road and we'll be there in no time at all.'

'Good,' he said, turning his face deliberately to the dismal view through the window. He hoped she'd take the hint and leave him in peace, since there wasn't any place he could escape if she didn't.

The snub was deliberate enough to bring a flush of annoyance to her cheeks. There was nothing Darcy would have liked more than to let her moody passenger brood in peace; he wasn't her idea of the ideal travelling companion—not by a long chalk!

The problem was he'd had a bump on the head; for all she knew, he might have a fractured skull! If he dozed off, how was she to know if he'd just fallen asleep or lapsed into a coma? This alarming possibility made her search his face surreptitiously for signs of imminent collapse—she found none.

But she did discover that in the subdued light her passenger's to-die-for bone-structure had an almost menacing quality. Nick's outlandish hypotheses were still fresh in her mind, and Darcy reasoned that this explained the small bubble of anxiety which she sensibly pushed aside—at least she *thought* it was anxiety that was responsible for the adrenalin surge that had her body on red alert.

The idea of being stuck miles away from medical assistance with an unconscious man had limited appeal for Darcy. No, the fastidious and reserved Mr Erskine was going to stay awake whether he liked it or not!

Trying to keep her growing uneasiness from her voice, she asked, 'What brings you to this part of the world?' Only a comment on the weather, she decided, could be less innocuous—not that you'd think so by his tight-lipped, rude response.

'Solitude.' *Surely* she'd take the hint now.

With anyone else Darcy would have felt inclined to put down this display of boorish bad manners to pain and discomfort—*with anyone else*…!

He considered himself a tolerant, patient sort of bloke, but ten minutes and what felt like several hundred questions later Reece was having trouble controlling his temper.

'You can't possibly be spending Christmas at the Hall!'

He hadn't come right out and said so—actually the gorgeous but tight-lipped Mr Erskine hadn't come right out and said *anything* without prompting, and then it had been as vague and uninformative as he could make it—but by a process of elimination Darcy was now pretty sure the injured hunk was actually staying at the semi-derelict Hall for the duration of the holiday.

'Oh…?' Reece wasn't about to let on that he'd been thinking much the same thing himself. After all his furtive planning he was going to end up holed up in some tinsel-decked hotel again this year.

Darcy felt encouraged to pursue her point—by his standards, this response had been positively garrulous.

In the cramped conditions—the car hadn't been constructed with his length of leg in mind—he lost all feeling in his right foot. Reece slowly shifted his right leg, rotating his ankle. His muscle-packed thigh nudged against the blonde's leg.

A startled, gusty breath snagged in Darcy's throat. A sensation that was all fizzing sexual awareness and no common sense dramatically surged through her, coalescing in a squirmy mess low in her belly.

Help, where had that come from?

The momentary distraction almost had disastrous consequences.

'Hell!' She braked sharply to allow the bedraggled cat dazed by the headlights to cross from one side of the narrow lane to the other. The feral creature disappeared into the dark undergrowth. 'Whew! Close call.' Her heartbeat slowed down to a steady canter as they accelerated away.

You could say that again! The abrupt halt had sent Reece's head on a collision course with the windscreen—the seat restraint was the only thing that had stopped him making contact. The pressure against his damaged ribs was exquisitely painful. It was becoming obvious to Reece that his chauffeur was the type of bleeding heart who saw no conflict in risking life and limb to save a dumb animal—probably the less appealing the better.

'Are you all right?'

Now she asks! 'I'm fine!'

Darcy's dark brows shot quizzically towards her fair hairline; his taut tone had been several degrees to the right of brusque.

'You're obviously not.' No doubt such stoicism was admirable but in this instance not really practical. 'Have you hurt yourself some more…? Shall I stop the car…?'

And prolong the agony of sharing space with Miss Sweetness and Light? *Anything*, he decided, was better than that—even replying to her incessant questions for another five minutes.

She obviously wasn't going to be satisfied until he owned up to something. 'I jarred my shoulder. *Why* can't I be staying at the Hall…?' he asked before she could press the point any further.

'Well, leaving aside your injuries…'

'Yes, let's do that…'

Repressing the angry retort that hovered on the tip of her tongue, Darcy jammed her foot on the brake as the lights ahead turned red. 'And the fact that the place is uninhabitable…'

'I found it quite cosy.'

'It's Christmas!'

'Your point being…?'

'Time of good cheer and loving your fellow man… Does that ring any bells…?'

The cynical light in his hooded, secretive eyes intensified. 'And come the New Year I can go back to screwing the bastards…?' he queried hopefully.

The sound of an impatient car horn brought her attention to the green light. 'Are you always unpleasant just for the hell of it?'

'It does give me a nice glow,' he admitted glibly.

'I don't think you've got the hang of the Christmas-spirit thing, Mr Erskine.'

'It's Reece, and as far as I'm concerned, Darcy, Christmas is just like any other day of the year...'

'But...'

'...except, of course, for the exceptionally high hypocrisy factor.'

'You mean you don't celebrate at all?' Darcy knew that it was none of her business how this man celebrated or didn't during the festive season, but for some reason she just couldn't let it go. 'What about your family...?'

'I don't have a family.' Reece hardly even felt a twinge of guilt as he brutally disposed of his numerous relatives.

'Oh!' Darcy, who was pretty blessed in that department, felt guilty at her abundance. 'That's sad, but even someone like you must have friends,' she insisted earnestly. She heard his startled intake of breath. Oh, dear, that hadn't come out quite as she'd intended.

'Are you *trying* to wind me up?'

'Why would I?' Even if it was exhilarating in a dangerous sort of way.

'Sins of a previous life catching up with me...?'

Darcy repressed a grin. Sarcastic pig...!

'Maybe you *don't* have any friends,' she countered nastily.

'I have friends,' he confirmed tightly. 'The sort who respect my privacy,' he added pointedly.

'Then it's a religious thing...?'

Her swift change of subject made him blink. 'What is...?'

'Ignoring Christmas.'

'It's a personal-choice thing,'

'There's no need to yell,' she remonstrated gently.

Reece's nostrils flared. 'Hard as this might be for you to comprehend, I don't *like* the festive season.'

'It must be pretty spartan inside,' Darcy mused, thinking about the bleak aspect of the old Hall.

An image of walls stripped back to bare brick ran through his mind; the draught from the open window whistling down his neck wasn't the only thing that made him shudder.

'Depends on what you're used to,' he responded evasively.

He looked to her as if he was used to the best—of everything. In fact, Darcy thought, shooting another covert glance in his direction, she didn't think she'd ever met a man who looked *more* accustomed to the good life and all its trimmings than him.

That wasn't to say there was anything *pampered* or soft about him—in fact, the opposite was true. Even in his present battered and bruised condition it was obvious he was in peak physical condition, and he had the indefinable but definite air of a man who would be ruthless to achieve his own ends.

Of course looks weren't everything, and for all she knew he might be afraid of the dark and give generously to charities. Either way, why would a man like him choose to spend any time, let alone Christmas, alone in a dump like…? It made no sense…unless he was hiding out, or running away…? Perhaps Nick's suspicions weren't so crazy after all!

Well, even if he is a sex maniac I should be safe; he doesn't come over as the type who goes for women who can be mistaken for boys—*lucky me*!

Darcy gave herself a mental shake and shrugged off the self-pitying direction of her reflections. Whilst there wasn't much point pretending that physically this man hadn't seriously unnerved her, there was no point advertising the embarrassing fact—though no doubt he was used to women making fools of themselves over him. As the feeling was *obviously* one-sided, and they were going to stay strangers, there didn't seem much point getting bogged down with uncomfortable self-analysis.

'Well, obviously I don't know what the Hall is like inside at the moment, but I would have—'

Reece was not used to explaining his actions, and he decided it was time to call a halt to her interminable speculation once and for all.

'You do surprise me,' his acid drawl interrupted. 'I was under the impression the locals keep fairly up-to-date with *all* the developments around here. I imagined I'd discovered the net-curtain-twitching capital of Yorkshire.'

Two pink spots appeared on Darcy's smooth cheeks; she sucked in an angry breath and crunched her gears. The faintly amused condescension in his voice made her see red. Why not just call us nosy yokels with nothing better to do than gossip and be done with it? She'd have liked to bop him one on his superior nose.

'You'll have to make allowances for me— I'm only home for the holiday, so I'm not completely up to speed yet.'

'That accounts for it, then.'

Darcy's eyes began to sparkle dangerously; the man had a very nasty mouth and there were limits to how much she was willing to make allowances for his delicate condition.

'*We're* nosy? That's pretty rich coming from someone who was spying on me from up a tree!' She hadn't been going to mention it because of his injuries, but he was asking for it…

Reece, who hadn't been in a situation that made him blush for years, felt his colour rise for the second time today.

'I wasn't spying.'

'That's what all the peeping Toms say,' she cut back with a provoking little smile.

Reece gritted his even white teeth.

'I've been demoted from sex maniac, then?'

'You were eavesdropping!' she exclaimed accusingly, a rush of colour flooding her cheeks. Her memory in play-back mode, she tried to recall exactly how bad what they'd said had been.

'It was hard not to, the way you were yelling.'

'Yelling is better than spying,' she countered with un-deniable accuracy.

'I was investigating the noise pollution,' he gritted with the air of a man on the brink of losing his temper.

At that moment they approached a particularly savage bend in the road. His knuckles whitened as he braced his good hand against the dashboard.

'Will you do me a favour and keep your eyes on the road?' he pleaded grimly as her smouldering eyes showed a tendency to linger indignantly on his face.

'It's so hard,' she confessed apologetically, 'when there's you to look at.' She sighed soulfully, placing a hand mo-mentarily over her strongly beating heart.

Actually it was getting increasingly hard to treat the fact she was a long way from immune to his raw brand of phys-ical magnetism as a joke.

He shifted in his seat once more, as if trying to alleviate some discomfort, and his broad shoulders nudged against hers in the restricted space of the small car.

Darcy was conscious of a fleeting feeling of guilt that she was being so mean to someone who was injured and in pain. The other feeling the brief contact created was less fleeting and much more disturbing; the fluttery sensation low in her belly went into overdrive, and pulses had started hammering a loud tattoo in places she didn't know she had pulses! Her palms felt uncomfortably damp as she grimly gripped the cold steering-wheel.

'Ha ha.' Reece's nostrils flared as he watched the provoking little witch toss her bright head. 'You were making a racket and I came out here for peace and quiet.'

She'd never claimed to be Kiri Te Kanawa, but a *racket*—charming! What a great confidence-boost just when she needed it.

'If this is a sample of your usual behaviour I think I can guarantee you that,' she promised him drily. 'It's true that in the country we do take an interest in what our friends and neighbours are doing; perhaps it can be intrusive sometimes…' she conceded.

Reece found his wandering attention captured and held by the dramatic rise and fall of her well-formed bosom. The fascination bothered him—it was totally irrational: he'd seen bosoms a lot more spectacular. He worriedly recalled reading somewhere that head injuries could totally alter someone's personality.

'…but I'd prefer that to indifference…'

'God!' Reece groaned as if in pain and rolled his head from side to side in an effort to alleviate the increasing stiffness in his neck. 'I knew I should have taken a taxi.'

'My driving's not that bad,' Darcy muttered truculently. The fact he was treating the journey like a white-knuckle ride hadn't escaped her notice.

'I'm very grateful for what you've done,' he ground out. He sounded as if each syllable hurt.

'Save it! I don't want your gratitude.' With an airy gesture that caused the car to lurch slightly towards the centre of the road she brushed aside his protest. 'We may be nosy in the country, but we don't step over sick people yet, or ask for payment when we pick them up!'

She shot a disgusted glance at his perfect, slightly bruised profile; anyone would think his movements were front-page news, the way he was acting!

'I wouldn't like you to run away with the impression I give a damn if you get triple pneumonia. I was just making polite neighbourly conversation to take your mind off your pain.'

'I'm not in pain.'

With a lofty sniff Darcy dismissed this transparent untruth. 'You don't have to tell me anything if you don't want to.' An expression of fierce concentration on her face, she stared unblinkingly through the rain-washed windshield.

'No, I don't, do I?'

Another five minutes and the hospital came into view. Even as he broke the silence, Reece couldn't understand what made him do so.

'I'm being a great deal of trouble.'

As much as he liked to give the impression he didn't have one, it looked to her as if the cranky Mr Erskine's conscience was giving him trouble—she was in no hurry to ease it.

'Yes,' she agreed sweetly.

Reece was gripped by an urgent and irrational desire to make those wilful lips smile once more.

'And behaving like an ungrateful monster.' His efforts were rewarded: her lips twitched.

'Such perception.'

Truly kissable lips; shame about the sharp tongue that went with them. A nerve along the chiselled edge of his strong jaw began to throb.

'I came here to escape Christmas…'

'You should have said.'

'Should have said what?' he demanded in a driven voice.

Darcy drew up beside the Casualty doors with her engine running. 'Christmas has bad associations for you, doesn't it?'

He stiffened.

She had spoken on impulse; now she wished she hadn't. For an unguarded moment there she'd seen something in his eyes that made her feel like an intruder. The moment was gone; now there was only hostility and suspicion as he scowled at her.

'What the hell are you talking about?'

Darcy shook her head. 'I just got the impression… Forget it; I obviously got the wrong end of the stick. I'll drop you off here—less far to walk.' She thought about leaning across him to open the door but, recalling what she had experienced the time she'd touched him, she changed her mind.

When he'd gone Darcy drove around looking for a parking space, and even when she found one she wasn't sure whether or not her presence would be appreciated. But, personality clashes aside, it didn't seem quite right somehow to drive off without even finding out how he was. The family would certainly think it very odd if she returned with no news.

It was with mixed feelings she finally presented herself at the reception desk.

'I'm enquiring about a Mr Erskine,' she began tentatively as she approached the smart-looking female who presided over the empty waiting area. 'I came in w—'

'Did you really?' The young woman blushed and continued in voice absent of wistful envy this time. 'I mean, they're expecting you.'

Darcy looked blank. 'They are?' she said doubtfully. It occurred to her this was a case of mistaken identity.

'They said to send you right on in. Rob!' The receptionist flagged down a white-jacketed young nurse. 'Will you take Mrs Erskine through to cubicle three?'

Mrs…? God, they thought…!

'I'm not!' Darcy denied hoarsely, but nobody seemed to be listening to her as she trotted obediently along beside the young nurse.

My God, this was so embarrassing. She just hoped Reece Erskine didn't think the mistake any of her doing.

'I think there's been a mistake,' she began firmly as the young man drew back a curtain and stood to one side.

'Here she is…Darcy, *darling*.'

Darling…?

'Oh, God!' she breathed, her eyes riveted on the bare torso of the man who had greeted her with such a highly deceptive degree of warmth.

He was standing there, stripped to the waist, in the process of zipping up his trousers one-handed; her makeshift sling had been replaced by a more professional-looking collar and cuff arrangement.

Darcy didn't make a habit of mentally stripping casual acquaintances, but it seemed she must have made an exception with him because she found herself comparing the reality to that mental image stored in her head and finding it had hardly done him justice. With wide shoulders, amply endowed with muscle in a lean, athletic, unbulky way, his body was way better than good—it was sensational!

Her tongue clove to the roof of her mouth as her hot eyes went into exploration mode. No wonder her emergency stop had made him cranky—there were spectacular darkish-blue bruises all the way down one side of his ribcage.

'It looks a lot worse than it is,' he comforted her.

Blushing wildly, Darcy tore her eyes from his body. 'Good,' she croaked hoarsely.

'I could do with a hand here.'

Darcy almost choked when she realised he was talking about his zip. Eyes wide, she mutely shook her head. The alarmed backward step she took brought her into abrupt contact with a second person in the tiny cubicle, who until that moment she hadn't even been aware of. No, I was too busy leching over Reece Erskine, she thought shamefully.

'Sorry,' she mumbled incoherently.

'No harm done,' the white-coated figure assured her cheerfully. 'Just a few cracked ribs, lots of bruising and the dislocated shoulder, of course.'

'What?'

The doctor looked bemused for a moment by her alarm, then he grinned. 'I see what you mean…no, I'm talking about your husband, not me.' Chuckling over their crossed lines, the doctor held an X-ray film up to the light.

There was that husband thing again. Darcy waited expectantly, sure that Reece would take this opportunity to correct the error—he didn't, and her confusion deepened.

She felt obliged to respond. 'A *few* seems a bit vague.' Even as she spoke, she was overpoweringly aware of the tall, scantily clad figure who had moved up behind her.

'Point taken.' With an unoffended grin, the medic clipped the film onto an illuminated screen and pointed out the defects with his pen. 'One, two and here's number three.'

'I thought he might have broken his collar-bone.'

'I can see how you might, but no. It was a dislocation. Agony to pop back, of course.' The disgusting, bloodthirsty *popping* noise he made to illustrate the point made Darcy shudder.

'It sounds awfully painful,' she protested.

'It was,' Reece volunteered.

'We offered him an anaesthetic, but your husband *insisted* we do it right away.' The doctor hastily defended his actions. 'A few days and the shoulder should be back to normal,' he promised. 'Actually, it's on account of the head injury we'd like to keep him in overnight, Mrs Erskine, but he doesn't seem too keen.'

'I'm not…'

'She's not surprised, are you, darling?'

The warm, caressing note froze her to the spot without

the added trauma of hearing her addressed again as 'darling'. 'She knows how much I hate hospitals.'

She felt a large competent hand push aside the hair from the nape of her neck. Darcy's hair was plentiful and incredibly silky, but very fine and inclined to go kinky when exposed to moisture—it had definitely been exposed and right now it was a mass of crinkly curls.

Her breath expelled in a soft hiss as she felt the unmistakable touch of cool lips against the sensitive flesh of her exposed nape. Her eyes closed and the strength drained from her body.

The doctor only gave a slightly benevolent smile as he watched them. 'Of course, if he hadn't been going home in the care of an experienced nurse I'd have insisted…'

Darcy's eyes flickered open. He's married, married to a nurse, was her first thought. Then it clicked— Me, he's talking about me!

'Where are you working at the moment, Mrs Erskine?'

'I…I'm…' It was bad enough realising she had a whole new identity created by this madman without being expected to act in character too!

'Darcy is staying at home. Making a home is a full-time job as far as we're concerned, isn't it, darling…?' A firm hand beneath her jaw turned Darcy's head so that she was exposed to the full intensity of his green eyes. No desperate appeal for her co-operation there—on the contrary; if anything, there was a hint of challenge.

'*You're* a full-time job!' she breathed incredulously.

The doctor laughed. 'I'll send a nurse in to suture up that head wound,' he explained, scribbling rapidly on the sheet in front of him.

Darcy waited until he'd gone before she exploded.

'*Are you mad?*' she seethed. Why hadn't she just told the doctor he was lying through his teeth when she'd had the chance?

'Hush, *darling*, or they'll hear you.'

She saw that he was looking well pleased with himself—and why not? Her anger escalated rapidly as he calmly began to shrug on his shirt as if nothing had happened. The man had the gall to stand there looking as if butter wouldn't melt in his mouth, when… Her train of thought skittered to an abrupt full stop—it had been a bad mistake to think *mouth*; she could still feel the tingling area on her neck where his lips had been moments before.

'Let them!'

He directed a mildly irritated glance in her direction.

'I don't know what you're playing at…'

'Sure you do; you're not that stupid.'

Darcy's eyes narrowed. 'Let's pretend for the sake of argument that I am,' she suggested sweetly.

'I think I can just about make that giant leap. They were highly reluctant to discharge me without assurances I have someone responsible to take care of me. Whilst I could have just walked out of here, it seemed less stressful all round if I was married.' The longer he was here, the more likelihood there was of someone recognising him and then it was only a matter of time before the local Press showed up…in his experience these things snowballed pretty fast.

'And you thought of me. Naturally I'm *deeply* flattered,' she spat sarcastically. 'Why on earth did I have to be a nurse…?' she wailed.

'I thought that was a nice touch,' he agreed complacently. 'If the doc had been on the ball he'd have realised you're not old enough to be experienced.'

'You're mad…quite mad!' she announced with conviction.

'You're not a nurse, then?'

'Of course I'm not a nurse!'

'Just when your father said you were a great little nurse I thought…'

'I've got brothers—I can stick on a plaster. I'm not Florence Nightingale…!'

'True. Nobody with an ounce of caring in their body could stand there watching me struggle like this.' He stood there, one arm inserted in his shirt, wondering what to do next.

'If that was a hint, you're really pushing it!' she growled. 'What if someone asks me to do something…*nursey*?' she worried hoarsely.

'Is that likely?' he drawled, managing to project the distinct impression he found her complaints slightly hysterical.

It occurred to Darcy that they were drifting away from the real cause of her simmering anger. 'Don't try and change the subject,' she growled.

One slanted dark brow quirked. 'Which was…?'

'I'm not your wife!'

'This is true,' he conceded with an expression that suggested he was mightily relieved about this. 'I didn't think you'd mind—it's not like I'm actually asking you to marry me or anything drastic.'

'For your information, I've been proposed to *several* times!' she felt goaded into unwisely boasting.

'Congratulations,' he drawled, looking amused.

Darcy's cheeks were burning with humiliation as she discovered a major flaw in his manipulations. 'What were you going to do if I'd driven straight off?'

'I knew you wouldn't do that,' he stated confidently.

'How could you possibly…?'

'You'd be eaten up by guilt if you did. You're deeply into doing the right thing.' He made it sound like a flaw in her character. 'Be a sport, Darcy,' he cajoled.

'I'm not lying for you.'

He sighed. 'Just don't say you're not, that's all I'm asking. It's no skin off your nose. Walk out of here with me and then you'll never have to see me again.'

Darcy's shoulders slumped in defeat. 'I must be mad...'

A wolfish grin split his lean, dark face. 'Good girl,' he approved.

Further comments were made impossible by the arrival of the nurse who'd directed Darcy here originally.

'I've come to suture your head wound,' the young man explained.

Darcy took the opportunity to excuse herself. 'I'll wait outside.' Halfway through the curtain, she paused. 'Are you going to give him a local anaesthetic?' she asked the young nurse.

He looked confused. 'Well, yes,' he admitted.

'Pity!' Darcy declared maliciously.

The sound of husky laughter followed her down the corridor.

CHAPTER THREE

'GOODBYE, Mrs Erskine…Mr Erskine,' the young receptionist gushed breathily as she left them with obvious reluctance at the swing-doors.

Darcy gave a sigh of relief as the doors swung shut. The red carpet was about the only thing that had been missing and, given enough time, she had the impression the smitten young woman would have produced that too. At least she could drop the wifey act now.

'What are we?' Darcy grouched, intensely relieved to be out of the place and out of her role. 'Visiting royalty? Do you always have this effect on people?'

'What effect is that?'

Darcy raised a sceptical brow. 'Like you didn't notice!' she hooted. 'The woman was deferential, bordering on obsequious.'

Despite the enigmatic smile she received in reply, Darcy got the impression he was even less pleased than she was by the VIP treatment.

The rain had stopped, but it had started to freeze, making the pavement underfoot lethally slippery. Darcy moved cautiously past the men who were gritting the entrance to the hospital, smiling in a distracted way at them as she passed. The gravel was crunchy underfoot as they passed the tall, twinkly Christmas tree, and a layer of sparkling frost added to the festive look in a way that expensive ornaments never could.

She only just stopped herself mentioning how much she loved the smell of pine to the wet blanket beside her.

'Where are we parked?'

Even though she hadn't forgotten the tall, commanding presence at her side—chance would be a fine thing—she started when he spoke. It made her realise how uptight and wound up the whole play-acting thing in the hospital had made her. Her fellow conspirator, on the other hand, had seemed almost to relish his role, or maybe it was her discomfort he enjoyed…? Considering the glimpses she'd had of his warped sense of humour, the latter seemed the most likely explanation.

'*We…?*' She lifted her eyes to his face, but not for long—for some reason she felt oddly reluctant to maintain contact.

Like a silly, lust-struck teenager afraid to look the unattainable object of her fantasies in the eyes! Self-disgust curled in her belly. Grow up, Darcy!

By the time she had sternly told herself to stop acting so *wet*, he had paused under the blue-white beam of an overhead light and was making a careful minor adjustment to the jacket draped over his broad shoulders. His head was bent forward at an angle; she couldn't see his face, just the strong curve of his jaw and the sharp angle of his cheekbones, but even these sketchy details were enough to proclaim him as something pretty special to look at indeed.

'Are you going to abandon me…?' He contemplated his abandonment with what seemed to her unnatural composure.

'That was my plan, yes.' She could see the flaw in this plan even before he came over all pathetic and helpless.

'No wallet, no money or plastic. See for yourself.' He opened his jacket, inviting her to disprove his claim.

No way—she'd been there, done that and felt her hormones riot! She was not conscious of placing her tightly clenched hands firmly behind her back.

'There's no need to act like an endangered species; I believe you,' she told him gruffly. Her sigh of defeat had a long-suffering sound to it. 'Do I look like a soft touch?' she wondered, wearily running a harassed hand through her dampish curls.

Dark head on one side, he regarded her in a considering fashion. To add insult to injury, it took him bare moments to come to a decision.

'Actually, yes, you do.' She also looked extremely young, still full of youthful ideals, a soft target for unscrupulous operators—a student home for the holiday possibly…?

His own innocence and youth seemed a long way off at that moment. It seemed an opportune time, given the direction of his wayward thoughts, to remind himself how far removed she was from the females who temporarily lent a bit of variety to his solitary existence— Reece wasn't looking for anything other than temporary.

His candour made Darcy's face darken in annoyance.

'And you're the type to take advantage,' she accused rattily.

Taken advantage of by Reece Erskine—now, there was a thought! She was too busy being angry, flustered and ashamed of her thoughts to notice that a new expression had filtered into his eyes.

Soft… His mind seemed determined to explore this avenue and there was no lack of appropriate material to feed his interest—soft lips, soft curves. The compulsive nature of his speculation had none of the objectivity Reece took for granted in sexual matters.

Don't go there, he urged himself, repressing the sudden strong inclination to lean closer to all that *softness*, smell the flowery scent that enveloped her small person.

Darcy set off purposefully, reluctant to invite ridicule by admitting she'd forgotten where she'd left the car. She was too damned spooked at the prospect of being enclosed in a small space with him once more to think straight or accept defeat graciously. She heard his soft but firm footsteps shadowing her.

'You *said* I'd never have to see you again,' she reminded him crankily.

'I'm a great believer in telling people what they want to hear if that gets the job done.'

'Lying, you mean.'

Reece winced. 'I wouldn't have put it that way.'

'That I never doubted!'

Despite the fact she wasn't making any allowances for his delicate condition, his long long legs seemed to be having no problem keeping up with the cracking pace she was setting—*pity*!

'I'm not exactly thrilled to find myself obliged to beg a lift either,' he rasped huskily.

Of all the ungrateful rats! Darcy came to an abrupt halt and turned her wrathful gaze upon the tall figure who had almost collided with her.

'That makes two of us!' she retorted sharply.

Their eyes met.

It was at that moment Darcy felt *it*—*it* was a tense excitement so thick the air quivered with it, so thick her limbs were all but immobilised by it.

It didn't seem to be a one-sided situation. His burning eyes kept moving back to her parted lips as though they were being dragged there against his will. She felt as if she was being drawn in by that raw expression in his hungry eyes. The tightness in her chest finally found release in a fractured sigh.

The compulsion to reach up and press her lips to his was so strong her head spun. Would they be cold, warm…firm…? Wondering sent delicious little shivers skating along her spine.

She wouldn't do it, of course, because she wasn't the sort of girl who gave in to lustful base instincts…all the same, *thinking* about it—and she discovered her embarrassingly lurid imagination had a mind of its own—made her body temperature soar despite the sub-zero temperature around them. Her dry-throated excitement mounted with dizzying rapidity as her knees began to literally shake.

Seconds probably carried on ticking relentlessly away in the few moments after speculative green eyes had met startled blue—but Darcy was unaware of the passing time as they stood stock-still in a silence broken only by the distant wail of an ambulance.

No good will come of this, a sensible voice, to which she paid no heed, forecast in her head.

Reece felt his breath perceptibly quicken. Her mouth was just sensationally lush. The uneven sound of her breath catching in the back of her throat was driving him slightly crazy. He watched as her clenched fingers unfurled and she began to reach out…he thought about them touching his face…his hair…his…!

With a mumbled expletive he took a step backwards. '*Darcy…!*'

It was a verbal warning, the sort an adult gave a reckless child about to indulge in dangerous exploration.

Mortified, Darcy let her extended hand fall away, and she stood there feeling stupid and confused by what had just occurred—whatever that was… He had wanted to kiss her too—hadn't he…? It hadn't been a figment of her overheated imagination, had it?

The uncertainty only lasted a split-second; she hadn't imagined anything—it had been real. She thrust her softly rounded chin forward defiantly. As unlikely as it seemed, Reece Erskine had wanted to kiss her just as much as she'd wanted to kiss him! She raised her eyes stubbornly to his stony face and her heart sank—only he didn't now!

So he had gone off the idea; she was damned if she was going to let him make her feel ashamed!

'Darcy what?' She sniffed angrily. 'Darcy, don't kiss me...?' she suggested shrilly.

She watched his eyes widen as she gave an appalled gasp—*I can't believe I said that!*

'Were you going to?'

I asked for that, didn't I? What was she supposed to say...? Given a little bit of encouragement, *probably*...?

Darcy served up a withering look. 'What a tactless thing to ask,' she observed, resorting to disgust to disguise the extent of her dismay.

Spontaneous and asking for trouble would have been closer to the mark in his estimation. No wonder the brother wanted to keep her at home—if she was his sister he'd never let her out of his sight!

For the first time Darcy noticed the lines of strain around his sensual mouth—as if not kissing her hadn't been the easy option...then why...? A horrifying possibility occurred to her. 'Are you married?'

Unprepared for the tense, accusing query, Reece blinked, his jaw tightening. 'That's not relevant.'

Her mouth hardened with contempt; that meant he was. Not again! She didn't know who she despised the most at that moment—him or herself. 'To me it is!' she choked bitterly.

Reece gave an exasperated sigh; he could cope with a lot of things but he discovered—rather to his surprise—that being looked at as if he was some sort of moral derelict by those big blue eyes was not one of them.

'If it matters so much to you, I was, but I'm not now.' He saw her slender hunched-up shoulders slump in relief. 'Though why it should be so important to you I don't understand...'

And Darcy wasn't about to explain. Having an affair with a married man—even if she hadn't known he was at the time—was not the sort of thing she felt like sharing.

'I'd introduce the subject of morals if I thought you'd understand.'

'I don't see where morals come into it,' he drawled. 'You didn't do anything…'

'If I had…would you have…?' Cheeks flaming, she struck her forehead with the palm of her hand. 'Oh, God!' she wailed. 'Me and my mouth…!' How to take an embarrassing situation and make it ten times worse in one easy-to-follow lesson!

His eyes automatically moved to the object of her contempt. The muscles in his strong throat worked overtime.

'Yes, I'd have kissed you back,' he admitted throatily. The words seemed drawn from him against his will.

Her eyes widened. 'You would…?' She saw his lips twitch at the incredulity in her voice. 'I knew that.' A puzzled frown crinkled her smooth brow. 'Then why didn't you…?'

Reece's bark of rueful laughter brought her back to her senses—and not before time. He stared at her flushed face for a couple of moments before replying.

'You don't kiss married men; I don't kiss girls young enough to be my…kid sister.'

It was the very last explanation Darcy had expected to hear. 'How quaint that you've got principles.'

'It comes as as much of a shock to me as it does to you,' he assured her drily. 'It's getting cold out here.' He spoke abruptly now, as if the humour of the situation was wearing thin. 'If you really can't stomach the idea of giving me a lift back I should be able to make alternative arrangements.'

Darcy touched his arm; he didn't flinch but his rigidity didn't suggest relaxed and carefree—was it possible he was not entirely immune to the contact? This not unflattering possibility was heady stuff.

'How old exactly do you think I am?' Repressing a smug smile, she worked her way towards her grand finale.

Whilst it might have been wiser to leave him in ignorance, given the dangerous sexual chemistry in the air, she wanted the satisfaction of establishing herself as a mature woman of the world in his eyes. Perhaps for once in her life she wanted danger…? Her eyes slid over his tall, rangy frame before coming to rest on his face, and she gulped; he registered high enough on the danger scale to satisfy the most reckless risk-taker, she conceded.

'Nineteen…twenty maybe.'

'I'm twenty-seven.'

His chin came up and the dark veil of lashes lifted from his high, chiselled cheekbones. His narrowed eyes raked her face. 'Not possible.'

'Furthermore,' she continued, breathless after his intense scrutiny, 'I'm not some teenage virgin.' Like he really wanted to know that, Darcy.

'What are you, then?'

'Your best hope of getting home, mate.'

His mobile lips quirked; his expression was still rapt. 'I'd not forgotten that. I was actually wondering what you do when you're not doing the angel-of-mercy act.'

A wistful expression flitted across her face. 'At this moment I should be skiing.'

'But you were lured away by the glamour of deepest, darkest Yorkshire?'

His sneering irony brought an annoyed frown to her face. She took any criticism of her beloved Dales very personally.

'There was a family crisis,' she told him tersely.

'So they called you.' That would figure.

Darcy resented his tone. 'I don't mind,' she flared. 'Who else would they call?'

'You tell me. My recollection is a bit cloudy, but there didn't seem any shortage of family members from what I saw.'

'You don't know the half of it,' she mumbled. 'I get a panic attack every time I think about how many people I'm meant to be cooking Christmas lunch for.'

'Is this the same girl—sorry, *woman*, who considers every strand of tinsel sacred…?' he taunted gently.

'This is the woman,' she countered angrily, 'who is trying to step into her mother's shoes and failing miserably!' The instant the impetuous retort emerged from her lips she regretted it; she regretted it even more when she saw the curiosity on his face.

'Your mother's ill…?'

'No, she's not. She's…*away*.'

His dark brows lifted. 'Another man…' It might have been a trick of the light but Darcy thought his hard eyes actually softened. 'Bad luck, kid. It happens.'

Darcy was furious and horrified by his casual assumption that her mother would have an affair. 'Not to my family! My mother has gone to a retreat to recharge her batteries, that's all…' Tears prickled the backs of her eyelids and her voice thickened emotionally. 'And I'm not a kid.'

Reece looked down into her stormy upturned face. 'Want to talk about it?' he was surprised to hear himself offer; he wasn't prone to encouraging soul-baring.

'Not to you.' Darcy thought he looked relieved rather than disappointed by her blunt response.

'Fair enough.'

She eyed him suspiciously before she eventually nodded and blew on her icy fingertips. 'If the interrogation's over, perhaps we should get along before hypothermia sets in.'

Face burning with embarrassment and humiliation, she turned abruptly on her heel. She deliberately turned her face to the icy embrace of the cold north wind and, as luck would have it, found the car almost immediately.

'I can't find the keys,' she admitted after turning her pockets and handbag inside-out and upside-down.

Reece, who had watched her feverish attempts silently, walked around the car to join her.

'Might these be what you were looking for?'

Relief was mingled with chagrin as she saw he was indicating the familiar bunch of keys inserted in the driver's door. He pulled them out, and instead of dropping them into the palm she held out he placed them in a way that meant his fingers brushed against her wrist. The tingle that shot up her extended arm was neat electricity.

'Thanks,' she mumbled without looking at him. She couldn't decide whether or not that touch had been as artless as it had appeared.

He inclined his glossy head graciously. 'My pleasure.'

The fit inside the car was even snugger than she remembered. His head brushed the top of the car and in order to accommodate his legs he had to draw his knees up towards his chest at an awkward angle.

She went to turn the ignition key but he reached out and covered her hand with his, and if anything this time the sensation was even stronger.

Her eyes, wide and startled, lifted to his. 'What's wrong?'

Besides the state of imminent collapse of my nervous system, that is?

'This kissing thing.'

Darcy wriggled her hand from beneath his and clasped it protectively to her heaving chest. 'What kissing thing?' she asked, desperately affecting amnesia.

'You wanting to kiss me.'

'*You* wanting to kiss me.'

'That too,' he agreed. 'The point is, now that you know I'm not a married man and I know you're not a teenager...or for that matter a virgin...' A choking sound emerged from Darcy's throat. 'Incidentally we have that much in common. There's no actual reason we shouldn't.'

'Shouldn't…?' She hoped he wasn't going to say what she thought he was going to say—he did.

'Kiss.'

She almost kept the wobble from her cool response. 'Other than the fact I'd scream blue murder, probably not.' She sent up a silent prayer that her claim would never be put to the test.

'Ah…! You've gone off the idea… Maybe it's for the best,' he conceded casually, before leaning back in his seat and closing his eyes.

Just like that! Heavens, she didn't expect him to get suicidal because she'd said she didn't want to kiss him, but he could at least have the decency to look as if he cared! It was, she decided, eyeing his profile with loathing, a matter of simple good manners!

Darcy knew straight off she'd not fall back to sleep for some time—her feverishly active mind was racing like an overwound clockwork toy. She glanced at the illuminated fingers of the clock on the bedside table and groaned: it was only two a.m.

Her tiny bedroom set beneath the eaves faced due north, and the wind was battering against the window-panes, sneaking through every odd crack or cranny in the well-insulated room. The Hall wouldn't be well-insulated…

'Oh, hell, why did I go and think that…?' She rolled onto her stomach and pulled a pillow over her head to drown out the noise. I will not think about him, she told herself angrily.

Trouble was, she did.

Her family had been surprised when on her return she hadn't brought home the invalid to eat with them. Their collective comments to this effect had served to add to the burden of her own guilty conscience until she'd eventually exploded.

'If you want to feed him, feel free, but don't expect any thanks. Me, I've had enough of him for one evening!' she'd announced.

After that they'd let it alone, but she'd been able to tell that they thought she was being mean and she'd caught Nick regarding her speculatively several times during the evening.

Thirty minutes after she'd woken from her restless sleep Darcy, armed with a torch, blanket and a flask of coffee, made her way up the lane towards the Hall.

There was no front door to knock. The beam of her torch feebly illuminated a very sorry state of affairs. Horrified, Darcy explored further; things didn't get any better.

'And I didn't even offer the man a cup of tea,' she moaned, stepping over a pile of ladders that lay across her path. 'And why…? Just because he accepted no means no. If I find him dead from hypothermia or in a coma it'll be my fault.' The knowledge increased the urgency of her search for signs of life.

A room with a door seemed a logical place to look. Her efforts were rewarded with the sight of the smouldering embers of a large fire in the wide inglenook.

Tentatively she approached the large human-sized bundle on the floor. She put down everything but the torch and knelt down beside the figure. Her ears were straining for signs of healthy breathing—in her present frame of mind she'd have welcomed the odd wheeze or two!

One minute she was shuffling a little closer to the figure with her hand raised, the next she was flat on her back, pinned beneath a heavy figure. An ungentle hand was pressed over her mouth.

'If you don't want to get hurt, stop struggling,' an ugly growl advised her. 'Are you alone?'

How the hell did he expect her to reply with a dirty great

paw over her mouth…? It seemed her assailant's thoughts were running along similar lines.

'I'm going to take away my hand, but if you try and yell to your mates you'll regret it. Understood…?'

Heart pounding, Darcy shook her head as vigorously as her position would allow. If she hadn't known this was Reece she'd have already died of heart failure. To her relief the suffocating hand lifted.

'For heaven's sake, get off me, you idiot; I can't breathe!' she gasped.

'Darcy!'

The pressure across her ribs eased but he didn't shift completely. 'Of course Darcy,' she grumbled crossly. 'Who did you think it was?'

'A burglar.'

She heard sounds of him searching for something just before a strong light was shone in her face.

'Will you take that out of my eyes?' she pleaded, screwing her watering eyes up tight. 'I can't see a thing.'

She felt a hand tug at the knitted cloche she wore on her head and pull it off. The same hand ran gently through the soft waves that had been crammed beneath. Suddenly the pressure over her middle was gone, as was the hand… Disturbingly she had mixed feelings about her release; there had been something very soothing about those probing fingers—no, that wasn't quite the right word…

She struggled to sit up and managed it with both hands braced behind her for support on the dusty floor.

'I had a torch but I lost it when you leapt on me like that.' She squinted into the dusty corners, hoping to relocate it.

Reece regarded her incredulously. 'Well, what did you expect, woman, creeping up on a man in the middle of the night?'

Fair question if you stopped to look at it from his point

of view—something that Darcy hadn't done up to this point. She realised how foolish her impulsive behaviour might seem.

She watched nervously as he got to his feet and moved towards the fire, pausing to choose a couple of dry logs. The fire immediately began to sizzle as the flames licked the wood. Picking up a box of matches from the shoulder-high age-darkened oak mantel, he began to light half a dozen or so candles which were laid out there in various stages of demise. As they took hold he switched off the torch and slid it into his pocket—it came as no surprise that he'd been sleeping fully clothed.

'Don't you just love candlelight?' he drawled.

'Not especially.' His dark hair was mussed up and what had been the suggestion of a shadow over his strong jaw earlier was now a well-developed dark stubble. Neither of these factors altered the fact he looked devastatingly attractive—well, looking at him made her feel fairly devastated at any rate.

'Now,' he said in a don't-muck-me-about sort of voice, 'you can tell me what you thought you were doing.'

What had seemed a perfectly logical step to take at the time suddenly seemed extremely difficult to explain to her critical audience.

'If you don't speak I'll just have to assume you couldn't bear to be parted from me any longer...' he warned.

The satiric taunt made the colour flare in Darcy's pale cheeks. 'In your dreams,' she grunted, catching her lower lip between her teeth.

'Talking of dreams, you owe me one—you rudely interrupted a particularly...'

'I don't want to know anything about your dreams,' Darcy assured him, drawing herself up on her knees and dusting the seat of her trousers with a vigorous hand.

'Even if you were involved...?'

He seemed to take a malicious delight in winding her up. '*Especially* if I was involved.' Thank goodness she had a thick sweater and a windcheater over her pyjama top, because things were happening to her nipples that couldn't be blamed on the temperature.

Reece laughed then and went to sit down on an upturned packing case. 'I'd offer you a seat, only this is the only one.' He fingered the rough surface. 'It's thc only table too, for that matter.'

Darcy gathered the drifting threads of her wits—she hadn't come here to talk furniture. 'I only came to look at you,' she gritted, wondering why she had ever cared if he expired in his sleep.

'Not touch…?' he muttered.

'Will you stop interrupting me?'

'Sorry,' he responded meekly.

Meek, him…? That was the best joke she'd heard in ages.

'I shouldn't have let you spend the night alone just because you irritated me.'

Now that she had his complete attention, Darcy wasn't sure that was what she wanted… She didn't trust that innocent expression in those green eyes either.

He rapidly proved her distrust was well-placed!

'So you decided to spend the night with me after all, Darcy. I don't know what to say…'

Her jaw locked tight as she tried to act as if his wolfish grin didn't do anything to her at all.

'I'm sure you'll manage to come up with something suitably smutty,' she predicted acidly, rubbing her sweaty palms against her jeans.

His low chuckle was not only genuinely amused, it was also deeply, devastatingly sexy.

'The doctor said you needed to be carefully observed. I just thought I'd pop round and see if you were all right.'

'You thought you'd *pop round* at,' he glanced down at the slim-banded wristwatch on his wrist, 'three a.m.,' he read incredulously.

'I didn't know if you could cope, with your ribs and the shoulder…' She gave an exasperated sigh. 'If you must know,' she said, gathering up the flask and blanket and thrusting them out to him, 'I was worried about you.'

Reece looked from her angry, flushed face to the offerings in her hand and back again. 'I'm touched.'

'There's no need,' she said with dignity, 'to be sarcastic.'

'I'm not.'

Darcy tapped a pearly fingertip nervously against a white tooth and eyed him with an exasperated frown. 'It's perfectly simple,' she began to explain patiently. 'I was lying there, listening to the wind, thinking about you…'

'Snap.'

It took two seconds' exposure to his wickedly explicit eyes to extinguish the innocent look of enquiry on her face. 'I wasn't doing *that* sort of thinking,' she gasped, horrified.

'What sort of thinking would that be, Darcy…?'

'If you'd got ill in the night nobody would have known. I would have felt responsible.'

'You've got a thing about responsibility, haven't you, Darcy?' he mused softly. 'Don't you ever get the urge to do something irresponsible?' The humour faded abruptly from his eyes.

Darcy swallowed, and waited for the worst of the spasms in her belly to pass. It must be the candles, she reasoned desperately. 'No, never.' Her stern denial emerged as a hollow whisper.

Her fingers, still curled around the blanket and Thermos, trembled. It didn't occur to her to release her grip on them as he pulled them—and her—slowly towards him. Finally he removed them from her weak grasp and placed them on the floor. His eyes never left hers all the time.

An image of the livid bruising she'd seen on his body came into her head, but her imagination didn't limit itself to damage; it conjured up some impressive muscles, smooth olive-toned flesh and crisp body hair too. She ran the tip of her tongue over her dry lips to lubricate them and gave her head a tiny shake, but neither act totally dispelled the disturbing image.

'Did I hurt you?' she asked hoarsely. She knew she hadn't been a submissive victim.

He touched the side of her face softly and sent an illicit little shiver through the tense body. Darcy couldn't afford the time to worry if the tremor had been transmitted through his fingertips—it was taking all her energy convincing her knees they didn't want to fold under her. To make matters infinitely worse, the debilitating weakness wasn't just affecting her limbs…at best, her brain was functioning on a very basic, fuzzy level.

'Do you want to?' Finger on the angle of her jaw, he tilted her face up to his.

Darcy shook her head—she didn't want to think about what she'd like to do to him; it wasn't decent. His face was swimming in and out of focus as she stared back at him.

'I don't like hurting people. Do you…?'

Reece didn't reply; he simply took her by the shoulders and drew her unresisting body towards him, parting his thighs to let her rest within their confining circle.

'Are you quite sure that concern for my health was the only reason you came here, Darcy…?'

She had to do something to throw cold water on the escalating intimacy and danger of a situation that was fast getting out of hand.

'What other reason could there be?'

Underneath the faint antiseptic hospital scent and a distinctive male fragrance she could smell him—not just his soap or cologne, but *him*! Panic was just a heartbeat away—or was it capitulation she could sense…?

'This one…' His intention was written clear on his dark, impassioned features.

Desperation and panic flared in her wide eyes just before they reflexly closed. The uncoordinated flailing movements of her hands brought them in contact with the iron-hard thighs pressed either side of her hips; she froze and her fingers spasmed, relaxed, then tentatively spread out over the hard-muscled expanse.

'That's good,' he approved.

Darcy gave a sigh; it was. She felt his breath as it moved over her cheek, felt it tease the quivering line of her trembling lips in the moment before his lips purposefully parted hers. The sensual, silken, smooth stab of his tongue melted her last resistance.

Darcy gave a lost little cry and sank deeper into the seductive velvet blackness inside her head. The explosive force of his hunger was something she'd never encountered before. Almost more shocking was the equally unexpected raw response that uncoiled within her. She gave herself up totally to the seductive exploration, only stopping when she could no longer breathe.

They drew apart, but not very far. Her forehead was resting against his, her fingers were twisted in the glossy strands of his dark hair.

'I forgive you totally for waking me up.'

And, given he kissed like an angel, she was prepared to forgive him for sounding so smug. He knew all the moves all right; even now Darcy didn't want to admit even to herself that it wasn't simple slick technique that had made her respond to him that way.

'Ever undressed inside a sleeping bag?'

Darcy stiffened slightly but didn't draw back. She only

had herself to blame for this situation—if she hadn't kissed him back like that…

'Isn't that a bit of a leap from a kiss?'

'There are kisses and then again there are *kisses*.'

Again he was right. Until that particular moment Darcy hadn't known how great the gap between the two was. She was pink all over already, and the shade deepened perceptively as she encountered the sensuous warmth of his eyes.

'It's a challenging proposition…' she admitted, a responsive smile in her voice. Yesterday she would have laughed her socks off if someone had suggested she would be seriously considering sleeping with a man she barely knew.

'I can hear a "but" coming on,' Reece predicted gloomily.

Reluctantly Darcy released her hold on his hair and straightened up. She became aware for the first time that at some point during the embrace Reece had removed her windcheater. She stood there shivering, but not from cold.

'I think it would be a safer bet all round if you invest in a heated blanket,' she explained regretfully.

'No electricity.' His gesture caused the candles to flicker and dance in the draught he created. 'And if you're worried on a safety basis I'm a prepared sort of guy.'

'I wasn't.'

'You ought to be; you don't know me.'

She blinked. Is he lecturing *me* on safe sex…? 'Which is one of the reasons I'm not about to sleep with you.'

'The others being…?'

'You have several broken bones.'

Reece impatiently disposed of this objection. 'We can work around that.'

Just imagining what 'working around' might involve made her skin burn.

'You know you want to.'

Darcy gasped. 'That,' she bit back with tremulous contempt, 'is an incredibly arrogant thing to say.'

'Maybe, but it's true,' he returned imperturbably.

'What are you doing…?' she squawked as he got to his feet.

'I can't make love to you if we're on opposite sides of the room.'

This would have been even truer if I had stayed safely tucked up in my own bed—only I didn't. Why didn't I…? Did I want this to happen…? She shook her head in feverish denial but the idea clung stubbornly on.

'I find you quite incredibly exciting.'

His honeyed drawl froze her to the spot, the dark reckless glow in his eyes liquefied her bones, and held her there. Eyes a little wild, she tilted her head to maintain eye contact as he came closer…and closer.

'I think you must be thinking of someone else…'

'You smell like summer.'

'I do…? When you said we could work around it…are you sure…?'

Reece took her small face between his big hands. 'I don't say things I don't mean.'

'You're quite sure…' Darcy felt his low laughter against her ear, smelt the male muskiness of his arousal.

'Shut up and kiss me, woman.'

CHAPTER FOUR

THE impetus of the kiss made them stagger backwards into the makeshift table. A small bottle of tablets fell onto the dusty floor; Darcy automatically tried to avoid stepping onto the contents.

'Your painkillers…' Fortunately the bottle of whisky set beside it on the table hadn't fallen.

The arm around her waist didn't slacken.

'To hell with them,' he slurred.

'Good God!' she gasped. 'You've mixed tablets with booze, haven't you?' she accused hoarsely. 'That explains it.'

'Explains what?' He didn't sound terribly interested in her reply.

'This!' she indited shakily, stabbing a finger at her chest and discovering in the process that at some point during the kiss he'd managed to remove her sweater.

If undressing women ever became an Olympic event he would win gold with one hand tied behind his back—quite literally, she thought, her eyes sliding to his immobilised arm.

Flushing deeply, she gathered the lightly elasticated neckline of her pyjama top in one fist, which didn't so much conceal what was going on underneath the thin, silky fabric as draw his hot-eyed attention to it.

'I've no idea what you're talking about, but hell, you taste good.' He pushed a hank of her silky hair aside to press an open-mouthed kiss to the pulse point on her neck.

Darcy's head fell back and she groaned, the sensual shock of his touch juddering through her responsive body.

'You don't understand.' She valiantly struggled past the passion barrier to make him listen.

'Reece, I think it's probable you're having a reaction to your medication.' Depressing as it was, it did perfectly explain away the inexplicable—a man like him being so deeply in lust with an average type like herself.

'So that's what this is.' He firmly unglued her fingers and peered down the open neckline; what he saw seemed to afford him considerable pleasure.

She got even hotter. 'I don't think you're taking this seriously.'

'Believe me,' he grated hoarsely, 'I'm taking this very seriously.'

'You don't really want me,' she whimpered.

Reece's jaw tightened. 'Is that a fact...?' He slid the silky fabric clear down her shoulders and with a muffled groan pressed his lips to the heaving contours he'd revealed. 'Absolutely incredible...'

'Sweet...sweet...mercy...' Darcy tried to regroup but it was an uphill battle. His tongue had begun to travel very slowly over the slope of one breast. Did it really matter that he wasn't in full possession of his senses...? *'Listen!'* Fingers in his hair, she pulled his head back.

'What the hell's wrong now?' There was a light sheen of sweat covering his taut, lean features, the dampness extending down the glistening column of his throat. His hot eyes kept sliding from her face in the general direction of her heaving breasts.

'It's the medication. I think you've had some sort of reaction to it. You can't take alcohol with some sorts of analgesia. That's why you're acting like this.' Miserably Darcy brushed a strand of hair from her damp face and found she couldn't look him in the eyes—it was too humiliating... Her body was literally throbbing with arousal, aching for his touch.

'You can't think of any other reason…?' The blood in her temples roared as his eyes slid in hot, sensual appraisal over her body. 'A reason like I'm sexually attracted to you!' She audibly caught her breath. 'A reason like I've been lying here alone all night, wondering what it would be like to have you beside me, warm and soft, to be inside you. Then you're here…' His throat muscles worked. 'And you want to stay.' He smiled with grim satisfaction when she didn't respond to the challenge.

Darcy couldn't speak; the sound of his low, vibrantly masculine voice saying things no man had ever said to her was like a fist tightening inside her belly. She felt light-headed and dizzy and her blood seemed to hum hotly, pooling; the ache between her thighs was so intense she could hardly stand up, and, her breathing shallow and fast, she stared breathlessly up at him.

'But the—'

'Paracetamol. You can buy it anywhere over the counter.' His sensuous lips curled contemptuously as her eyes widened. 'The doc wanted to give me something stronger but I've never been keen on having my senses dulled.'

'Then this is…'

Reece nodded. 'The real thing. Unless you're going to tell me you're taking hallucinogenic drugs?'

The dazed look still in her eyes, she shook her head vigorously.

'Does this feel real enough for you?' he asked, pressing his lean, hard body tight against hers.

Darcy could feel him, thick and hard, pressing into the softness of her belly. 'It…you feel incredible,' she gasped.

'Take my shirt off, Darcy?'

'Because of your shoulder.'

'Because I want you to.'

That seemed a good enough reason to Darcy.

Her hands were shaking as one by one she slid free the buttons and pushed the soft cord fabric aside to reveal his broad chest and flat belly. Expression rapt, she spread her fingers and felt the fine muscles just beneath the surface of his taut skin twitch and tighten.

Her hair looked silver by candlelight and all Reece could see of her as she leant closer was the top of her head and the exposed nape of her slender neck. It wasn't an area he'd previously considered erotic—was it napes in general or this nape in particular…? That was a question for later—right now he needed to assuage the fire in his blood, the ache in his loins.

A deep line bisected her smooth brow as she examined the bruised area. 'Tell me if I hurt you,' she whispered, tracing a line across his belly with her fingernail.

'I'm hurting,' he told her thickly.

Alarmed, she raised her eyes questioningly to his. 'Where…?' she began. She saw the expression on his face and her voice faded away.

'Here…' he took her hand and showed her '…here and here,' he elaborated thickly.

Darcy whimpered, the last remnants of her control evaporating.

'I want to see you. Take your clothes off for me. All of them.'

Not doing as he requested—or was it a demand?—was never an option. Like someone in a dream she crossed her arms and began to lift the hem of her top up over her smooth stomach.

'And, Darcy…?'

She paused.

'Look at me.'

Darcy did. She could hear the harsh, uneven sound of his breathing, loud in the quiet room. Even in this light she could make out a definite flush of colour along his slashing cheekbones and the fire in his eyes— Did I really put it there…? How strange…how marvellous.

Their eyes locked, and her anxiety was instantly soothed; he looked just as needy as she felt. Despite the new confidence, her hands trembled uncontrollably as she did as he had bid. It was no slow, seductive striptease because even with a fire now blazing in the hearth it didn't seem such a good idea to linger over disrobing.

'You're beautiful.' She almost believed him.

He closed the small gap between them. Where he touched her Darcy's skin tingled, and pretty soon she tingled all over. 'And cold.' He began to briskly massage her cold extremities. 'Come on, get in here.' Taking her by the hand, he led her towards the sleeping bag and blankets.

The cotton lining still retained the last remnants of his body heat. Darcy drew her knees up to her chin and waited for him to join her, anticipation pumping darkly though her. She watched as he shed his clothes, ripping the shirt as he tried to ease it too quickly over his injured arm; he was lean, lovely and very, *very* aroused.

He was actually so beautiful she wanted to cry—she *was* crying, hot tears sliding over her cheeks. He wiped away the dampness with his thumb when he finally came to join her but didn't question their presence.

'Come here,' he whispered.

Darcy did; there wasn't very far to go. They lay side by side, close but not touching, until with a hoarse groan he reached across with his good arm and drew her on top of him. His mouth reached hungrily for hers.

Darcy responded joyfully to the demands of his lips and thrusting tongue. It was intoxicating to have nothing to separate them any longer. Darcy wriggled to fully appreciate the sensation. His skin was warmer than hers; it was harder, and she discovered it had a deliciously smooth texture roughened by drifts of body hair that prickled against her breasts and thighs. Every detail delighted her and increased the pressure of excitement building inside her to detonation point.

'For a one-handed man,' she remarked a hundred or so gasps later, 'you manage pretty well.'

A savage grin split Reece's face as he looked into her flushed, aroused face. 'If you think that was good, wait until you get a taste of no hands.'

A confused frown drew Darcy's feathery brows together as she puzzled over his words, the meaning of which was brought crashing home to her seconds later.

Shock tensed her muscles for a split-second before she gave a languid sigh and relaxed. She moaned his name out loud and writhed restlessly as his tongue flickered lower over the soft curve of her abdomen. The excitement built to fever pitch as he continued his merciless ministrations.

The zip on the sleeping bag gave way as he brought her knees up and knelt between them, but Darcy didn't register the blast of cold air. The pleasure was so intense it bordered on pain; she cried out in protest but she cried out even louder when he stopped.

He kissed her, stilling her inarticulate protests.

He tasted and smelt of her and sex; it was a mind-shattering combination.

'I want you so badly!' she moaned, leaning her face into his neck.

'Then take me, sweetheart,' he urged throatily. 'Take me.'

Darcy lifted her head. 'I can. Can I…?' she gasped wonderingly. He whispered things in her ear that convinced her she could—she could do anything she wanted to.

Darcy stared down gloatingly at the magnificent man beneath her—his eyes were closed, his skin glistened with sweat. Her muscles tensed, she bore downwards. The cry of relief and triumph that was wrenched from her throat as she lowered herself upon him echoed around the room.

Reece's eyes snapped open. 'Oh, my God, sweetheart!' he groaned. 'You are…' A red mist danced before his eyes; he couldn't speak, he couldn't think, he could just thrust and thrust…

She rubbed her gritty-feeling eyes. Someone had carefully tucked the sleeping bag around her while she slept. Someone nothing. Her eyes went to the only other person in the room.

'Sleep well?' The fully clad figure bent over a portable keyboard didn't lift his dark head, but seemed to sense her wakefulness.

'Yes, thank you.' She tucked her nose below the covers. So this was that embarrassing morning-after feeling. 'What are you doing?'

'Sending a few e-mails.'

What sort of person sent e-mails at this time of the morning…? The sort of person you slept with last night—a *stranger*, her mental critic added, just in case she didn't feel bad enough already, a beautiful stranger.

'Right…' She cleared her throat. 'What time is it…?' she asked, more out of a desire to fill the yawning gap in their conversation than a genuine desire to know.

'Almost seven.'

'Seven!' she yelped, shooting upright. 'Oh, God!' she groaned, clasping her hands to her bare breasts.

Reece closed the lid of the laptop with a click and turned to face her. His gently ironic expression made her even more aware of the absurdity of displaying inhibitions the morning after the night before—especially when the night before was the one they'd shared!

'Is that a problem?'

'Dad and the boys will be up for breakfast,' she agonised.

'Can't they do *anything* without you to take charge?'

'Of course they can,' she responded, exasperated. 'And I don't "take charge".' Did she really strike him as a bossy, *organising* female? 'I just want things to be…' A frown puckered the smooth skin across her broad, seamless brow.

'The same?' he put in gently, drawing her startled gaze.

'I don't know what you mean.'

'Sure you do—you're trying to step into your mother's shoes. Has it ever occurred to you, Darcy, that maybe she wants her absence to be noticed…?'

A flicker of uncertainty made the soft corners of her mouth droop for a few tell-tale seconds before her expression hardened. 'You know nothing about it,' she blustered angrily. 'Mum isn't a frustrated housewife and she isn't menopausal.'

'Is that what the menfolk think…?'

Nick had put forward this theory but Darcy had soon put him right. 'Anyway, you're missing the point.'

He looked mildly perplexed. '*I* am…?'

'They'll wonder where I am.'

She watched his sensual lips twist. 'And you don't want to broadcast the fact you spent the night with me.'

The sad part was her reputation could probably survive intact. She'd learnt a long time ago that people didn't think of her and steamy sex in the same thought. She was doomed to be the eternal Mary Poppins figure. Which was pretty ironic when you had an almost ruined marriage on your conscience.

'Do you blame me?' she asked him scornfully. He didn't respond but a nerve along his jaw-line did some flexing. 'Relax,' she sighed disconsolately. 'Even if I did want to tell, nobody would believe me.'

Reece got to his feet and strolled towards her. 'Put this on—you look ridiculous.' He handed her her pyjama top.

His scornful contempt of her maidenly modesty was even more infuriating because she shared his opinion; even so, she couldn't bring herself to expose herself to the full glare of his scrutiny, which was, she reasoned gloomily, bound to be a whole lot more objective than it had been last night.

'If you're waiting for me to turn my back you'll be waiting a long, long time,' he drawled, taking up a grandstand seat on the packing case. He stretched out his long legs and casually crossed his booted feet at the ankle.

'You're no gentleman.'

He seemed to find her accusation amusing.

With an angry toss of her tousled hair she pulled the garment over her head.

It was a classic case of more haste, less speed. With her head halfway through the arm-hole she took a deep breath and told herself to calm down. So she didn't have the best boobs in the world—they were more than adequate…some might even say ample…what did it matter if he didn't grade them in the top ten per cent…? After all, they were only ships that had passed—and collided—in the night.

The rest of the manoeuvre was performed with a bit of belated dignity. She smoothed the fabric into place.

'I'm perfectly at ease with my body,' she declared defiantly. Why not just give him a list of your insecurities to peruse at his leisure and be done with it, you *idiot*!

'Oh, it shows, sweetheart, it shows,' came the bone-dry response.

Whilst his facial muscles didn't budge an inch, the sardonic amusement in his eyes said it all. Then suddenly he wasn't smiling any more and something was added to the atmosphere that hadn't been there a second before—something that made her heart-rate pick up tempo.

'Last night…' he began heavily.

Here was the point where he explained it had been great *but*... She jumped in to beat him to the punchline; no way could she endure the big brush-off she sensed was heading her way!

'Last night!' For some reason she found herself grinning in a manic kind of way across at him. 'Yes, mad wasn't it...?' She shrugged in a way that suggested that kind of madness came her way on a regular basis.

'Mad, bad...' his deep voice lovingly caressed each syllable and became diamond-hard as he continued '...mind-blowingly great sex...is that what you are trying to say?'

Darcy wasn't trying to say anything; she was trying to remember how to breathe! Not only did he sound as if he meant it, he looked it too. In fact, that mean, hungry look on his rampantly male features made her shudder inside and blush hotly on the outside—she wished she could have reversed the scenario; it would have shown less.

Now, here was something she hadn't bargained for. Was it a good or bad thing...?

With a rush she got to her feet and tugged the pyjama top down as far as it would go over her thighs.

'I'm glad you enjoyed yourself.' Of all the *moronic*... With a sigh of relief she located her clothes folded in a neat pile—Darcy retained a very definite memory of throwing them along with her inhibitions to the four winds the previous night. She found the thought of Reece retrieving and carefully folding her clothes somehow strangely unsettling.

'Did you?'

'You know I did,' she choked.

'I seem to recall your mentioning something to that effect,' he agreed.

Darcy choked some more.

'Why are you running away?' His languid tone suggested

casual curiosity rather than a driving desire to discover the reason.

Darcy zipped up her jeans, swearing softly as the zip snagged in the fabric of the pyjama trousers she had on underneath. 'That's rich coming from you!' she said, going into attack mode.

There was a tense silence.

'Meaning…?' Darcy had never heard that dangerous note in his voice before but she didn't doubt he used it often—and no doubt it had the desired effect of cowing the recipient. Well, not this time, mate…!

A mulish expression settled on her soft features as she planted her hands on her hips and laughed. 'You've got to be kidding…? You're holed up here; what's that if it's not running away?'

She watched the anger slowly fade from his eyes. 'Christmas. I'm running away from Christmas…'

A startled laugh was drawn from her. 'There's a lot of it around.' If all Mum was running away from was Christmas she'd be delighted—the complications arose if it was her life or, nasty thought, her family that had made her flee!

'Pardon…?'

Darcy shook her head. 'Nothing,' she prevaricated, her eyes sliding from his.

'Then why are you looking so shifty?' he wondered, displaying an unforgivable and highly worrying degree of perception.

'I've got that sort of face,' she snapped back badtemperedly.

'You wouldn't make a poker player,' he agreed.

'I was just thinking.'

'Dare I ask what?'

'If you must know, I was thinking you don't strike me as the sort of man who runs away from anything. And even if you did, why on earth would you run away here…?' Her eyes did a quick, highly critical circuit of the room.

He shook his head and clicked his tongue. 'Don't let the Yorkshire Tourist Board hear you say that,' he chided.

'I meant this house.'

'Why not…?' he drawled.

'No electricity, I'm guessing poor plumbing…?' She began to tick off the reasons on her fingers.

'Diabolical,' he conceded ruefully. 'If you want the bathroom I'd wait until you get next door if I were you.'

'Thanks for the advice.' She refused to be sidetracked. 'You still haven't told me why.'

The imperious angle of his head made it seem as though he was looking down his masterful nose at her—Darcy didn't relish the sensation.

'Could that be because I don't think it's any of your business…?'

Darcy relished this sensation even less! She caught her breath angrily at the calculated rebuff.

'Well, that put me in my place, didn't it?'

A spasm of something close to regret flickered across Reece's features.

'Hold on.' He moved to intercept her before she reached the door. 'My friend's builders have been a little less than truthful with their reports to him,' he explained abruptly. 'I'd say they've fallen behind schedule by a couple of months. I was expecting something less…basic.'

'Then you're not staying?' Of course he's not, dumbo.

'I wasn't…'

Sure she must have misheard his soft response, Darcy raised her startled eyes to his face. 'What's changed?'

He was watching her with that infuriatingly enigmatic smile that told her absolutely nothing. 'I like the neighbours.'

Their eyes met and a great rush of sexual longing

crowded out sensible coherent thought. She never figured out how long she stood there staring at him like a drooling idiot.

Does he think all he has to do is click his fingers and I'll…? Why not, Darcy, girl, that's all he had to do last night! Her face flushed with mortification.

'Like the idea of sex on tap, you mean!'

His mouth tightened.

'Well, let me tell you, if you think last night was anything other than a one-off, think again!' she advised hotly.

'Does the idea of a relationship based on sex frighten you, Darcy?'

'No,' she told him candidly, 'it appalls me!'

'And excites you,' he interjected slyly.

'No such thing!' she blustered.

'Liar…you want me and we both know it.'

Darcy gave a hoarse, incredulous laugh—talk about Neanderthal. 'Why not just thump your chest and drag me off to your cave?'

Reece thought the general idea was sound, although he was thinking more along the lines of a nice hotel room with good plumbing and Room Service.

'It may not be a particularly politically correct thing to say, but—'

'May?' she squeaked. 'There's no "may" about it!'

'Tell me, do you regret last night happened? Do you regret we made love, Darcy?'

She lifted her chin, met his eyes scornfully, and opened her mouth. 'You bet I…' The blood drained dramatically from her face. 'I…*no*,' she admitted with the utmost reluctance—now would have been a good time to lie.

'As I was saying, from the first moment I saw you…'

Perhaps the significance of her confession was wasted on him…? Then again, perhaps this was wishful thinking on her part.

'The first moment you saw me you thought I was a boy. Is there something you're not telling me…?'

He eyed her with signs of irritation. 'So, not the *first*,' he gritted. 'We're not talking about *then*, we're talking about *now*.'

Darcy didn't want to talk about now—actually, she didn't want to talk about anything with this infuriating man who seemed to have the knack of making her say incriminating things.

'And now,' she announced coldly, 'I'm going home—or I would be if you'd shift yourself.' She looked pointedly past his shoulder at the door.

Reece immediately stepped to one side with a fluid grace that made her stomach muscles quiver; perversely she found herself reluctant to take the escape route offered.

Whilst she hovered indecisively he moved to her side. 'I'll walk you home.'

Darcy's eyes widened. 'You're joking—right?'

'Actually,' he confessed, 'I was hoping you'd let me have the use of your shower, or, better still, a long, hot bath.'

'My God, but you've got a nerve!' she gasped.

'I've also got several broken ribs, extensive bruising and a bust shoulder, but don't let that influence your decision.'

Despite herself, Darcy felt a smile forming. 'We're not a hotel!' she told him severely.

'Is that a no?'

Darcy's eyes narrowed. 'It should be.' He didn't look surprised by her capitulation, but then, why would he, when you've already proved you're a push-over in every sense of the word? 'If you say *anything* to my family about…you know what…'

'So, Darce…?'

'So what?' Darcy waved her secateurs in her brother's

face. 'If you're going to get in my way you might as well carry this lot.' She indicated the large pile of freshly cut holly at her feet.

'Me!'

My God, but men were hopeless. 'I suppose you'd just stand there and watch me shift the lot.' They'd certainly stand by and watch her decorate the house with boughs of festive greenery, not to mention decorate the enormous tree that by family tradition they collected from the local garden centre owned by her godparents.

'It's sharp.'

'It's holly, Nick; of course it's sharp.'

'This sweater cost me a fortune,' he grumbled, preceding her up the garden path. 'Where do you want it?' he asked when they eventually reached the house.

'Leave it in the porch. Feel like a cup of coffee?' she asked as her brother followed her into the house.

'I feel like some answers.'

Darcy, her expression suspicious, watched as he plucked a couple of stray glossy leaves from the fine rib of his sweater.

'About what?' she asked, trying not to sound defensive.

'About what you were doing with our neighbour. I thought you couldn't stand him.'

'I can't,' Darcy asserted stoutly. 'The man had a serious accident. What was I supposed to do—say he couldn't take a shower?' She turned away, crashing the cups and saucers. 'Did you say you wanted tea or coffee?'

'Neither. It would be when you bumped into him while you were walking the dogs that he asked to use our facilities, would it, Darce…?'

'Yes, that's right,' she agreed quickly, not turning around.

'Since when, little sister, did you take the dogs for a walk wearing your pyjamas?'

Darcy started and spilt the milk over the work surface.

'Language!' her brother reproached.

She shot him a withering glance and wiped her clammy palms on the seat of her jeans before she picked up the cup; the faint tremor in her fingers was barely noticeable—though eagle-eyed Nick had probably spotted it.

'Since when did you become Miss Marple?' She laughed lightly as she planted herself on a chair and raised the scalding drink to her lips. Playing it down was the best way to go…

'Since I looked into your room after I took the dogs for a walk around seven and found you weren't there.'

All the colour bar a small pink circle over either cheek fled Darcy's guilty face. 'What were you doing in my room?'

'Fetching you a cup of tea.'

It was typical of Nick to discover his considerate side at the worst possible moment. 'Oh…' What else could she say? She certainly wasn't going to volunteer any more information if she could help it!

'What is a guy like him with that sort of serious money doing hanging around someone like you?' Nick wondered suspiciously. 'No offence intended, Darce…' he added casually.

Darcy wondered what he'd say if she told him she took offence—serious offence. She was about to quiz her tactless sibling on the 'serious money' statement when his next comment distracted her.

'Has he followed you here, Darcy, is that it? I'm assuming you'd already met before yesterday.'

'Why on earth would you think that?' There was no way he could have picked anything up from her attitude when she'd brought Reece back earlier. She'd been very careful about that—so careful, in fact, that her behaviour had bordered on the catatonic, before she'd swiftly excused herself and nipped off to the church to do the flowers—it was Mum's turn on the rota; Adam would probably have a fit when he saw her efforts.

'I think that because I didn't think you were the sort of girl who would spend the night with a complete stranger.' If what he had said wasn't bad enough, Nick had to go and make it even worse by adding, 'Even if he is rich and powerful.'

For several moments Darcy didn't do anything, but when she finally lifted her eyes from the rim of her coffee-cup they were sparkling with anger.

'How dare you?'

Nick looked taken aback by the rancour in his sister's shaking voice. 'Come on, Darce, you must admit it was pretty sus...'

'I don't have to admit anything!' she said in a low, intense voice that throbbed with emotion. Carefully pushing her seat back, she rose to her feet. 'Not to you at least.' She ran her tongue over the bloodless outline of her pale lips. 'Just for the record, Nick, you're the biggest hypocrite I know.'

His eyes filled with concern, Nick rose to his feet. 'Darce, I didn't mean—'

Darcy cut him off with a flash of her narrowed eyes. 'Incidentally, I'll sleep with who the hell I like!' she yelled, sweeping from the room.

Her dramatic exit was ruined by the fact she narrowly avoided colliding with the solid bulk of Reece Erskine on her way out.

'Whoa there.' She'd have fallen rather than accept the arm he tried to offer her; it wasn't easy, as he was carrying a large wicker hamper balanced on the crook of his functioning elbow, and his solicitous action almost sent it to the floor.

'What are you doing here?' The tense, scratchy thing

didn't sound like her voice at all. Making a superhuman effort, she pulled herself together and stepped back away from his chest—and the temptation to lay her head on it. Even holding her breath, she could still smell the fresh male fragrance that emanated from his warm skin, so she gave up on what was not really a practical long-term solution to her problem to begin with.

'That's no way to greet a guy carrying gifts, Darce.'

Darcy hadn't even noticed the twins and Jack, who had entered the kitchen behind Reece—when he was around she didn't tend to notice much else.

'Cool!' Harry cried, holding up a large box of Belgian chocolates and adding them to the pile of luxury items he and his twin were extracting from the hamper they'd set down on the table.

Darcy glanced at the growing pile—there was no way he'd got that little lot from the village shop.

'This is mine,' Charlie crowed, discovering a bottle of champagne.

Clicking his tongue tolerantly, his father removed the bottle from his crestfallen son's hand. 'This is really very generous of you, Reece…'

'A small thank-you for everything you've done for me.'

'It really wasn't necessary,' Jack insisted.

'Dad, you're not going to give it back, are you?' Charlie asked in alarm.

'How did we raise two such avaricious little monsters…?' The twins exchanged rueful grins. 'What the boys are trying to say, Reece, is the gift is much appreciated. Can we offer you a drink—it looks like there's one on the go… Darcy…?'

'In case nobody noticed, I'm busy,' she responded shortly.

If her stepfather had looked annoyed by her unneighbourly response she could have coped, but no, he had to go and look hurt and guilty.

'I suppose,' he responded worriedly, 'we have let a lot of things fall on your shoulders.' He turned to Reece. 'It's just my wife usually...'

'I enjoy it, Dad,' Darcy interrupted hurriedly, hating the forlorn expression on her stepfather's face and despising herself for putting it there. 'Actually, I was just off to pick up the tree. Anyone like to come?' she enquired. She was predictably underwhelmed by the response. 'Right, I'll be off, then.'

'If you don't mind, I wouldn't mind coming along for the ride.'

Darcy spun around, horror etched on her pale features. 'You!'

'I'm getting a bit stir-crazy, unable to drive,' Reece explained glibly to the room in general.

'You'd be bored,' she said several shades too emphatically.

'I think it's an excellent idea,' Jack responded firmly, reproach in his eyes.

Nick spoke for the first time. 'I'm sure Darcy will enjoy having company.'

Darcy shot her treacherous narrow-minded brother a seething look from under the sweep of her lashes. 'There will be lashings of mud.' Nobody paid her any heed.

'Borrow some Wellingtons—the twins look about the same size as you.'

With a sigh Darcy subsided into a resentful silence whilst her eager family—with the notable exception of Nick—equipped their neighbour.

'You look awfully pale, Darcy.'

Thanks, bro, she thought as Nick's contribution to the conversation brought her a lot of highly undesirable attention.

'Yes, she does, doesn't she?' her stepfather agreed. 'Are you feeling all right?'

'Absolutely fine.'

'It's probably sleep deprivation,' Nick continued smoothly. 'She's not been sleeping too well.' He wasn't looking at his sister as he spoke but at the tall figure who stood beside her. The two men exchanged a long look.

'Is that right? You didn't say so, Darcy.'

'Lot on my mind, Dad...' she muttered. 'Holidays are always the same—it takes me the first week to wind down.'

'Darcy is a computer analyst,' her proud stepfather explained to Reece. 'She has a *very* responsible job.'

Darcy cringed. 'Give the man a break, Dad,' she laughed uncomfortably. 'I'm sure Mr Erskine doesn't want to know about my work.'

Nick, of course, couldn't resist stirring the pot. 'You mean, he doesn't already?'

'If you've got nothing better to do, Nick, you could take a look at the Christmas lights for me.' She felt a surge of satisfaction as her brother looked suitably horrified at the prospect. 'They don't seem to be working.'

'I think,' Nick announced hopefully, 'that it's time we bought some new ones.'

'You can't do that, Nick!' Charlie protested. 'We've had them for ever...'

'My point exactly,' Nick muttered. 'It's the same every year—they never work.'

'I remember the time the cat—that one that had no tail—' Harry began.

'Oscar,' his twin supplied.

Nick decided to inject a little reality into this trip down memory lane. '*I* remember the time they fused the electrics while Mum was cooking Christmas dinner...'

There was a collective subdued gasp of dismay and all eyes turned to Jack.

'Far be it from me to break with tradition,' Nick put in quickly. 'I'll fix the damned things.'

'You all seem pretty protective of your father,' Reece observed as he trailed Darcy outside.

'Stepfather, actually, but yes, I suppose we are.'

'Stepfather; that makes the twins your...?'

Darcy gave a resigned sigh. 'Jack adopted Nick and me when he married Mum—I was five. Not that it's any of your business.' She stood beside the Land Rover, jingling the keys. 'You can't *want* to come...' Please...please, let him say he doesn't. She always had been a hopeless optimist!

CHAPTER FIVE

'DID you have to bring this thing?' Reece scowled as the big dog, his paws planted on the back of the passenger seat, licked his face ecstatically.

'I wanted *him* to come,' Darcy, tight-lipped, pointedly replied. 'Sit down, Wally!' Reluctantly the big animal curled up on the back seat of her stepfather's Land Rover, his eyes reproachful.

Reece wiped the excess canine saliva off his neck with a pained grimace. 'A man could get to feel unwanted.'

'Not by Wally.' The dog's ears pricked up at the sound of his name. 'Or my family,' she reflected with a frustrated little snort. 'You've certainly weaseled your way into their affections,' she hissed nastily. 'It was a master stroke to appeal to the twins' stomachs.'

Reece, who wasn't really interested in the direct route to the twins' hearts, responded with a slightly distracted smile.

'I take it the way to your elder brother's heart is not through his stomach…'

'You noticed that, did you?' Darcy had not yet forgiven Nick. How dared he lecture her on morality, she fumed—the man who had had, much to his parents' dismay and her awe, an affair with a thirty-year-old divorcee when he was just seventeen?

'Let's just say I didn't feel warm and welcome when he looked at me,' Reece responded drily. His eyes narrowed. 'Is he giving you a hard time?' he wondered suspiciously.

'I don't give a damn what Nick thinks!'

'Yeah, I heard that bit.'

A deep tide of colour washed over her fair skin as she

worked out what he must have heard. 'Don't go reading anything into that. I was establishing a principle. Sex isn't a high priority for me.'

Darcy knew she was wasting her breath; the man obviously had her down as some sort of sex junkie—I could always refer him to Michael, she thought. He would set the record straight. Not that Michael had ever come right out and complained about her sex drive, or lack of it, but that was probably because the man had still had a wife at home to keep happy. From his point of view, the fact she hadn't made excessive demands had probably been a godsend!

'You got many other prospects lined up?'

'Has anyone ever told you you've got a very crude mouth, and a one-track mind?' He wasn't the only one, she thought, struggling hard to banish the image of his big, sexy body shifting beneath her…his skin glistening…the ripple of muscle… The heat travelled like a flash-flood up her neck and bathed her face. The empty feeling in the pit of her belly got emptier and achier.

Despite her determination to think of anything else but the man beside her, Darcy couldn't have stopped her eyes from furtively fluttering to the mouth she'd criticised if her life had depended on it. Perfection didn't seem too extravagant an adjective for that wide, mobile curve which intriguingly managed to combine both sensuality and control.

'Actually,' she mused, her voice husky, 'the new vicar did ask me to the Christmas dance.' She'd almost forgotten this unexpected event, which had occurred only this morning, but then she had other things on her mind. How her little sister would laugh if she ever discovered what a man-magnet the sister she despaired of had become.

'New vicar…' Reece didn't look as though he was taking the opposition seriously. 'I'm seeing tweed jackets, maybe a goatee—looks aren't everything, of course…'

'Actually, Adam played rugby for Oxford,' she was pleased to announce.

'In the Sixties...?'

'I'd say he's thirty...'

'Broken nose...?' Reece suggested hopefully.

Darcy's lips twitched. 'No, he was a back-row man. It was a toss-up between male modelling and the church,' she lied outrageously. Her expression sobered. 'Reece, are you?' she began.

'Am I what?'

'Nick said...' she began.

'Nick said what?' Reece thought he could guess.

'He said you were rich—super-rich, actually. Is that true?'

Reece didn't prevaricate. 'Yes.'

Deep down she'd always known he didn't live in the same world as she did. Darcy tried not to let her disappointment show; she'd been secretly hoping that Nick might have got it wrong. Now there was no point even dreaming this thing might be anything other than a one-night stand.

'I suppose you're famous too?' she accused bitterly.

She made it sound as though he'd been concealing the fact he was wanted by Interpol. Reece had never met a female who had reacted in quite this way to his social position and wealth before.

'Obviously not,' he drawled, amusement in his voice.

'Don't be offended,' she soothed absently. 'I don't read the financial pages.'

'But Nick does?'

'Hardly; he's a sports journalist.'

Reece laughed. 'I think you're being a bit severe; I knew a sports writer once who had read a book.'

Darcy couldn't summon the necessary smile to respond

to his raillery. 'Are you involved in property development? Is that why you came to the Hall?'

'My company is involved in property development,' Reece agreed, not mentioning that this property development didn't include small country houses being renovated on a shoestring.

It did involve a string of brand-new hotels in various capitals of the world which the leisure arm of his empire now ran. A good many office complexes and several sports stadiums which had popped up all over Europe had also begun their existence on a drawing board in the Erskine Building—he didn't mention this either.

'Then you're some sort of property developer…?' she prodded.

'That was one of the areas we've diversified into during the last few years.'

'We?'

'Well, it's not a one-man show; my sister Kate is heavily involved in the running of the hotel chain, and my cousin Declan has just joined us. My kid brother has just finished his stint at Harvard, so hopefully he'll—'

'You told me you didn't have a family!' Darcy twitched her rear-view mirror and saw an almost comical grimace of dismay register on his drop-dead gorgeous features.

'I did…?' he echoed evasively.

'Yes, you did.'

'They're a lovely bunch but a bit…overwhelming *en masse*—like at Christmas time. Don't you ever wish you were an only child…?'

The encounter with Nick still fresh in her mind, Darcy found herself nodding. 'When I'm around Nick, yes, I do.'

'The guy's only trying to protect you.' Reece had a sister of his own, and a real headache she was too.

Darcy could hardly believe her ears—Reece, defending Nick of all people! 'This male bonding is all very sweet but have you forgotten it's you he wants to protect me from?' she reminded him.

'I'd not forgotten. I have this nasty feeling when he gets me alone he's going to ask me what my intentions are.'

Did he really expect her to appreciate the humour of this remark? 'He already knows. That's the problem.'

She sensed his looking at her, and couldn't stop herself taking her eyes off the road for a split-second…he was pushing an unruly hank of glossy almost black hair from his eyes. Did he always have to look so damned pleased with himself? she wondered, resenting the way just looking at him sent her temperature rocketing.

Reece would have been astonished if he'd been privy to her thoughts. He had rarely felt less complacent in his life; things were happening to him that he didn't want or need—his eyes were drawn to the shell-like shape of her ear—cancel 'didn't need'. Every time he looked at this woman he *needed* with a capital N.

'Perhaps he could tell me,' he muttered under his breath.

'Pardon?'

She wanted to know; well, he'd tell her! 'I can't look at your ear without wanting to whisper in it. I can't look at your mouth—'

'Stop!' Darcy yelled, her stressed heart pumping out adrenalin like a pneumatic drill. 'If you say things like that I'm likely to crash the car.'

'In that case, wouldn't it be far safer if you parked somewhere? Somewhere quiet and secluded would be good.' From what he'd seen, that shouldn't be too difficult—they'd barely passed another car.

Darcy broke out in a cold sweat. 'You can't say things like that to me!' She could hardly hear herself speak above the frantic clamour of her heart.

Reece sighed. 'I can't *not* say things like that to you. Do you think it's possible they've put something in the water...?'

'I think it's possible you've got nothing better to do than harass me,' she responded weakly in a strangulated version of her own deep, husky voice.

'Actually, I brought a heap of paperwork with me.'

'I'm flattered no end.'

'Do your boyfriends always have to work so hard?'

She could have said What boyfriends? but she didn't want to reveal the disgraceful lack of sexual encounters in her work-orientated life. 'You're not a boy or my friend.'

'I'm your lover.'

This man was the master of the one-liners; there was no doubt about it. Darcy dabbed the beads of sweat from the full outline of her upper lip with the tip of her tongue and tried to coax her respirations into a more manageable rate.

'You're my one-night stand,' she bit back coldly. He would never know that this admission hurt her more than it did him. 'Listen, I can see why you might think I'm up for...that I might want you to...' Darcy's voice dropped to an agonised whisper. 'You know what I mean.' Still he didn't respond. 'Last night wasn't me...'

Even though her eyes remained rigidly fixed on the road, she could feel his eyes travelling over her body, her skin prickling in response to the unseen scrutiny.

'I have to dispute that.'

The low rasp of his voice was like a caress, and she could picture his slow, sensual smile in her head. She ground her teeth in frustration.

'I don't normally act like that,' she insisted.

'Then last night was special...?'

'Last night was mad, a mistake!' she yelled. 'I'm not passing judgement on people that do act like that, but it's just not me.'

'I think it is you.'

'Haven't you heard a thing I've said?' she asked shrilly.

'You've made a lot of noise but you haven't come right out and said no.'

She gave a contemptuous laugh. 'And I'm supposed to believe that's all it takes...?'

'Believe it or not, it's true.'

You could have taken a chainsaw to the tension in the air.

'Will you fasten your seat belt?'

Reece smiled, but didn't push his advantage. 'It hurts the bust ribs,' he explained mildly.

So would being thrown through the windscreen. 'Don't be such a sissy!' she admonished sternly.

'You're the boss.'

If only, she thought wistfully. I should have said no—why didn't I say it...? 'If the word ''mouth'' crosses your lips once more I'll make you walk back,' she warned him sternly. Darcy had no intention of becoming a rich man's plaything—no matter how tempting the notion was.

'Last night—'

Darcy cut him off. 'That too.'

'I have a very extensive vocabulary, Darcy.'

'And I have a very low tolerance level.' Her angry sneer morphed into a weak scowl. 'Why the hell did you come here?' If he hadn't been doing so she'd never have met him and her life would have been a lot simpler.

'Maybe I got tired of well-meaning people trying to rehabilitate me.'

Darcy puzzled over his obscure reply. 'I don't understand.'

'That's the way I'd like to keep it for the moment.'

There was only a handful of people in the garden centre, but Reece suspected they'd have come in for personal attention even if the place had been packed out. As if he'd been expecting them, the guy Reece assumed ran the place appeared as soon as they drew up. He greeted Darcy warmly and enfolded her in a bear-like hug. When she emerged she reluctantly acknowledged his presence.

'This is Richard Stenning, my godfather. Uncle Rick, this is Reece, and, before you say anything, he's *not* my boy-friend.'

'But I'm working on it.'

Both men seemed to find this crack amusing; Darcy didn't.

'I was thinking between six feet and six feet six…?' she said briskly, eyeing up the swathes of green pine.

'I'm six four and a half actually.'

'Not you, *stupid*, the tree.'

The older man looked at the bickering couple with a benevolent smile. 'Come along this way, Darcy, I think I've got just what you want.'

Darcy doubted this very much unless he had a supply of six-foot-four-and-a-half males with fascinating green eyes, black hair and sex appeal that went off the scale! Despite this, she stomped obediently after him.

Despite Reece's unhelpful contributions, she eventually selected one that was neither too bushy nor too straggly and didn't have any bare bits. The tree was bagged in a net and installed in the back of the Land Rover beside Wally.

'You'll have a mince pie, of course?'

Reece bent downwards to enquire in her ear, 'Is this another family tradition?'

Darcy ignored him and the tantalising male scent of him that teased her receptive nostrils—she was partially successful.

'Wouldn't miss it for the world,' she agreed, following their host into the shop area, which was dripping with both tasteful and gaudy Christmas decorations—not the place for a man who was trying to avoid Christmas, although Reece seemed to be taking the festive surroundings in his stride. 'But no sherry for me,' she added hastily, with an expression of regret, 'I'm driving.'

'But you'll have some, Mr Erskine?'

'Reece. Yes, I'd love some.'

Darcy was watching from under the protective sweep of her lashes, so she had the satisfaction of seeing his eyes widen in shock as he took a robust bite from his innocent-looking pie. Her lips twitched; she was far more tentative in her approach.

'Delicious as usual,' she mumbled, chewing away valiantly; Uncle Rick must have a stomach of cast iron, she decided, watching him munch his way through two for her one. The problem with Aunty Grace's mince pies was that they looked totally delicious and had the consistency of concrete. 'Aunty Grace has surpassed herself this year.'

'Delicious,' she heard Reece agree faintly after he very visibly swallowed.

'Would you like another, Reece?'

Reece patted his stomach. 'Love to, but I don't want to take the edge off my appetite—I'm taking Darcy to lunch,' he explained glibly.

'First I've heard about it.'

'It was meant to be a surprise, darling.' He glanced at the steel-banded watch on his wrist. 'Talking of which, we should be making a move—I've booked a table for twelve.'

'Where would that be...*darling*?' she wondered innocently. The man was entirely too slick.

'Why, where else but your favourite, *daaarling*?' Reece drawled smoothly.

'Twelve...? You'd better get a move-on, Darcy; it'll take you twenty minutes to get to the Bull's Head. You give my best to the family.'

Darcy bent forward and kissed the older man's cheek. 'I will, Uncle Rick. Why, Reece!' she exclaimed, picking up the glass carefully secreted behind a potted palm. 'You've forgotten your sherry,' she reminded him spitefully.

'So I have.' He met her eyes and, nostrils flared, tipped back the glass, downing the contents in one gulp—like taking nasty medicine, she thought, stifling the urge to giggle.

'Was that a test, or an initiation ceremony?' he muttered under his breath as they walked together back to the Land Rover.

If it had been he'd have passed with flying colours. 'Uncle Rick only hands out the mince pies and sherry to valued friends and customers.'

'I'm surprised he still has any.'

'Shut up,' she hissed, waving through the window. 'He'll hear you.'

'What was that I just drank?'

'Sherry.'

'I've tasted sherry, sweetheart, and that wasn't it.'

Darcy, who had sampled the sweet, syrupy concoction in the past, had some sympathy with his view. 'It's probably safer to call it fortified wine,' she conceded.

'How about we head for the Bull's Head, your favourite watering hole?' he reminded her drily.

'How about I drop you at the nearest bus station? Oh, sorry, I forgot I'm talking to limo man.'

'Helicopters are my preferred mode of transport. Do you realise that nearly all our conversations have taken place while you're at the wheel of a car—?'

'Is there anything wrong with my driving?' she asked belligerently.

'Not a thing—when you're looking at the road. It would make a nice change to be able to have a conversation that doesn't prohibit the odd physical gesture.'

Darcy swallowed nervously and decided it would be safer to never relinquish her place at the wheel. 'Your problem,' she announced scornfully, 'is you think I'll agree to anything if you kiss me.'

'From where I'm sitting that's a revelation not a problem.'

It was one revelation too many for Darcy; she couldn't concentrate on the road when her mind was full of forbidden images. The battle of words, at times undeniably stimulating, had lost all appeal. With a muffled plea for heavenly intervention she brought the Land Rover to an abrupt halt on the grassy verge. Without even bothering to switch off the engine, she leapt from the driver's seat.

Reece switched off the engine and pocketed the keys before following her.

Darcy, who was hunched over, her hands braced against her thighs, turned her head to look at him.

'Go away!' she pleaded hoarsely. She didn't actually hold out much hope of his doing as she requested.

'Are you all right?'

'Very obviously not.' She took another deep breath and slowly straightened up. She brushed a few stray strands of hair from her face; it was an intensely weary gesture. 'If you must know, I couldn't stand being in that car with you any longer.' She was past caring what he thought.

Reece didn't seem to take offence in her anguished observation. 'It's pretty intense, isn't it?' he commiserated.

Darcy's brows drew into a suspicious line above her wide, startled eyes. 'Are you saying that *you*...?' She moved her head in a scornful negative gesture, rejecting the idea that Reece could be similarly affected by her proximity.

'I can't stop thinking about last night or wanting it to happen again.' His tone might have been matter-of-fact bordering on rudely abrupt, but the lick of flames in his deep-set eyes was not!

Darcy was shaking so hard she had to fold her arms tight

across her middle to hide the tremors. In the process she unwittingly drew attention to her full, heaving bosom. 'That was sex.'

'That was *exceptional* sex,' Reece contradicted firmly. 'A relationship has to start somewhere.'

Darcy looked at him blankly. 'Relationship…? You don't want a relationship.'

'How do you know what I want?' he demanded.

'Well, do you?'

'Maybe not. Well, actually, no, I don't want a relationship. I don't want to be celibate either.'

He didn't even have the guts to look her in the eye when he said it, she thought wrathfully. The perversity of the average male was simply breathtaking. But it had shut up the voice in her head, the one recklessly shrieking 'Go for it! Go for it!', and a good thing too, she decided glumly.

'The only thing I know for sure I want is you.'

She couldn't legitimately complain about eye-contact now—an earthquake couldn't have broken the grip his dark-lashed eyes had on her. The air escaped her lungs in one long, sibilant hiss; her eyes, huge in her pale face, were glued to his face. Her thoughts were in total chaos. You can't let yourself be seduced by someone saying he wants you—even if that someone is Reece Erskine, she told herself angrily.

'Naturally I'm flattered,' she drawled, giving a scornful, unnatural little laugh that implied just the opposite.

His jaw tightened. 'I'm not trying to flatter you.' Reece, who prided himself on self-control, discovered he couldn't take his eyes from the lush curve of her lovely lips, even though the looking caused the distant buzzing in his head to increase significantly.

'What are you trying to do, then?' Other than drive me out of my mind, that is…? It just didn't seem possible for a man to walk into her life and turn everything upside-down. 'You may be in the mood for some sort of holiday romance, but I simply don't have the time, energy or inclination.' Well, the first two at least were true.

'I thought you were on holiday too.'

Some holiday! 'My mum's gone walkabout, my stepfather, who I happen to be crazy about, needs constant reassurance, several hundred members of the family are likely to descend on us at any second and I can't even bake a mince pie, let alone feed and entertain them!' Stupidly it was the last deficiency that made her eyes fill with tears.

Reece moved towards her and she ached to throw herself into his arms. With a stiff little gesture that shrieked rejection she swayed backwards; it stopped Reece in his tracks.

'Are you trying to tell me this isn't a good time for us?' There was no smile to match the flippancy of his tone.

Darcy wanted to cry from sheer frustration, but she didn't have the luxury. As right as it felt to have his arms close around her, she knew it was all an illusion created by her overactive hormones. If she had been after casual sex she wouldn't have looked any further than this man: he fulfilled every criteria for the role.

The problem was she couldn't be that casual about sex, and when she got involved serious disaster usually followed—she was thinking about the rat Michael here, the one who had forgotten to mention his wife and children. His wife with kids in tow landing up on her doorstep pleading with Darcy not to take her husband away was one of her least favourite memories. Just recalling Michael's defence made her blood boil— 'I wanted to tell you, Darce, but I didn't want to hurt you'.

'There is no us!'

'There could be if you let it happen.'

And letting it happen would be so easy. Darcy sighed; his voice had a dangerously mesmeric quality…it was so hypnotic and attractive, in fact, that a person was inclined to forget just how outrageous the sentences formed by these perfect lips were.

'You're really worried about your mother, aren't you…?'

This observation brought her back to reality with a resounding thump.

'Am I supposed to believe you care about what I'm worried about?' she sneered, eyeing him with open contempt. 'The only thing you care about as far as I can see is getting me back into your bed!'

It was true, but that didn't alter the fact her words made him mad as hell. The flare of something close to fear in her eyes made him realise that his feelings must have been reflected on his face, so he made a conscious effort to control his anger.

'Listen, sweetheart,' he said after he'd counted to ten a couple of times, 'I've absolutely no idea if this thing is going to run its course in a matter of days, weeks or months but I think for both our sakes we should find out. If we don't we'll always wonder…' He paused long enough for her to appreciate the truth of what he was saying. 'I know you've some sort of guilt trip about sleeping with me last night, but it happened and I don't see much point beating yourself up over it.'

'Maybe I wouldn't if you didn't keep throwing it back in my face. Just for the record, I'm not…easy!'

'Just for the record,' he retorted drily, 'I don't think you're *easy*…anything but, as a matter of fact,' he added in a wry aside. 'This isn't the sort of attraction you can pretend isn't there, Darcy.'

That was true.

'I may want to get you into bed,' he continued with a candour that made her mouth grow dry and started up the distressing palpitations once more, 'but it doesn't mean we can't communicate outside the bedroom.' Darcy had no way of knowing how extraordinary this statement was coming from Reece Erskine, and Reece wasn't about to tell her—the truth was, it made him uneasy to acknowledge it. 'You're obviously worried about your mother and I thought it might help to talk to someone not personally involved. I may be shallow but I'm not totally insensitive.'

He sounded genuine. She searched his face—he looked genuine. 'I was only talking to her the day before; she didn't give a clue anything was wrong.' Her fingers clenched tightly.

'And you think you've done something?'

'Not me personally maybe—but us, the family. Why else would she walk out like this just before Christmas? She's made sure we can't contact her…' She gnawed away silently on her lower lip as she puzzled over the bizarre, bewildering behaviour of her parent.

'It's possible this is *her* problem.'

Darcy regarded him with disdain. 'Families are there to help you with your problems; you don't shut them out when you most need them.' An expression she didn't understand flickered across his handsome face. 'It's not at all like her—she's so *responsible*. Poor Jack is convinced it's something he's done.'

'But you don't think so.'

Darcy shook her head jerkily; now she'd started to talk it was hard to stop. 'Why couldn't she talk to us…?' she wondered unhappily.

'I expect you'll be able to ask her yourself when she comes home.'

In front of Jack and even her brothers she had to act optimistic and upbeat, and it was a relief almost to stop being so damned cheerful. 'Whenever that might be.'

'You've no idea at all how long she's likely to be away?'

Despondently Darcy shook her head. 'I'm really trying hard to make everything the same as it usually is…' It seemed important somehow not to let things slip, to keep a sense of continuity.

'And driving yourself into an early grave in the process,' he observed disapprovingly. 'The secret of a successful manager is delegation, Darcy.' She looked so transparently touched by his comment that he felt impelled to add, 'You ought to try it; you might even find you've got time for a personal life, and, as you already know, I have a vested interest in that.'

She stared wonderingly up into his face. It sounded as if he was saying he wanted to be part of her personal life, which didn't fit with what he had said about not wanting a relationship—in fact, it seemed to directly contradict it. The warmth in his eyes made her lose track for a few moments. 'How would I go about doing that?'

'You really want to know?'

Darcy gave a rueful smile. 'I wouldn't have asked otherwise.'

'Make a list of things you need to do and halve it.' She opened her mouth to protest but he didn't give her the opportunity. 'Divide the remaining tasks amongst the others. And don't tell me you can't give orders because I've been on the receiving end. Actually,' he admitted, his firm tone gentling, 'I quite liked it. Some of the time I quite like you…'

Darcy gulped. 'And the rest…?' she prompted huskily.

'I want to throttle you.'

'Which is it now?'

'Neither. It's been a hell of a long time since I wanted to wake up beside someone.'

'You're not trying to tell me you're celibate?'

'No, I'm not,' he agreed tersely. 'Sex is one form of recreation that I've made a point of including in my schedule,' he explained casually.

There was an appalled silence.

'That sounds pretty cold-blooded.' If she'd any sense she'd get back into the Land Rover and drive away. Darcy knew she wouldn't—she *couldn't*.

'It's an accusation that has been levelled at me before.'

'You want to kiss me.' It was a statement, not a question—it was the sort of statement that a girl who didn't want to be kissed didn't make.

'For starters,' he growled.

'Then for God's sake,' she pleaded in an agonised whisper, '*Do it!*'

My God, but the man could move fast with the right motivation. She barely had time to draw breath let alone change her mind before his mouth was hard on hers, and his tongue began to make some electrifying exploratory forays into the warm, moist interior.

The sheer pleasure of his touch as his fingers slid surely under the woollen jumper she wore made her whimper and sag, weak-kneed, against him. His hand worked its way smoothly up the slender curve of her back. Darcy grabbed for support and then remembered his injuries.

'I forgot.'

Reece's mouth came crashing back down on hers and stole away the rest of her words.

Eyes closed, she gave a long, blissful sigh when his head eventually lifted. 'I've hurt you.' She made an agitated effort to pull back, but he had other ideas.

'If I can't cope I'll tell you,' he breathed into her mouth.

'I don't think I can cope with much more of this!' she breathed back, touching her tongue to the fleshy inner part of his upper lip. She shuddered—they both did.

'Cope with what?'

Darcy laid her hand flat against his chest, feeling his heart beat through the layers of clothing. She'd known him for less than forty-eight hours and already he'd taken over her thoughts. If she had any sense she'd call it a day now before things got any worse.

'Cope with…*wanting*.' She put all the aching longing in the one word.

What was happening to her—where had this wilful recklessness come from? After Michael she'd been cautious—pathologically so, Jennifer had said. Would Jennifer approve of the new Darcy? The one who saw the flare of fierce possession in his eyes and felt the heat melt her bones and didn't even once contemplate running for cover? Hell, what did it matter? She needed action not analysis, and she needed Reece.

'Does that mean you've stopped trying to push me away?'

'I don't recall doing much pushing.' Grabbing, that was another matter.

'Why fight…?'

'My thought exactly.'

'It'll burn itself out soon enough.' Wasn't that the way with hot things? 'And I can get back to normal.'

Though his own thoughts had been running much along the same lines, Reece found that her sentiments filled him with a sense of discontent. He was perfectly aware that for a man who had a policy of never spending the entire night with a woman this was a pretty perverse response. Knowing it made no sense didn't lessen the gut feeling.

'And normal is…?' He slid his thumb down the soft curve of her cheek.

There was danger and raw, unrefined charisma in his smile. Without waiting for her to reply, he dipped his head and parted her lips with masterful ease.

'This normal…?' His tongue stabbed and she moaned low in her throat and pressed herself tight against his hips. She wondered vaguely if he was permanently aroused—not that she had any major objections if this should be the case. 'Or this…?' He withdrew.

Darcy gave a whimper of protest as he lifted his head.

'I preferred the first,' she admitted huskily.

'That being the case, perhaps we should…' He dangled the Land Rover keys in front of her. 'Can you drive…?'

Darcy nodded her head vigorously. So fierce was her need that if flying had been the only way to get into bed with him she'd have sprouted wings!

CHAPTER SIX

DURING the afternoon there had been several flurries of snow, and by the time Darcy got back home complete with the Christmas tree and a slightly guilty conscience a little of the powdery whiteness had begun to stick to the damp ground.

She stamped her feet to loosen the snow on her boots and lifted the old-fashioned iron latch on the kitchen door, hoping as she did so that there was nobody about; it wasn't that she intended to be *furtive*, exactly. 'Furtive' implied she had something to hide or be ashamed of, and, whilst Darcy acknowledged she was deeply confused and wildly exhilarated by what had happened to her, shame didn't feature at all. It was just that there were some things you couldn't share with your family, no matter how close you were, and Darcy didn't see much point in drawing unnecessary attention to her extended absence.

'Where have you been?'

So much for subterfuge.

Her entire family minus only one important member were seated around the long farmhouse table, but that absence brought an aching lump to her throat—if there was ever a time she'd needed her mum it was now. Darcy swallowed; she didn't need this, not when her mind was still full of the passionate coupling which had just taken place next door. She felt as if the evidence of her abandoned behaviour was written all over her face.

'Clare, you're home.' If Clare noticed her half-sister's greeting was lacking a certain warmth she didn't show it.

'Finally,' Nick contributed drily. 'Had trouble choosing the right tree, did you?' he wondered guilelessly.

Unexpectedly it was Clare who came to her rescue. 'Never mind about that, Nick.'

I'll second that, Darcy thought, pulling off her mittens. 'Good journey, Clare?'

'In case you hadn't noticed, it's snowing.' Clare's expression suggested that Darcy was in some way to blame for this.

I didn't notice because I've spent the afternoon making wild, passionate love to a gorgeous man. How, Darcy wondered, would that explanation go down…?

Clare shook back her rippling waist-length mane of hair and looked impatient. Like her half-sister, she was blonde and blue-eyed, but that was where the resemblance ended.

'I arrive to find that my mother…' she choked tearfully.

'She's ours too.'

'Shut up, Harry! Why didn't anyone tell me what was happening?'

'We didn't want to upset you, darling,' Jack soothed.

Nobody, Darcy reflected, feeling a twitch of resentment, ever wanted to upset Clare.

'Well, I'm upset now.' Clare sniffed.

'Did you remember to pick up the order from the farm, Nick?' Darcy asked, shaking her hair free of a few stray snowflakes, which were rapidly melting in the warm room. She hung her damp coat on the peg behind the door.

'How can you act as if nothing has happened?' Clare tearfully accused Darcy.

The implication that she didn't give a damn made Darcy turn angrily on her sister. 'What do you expect me to do, Clare?' she snapped. 'Mum's a grown woman; we can't bring her back against her will. We just have to wait.' Patience never had been one of her younger sister's most obvious qualities—when Clare wanted something she wanted it *now*, and more often than not she got it! 'Sitting about whining isn't going to help anyone!'

There was an almost comical look of shock on Clare's face as she recoiled from her sister's anger—Darcy was a bit surprised herself, as she rarely raised her voice to her sister. Instantly she regretted her outburst, not to mention her ungenerous thoughts. Clare could be thoughtless and selfish, but her kid sister could also be generous and loving, and not nearly as hard-bitten as she liked to make out.

There was a scraping sound as the younger girl rose gracefully to her feet. Darcy was happy being herself, but she wouldn't have been human if she hadn't felt the occasional touch of wistful envy when she looked at her spectacularly beautiful sister. Occasionally on bad days, when her hair was particularly unruly and the bathroom scales told her things she'd rather not know, she couldn't help but think that it would be nice if—just once—someone took notice of *her* when she walked into a room beside her gorgeous sister.

Seeing her sister stand there, tall, willowy and with a face and figure that would have stood out as exceptional on any catwalk, Darcy knew this was only going to happen in her wildest dreams.

Clare had no qualms about using her looks when it suited her, but she'd never had any intention of making her living out of them. Thanks to a big injection of capital from her parents, her dreams of becoming a fashion designer were well on the way to becoming a reality. She'd started her own business straight from art college and she had ambitious plans for her fashion label.

'We're all missing her, Clare,' Darcy said quietly. From the corner of her eye, she saw Harry reach across and hug his dad and the emotional lump in her throat ached.

'I know,' Clare admitted huskily. 'Sorry. Is the other thing true, or is Nick winding me up…?'

'Is what true...?' Darcy responded cagily. What had Nick the wind-up artiste been saying this time? she wondered, shooting her brother a suspicious glance. She didn't have to wait long to find out.

'Nick says that *Reece Erskine...*' Clare murmured the name in a dreamy, reverential way that made Darcy stiffen in alarm '...is staying next door—which is very obviously impossible,' she added quickly. 'I suppose he *is* having me on...?' Despite her conviction that this was a wind-up, there was a gleam of hope in her eyes as she appealed to her big sister.

'Yes, he is staying next door,' Darcy disclosed reluctantly. She watched her sister go pale with excitement.

'Why would...?' Clare began. 'No, it doesn't matter. Let me think... This is too marvellous...!'

Darcy thought so, but she had mixed feelings—no, actually, they weren't mixed at all; she didn't like the idea of Clare thinking Reece's proximity was marvellous one little bit.

'It is?'

'Of course it is, silly!' Clare exclaimed. 'Did you invite him for dinner, Darce...?' Her lovely face creased with annoyance. 'Of course you didn't,' she predicted critically. Her exasperation increased as the jerky little movement of Darcy's head confirmed her suspicions. 'Honestly, Darcy! What were you thinking of?'

Reece's tongue sliding smoothly skilful over her stomach...his burning eyes devouring her, the tiny quivering contractions that tightened her belly as she was overwhelmed by an almost paralysing desire to have him deep inside her.

'Are you listening to me, Darcy?'

The shrill, indignant sound of her sister's voice broke through the sensual thrall of her recollections. Darcy was appalled and slightly scared by her lack of self-control.

Sweat trickled damply down her stiff spine, and her cheeks felt as if they were on fire.

'I haven't got the time to have a dinner party, Clare,' she told her sister gruffly.

Her words fell on selectively deaf ears.

'Better still!' Clare, the bit firmly between her pearly teeth, enthused excitedly, 'We could invite him to stay. Yes, why not…? According to Dad, the Hall is not fit for human habitation.' She clapped her hands, her eyes glowing with enthusiasm. 'Yes, that would be perfect! Is anyone going to answer that?' she exclaimed, irritated by the persistent ring of the phone in the hallway.

Jack rose from his chair and put his hand on Darcy's shoulder. 'I'll go.'

'Perfect for what?' asked Charlie, who was growing bored with the subject, when his father had left the room. 'I don't see what's so great about the guy next door. You haven't even met him.'

Clare turned to her young brother, her expression one of supreme scorn for his ignorance.

'Don't you know anything…? He's one of the richest men in the country—he inherited a fortune from his grandfather and he's doubled it, or trebled it, whatever.' With a graceful flick of her wrist Clare dismissed the odd million or ten.

'That would explain the Merc in the shed,' Harry remarked thoughtfully to his brother.

'Have you two been spying?' Darcy exclaimed in a horrified tone.

'No harm done, Darce,' Harry soothed. 'Nobody was around. We saw some guys delivering this bed, though—gigantic thing it was, so he must be thinking about staying.'

Darcy, who knew all about the bed, tried to blend in with the furniture. If anyone looked at her now they would know—they'd just *know*…!

'Is he as good-looking as he looks in the photos I've seen of him?'

'I thought it was his money you were interested in.' Harry received an annoyed glare for his insensitive comment. 'I suppose you think he's going to take one look at you and propose you share his bed and bank account,' he sniggered.

'It has been known,' Clare confirmed calmly.

The awful part was that her sister's complacence was perfectly understandable—Darcy could see it all: Reece blinded by Clare's beauty, wondering what he'd ever seen in the dowdy little sister with the funny nose. Why hadn't she foreseen this? she wondered bitterly.

If the loud, realistic gagging noises Harry made as he headed for the door dragging his twin with him were anything to go by, her comment made him feel sick too.

Charlie seemed perfectly willing to follow his twin but he couldn't resist a taunting parting shot. 'What makes you think he's not already got a girlfriend or a wife even…?'

'Those boys get worse!' Clare exclaimed angrily as the door slammed behind them. 'He hasn't, has he, Darce?' she added worriedly.

'How should I know?' Helping her sister seduce her own lover was above and beyond the call of sisterly duty.

'Well, you have seen more of him than everyone else.'

'Something gone down the wrong way, Darce?' Nick asked solicitously.

'Do you want a drink of water?' Clare asked

Darcy wiped the moisture from the corner of her eye. 'I'm fine,' she protested hoarsely. The image in her mind of Reece's powerful body slick with sweat, his powerful thighs quivering with need and power, made it difficult for her to formulate a suitable reply. 'He didn't discuss his personal life with me, Clare.'

The indentation between her brows deepened as it struck

her forcibly just how adept he'd been at distracting her when their conversation had begun to touch on personal areas, but then his methods of distraction were in a class of their own. Married men acted like that...what if he'd been lying all along...? Clammy perspiration broke out along her brow as her tummy tied itself in knots of apprehension.

Darcy took a deep breath and firmly pushed aside her fears; this was her own insecurity at work. Reece wasn't the type to resort to subterfuge—let's face it, she thought, he doesn't need to! He'd been upfront enough—he wanted sex and nothing more.

'I can't believe you wasted all that time.'

'I wouldn't call it wasted exactly.' The way she recalled it, there hadn't been a second they hadn't filled with touching or tasting or *taking*... Darcy was confused on any number of matters but one thing was clear to her—she was glad they'd been lovers. She would always treasure the memory and no matter what the outcome that much at least wouldn't change.

'Oh, you're hopeless, Darcy!'

Hopelessly in love. Darcy felt as though a large fist had landed a direct hit on her solar plexus. Suddenly the missing pieces of the emotional jigsaw fell into place. Her mouth opened and closed several times as she gasped for air like a land-locked fish. If anyone had noticed her condition they would no doubt not have considered it attractive—but nobody did.

'I have made some enquiries...'

Clare squealed and gave her older brother her immediate approving attention. 'Why, you clever old thing, you. And...?'

'He's a widower.'

'Excellent!' Clare exclaimed gleefully; unlike Darcy, she didn't detect any undercurrent in Nick's words.

'Clare!' Darcy exclaimed, unable to hide her shocked disapproval.

'There's no more edifying sight,' Nick drawled to nobody in particular, 'than a woman in full pursuit.'

'I thought hunting was your favourite pastime, Nick…? But, silly me, you're a man, so that makes it all right, doesn't it?' Darcy heard herself perversely defending her sister.

Nick grinned. 'Sexist down to my cotton socks,' he conceded good-naturedly. 'I can't help myself any more than you can help yourself being scrupulously fair, Darce—even when it's not in your best interests,' he added in an amused but not unsympathetic undertone.

'Thank you, Darce. There's no need for either of you to look like that,' Clare insisted with a moody little pout. 'It's just such an excellent opportunity for me. It's not as if I'm going to marry him or anything.' A naughty grin flickered across her face. 'Unless, of course, the opportunity arises,' she added with a husky laugh. She shrugged when neither of her siblings showed any appreciation of her joke. 'Can you imagine how much free publicity I'd get being seen with Reece Erskine? It could really be the break I've been waiting for. It's perfectly legitimate,' she announced, a shade of defiance entering her voice.

Darcy couldn't help but wonder if her sister actually believed that. 'Dad would go spare if he could hear you.'

'Well, he can't, can he?' Clare pointed out unrepentantly. 'And what he doesn't know won't harm him—unless you tell him…'

'I can see it would put the spotlight on a brilliant new designer who is just starting out if she was seen in all the right places with someone the media love to write about,' Nick agreed.

'Don't encourage her!' Darcy pleaded.

'At last, someone who understands!' Clare sighed in a long-suffering 'nobody understands me' sort of way.

'But doesn't it rather spoil your plan if the guy in question bends over backwards to avoid the spotlight?' Nick wondered.

'These things have a way of leaking out—you of all people should know that, Nick.'

Darcy, who knew how ambitious her sister was for her business, was shocked by this display of casual ruthlessness.

'You mean you'd leak things to the Press…? Plant a story…?'

'Don't you worry your head about the details, Darce.'

The patronising comment brought an angry flush to Darcy's cheeks. 'I think you're getting a little bit ahead of yourself, Clare,' she bit back coldly. 'You haven't even met the man yet.' If she had her way that situation was not about to change. 'And there's no question at all of his staying here. Once Beth and the children arrive, not to mention Gran, we'll all be doubling up, if not trebling up!'

'I've thought about that,' Clare replied smoothly. 'You could share with the children in the attic room, and I suppose under the circumstances I could share with Gran.'

'That's mighty big of you.'

'There's no need to be like that, Darcy. I think it's the least you could do—'

'Whatever gave you the impression that I want to help you? I think what you're planning to do is callous and calculating…'

Clare looked blankly astonished by her placid sister's fresh outburst. 'But you said to Nick…' She was starting to think Darcy might be sickening for something—it wasn't like her to be so belligerent.

'I pointed out that Nick is a sexist pig.' She paused to glare at her unmoved brother. 'Which he is. But that doesn't mean I don't basically agree with him. What you're planning to do is cold-blooded and unethical.'

Clare's lips tightened. 'I think you're being very selfish. Mum and Dad invested a lot of money in my business, and I owe it to them to make it a success. I'm not trying to trap the man, but if meeting him happens to oil a few wheels, where is the problem?' Slow tears began to form in her lovely eyes; she sniffed and one slid artistically down her smooth cheek.

Even though she knew her sister could cry on cue, Darcy knew that it wouldn't be long before she'd be saying soothing things to drive that tragic expression from her lovely face. The pattern of behaviour had been laid down early on in childhood and was nigh on impossible to break at this stage in their lives. Somehow Darcy always ended up stiffly apologising and in her turn Clare would accept it and emerge looking gracious and generous.

'Maybe I don't have your lofty principles, Darcy,' she added huskily, 'but I do have fun...and so will he.'

The thought of Clare having fun with Reece made Darcy lose all desire to pour oil on troubled waters.

'What is it, Dad?' It was Nick who had noticed Jack's return.

'It was your mother.' Jack smiled a little dazedly at their expectant faces. 'She's coming home.'

Darcy closed her eyes. 'Thank God,' she breathed. Only just blinking back the emotional floods, she opened her eyes and saw Clare hugging their father while Nick, an imbecilic grin on his face, was pounding him on the back.

'Did she say why she...?' Darcy began huskily.

Jack shook his head. 'No, she said she wanted to talk. That's good, isn't it...?'

'Very good,' Darcy said firmly, hoping with all her heart that she was telling the truth.

Jack nodded. 'She'll be here tomorrow morning.'

Darcy had reached the point when she couldn't hold back the tears of relief any longer. 'I'll go get the tree in,' she announced huskily.

She was struggling with the evergreen when Nick joined her.

'Good news…?' He stood, his back against the garage door, watching her efforts and making no reference to her puffy eyes.

'The best,' she agreed.

'Personally I'm keeping all extremities crossed just in case.'

'A wise precautionary measure,' Darcy agreed with a tired smile.

'About Clare…'

'I don't want to talk about Clare.'

'You know she doesn't mean half of what she says.'

'The half she does mean is enough sometimes,' Darcy responded drily.

'Things aren't going as well as she'd hoped with the firm. I don't know the details, but I do know it's not good.'

Darcy's eyes widened in sympathy. 'I didn't know.'

'Only knew myself because she was in a bit of a state when I dropped in the other week. It does explain the conniving-bitch act.'

'You don't think she's desperate enough to…?'

'Sleep her way out of trouble?' Nick considered the idea. 'Shouldn't think so.'

Darcy was torn; she knew she ought to be more concerned about her sister's welfare than the possibility that Clare might find the solution to her problems in the bed of her own lover. Jealousy was not a nice feeling.

'Do you think you could give me a hand with this?'

Nick took the tree off her. 'All you had to do was ask. There's never a twin around when you want one,' he added, hefting it into his arms.

'And there's always two around when you don't want one,' Darcy added with feeling.

They were halfway up the driveway when Nick planted the rootball on the ground. His expression as he turned to face her suggested he'd come to a decision about something.

'I didn't tell Clare all the things I learnt about Erskine.'

'From a reliable source, no doubt.'

'It's all on file, Darce. Do you want to know?'

She shrugged her shoulders, affecting uninterest, while she was just bursting to shake the information out of him.

'Well, in that case…' he began, balancing the tree against his hip.

'I'm interested!' she snapped, grabbing his shoulder and spinning him back to her.

'Apparently the guy married his childhood sweetheart. Five years ago this Christmas Day she was killed.'

Darcy closed her eyes. Now she had the answer to his distaste of all things Christmassy. How awful to have such a powerful reminder year after year of his personal tragedy. Her tender heart ached for him.

'That's not all. She was pregnant…'

Oh, God, there was more to come! She could hear it in Nick's voice. Her eyes flickered open; she met her brother's eyes—not only more but *worse*. Darcy didn't see how that was possible but she waited tensely, her stomach tied in knots for him to deliver the clincher.

'A motorbike mounted the pavement—it was crowded with people coming out of midnight mass. They were holding hands, but it didn't touch him, just her.'

Darcy was seeing the horror of it; her chest felt so tight she could hardly breathe. 'He saw her die.' She blinked back the hot sting of tears; she ached with empathy. She turned away from her brother and fought to master her emotions. Losing a wife he loved and his unborn child—how did a person come back after a cruel blow like that?

'She died instantly, but he tried to revive her. When the paramedics got there eye-witness reports said that it took five guys to eventually persuade him to let her go, and, Darcy…' he touched her arm '…he made the biggest deal of his life on New Year's Eve. Makes you think, doesn't it…?'

'What are you suggesting—?' she began, hotly defensive.

'I'm not suggesting anything. I'm just saying that a man like that needs handling with care…'

Darcy's eyes slid from her brother's. 'Shouldn't you be telling Clare that?' she muttered evasively.

'Clare thinks she's a lot more irresistible than she is.'

'You only think that because you're her brother,' Darcy retorted. Jealousy tightened its grip on her—Reece wasn't Clare's brother.

Darcy tucked her hair behind her ears and stood back to get the full effect of her decorative efforts. She heard the door open behind her.

'Switch on the lights, will you?' she called without turning around. She gave a satisfied sigh as the tree was illuminated. 'It's a bit lopsided.'

'It's got character,' a very familiar deep voice replied.

Darcy gave a startled yelp and dropped the bauble in her hand as she swung around. 'What are you doing here?' Her body temperature seesawed wildly at the sight of the tall figure, as did her emotions.

'Do you give all your lovers receptions this warm and welcoming?'

Lovers. A sensual shudder rippled down her spine. 'Hush!' she hissed, reaching up and pressing her hand to his lips. 'Someone will hear.'

His disdainful expression was that of a man who didn't care what other people thought. Darcy would have taken her hand away, but he caught hold of her wrist and held it there against his mouth. The giddiness that had begun to recede came rushing back with a vengeance as his lips moved along her flexed fingertips, then equally slowly returned to the starting point.

Reece couldn't get over how incredibly fragile her bones were as he circled her wrist with his fingers. With the utmost reluctance he removed her hand from his lips, but not before he'd touched the tip of his tongue to the palm of her hand and felt her shiver with pleasure.

'And that matters…?' The shiver inclined him towards indulgence.

'How did you get here?'

He got the impression from the way her eyes were darting wildly around the room that she wouldn't have been surprised if he had announced he had materialised out of thin air. The truth was far more prosaic.

'I knocked on the door and was kindly directed this way.'

'Who by?'

'A twin; which one, I wouldn't like to say.'

'Oh, I thought maybe Clare had brought you?'

'I brought myself, and who might Clare be?'

'She's my sister.'

His eyes narrowed. 'Tall, blonde, persistent…?'

He'd missed out 'beautiful', which was tactful of him. 'You've met.' Of course they had—when Clare set her mind on something she didn't hang around.

'Not *met* precisely. I saw her through the window; she was knocking on the door.'

'You don't have a door.'

The bed to make love to her in, the door to keep out the world—he was a man who believed in prioritising.

'I do now.' A few phone calls had improved the conditions to bearable. 'I also have electricity. If I'm staying around I see no reason to suffer unnecessarily.'

How big an 'if' are we talking about here, she wondered, and do I have any influence on it?

'Why didn't you answer the door?' she puzzled abruptly. One sight of Clare would have most men tripping over themselves to let her in.

'I came here to escape people.'

Darcy knew what he'd come to escape, and she also knew that memories were not so easy to shake as flesh and blood people. It wasn't her place to share this with him—if he'd chosen to confide in her it might have been different, but he hadn't.

'I thought it was just Christmas,' she reminded him as with a grin she draped a strand of tinsel around his neck.

'Slip of the tongue.'

It could slip in her direction any time. 'Freudian…?'

'You tell me; you seem very well-versed.' His expression didn't suggest his opinion of psychoanalysis was high.

'This is Christmas.' Her gesture took in the room. 'And I'm people,' she reminded him.

He reached out and cupped her chin in his hand. 'You're a special person,' he contradicted firmly.

The breath caught in her throat. It didn't mean anything; there had only been one special person in Reece's life and he had lost her.

Darcy had promised herself she wouldn't allow herself to fall into this trap. When he wasn't here it had been easy to tell herself she wasn't going to see desire in his face and read love. Now he was here she had to keep reminding herself he was out for a good time and that was all; she had to accept that because the only alternative to not seeing him at all was even less acceptable—wasn't it…?

'Why are you here, Reece?'

An alertness flickered into his eyes. 'Here as in this

room? Or are we talking bed…life…?' His voice hardened. 'What's happened, Darcy?'

'Nothing.' Nervously she withdrew the hand he held and nursed it against her chest.

'Then why won't you look at me?' He took her chin in his hand and forced her face up to him. 'Look at me, Darcy,' he commanded. His eyes scoured her face, reading each line and curve. 'Someone's told you about Joanne.'

Joanne…so that had been her name. It struck her afresh that his perception was nothing short of spooky.

'Nick,' she admitted, half-relieved. 'I'm so sorry, Reece.'

'And now you want to comfort me, offer me solace and make me forget…'

It was hard not to recoil from the arid harshness in his voice.

'You'll never forget; why would you want to? I'm sure you have a lot of precious memories.' She could almost see the barriers going up—she had to do something to stop him retreating behind them. 'And actually,' she improvised wildly, 'I'm concerned about getting…*involved* with someone who has so much unresolved…' Her underdeveloped lying skills deserted her.

'Angst…? Baggage…?' he suggested with a quirk of one dark brow.

Darcy had the distinct impression he was relieved by what she'd said.

'I don't mean to be callous.' It horrified her that he found it so easy to believe she was that shallow.

'Don't apologise for being honest, Darcy.'

Ouch!

The lines bracketing his sensual mouth suddenly relaxed. 'Sorry.'

Her eyes widened. 'What for?'

'I get defensive.'

And I'm not defensive enough, she thought, staring longingly up into his strong-boned face—she loved every inch of it.

'I was afraid at first you might be the sort of girl on the look-out for marriage and children.'

It was coming over loud and clear that he didn't want either—at least, not with her!

'Me…?' she gave a jaunty laugh and shook her head. 'That's not on my agenda for years and years yet!'

'It's hard to timetable these things. Sometimes it happens when you least expect it.'

'Is that how it happened…with you and your wife?' She seemed to have tapped into some hitherto unsuspected streak of masochism in her nature. 'Sorry, I didn't mean to pry.'

His taut jawline tensed. 'Jo and I were as good as brought up together; her parents and mine were… You know the sort of thing.' Darcy nodded. 'She proposed to me when we were seven.' For a moment his expression softened and grew distant. 'I did the proposing the next time. Keep your eyes wide open, sweetheart,' he recommended gently. 'It would be a shame to miss a once-in-a-lifetime experience because you were concentrating on your career.'

The irony was exquisitely painful. 'You think it only happens once?'

'I *know* it only happens once.'

Darcy's thoughts drifted to her mother and Jack; they might not seem to be the world's most perfect couple just now but she had total faith in their love for one another. And significantly both of them had had previous marriages. It was hard to bite back the retort that hovered on the tip of her tongue.

'And if, like you, something happens to…?' she probed clumsily.

'Then that part of your life is over,' he bit back abruptly.

'There are other things…' his restless eyes wandered hungrily over her trim figure '…like *sex*.'

He was condemning himself to a very bleak future—not to mention herself. Despite the rebellion which she sensed building up inside her, Darcy had no control over her physical response to the smoky, sensual invitation in his eyes.

'And that's enough for you?' How sad—how horribly sad. Is that what she wanted to be? A distraction to temporarily fill the gaping hole in his life?

'You sound like my mother.'

A person that Darcy was beginning to have a lot of sympathy for. How did you help someone who didn't think he needed helping?

'It's not enough for me, Reece.' Fundamentally you couldn't change yourself, not even for love. It was a relief to recognise that she'd only be pretending to let him think otherwise, and, as tempted as she was to take what he had to offer, she knew that in the long run it would be more painful.

With a sinking heart she watched his expression shifting, growing harder and more remote.

'I thought you enjoyed uncomplicated sex.'

His tone wasn't quite a sneer but it was painfully close to it. Darcy flushed and lowered her eyes. Letting her mind drift back over her recent uninhibited behaviour, she wasn't surprised he'd arrived at this conclusion.

'At the time, but not later on.'

'That morning-after-the-night-before feeling—you're very frank.'

'It's no reflection on you, on your…'

His mobile lips curled as she floundered. 'Technique?' he suggested. 'Don't fret, Darcy, I'm not plagued with doubts in that direction.'

'You might be a nicer person if you were!'

'Would it make any difference to your decision if we were to put this arrangement on a more formal footing?'

'Formal!' she echoed, startled.

'Formal as in exclusive.' He hadn't planned to say this and in fact had been almost as surprised to hear himself say it as she appeared to be. Now he had, he could see the practical advantages of the idea—the idea of her being with other men was one he'd been having major problems with.

'As in, you don't sleep with anyone else?'

'As in, neither of us sleep with anyone else,' he corrected blandly. Darcy's eyes widened. Was that a hint of possessiveness she was hearing, and, if it was, what did that mean?

'That would be a major sacrifice.' Did the man think she cruised the single scene in a bid to add fresh scalps to her belt?

He seemed to find her sarcasm encouraging. 'It makes sense; we both want the same things…you're not at the stage where you want a commitment, and I'm past it.'

Darcy gazed up at him, speechless with incredulity. You dear, delicious, *deluded* man, she thought bleakly.

'Are you still worried I'm a loose cannon, emotionally speaking?'

I'm the only emotional basket case around here. 'You seem to have got your life on track very successfully,' she choked. 'Your work-life, anyhow.'

Reece's eyes narrowed shrewdly. 'Nick again…'

'He mentioned you didn't take any time off after the…accident.'

'Very tactfully put,' he congratulated her. 'A certain section of the Press never forgave me for ruining a great tragic story by not falling apart in public. I'm not comfortable with the role of tragic hero,' he explained, a spasm of fastidious disgust crossing his face. 'After Joanne died the Press had a field-day. The public appetite for the personal tragedy of people who have a high public profile is almost limitless. They wheeled out the experts to pontificate on the grieving process, interviewed every person I'd ever said good morning to…'

Darcy could feel the pain behind his prosaic words. It must have been agony for a very private man to have his grief dissected and analysed.

'And when you were working you weren't thinking.'

Reece shot her a startled look. 'That was the theory—it didn't always work,' he admitted wryly. 'After Jo's death the Press pack were their usual rabid selves, and my lack of co-operation only increased their appetite. Of course when I didn't oblige them by drowning my sorrows in a gin bottle they were even less happy. Chequebook journalism being what it is, any ex of mine can look forward to making a tidy profit—several have.'

Darcy's face froze. 'Is that meant to be an incentive?' she breathed wrathfully.

'Hell, no, I didn't mean you!' he exclaimed—she seemed to be remarkably lacking in avarice.

Darcy's hands went to her hips as she tossed back her hair. 'You'd better not.'

'I've made you mad, haven't I?'

'Whatever gave you that idea?' she snapped sarcastically.

'Let me take you to dinner; we can talk more.'

Darcy didn't want to talk more—she'd already had more *talk* than she could cope with. 'I c-can't go to dinner with you,' she stuttered.

'Why not?'

'Well, I've got a lot to do.'

'You have to eat.'

'And it's Clare's first night home.'

He looked palpably unimpressed by her clinching argument. 'The table's booked for eight-thirty.' He consulted his watch. 'That gives you twenty minutes to get ready.'

'Do people always do what you say?'

The lines that fanned out from his eyes deepened as if he found her futile resistance amusing—Darcy couldn't shake the uneasy notion that pursuit had a lot to do with his interest; perhaps his interest would cool rapidly once she'd settled for his terms.

'Nineteen minutes,' he said, not taking his eyes off her face.

'I don't react well to ultimatums,' she told him, smiling grimly through clenched teeth. 'Anyhow, you can't drive and I've promised the car to the boys tonight.'

'Nice try, but I've hired a driver.'

'Doesn't the driver think it's bit sus that his employer is sleeping in a derelict mansion?'

Reece's dark brows moved in the general direction of his dark hairline. 'I didn't ask him,' he replied. 'Eccentricity is only frowned upon if you don't have money, Darcy.'

'That's a cynical way of looking at things.'

'Whether you like it or not, that's the way the world works.'

'I don't have to like it,' she snorted.

'No,' he agreed, 'you don't have to like it—just me. *Do you?*'

The clipped abruptness of his question was unsettling, but not as unsettling as the peculiar intensity of his expression.

'Like you…?' Was this a trick question? 'I…I don't know you,' she blurted awkwardly. For a moment she thought he was going to push it, but much to her relief he dropped the subject.

'You're cutting things fine, and I'm hungry—in case you've forgotten, you did me out of lunch.' A slow, sensual smile curved his lips. 'Not that I'm complaining,' he added huskily.

Reece wondered if all her skin had turned the deep shade of crimson that her face had—he made a mental note to test the theory some time soon…very soon.

She looked just about everywhere but his face. It was while she was looking at the Christmas tree she thought of another excuse—feeble, but a drowning person wasn't fussy.

'I haven't finished decorating the tree.'

His attention was promptly diverted to the twinkling tree set beside the window.

'It looks as though it will collapse under the weight if you add another thing,' he commented after a moment's silent contemplation of the overladen branches.

Darcy rushed to defence of her efforts; it might not be fashionably minimalist, and it was light-years away from being colour co-ordinated, but every item that adorned it had sentimental value.

'Mum never threw away any of the things we made at school, not a thing; everything on that tree has a history.' She grabbed the fairy that had been gracing the top of the tree for as long as she could remember.

'There's a limit to how much *history* one little evergreen can take.'

There was also a limit to how much proximity she could take, Darcy thought as his hand brushed her shoulder—it was electric. The fizzling surge of sexual desire stole her breath. She took a stumbling step backwards.

'I can't…' she began stiltedly. Her eyes, which had been fixed on his expensively shod size twelves, started to travel upwards as if obeying an unspoken command. Long legs, more than a suggestion of muscle in the thigh area, and the loose cut of his tailored trousers couldn't disguise the fact he was aroused…as was she…*help*!

No benevolent force came to her aid. She could feel the glazed expression sliding into her eyes, feel the prickle of heat travelling over her body, and the worst part was being totally incapable of preventing it.

'Not touch—me neither.' His low-pitched voice carried an indecent amount of sensual suggestion.

She fought hard to master her seething emotions. 'I wasn't going to say that,' she managed to protest weakly. Her throat closed up as her wide, fearful eyes meshed with hot, determined green.

'You didn't need to.'

'That obvious, am I?' she asked, her throat clogged with shame. His thumb moved slowly down the extended column of her throat. Darcy, her eyes still melded with his, shivered and swayed far more violently than the overladen tree. She shook her head in an attempt to clear the sexual lethargy that had permeated her entire body.

'I'm not coming to dinner with you.'

His indulgence had a feral quality to it. 'Of course you are.'

Darcy bared her teeth. 'I'm not coming,' she continued, trying to keep a grip on both her temper and determination—at the last second she lost her nerve. Telling him she was in love with him would have the desired effect of sending him running, but it would also leave her without a shred of pride. 'Because we have nothing to talk about,' she finished limply.

'Fine; we won't talk,' he responded amiably. 'We'll do this instead.'

Darcy closed her eyes as his mouth came down hard on hers, and the wild wave of longing that washed over her sent her spinning out of control. She gave a discontented sigh when he lifted his head.

Finally Darcy heard what he obviously already had; she

recognised the click-clack of the ridiculous high-heeled mules that Clare wore around the house.

'Darcy... Sorry, I didn't know we had company.'

Sure you didn't, Darcy thought as her sister made a graceful attempt to pull together the sides of the gossamer wrap she wore, so graceful in fact that they were granted several tantalising glimpses of what was underneath; Darcy didn't actually feel very tantalised—she felt as mad as hell! She cringed at her sister's painful *obviousness*.

As you could see right through the wrap and she wasn't wearing a stitch underneath, Darcy didn't see why she'd bothered to put it on in the first place. In fact, she didn't see why she'd bothered to put on anything at all—surely a towel dropped at the right moment would have achieved her purpose just as well. Reece had got an eyeful of the celestial body. She gritted her teeth and felt anger bubbling within her.

He was staring...major surprise—*not*! It was the moment that Darcy had been subconsciously dreading; now it was here it was even worse than she'd imagined. In that moment she knew what it would feel like if she accepted his offer and became—for want of a better word—his mistress. There would be the constant fear that he would tire of her, or cheat, or... No, she couldn't cope on his terms.

'Your hair's sticking up,' she snapped abruptly. And I mussed it up, she wanted to shout at her sister.

'Thanks.' Reece smoothed down his dark hair with his good hand and turned to smile at Clare.

Clare, who had looked a little startled by Darcy's abrupt tone, began to look more confident.

'You must be Clare. Run along and get changed, Darcy.' The man had the unmitigated gall to absently pat her on the behind. 'Clare will entertain me.'

I just bet she will!

'Darcy missed her lunch on account of me, so I thought

the least I could do was take her to dinner,' he explained smoothly.

'What's wrong with the way I look now?' Darcy asked mutinously.

It occurred to Darcy too late that to invite a man to look at her when he'd only just feasted his eyes on Clare was a bad move—the comparison was hardly likely to do her any favours. She'd invited the scrutiny, though, and she was getting it; it took all her will-power not to drop her gaze under the searching intensity of that raw sexual appraisal.

'Not a thing.'

A gratified glow spread through her electrified body, but she didn't let herself respond—she couldn't.

'Here you are.' Nick strolled past the frozen figure of his younger sister in the doorway, apparently oblivious to the electric atmosphere.

Darcy gave a sigh of exasperation. 'I suppose you didn't know we had a visitor either?'

'As a matter of fact, Charlie mentioned Reece had come here to snog you.' He picked up an apple from the selection in the fruit bowl and polished it on his jumper.

'He mentioned *what*?' she yelped.

Reece cleared his throat. 'He asked me whether I was going to,' he admitted. 'What was I supposed to do—lie?'

'Yes!' Darcy responded with feeling.

Nick did some more apple-polishing. 'I suppose you know you can see right through that thing, Clare?'

Clare shook her head like someone emerging from a trance. 'What? I…' With a muffled sob she ran, clicking and clacking, from the room.

'Was it something I said?' Nick wondered innocently.

'Don't be facetious, Nick!' Darcy snapped. 'I should go after her…'

'And rub salt in the wound…?'

'What wound?'

Brother and sister looked at one another but didn't reply.

'I'm taking your sister for a meal.'

Nick bit down hard into his apple. 'So long as you don't take her for a ride, mate, be my guest.'

'He won't be your guest, because I'm not going, and I'm sure you mean well but I don't need a chaperon, Nick.'

Nick looked from his sister to the tall man at her side, but didn't budge.

'For heaven's sake, Nick!' she cried, totally exasperated. 'I'm quite capable of taking care of myself.'

'Not always, you weren't,' Nick reminded her quietly.

'What did he mean by that?' Reece asked the moment they were alone again.

'I got involved with someone who forget to mention he was already married.' If he despised her for what she'd revealed he was hiding it well; maybe he was reserving judgement, which was more than most people did. 'I thought he wanted a wife, but he wanted a mistress…is this ringing any bells?'

There was a guarded expression in his lushly lashed eyes. 'Do you still see him?' he fired abruptly.

'Who?'

'The married guy!'

The implication that she would knowingly continue an affair with a married man brought a furious sparkle to Darcy's eyes.

'I don't know why,' she gritted, her voice dripping sarcasm, 'but once I've broken up a marriage the excitement goes clear out of a relationship.' Her icy blue gaze swept contemptuously over his face. *'You're as bad as him!'*

'I haven't lied to you…I haven't asked you to marry me…'

You haven't fallen in love with me, she wanted to wail.

'But you have asked me to be your mistress—not in so many words, but it amounts to the same thing.'

'But you're holding out for a ring?' he speculated scornfully.

Darcy shook her head and smiled sadly. 'No, I'd settle for a lot less than that.'

'Such as…?'

She met his eyes, her own gaze steady and clear, and, holding her breath, jumped in with both feet. 'Love.'

His big chest rose sharply. 'You know—'

'I know you loved your wife and you'll never love anyone else, or that's what you tell yourself. I think the truth is you're too afraid to look forward, so you keep on looking back—'

Reece, who'd been holding his breath, exhaled noisily. 'And you'd know all about it…'

'The only thing I know for sure,' she returned with an emotional catch in her husky voice, 'is that I'm in love with you.' There, I said it.

'You're *what*…?' For once his effortless air of command had totally deserted him.

There was no way she was going to say it again. 'You heard me.'

He opened his mouth, closed it again and then abruptly turned on his heel and left her standing there beside the sparkling Christmas tree.

She made it to her room before she started crying in earnest. This orgy of misery was interrupted by her sister's entrance.

'Go away, Clare!' she begged gruffly without looking around.

'Are you getting ready to go out?'

'The dinner date's off,' Darcy explained with a quiver of high-pitched hysteria.

'I wanted to explain about the way I acted… I had the most awful interview with the bank manager yesterday and…I didn't know that you and Reece…'

'There is no me and Reece!' Darcy sobbed, lifting her downcast face.

'Darcy, have you been crying?' Clare exclaimed, lifting the tissue from her own pink nose. 'Oh, Darce, what's wrong?' she cried, wrapping her arms around her sister's shaking body. 'He's not worth it!' she cried soothingly.

If Darcy could have brought herself to truly believe that, she'd have felt a lot happier.

CHAPTER SEVEN

'THAT'S it. I'm going in!'

Darcy caught hold of her sister's arm. 'No, Clare,' she hissed urgently. 'We can't barge in—Mum and Dad need to talk…'

'They've been talking for over an hour!' Clare pointed out. 'How long can it take?' she wailed, wringing her slender hands. 'Darcy, I just can't take not knowing what the hell is going on for another minute.'

There was a murmur of general assent from their brothers.

Darcy sighed. 'Well, actually,' she admitted, letting go of Clare's arm, 'neither can I.'

Nick placed his hand on the doorknob to the sitting room, where their parents had been ensconced since Cathy Alexander had returned home earlier that morning, and looked questioningly at his siblings.

Darcy shrugged and Nick, taking this as encouragement, pushed the door open. The twins and Clare pressed from behind, sending Darcy headlong through the door with a precipitate rush.

'Come along in, children,' Jack said drily as his family stood there, all displaying varying degrees of sheepishness and a uniform level of anxiety.

Darcy looked at her parents' faces and gave a sigh of relief—everything was going to be all right! Until that moment she hadn't known how apprehensive she'd been. Jack looked dazed—but good dazed, like a man who'd just won the lottery as opposed to one who'd just been told his marriage was over. As for her mother, Cathy was positively glowing.

'Your mother's got some marvellous news for you all.'

'Jack, they might not think it's so marvellous.'

Jack Alexander clasped his wife's hand as if he was never going to let go. 'Of course they will. Your mother is going to have a baby.'

His news was greeted by a stunned silence.

'You're joking, right…?' Darcy heard Nick say, his tone suggesting he was just as gobsmacked as she felt.

'This is no joke, Nick,' his mother said quietly. 'It was a shock to me too…'

Darcy recognised an understatement when she heard it. Take what I'm feeling and times it by the odd million or so… No wonder Mum bolted!

'…and it's taken some time for me to get used to the idea,' Cathy admitted, casting an apologetic sideways look at her husband. 'I know it will mean a lot of changes…'

'Not to us—we'll be at university… But you know, Mum, I thought you were past that sort of thing.' Charlie winced as his twin kicked him in the shin.

'She's only forty-seven, idiot!' Harry hissed.

Clare was the first to recover. 'Why, Mum, that's marvellous!' she cried, running gracefully forward to embrace Cathy. *'Isn't it…?'* she said pointedly to Nick and Darcy.

Her words seemed to shake Nick out of his trance-like state. 'It's a relief, is what it is!' he sighed, surging forward to join his sister.

Cathy looked at her elder daughter over their heads, and there were tears in her eyes. 'And you, Darcy…? Do you mind…?'

'Mind…?' Darcy echoed hoarsely. *'Mind…?'* She saw for the first time what Clare had seen right off—their mother was desperately embarrassed by the situation and seeking their approval.

'She means no, Mum,' said Nick, directing a playful punch at his sister's shoulder, which almost knocked her off her feet.

Darcy rubbed her shoulder. She knew she was grinning like an idiot but couldn't seem to stop; the relief was so intense she felt weak.

'God, Mum, it's so good to have you home. Now tell us, what has the doctor said…?'

'Yes, you'll need a hospital with all the facilities,' Clare began thoughtfully, perching herself on the arm of the sofa to let Darcy move forward and get in on the hugs.

'Because of my age…?'

'Age nothing!' Clare denied robustly. 'If it was me I wouldn't set foot in a place that didn't offer every pain-killing device known to man, and don't let Beth brainwash you with all that stuff about natural childbirth when she gets here,' she warned. 'Just keep in mind that it was Beth who ended up giving birth in the back of the Land Rover.'

'I never knew you were so clued up, Clare!' Darcy exclaimed. 'I'd sort of assumed—'

'Just because my career is important it doesn't mean I don't like babies, Darcy, and wouldn't mind having a few—when the time is right.'

That put me in my place and quite right too, Darcy conceded, aware she'd been guilty of pigeon-holing her sister.

The males of the Alexander family began to drift away as the discussion on modern childbirth got increasingly technical—or, as Harry put it, *yucky*!

The piped music in the lift was working its way through a Christmas medley and Reece was working his way through the enamel on his white teeth. Having taken the penthouse suite—thanks to a last-minute cancellation—he had no option but to endure the agony longer than anyone else.

He reached the foyer and was immediately spotted by the assistant manager, who hastened discreetly to his side.

'I hope everything—'

'Fine, fine…' Reece murmured without slackening his pace. He seemed genuinely oblivious to the fact that his tall, distinguished person was a magnet for numerous curious and admiring eyes.

'Will your wife…?'

This stopped Reece.

'I have not got a wife!' Without raising his voice above a low murmur he managed to give his words the impact of a blood-curdling yell.

It might have been that his ears had become supersensitive, but the more often he denied it the less convincing it seemed to sound. Perhaps that was what happened when you were forced to repeat yourself ad nauseam to disbelieving people all morning—first his mother, then his sister. The rest of the family would no doubt have got in on the act too if he hadn't instructed the switchboard to say he wasn't taking calls from *anyone*!

He didn't know what was worse—their initial reproaches that he'd slunk off to marry someone they'd never met and cheated them out of a wedding, or their bitter disappointment when he'd finally convinced them it was all lies.

He wouldn't have had the ear-bashing at all if he hadn't allowed himself to weaken and ring home to tell them where he was—and that weakness too could be laid at the door of Miss Darcy Alexander, with all her idealistic claptrap of families and sharing!

'No, sir.' The poker-faced individual couldn't stop his eyes from straying to the newspaper poking out of Reece's pocket which had announced very authoritatively that he was:

Billionaire head of the Erskine Empire secretly wed. Honeymooners involved in accident.

'Damn you!' Reece said without any particular conviction as he strode off.

'Where are we going, boss?' his driver asked as he produced the Mercedes—as requested, fully fuelled—in front of the hotel.

'We're not…I am.'

'The arm—'

'Is fully functioning,' Reece snarled belligerently.

'If you say so.' The driver, who had found his employer to be punctiliously polite, looked startled.

'I do,' Reece replied in a more moderate tone as he slid into the driver's seat. 'Take Christmas off.'

'Thanks very much.'

'And, Andy…' he picked up the newspaper spread out at the appropriate page on the front seat and screwed it into a tight bundle before pressing it firmly into the driver's hand '…take a different newspaper while you're at work.'

'Does this mean that job with your mother is off?' the young man asked with a rueful grimace.

'Do I look like the vindictive type? No,' he said, adjusting the mirror, 'don't answer that.'

'I wasn't going to.'

'If you can put up with my mother the job is yours,' Reece yelled over his shoulder just before the window slid silently down and the car drew smoothly away.

Cruising in the outside lane of the motorway, the man without a vindictive bone in his body contemplated the awful retributions he was going to visit on Darcy Alexander.

Having so-called 'friends' leak stories to the Press was an occupational hazard as far as he was concerned—even when that stupid kiss-and-tell story had appeared last Christmas he'd been able to shrug it off; this was different, though. He'd *believed* in those big blue eyes—hell, he'd even believed it when she'd said she loved him; that fact was largely responsible for the fact he hadn't had a moment's peace since. And now she turned out to be the sort of girl that ran to the newspapers with a fake but eye-catching story… Why…? Was she deluded enough to think that this would in some way obligate him to actually marry her…?

Before long he'd find out—even if he had to wring the truth out of her!

'I don't know what the fuss is about; in my day plenty of women had babies well into their forties.'

'Yes, Gran,' Darcy replied meekly, deciding on reflection that this probably wasn't the moment to point out the lamentably high maternal death-rate enjoyed by women of that rosy bygone era. When Gran was in full nostalgia mode it was better to let her run on…and on…and on…uninterrupted.

'If anyone had seen fit to ask my advice…but of course they didn't…'

'You won't believe how much little Jamie has grown, Gran!'

'Grown into what, is the question,' the old lady retorted, suitably diverted but not placated. 'I told that girl of Jack's she was making a rod for her own back, picking the child up every time he whimpered. Worn to a frazzle she looked, last time I saw her.'

'Well, she looks pretty marvellous now,' Darcy replied uncooperatively, 'and Jamie is a dear little boy, so why don't you stop being such a grouch, Granny Prue,' she coaxed gently, 'and get into the Christmas spirit?'

The lady, who was neither particularly old nor infirm, but a modern-minded, sprightly sixty-nine, sniffed.

'In *my* day I wouldn't have dared speak to my elders that way, young lady. You always did have far too much to say for yourself,' she mused, unable to totally disguise her approval of this character flaw in her granddaughter.

The entire clan, minus little Jamie, who, Darcy assumed, was taking a nap, was dutifully lined up to greet Prudence Emery. It was a noisy, boisterous occasion, during which the lady in question hid her pleasure by criticising the new décor in the room and offending Nick by falsely claiming he was losing his hair.

Taking advantage of a lull in the clamour, Cathy drew her daughter to one side. 'You've got a visitor, Darcy,' she explained quietly. 'He's in the sitting room, if you want to slip away.'

'He…! Who he…?' Darcy demanded, grabbing hold of Cathy's sleeve.

Aware of her mother's startled response to her shrill reaction, Darcy took a deep breath and tried to regain her serenity—actually she'd never been particularly serene to begin with, and lately not at all! Contemplating the way she'd been lately wasn't going to improve her mental well-being, so Darcy wisely decided not to go there.

With a self-conscious grimace she released her mother's sleeve and brushed down the creased fabric. If she couldn't manage serene she could at least rise to sane! People lost out in the love stakes every day of the week and they still carried on functioning as useful members of society; only wimps curled up in a corner and moaned about their tough break.

There wasn't even any reason to assume that this visitor was Reece, and even if it was that wasn't necessarily significant. He could have come calling for any number of reasons—none of which she could bring to mind at that particular moment. The 'he's discovered he can't live without me' reason was one she forbade herself to think about even in the hypothetical sense.

'Is it anyone special?' she asked, overdoing the languid

unconcern like mad to compensate for her previous behaviour.

'You tell me, dear.'

Darcy gave her mother a pained look; it was a burden having a parent who could read you like a book.

'I'd be surprised if he wasn't special to someone,' Cathy volunteered innocently.

'Does this *special* man have a name?' Darcy wasn't in the mood for enigmatic; her brain was aching.

'It's the gentleman who I believe was staying next door—Reece Erskine; a nice boy,' Cathy mused innocently.

Nice! Darcy choked with quiet restraint; her heart felt as if it was trying to climb up her throat. The anticipation rushing through her veins made her head buzz loudly.

'Right.' She made a vague fluttery motion with her hand. 'Well, I suppose I'd better… Couldn't you just say I'd gone away, Mum?' She blushed deeply and lowered her eyes. 'No, of course you couldn't,' she mumbled, shamed by her display of cowardice. 'The sitting room, you said…? I'll just go and…' Darcy made a hasty dive for the door; her mother was quite capable of asking any number of uncomfortable questions if she hung around any longer.

He didn't hear the door open, which, considering the racket they were making, wasn't entirely surprising. Darcy had taken the intervening minutes to compose herself sufficiently to avoid looking a total fool when she came face to face with him.

Her mental preparations had not, however, prepared her for the sight of Reece, sharply dressed in a beautifully cut mid-grey suit, crouched down on all fours with her small nephew riding on his back. It was only a matter of forty-eight hours since she'd last seen him but the wave of longing that hit her was so intense that for several seconds it drove all other considerations from her mind.

He had the sort of earthy sex appeal that a memory could

not fully do justice to, or maybe she'd made some subconscious effort to spare herself pain by playing down the details. In the flesh he was bigger, leaner and more good-looking than any male had a right to be—definitely more good-looking than a girl in love could be expected to cope with.

As she watched an excited Jamie grabbed a hank of Reece's dark hair and ordered him to stop in his baby treble. Reece promptly fell down flat on his belly, flipped over and with straight arms lifted the laughing little boy above his head. She only just stopped herself crying out a warning for his poor shoulder, or maybe she didn't because his head suddenly turned. Their glances clashed warily.

In that second all Darcy's hopes faded and died. The world had become an even more confusing place—why anger…? Well, at least I know why he *hasn't* come to visit—a look of love that was not.

'Hello, Reece; your shoulder's better?' She nodded her head towards his arm, unable to take her eyes off his face.

'Full working order,' he agreed, flexing his shoulder to illustrate the range of movement. Underneath the commonplace response she was deeply aware of his seething anger.

'Aunty Darcy!' Jamie cried, catching sight of his favourite aunt. 'Come and play with us.'

'Not now, Jamie, darling. Granny has arrived—why don't you go and see her?'

'Has she got me a present?' the little boy wondered with innocent avarice.

Darcy smiled in a distracted manner and patted his curly head. 'It's very possible,' she told him drily. As she spoke she was very aware of Reece agilely leaping to his feet, and the room suddenly felt too compact for comfort—far too compact to take all the turbulent emotions seething around them.

'I'll go, then,' the child agreed graciously. 'Don't go

away!' he added imperiously to Reece, who was smoothing his sleek black hair away from a broad heroic-looking forehead.

Reece smartly saluted the little boy, who solemnly saluted back after a fashion.

'You can play with Darcy while I'm gone,' Jamie announced in a spirit of generosity before he left.

A choking sound emerged from Darcy's throat as her cheeks fairly exploded with mortified colour.

Reece's eyes ran insolently over her slender figure from head to toe. A muscle leapt in his rigid jaw and disturbed for a moment the smooth, sardonic mask he wore.

'I'll pass, if you don't mind,' he drawled with languid contempt as he slid the loose knot on his tasteful silk tie up to his brown throat.

The deliberate insult made the colour ebb from Darcy's cheeks. An expression of hurt confusion appeared on her face as she watched him refasten a single button on his jacket with equal precision. This was the first time she'd seen him dressed formally; perhaps he donned a hostile personality along with the suit...?

Reece saw the hurt and the bewilderment—both were hard to miss; fortunately he knew what a duplicitous little creature she was, otherwise he might have been foolish enough to respond to the urge to kiss away the hurt.

The icy glitter in his eyes was pure, unadulterated contempt—to put it mildly, Darcy was disconcerted. She responded accordingly.

'Mind...?' she laughed. 'I *insist*.' She bit back further retorts; they'd get nowhere if this thing degenerated into a childish round of insults. 'You've come a long way just to be nasty, Reece...'

He thrust his hands deep into the pockets of his loosely tailored trousers and viewed her from under the protective shield of lush dark lashes.

'I've had to wait a long time to be nasty.' He looked pointedly at his wristwatch as if she'd deliberately kept him waiting—an attitude which struck Darcy as being perverse in the extreme, considering she hadn't known his plans.

Maybe he didn't like children? Perhaps Jamie had driven him crazy…? It wasn't likely, considering the fact the atmosphere had been pretty convivial until she'd walked in, but she couldn't think of anything else to explain his hostility.

'You met my mum…?'

'She was very kind.' So much so that it had been hard to maintain his crusading rage in the face of such genuine warmth. 'You must be relieved she's home. I'm happy for you.'

She'd rarely heard or seen anyone displaying fewer symptoms of happiness.

'I don't mean to be blunt, but why exactly are you here, Reece? It's not that I'm not over the moon to see you…' Irony was an excellent disguise for the truth.

'Like you don't know…?' he drawled.

Darcy had the uncomfortable feeling she'd walked into this conversation halfway through.

'I've not the faintest.'

He shook his dark head, regarding her with disdainful distrust. 'What I don't understand is what you thought you'd gain by it.'

Her bewilderment increased. *'It?'*

Reece breathed heavily, his nostrils flaring, before he turned abruptly away, dragging both hands viciously through his hair.

'If what I've done is so awful that you can't even look at me, it only seems fair I get to know what it is.'

He'd have thought better of her if she'd not tried to pretend, if she'd been frank about it. 'You want to play it like that—fine.'

Something inside Darcy snapped; this was the man she'd fallen in love with, the man she'd spent every miserable second they'd been apart craving for. The sound of his voice brought her out in goosebumps, the touch of his hand or, for that matter, any part of his body set her nervous system into meltdown, and here he was, treating her as if she was public enemy number one! Surely this couldn't all be because she'd said she loved him—surely walking away had been punishment enough for that transgression.

She planted her hands on the gentle curve of her hips and raised the angle of her chin an aggressive few degrees.

'Don't take that tone with me!' Unless he considered falling in love with him to be a betrayal of trust, Darcy's conscience was clear.

'What tone did you expect me to take after you fed that ridiculous story to that filthy rag?' he spat in disgust.

'What story?' For that matter, what filthy rag? She now knew that Reece, who might well be the financial genius everyone said he was, could mess up like everyone else. Human fallibility could be charming in a way, but not on this occasion.

He produced a screwed-up newspaper from his pocket and waved it in front of her. 'I expect you've had your copy framed. Did you get a kick out of seeing your name in print?' he asked, ignoring for the moment the fact her name hadn't appeared in the article.

'You can carry on talking in riddles if you like, but we'll get nowhere fast, and if you think I'm going to oblige you by being intimidated by this pathetic display, think again!' she flung for good measure.

Reece surveyed her through disillusioned eyes. 'You fed the paper a story about me being married—to you.'

The accusation was so ridiculous that she couldn't even be angry any more. 'Don't be stupid.' With a frown she impatiently snatched the paper from his hand.

'Page five,' he told her curtly. 'Have you any idea what havoc you've caused...?' he ranted. 'It took me three-quarters of an hour to convince my mother I haven't got married, and even after I'd managed to do that she still wanted to know what you were like...'

Darcy was bewildered but intrigued by these revelations. 'What did you say?'

Reece shot her a murderous glare. 'As for my sister, she insisted on giving me the number of the lisping idiot who designed her friend's wedding dress...! I wouldn't let that fawning creep within ten miles of my inside leg!'

Darcy giggled; it was inappropriate but she couldn't help herself, he looked so outraged. A blast of raw wrath from his spectacular eyes had her hurriedly spreading out the paper on the floor and squatting down beside it.

'You didn't make the front page—I can see why you're so miffed,' she mocked flippantly. 'I'm pretty miffed myself,' she added, solemnly quoting, '"Witnesses tell us that the distraught young bride temporarily separated from her husband was comforted by the hospital staff after she collapsed." *How wet!*' she exclaimed in disgust. 'I might sue.'

'Get in line.' It was slowly dawning on Reece that she wasn't reacting like the guilty party here—in fact, nothing had gone as he'd envisaged so far. He'd sailed in here, determined to deal out a retribution that was both swift and awful—the details of which he hadn't quite worked out—and he'd been taken to the family bosom and treated like a long-lost son.

Darcy tucked her hair behind her ears as she bent over the paper. The grainy picture didn't do him justice. Rapidly she scanned the rest of the print beneath. It only took her a few moments to digest the salient details. She sat back on her heels and lifted her face to his.

'Well, you've only yourself to blame.'

'Me!'

'Well, you're the one who made up that stupid story about me being your wife, and it was obvious that that girl on the hospital reception recognised you...'

She saw his eyes widen fractionally as he absorbed what she was saying.

'You're saying that *she's* the source of this story...?' My God, why hadn't he thought of that? It was so damned *obvious*. It made no sense...it was entirely out of character for him to jump to a conclusion the way he had.

Darcy shrugged. 'Well, let's face it, she's a hell of a lot more likely a candidate than me. If I did want my five minutes of fame I can think of better ways to get it than that!'

There was a startled silence.

If she'd been the sort of girl to gloat, now would have been the time to do it. The expression on Reece's taut face revealed he had accepted her explanation and accepted the fact he had egg all over his handsome face, and Darcy suspected this wasn't a situation he'd had much experience in dealing with. In her opinion a dose of humility wouldn't do the man any harm at all—loving him didn't stop her recognising the character flaws in his personality.

She held up her hand and after a fractional pause he grabbed it and hauled her to her feet.

'I might,' he conceded slowly, 'have been a trifle...*hasty*.'

'You weren't a *trifle* insulting and rude?' She withdrew her hand from his firm grasp even though every instinct told her to cling for all she was worth.

'I suppose you want me to apologise,' he growled belligerently, his colour slightly heightened.

'Grovelling would be a start,' she conceded, symbolically wiping the fingers that had moments ago been enfolded in his on the seat of her skirt. 'I thought you were supposed to be clever—even Jamie could have figured it out. I had no reason to plant a story; if you recall, I wasn't too keen on the idea of being Mrs Erskine to begin with.'

'I was under the impression that was exactly what you wanted. No ring, no sex—classic case of carrot-dangling.'

'How like a man!' she gasped contemptuously. 'I didn't propose to you, I just told you how I felt.' She glared bitterly at the outline of the broad back he presented her with. It struck her as representative of his attitude. 'I only wanted a relationship where both parties are open to the possibility of natural development. We're talking *possibility* here, Reece! Is that so outrageous? I suppose it is,' she mused thoughtfully, 'if you're an emotional coward.'

In the act of pacing over to the opposite side of the room, as though he couldn't bear to be close to her, Reece stopped and spun back towards her.

'What exactly do you mean by that?' he demanded, his pent-up frustration clearly illustrated in every tense, dangerous line of his lean body.

'You loved your wife, and what happened was a terrible tragedy, but it isn't loyalty to her memory that prevents you from having feelings for anyone else.'

'Is that a fact?'

'Yes, it is,' Darcy reiterated bravely in the face of his simmering displeasure—she'd given the matter a lot of thought and had promised herself that if she ever saw Reece again she would share her conclusions with him. 'You're afraid to feel in case you get hurt again—it's only natural for you to be wary...'

'So it's a simple matter of cowardice?' He released a short incredulous gasp as his dagger-sharp glare bored into her.

Darcy refused to be intimidated—after all, what did she have to lose by speaking her mind? 'After my experience with Michael I could have decided to mistrust all men, but I didn't.'

'You're an example to us all. You asked me if it's outrageous for you to be so uncomfortable with your sexual desires that you dress them up with socially acceptable labels like *love* and *relationship*.' He skimmed her pale face with a provocative sneer.

Indignation shot through Darcy, who barely recognised this translation of her earlier appeal to him.

'I'll tell you what's outrageous, shall I?' He didn't wait for her to respond but plunged furiously onwards. 'You playing amateur shrink… Of all the glib…!' The fire died from his eyes as abruptly as it had ignited, leaving a bleakness that swiftly delivered an emotional ache to her throat.

He groaned suddenly and, with the appearance of a man in acute pain, brought his hands up to his head. She watched his long fingers curl deep into his hair as if he was contemplating tearing out the odd fistful or two.

'God, but I hate the way you make me feel.'

Whilst she empathised wildly with his pain, she couldn't help but be cheered by this news—at least he wasn't indifferent to her.

'Sorry,' she murmured softly.

Reece lowered his hands. 'What for?'

'For not planting the story.'

Her neutral calm was beginning to irritate him deeply.

'If I had you'd have a legitimate reason to dislike me,' she explained. 'And that would be very convenient for you, wouldn't it, Reece?'

'I *do* dislike you.' There was a shade of helplessness in his strong face as he watched her catch her full lower lip between her teeth and gnaw thoughtfully on the softness.

Darcy shook her head. 'No, you like me—you *definitely* like me,' she added firmly, raising her clear blue eyes to his. 'And I think you're afraid you could get to like me more. That's why you skipped town.'

'What town?'

He sounded amused by her claim—on balance she preferred hostility. Amusement opened the possibility she'd badly misjudged the strength of his feelings. It had been a calculated risk to directly challenge him and she was beginning to wonder if it hadn't backfired; she might emerge from this looking a total fool.

'A figure of speech.' What possessed me…? Why didn't I keep my big mouth shut…?

'Have you always considered yourself irresistible?'

A wry laugh was wrenched from her throat. 'With a sister like Clare? Do me a favour.'

'Clare is a clothes horse.' Darcy stood, her mouth slightly ajar, whilst he casually dismissed her beautiful sister. His glorious eyes sought, found and clung to hers. 'You're a *woman*.'

The hoarse observation was uttered with total conviction.

'*Reece*.' Darcy hadn't even been conscious of moving towards him like a heat-seeking missile until his big hands came up on her shoulders, preventing her from pressing herself closer.

This close she could see the beads of sweat across his upper lip and feel the fine febrile tremors that were running through his greyhound-lean frame.

'You were right, Darcy, there's no future for someone like you with someone like me.'

'What's someone like me…?'

'Warm, giving…' His big, capable, clever hands left her shoulders and slid all the way down the smooth curve of her back before closing over the tight swell of her buttocks. Darcy quivered as hard as a highly strung thoroughbred and pressed closer.

'In that case,' she murmured huskily into his mouth, 'why did you just kiss me…?' Her head was tilted backwards, exposing the long, graceful line of her pale throat.

'Because I have no moral backbone at all.' His hot eyes

lingered smoulderingly on her slightly parted lips. 'And you have the world's most sexy mouth.'

'I do?' she exclaimed, lifting a hand to her lips and provocatively tracing the full outline. She could almost hear the satisfying sound of his control snapping.

'You know you do,' he ground out savagely before he kissed her again, bending her backwards from the waist with the raw force of the embrace. She felt one arm steal around her waist, hauling her upwards until their hips were level. His free hand slid under the hem of her skirt and moved confidently underneath.

The frantic flood of feeling generated by the intimate contact sent her spiralling out of control. She started babbling—she had no accurate recall later of what she said, which was possibly a good thing, but she knew it featured his name and 'please', and both more than once.

It was a major shock to her system when he suddenly released her and placed her back on her feet.

'I can't give you what you want, Darcy.'

She shook her head, refusing to hear what he'd said, refusing to hear the horrid coldness in his voice. Stretched up on tiptoe, she let her tongue slide along the firm, sensual line of his lower lip. A husky little laugh rolled off her tongue.

'You can give me some of the things I want,' she assured him, plastering herself sinuously up against him in a manner that left no doubt to her meaning.

'Darcy, stop that!' he rapped unsteadily as she slid her hand between the buttons of his shirt. He grabbed her wrist and firmly removed it.

Darcy gazed indignantly up at him as he moved her bodily away from him. The heat of arousal died from her eyes, leaving a bemused, resentful expression.

'You stopped!' she wailed.

'I stopped what?' he snapped, making unnecessary adjustments to his tie.

'Kissing me,' she elaborated disapprovingly. Her body had responded to the promise of sensual satisfaction; now it responded just as swiftly and equally violently to being so rudely deprived.

Reece's eyes slid to her face long enough to take in the sexy pout but didn't linger. 'You don't want me to kiss you; I'm not husband material and I'm emotionally stagnant—remember…?'

Darcy remembered but somehow it didn't seem so important any longer. Glutting her hungry senses on the taste, touch and scent of him was.

'What if I can live with that?' She caught hold of the lapels of his jacket and forced him round to face her. 'What if I want to be your mistress…?' This wasn't a perfect world; a girl had to take what she could get, she told herself, rationalising her about-face.

'I don't want you for a mistress, Darcy.' He delivered the uncompromising verdict with a stony face.

There was a period of total, disbelieving silence.

Darcy felt the hot blood rush into her cold face. Now would be the time to retire, beaten, but with a token degree of dignity intact—Darcy never had known when to quit.

'I don't believe you,' she whispered.

'You make too many demands.' She flinched as if he'd struck her. That look in her eyes was one that would haunt him to his dying day. 'You were right—I need a low-maintenance mistress, and frankly that's not you.' He had to get out of here before this bout of selflessness wore off.

Darcy's stomach was a churning mess of misery. Pride was the only thing that enabled her to lift her head and look him bravely in the face; he looked interestingly pale, she noted irrelevantly.

'I'm sure you're right.'

'Yeah, right,' he agreed with a noticeable lack of enthusiasm.

'It's probably best you go now; I'll explain to Jamie.' Perhaps someone will explain to me why I keep inviting rejection. Perhaps someone will explain to me how a person is meant to cope with humiliation on this mega scale.

'Great kid,' Reece observed flatly as she led the way to the front door.

Darcy, normally a besotted aunt, couldn't even manage a smile.

'So this is your young man, Darcy.'

Darcy only just stopped herself pushing his solid bulk through the front door and slamming it safely shut as her grandmother, who had an honours degree in making awkward situations worse, materialised as if by magic.

'This is Reece Erskine, Gran, and he's not my man, young or otherwise,' she explained quietly. 'This is my grandmother.' She pressed her back against the exposed stone wall in the hallway to allow Reece an uninterrupted view of her grandmother, and the support the cold stone afforded was actually quite welcome.

'Mrs…?' He looked to Darcy to help him out and wished he hadn't, she looked so desperately pale.

'Prue.' Prudence Emery held out her hand. 'You can always tell a lot about a man from his handshake.'

Reece wondered if it had told her he was the sort of man who played fast and loose with lovely young women just because he didn't have the self-control to keep his lust under control.

'Mr Erskine was just going, Gran.'

'I read that article you wrote in the *Economist*—the one about ethical investments; very interesting. Though I thought you were a little unrealistic when you said—'

'Gran!' Darcy wailed, unable to contain herself any longer.

'Well, really, Darcy!' Her grandmother was not slow to express her disapproval at this interruption. 'I don't often have the opportunity to speak with someone who actually—'

'Actually, Prue, I do have to be going; it was very nice meeting you…'

'Is he always so abrupt?' Prudence asked her granddaughter.

'Only when he's just had to fend off the amorous advances of stupid women!' Darcy explained before excusing herself.

CHAPTER EIGHT

'ISN'T this just perfect?' Clare exclaimed, holding up a cute baby-blue sleepsuit.

'But is it entirely practical?' Darcy wondered, fingering the velvet teddy bears.

Her half-sister gave a sigh of exasperation as Darcy diligently searched for the wash label. 'Does it matter? It's cute, it's gorgeous—I'm going to buy it.'

Darcy grinned. 'I give in. Perhaps we should pick up some of those nice little vests…'

'Nice *practical* little vests. You're hopeless,' Clare complained, adding the sleepsuit to their overladen shopping basket. 'Don't you ever just throw caution to the winds and buy something totally frivolous, or do something you'll definitely regret?'

Would falling for the wrong man qualify? Darcy wondered bleakly. 'Let's be really silly and get the pink dungarees with elephants.'

'What if it's a boy?'

'He can blame his big sisters for any gender issues that arise in later life.'

'While you're about it,' Clare said, catching on to this reckless mood quickly, 'why don't we go back and buy that dress?'

'I'd never dare wear it in public.'

It was only her sister's pushiness that had got her into the designer shop—it had taken the joint persuasive powers of Clare and the elegant assistant to get her into the dress. Strapless black and deceptively simple. Darcy was inclined to think their flattering reaction had been a put-up job by

Clare to boost her flagging ego—besides, there was no way she could wear something that could be fitted in her wallet.

'Who'd want to?' Clare scorned. 'If you play your cards right, it's not the sort of dress that would see the outside of a bedroom—private viewings only,' she giggled huskily.

Darcy's expression drew taut. If she thought bedrooms she thought Reece.

'Let's pay for these.'

'You're changing the subject, Darce.'

Darcy changed it some more. 'If we want to find a table for lunch we'd better get a move-on.'

The streets of York were crowded with shoppers buying last-minute gifts, but even in the mêlée the couple drew a lot of attention—they were an extremely handsome pair. This man was the rare breed that people didn't barge into and bustle, and the girl by his side benefited from the invisible exclusion zone around them.

'Hold up—progress check.' The girl placed her list on the broad back of her companion and began to tick off the list she carried.

'Mum'll love that pashmina. She'd love it even more if you came home for Christmas,' she added slyly.

'Kate, don't push it…'

The young woman straightened her felt hat to a jaunty angle. 'It was worth a try,' she explained with a philosophical shrug. 'And stranger things have been known to happen.'

Stranger things like her brother ringing her up two days before Christmas to ask her to help him buy Christmas gifts for the family. The fact that her brother was intending to buy Christmas presents *personally* definitely constituted strange, if not miraculous.

Displaying tact and restraint she wasn't renowned for, Kate had only asked, 'Why York?'

She was still, however, eaten up with curiosity to discover what had brought about this dramatic thaw in her big brother's attitude to the festive season. He did after all have more reason than most to be cynical and disillusioned about this time of year.

'Who's Jamie?' she asked, consulting the list once more.

'A kid I know.'

'How old is he?'

Reece leaned down and drew a tentative line about knee-level.

'You don't know how old he is?'

'Not old.'

'I know I make shopping look easy…but *really*, Reece.'

'I thought you liked shopping.' He looked nonplussed by her attitude.

Kate was unable to deny this. 'Perhaps we should take a lunch-break—*Reece*!' she called out, hurriedly grabbing the bundles of brightly wrapped gifts he'd left on the cobbled pedestrianised road before plunging through the crowd after him. If he hadn't been so tall she'd have lost him almost immediately.

'What on earth are you doing?' she cried, as panting, she eventually caught up with him.

Her brother didn't reply, and she'd have laid odds he hadn't even heard her—he was gazing with a fixed, hungry expression at a point across the street. She automatically checked out what had caught his attention.

'Oh, my!' she exclaimed once she had zeroed in on his target—a tall, willowy blonde dressed in an outfit that had 'designer' written all over it. A dedicated follower of fashion, Kate couldn't place the distinctive style. 'She is incredibly gorgeous,' she conceded reluctantly, 'if you like blondes.' She touched the deep copper tendrils of hair that artistically surrounded her face a shade defensively.

Reece, it seemed, obviously did like blondes—or at least

this one—because, ignoring her completely, he was crossing over the street with scant regard for the traffic flow.

'Heavens!' she exclaimed when she realised her brother was going to approach the young woman. This was a major departure for him! For the past few years Kate hadn't seen her big brother so much as raise a finger to make a woman notice him—of course they noticed him when he did nothing! 'This is not typical behaviour,' she explained to a startled-looking passer-by before she gathered up the parcels and resignedly followed him.

Kate's amazement escalated when her brother walked straight past the drop-dead gorgeous blonde as if he didn't see her and right up to the girl she was with, a girl that Kate hadn't noticed until now.

As she got closer Kate could see that the girl wasn't unattractive, and in fact if she hadn't been with the stunner you'd have thought she was a very pretty young woman, though at that moment she looked as if she wouldn't have minded being invisible. The way Reece was behaving, Kate didn't really blame her; he was her brother but even she could recognise he could be pretty intimidating on occasion.

Darcy retreated into the doorway as the large, life-like mirage moved steadily towards her. Her stomach muscles spasmed painfully and the blood drained from her face.

'Hello, Darcy. How are you…?' The mirage spoke; his voice was deep and vibrant, and it made the hairs on the nape of her neck stand on end. Either this was a cruel coincidence or he'd been following her, which, given the way they'd parted, seemed extremely unlikely.

Kate saw the expression on the young woman's face and her own eyes widened—she wasn't screaming for help, but she did look as if she was about to faint. Not strangers—not by a long way!

It was no surprise to Darcy that he was with a beautiful young woman; Reece and beautiful women went together naturally. She couldn't help but notice he appeared to have overcome his qualms about very young women because there was no way this redhead was more than twenty. Presumably if she was low maintenance he was willing to overlook the age-gap.

By avoiding directly meeting the bone-stripping blaze of his emerald scrutiny, Darcy managed to respond stiltedly.

'What a surprise, Reece; how are you…?' She was beginning to understand how relatively mild-mannered creatures could turn feral and dangerous if cornered.

'I'm fine.' A spasm of irritation crossed his patrician features. 'No, I'm not fine, not fine at all!' he bellowed harshly. 'In fact I'm awful.'

I'm not so crash-hot myself, Darcy wanted to yell back. She drew herself up to her full height; it alarmed her that, despite the fact her defences were on full red alert, her skin prickled with sexual awareness and it smothered her like a rash. After the emotional mauling she'd received at their last encounter she didn't fancy a repeat performance. The nasty truth was she didn't trust herself in his company. It wasn't as if she'd planned to act like some willing sex slave last time! She squirmed, recalling that awful moment of rejection.

'Well, don't look at me like that—it's not my fault!' she yelled. '*I* didn't run away.' She bit down hard on her lip, hating the *needy* sound of this last tellingly bitter comment.

Kate was aware that the tall blonde, just as curious a witness to this exchange as she was, had moved beside her to get a better view.

'Kate,' she whispered, thrusting out her hand. 'Sister.' She nodded towards Reece.

There was barely a pause before the other girl responded.

'Clare,' came the hushed, hurried response. 'Sister.' She nodded towards Darcy.

'I want to look at you...!' Reece announced defiantly. The line etched above his nose deepened. 'I need to look at you...I *have* to look at you!' he finished on a startled note of discovery.

Darcy was more shaken by this announcement than she was prepared to admit even to herself. 'Well, you've looked,' she sniffed. 'So now you can go away, and if you follow me,' she added rebelliously, 'I'll call the police. They take a very dim view of stalkers. *Clare!*' She looked around wildly for her sister.

'Coming, Darce!'

'Darcy, you can't go!' Reece began urgently.

I can't *not* go! Darcy ignored his plea and made a neat side-step around him; unfortunately his elbow caught the parcels she carried and sent them flying.

'Let me.' Reece joined her on his hands and knees and began to place the tiny items back in the numerous bags. 'We should talk...' The steady stream of busy people divided, leaving the couple to form an island as the flood moved around them.

'Talk...?' Darcy responded in a low, bitter voice. 'Aren't you afraid I'll embarrass you by doing something silly like offering myself up to you unconditionally...?' Gulping back the tears, she continued to feverishly ram tiny baby items back in the bags any which way.

For once in his life when he really needed to say something Reece was speechless. When you heard it put like that it was pretty hard to escape the conclusion that he'd been a prize fool. What had seemed like noble self-sacrifice now seemed like cowardly caution.

'What's the point?' she added, snatching the last item from his hand and getting to her feet. 'Nothing's changed.' If he'd denied it she might have hung around to hear what he had to say, but he didn't, he remained on his haunches, staring blankly at the hand she'd ripped the soft booties from. 'Come on, Clare.'

'Reece,' Kate murmured after she'd endured several curious stares of passers-by. 'It might be a good idea to get up some time soon unless you want to be charged with causing an obstruction.'

Prone to clumsiness, Kate felt a brief surge of envy as her brother, who, even in moments of extreme stress—and this was obviously one of them—was beautifully co-ordinated, rose to his feet.

'Kate, what do you know about babies...pregnancy...that sort of thing?'

'Well, I read the book Mum gave me, and I attended all the classes at school, but...' She paused; there was no flicker of answering humour in her brother's eyes. 'Could you be more specific?'

'How long does it take before you'd know you were pregnant?'

'Well, I suppose that would depend on when in your cycle you conceived, but I do know you can tell almost straight away these days with the kits they've got. Never had call to try them out myself but I hear they're pretty accurate.'

'Oh, my God!'

At moments of emotional crisis in her life Reece had always stood out as a comforting figure of calm authority to Kate. Now she was shocked to discover that even her self-contained brother knew what panic felt like.

'What is it, Reece? What's wrong?'

He raised a distracted hand to his forehead, his skin deathly pale and clammy to the touch. 'All those bags were filled with baby clothes,' he said in a voice wiped clean of all emotion.

'Then you think...and it's yours...*hell's bells*!' No wonder he looked stunned. 'Anyone can buy baby clothes—it doesn't mean she's pregnant. They're probably presents.'

'There were dozens of them.'

Kate wondered whether now would be the right time to say congratulations.

Reece turned to his sister, a zealot-like gleam of purpose in his eyes. 'I've got to go.'

'I thought you might,' she responded drily. 'What shall I—?'

'See you later.'

No 'when' later, no 'where' later; how typical, Kate thought, watching her tall sibling weave his way skilfully through the shoppers.

There were no signs of life at the Alexander house. Frustrated but not deterred, Reece pondered his next move—he could wait, but inactivity didn't recommend itself to him in his present frame of mind. He decided to drive down the road to the nearby village to see if there was any clue to their whereabouts.

There was a noticeably large collection of cars in the cobbled village square; Reece joined them. Leaving the car, he shadowed the handful of recent arrivals. Their destination proved to be a small hall with a tin roof set just behind the church.

'Two pounds fifty, please,' the large female at the door demanded, blocking his way into the glorified tin shed.

Impatiently he handed her a ten-pound note from his wallet. His impatient direction of 'Keep it' as she began to meticulously count out the correct change seemed to shock her Yorkshire thriftiness, but he got in, that was the main thing—into what, he wasn't quite sure, but instinct told him there was a strong possibility, given the scarcity of social occasions in the area, that Darcy would be here.

The place was heaving, but thanks to their height he spotted the twins almost immediately; their blond heads were easy to identify above the audience, who were seated in rows of uncomfortable wooden-backed chairs. He slid into the back row and waited.

He waited all the way through the infants' nativity play and the resonant recitation by a large bearded individual. His patience was rewarded when the choir trouped onto the small makeshift stage. In the front row, looking angelically sexy and terrified, was Darcy.

'You were marvellous, Darcy.'

'I think I'm going to throw up.'

'What you need is a drink.'

'What I need is several,' Darcy, whose knees were still shaking, informed the pushy cleric firmly. 'And, considering it's your fault I was up there to begin with, you're buying.'

Adam Wells grinned. 'Sounds reasonable to me.' He gave her a quick hug. 'You're a trouper.' With a display of sensible caution he moved away. 'Not still feeling sick, are you?' he enquired warily.

'That's passed, but it was a close call. I'll hold you to that drink.'

'How about now?' Adam suggested, looking around the dimly lit empty hall.

Darcy, who hadn't really taken the offer seriously, looked surprised. 'Mum and Dad are waiting.'

'They're not the only ones.'

Thanks to the excellent acoustics, the words uttered by the tall, sinister figure who rose from the shadows at the back of the hall reached the front with no problem.

'That's excellent voice projection you have there...?' Adam commented as the tall figure came to a halt just in front of the low stage.

'Reece Erskine.'

The vicar leant down to offer the newcomer with the unfriendly expression his hand. 'Adam Wells.'

After a pause Reece responded. A closer inspection confirmed his suspicions that this Adam chap was far too young and flashily good-looking to project the right sort of gravitas required for his chosen career.

'Hello, Darcy.'

Darcy's only reason for grabbing Adam's sleeve was a desire to stay on her feet. The expression in Reece's eyes as they rested on her slender fingers curved tightly over the dark sleeve suggested he wasn't considering extenuating circumstances—he was considering homicide! This example of male perversity brought a spark of rebellion to Darcy's face. It seemed he didn't want her but he didn't want anyone else to have her either! 'What are you doing here?'

'I'm a music-lover.'

Darcy snorted. 'I thought your opinion of my voice would have been a good enough reason to give the place a wide berth!' She stopped short, her eyes widening. 'Were you sitting there all the way through?' she asked hoarsely.

Reece nodded.

Darcy swallowed and went cold all over; it was just as well, she reflected, that she hadn't known that. The idea of Reece watching her made her feel ridiculously exposed and vulnerable. No, that would definitely have been one critical pair of eyes too many. She turned to Adam.

'Reece thinks I have a terrible voice,' she informed him, sparing an unfriendly glare for the figure standing just below them.

'I'm sure that's not true, Darcy.'

'It does lack a certain depth and power…'

Darcy took an outraged gasp. 'See, I told you! Who made you a music critic…?' she demanded, squaring her shoulders aggressively. The fact he was essentially right was no excuse in her eyes for his comment.

'But if you set aside technique,' Reece continued as if she hadn't spoken, 'it was the most moving thing I've ever heard.'

Darcy's aggressive stance wobbled. *'It was…?'*

'Of course, I'm not what you could call objective.'

The hunted, furtive expression on Darcy's face got more pronounced as his warm, caressing glance came to rest squarely on her face.

'You're not?' she squeaked.

'There comes a time in a man's life when he has to admit defeat.'

Darcy's heart skipped a couple of beats and she promptly forgot that only earlier that day she'd sworn that if he ever came crawling back it would afford her great pleasure to laugh scornfully in his face—at the time she hadn't actually expected the opportunity to arise.

'What are you saying, Reece?' she squeaked without the trace of a scornful laugh. She slid her bottom onto the edge of the makeshift stage and dropped hastily to the floor. A person couldn't hear something like what she suspected—*hoped*—he was about to say perched on this ridiculous platform.

For some inexplicable reason Reece seemed to find her action extremely alarming; he shot forward and clamped his hands around her waist, lowering her the last inch or so as though she were delicate china.

'You shouldn't be doing that,' he reproached huskily, as if she'd just done something wildly reckless.

Despite the distracting warmth of the hands circling her waist and the deliciously weak, tingling feeling that permeated her body, she had to ask. 'Why not?'

'I'd have thought that was obvious.'

The only obvious thing to Darcy was that she was destined to love this man for better or worse, in the for ever after sense. She shook her head in bewilderment. Amidst the emotional turmoil she clung to the tenderness she saw shining in his marvellous eyes—everything was going to be all right. Her vision blurred as she stared, mesmerised by that warmth, into his dark, strong-boned face.

'I'll let your parents know you're making your own way home, shall I, Darcy…?' Adam didn't act as if he expected a response—he wasn't disappointed.

'You should have told me,' Reece reproached throatily, running a finger over the soft curve of her cheek. His smile was strained as he tweaked a strand of her blonde hair.

'I thought I did,' Darcy murmured, turning her cheek into his open palm. He hadn't told her he loved her yet but surely that was only a matter of time.

It occurred to Reece that they were at cross purposes. 'What are we talking about here?'

'I did tell you I loved you…I even had a crack at hinting that you might love me too, but,' she brooded darkly, 'that wasn't a big success.' The humiliation of that occasion was still too recent not to hurt.

'Poor baby,' he crooned, placing a warm, wonderful kiss on her parted lips. 'I was an idiot.'

'I think so,' she agreed breathlessly.

'You should have told me about the baby,' he murmured, stroking the side of her diminutive nose with his.

Darcy shivered as his lips made sensual progress towards her ear. 'How did you know? Did Mum tell you?' she wondered, sinking her fingers into the marvellous lushness of his hair.

'Does she know? I'm glad you told her.' He hated the idea of her having no one to share the news with, no one to soothe her worries.

'Told her?' Darcy echoed, pulling a little away. 'I didn't have to *tell* her, silly.' She bit down gently on his lower lip before sliding the tip of her tongue inside. The judder that ran through his body was highly satisfactory.

'I suppose a mother just knows these things,' Reece agreed, breathing in the warm, fresh scent that rose off her skin and hair.

'Well, she was shocked to begin with,' Darcy conceded. 'But I think the idea's starting to grow on her.'

'And you, how do you feel about becoming a mother?'

'Oh, I feel…' Her dreamy smile faded; she stiffened. 'What did you say…?' A quiver of apprehension shivered down her spine.

'I know how you feel,' he sympathised, misreading her expression. 'I was pretty shocked myself to start off with, but I'm delighted, really I am.'

Darcy firmly detached herself from his arms. 'What exactly are you delighted about, Reece…?' A terrible suspicion was forming in her mind—and it was so horrible she didn't want to contemplate it. But she had no option.

'Becoming a father, of course.'

The suspicion solidified.

'You think I'm pregnant?'

His indulgent smile was tinged with a hint of concern; her skin had acquired a worrying, greyish tinge. 'Isn't that what we've just been discussing?' He pulled a chair forward. 'Perhaps you should sit down.'

'Maybe you should.' So this was what his sudden change of heart had been about—for some reason he'd got the idea she was carrying his child. That was what happened when you allowed wishful thinking to take the place of common sense! She felt as if a lump of ice was lodged behind her breastbone as she lifted her chin to face him.

'It might have been what you were discussing, Reece, but I wasn't.'

'There's no need to pretend, Darcy; I saw the baby clothes—I know.'

'You know!'

For some reason Reece couldn't fathom she seemed to find this comment hilarious. His expression was sombre and guarded by the time her wild laughter had died away.

'I'm not pregnant, Reece.'

'You mean it was a false alarm?' Reece was amazed at how bad this made him feel, but was determined not to let her see his disappointment.

'I mean that I never have been. I was buying the clothes for Mum—*she's* expecting the baby; that's what brought about her emotional crisis.'

'Then you're not…?'

'Not even a little bit,' she confirmed, shaking her head from side to side.

'But I thought…' His eyes moved to her flat midriff and the blood drained from his face. There was a lengthy pause. 'I did some jumping to conclusions, didn't I…?' he remarked ruefully. He didn't mention the degree of wishful thinking that had made him reach such a rash conclusion.

'You're not the only one.' Her smile was grim as she recognised the extent of her wilful self-delusion. 'I thought you came here because you'd realised you loved me—how silly is that?' She laughed bitterly. There came a time in a girl's life when she really ought to stop setting herself up for rejection—humiliation aside, it hurt too damned much!

'Don't look so concerned, Reece, I'm not about to hold you to anything you said while overcome by paternal feelings. Though actually I think you'll find you didn't actually say anything too incriminating.'

'I did come here because I love you, Darcy.'

Darcy backed away, evading the hand that tried to grasp her wrist. 'So the fact that you thought I was carrying your child had nothing whatever to do with it.'

His broad shoulders lifted; he knew how this was going

to sound. 'That was a factor, certainly, but only in that it acted as a catalyst.'

'So you mean you'd be here if you hadn't thought I was pregnant?'

The expression in his eyes said it all. At least he wasn't lying—that was something. Though it wasn't enough to make her feel anything less than deliriously unhappy.

'Not this soon maybe.' The cynical little twist of her lips escalated his growing sense of frustration.

'Don't panic, Reece; as entertaining as the spectacle of you trying to talk yourself out of this might be, I won't make you sweat. You didn't actually say anything that could be construed as a concrete proposal of any variety.' No need for that when I'm so eager to hear what I want. 'And if you feel a fool you can take comfort from the knowledge that I feel much worse.'

'I'm not trying to talk my way out of anything,' he grated.

'If you say so,' she drawled.

'I *do* say so.' She smiled again with faint, damning disbelief. 'Listen, Darcy, I was *happy* when I thought you were carrying my child. Don't you see what that means…?' he appealed, his taut expression urgent.

Her normally animated face was blank as stone. 'It means you want to be a father.'

'If it was that simple I could have done something about it years ago. When Jo and the baby died I swore I'd never…' His rich voice cracked and Darcy began to sweat with the effort of not rushing to comfort him—it was following impulses like that which had got her in this mess to begin with. 'Before today I thought the very last thing I wanted—other than to feel responsible for another human—was a child.'

His emotions when he spoke of his wife were obviously genuine, but anything else was suspect as far as Darcy was concerned—or at least her interpretation of them was. She could no longer trust her own judgement.

'I suppose I'm responsible in my own small way for this breakthrough.'

'Will you stop talking like that?' he bellowed.

'Like what?'

Reece took several deep breaths and when he replied it was with a calm he was far from feeling. 'I only want a child if you're the mother…' he said slowly, as if he was explaining something simple to a very small child.

'You expect me to believe that!' Darcy gasped, her face crumbling.

This reaction hadn't been the one he'd hoped for. In the face of her tears, his hard-fought-for calm deserted him totally.

'This is just plain ridiculous. I love you!' he yelled in a very un-lover-like manner as he advanced purposefully towards her. If words wouldn't convince her of his sincerity, maybe actions would.

'Don't touch me!' she breathed venomously, batting his extended hand away. She refused to be swayed by the flicker of pain in his deep-set eyes. 'I'm not interested in what you've got to say, not now, not ever!' She ran down the central aisle, knocking several chairs over as she went.

For a long time after the door had slammed shut Reece stood there in the dimly lit hall, thinking. By the time he left he had the outline of a plan in his mind.

CHAPTER NINE

'LET me get this straight,' Clare said, her smooth brow wrinkling in an incredulous frown. 'The man said he loved you, and you ran away? And this is because…you love him? Am I getting this right?'

Darcy hadn't confided in her sister in the hope of being mocked—where was a bit of sisterly solidarity when a girl needed it?

'He was lying.' The explanation emerged as hopelessly feeble with an unattractive hint of petulance. Even before she heard it Darcy had already been wishing she hadn't, in a moment of weakness, revealed the disaster that was her love-life to her half-sister.

'Don't talk!' Clare remonstrated sharply. 'You'll crack the mask. How do you know he was lying?' She picked up the damp ends of Darcy's hair. 'Have you ever thought of trying some of that serum that helps frizziness?'

'I like frizz!' Darcy snapped.

Unable to bear being the passive target of her sister's subtle but searching questioning technique for another second—first a hint on skin care, the next a 'Did you sleep with him that first night?' Darcy gave a grunt of exasperation and flung off the towel that was draped around her shoulders.

Her sister followed her to the bathroom and waited while she rinsed off the greenish face mask which had set hard as concrete.

'You won't get the full benefit—you didn't leave it on long enough,' she predicted as Darcy scrubbed at her tingling face with a towel. 'So what about Reece, then?'

Darcy scowled. 'What about him?' she said unencouragingly—problem was, when Clare had the bit between her teeth she didn't need any encouragement. 'I wish I hadn't told you!' she cried, throwing the damp towel at Clare's head.

'Let's say, just for the sake of argument, that he was telling the truth.'

Darcy buried her head in her hands. 'I've already told you he only turned up because he saw the baby clothes and got this stupid idea that I was pregnant!'

'So when you told him you were about to be a sister, not a mum, he did what any man who was only reluctantly doing the right thing by a casual lover he'd accidentally impregnated would…'

Darcy winced. 'You've got such a delicate way of putting things.'

Clare's grin broadened. 'He hung around saying he loved you…?' She gave a bark of laughter. 'Come off it, Darcy, why would he do that? If he really only cared about the baby he'd have been out of there as fast as his Merc would take him.'

'Reece has more style than that! Oh, don't look at me like that!' Darcy snapped. 'You didn't see his face when he realised—he was devastated. He was only trying to spare my feelings. If he was in love with me he's had plenty of opportunities to say so.'

'Perhaps he didn't know then?'

'I thought you were meant to be the realist.'

Clare shook her head. 'Listen, Darcy, I'm playing devil's advocate here because to be quite frank if you end up with him I'd be green with envy, and if you don't I might just feel inclined to… I don't suppose you could call it rebound if he never was in love with you.'

'You're so smart,' Darcy hissed. 'What about the redhead?'

'I told you, she's the sister. Go on—admit it; the idea of me making a move on your man makes you want to tear my hair out!'

'I'm not in the mood for mind games, Clare; I've fallen in love with him, that's no secret—*unfortunately*,' she added gloomily. It seemed that her love-life was the main topic of conversation in the locality.

'This isn't like you, Darcy…'

'What isn't like me…?'

'Wimping out isn't like you. You're not totally convinced he isn't in love with you, are you? Be honest.' She gave a crow of triumph as her sister's eyes slid away. 'I thought as much. You'll always wonder if you don't find out for sure.'

'How do you propose I find out?'

'Go next door and ask him.'

'What?' Darcy exclaimed, dropping the comb she'd been running through her damp hair.

'He's next door waiting right now,' Clare explained smugly.

'This is a set-up!' Darcy accused wrathfully. 'You've been got at,' she fumed. 'How much did it cost him?' The flicker of pain on her sister's face brought her back to her senses. 'I didn't mean that, Clare; I was mad. He's next door, you say…?'

'Waiting,' Clare agreed.

The shiny new door complete with a Christmas wreath swung open when she placed her hand on it. Chin high—Darcy didn't want anyone to get the idea this was one of the scariest things she'd ever done—she stalked towards the brand-new living-room door and pushed it open.

She opened her mouth to announce herself and it stayed that way as she took in the decor—actually it was hard to miss. Just about every possible surface had been draped with strings of twinkling, blinking fairy lights, there were singing Santas and clockwork reindeer, and the tree was so tall she decided it must have been erected with the aid of heavy-duty lifting equipment.

'Good God!' she gasped. 'What have you done?'

'Do you like it? All courtesy of Uncle Rick. I bought his entire stock.' Reece's tall figure moved out from behind the bulk of the towering fir. He was wearing dark jeans and a lighter cashmere sweater; the sleeves were pushed up to his elbows and she could see the fine mesh of dark hairs on his strong, sinewed forearms.

Darcy tore her eyes clear of this disturbing spectacle and focused her gaze on the very top of the towering Christmas tree. She briskly began to rub her own forearms, which, like the rest of her body, were covered by a layer of goose-bumps. She was incapable of disentangling the earthy sex appeal from the rest of the man, which meant she couldn't look at him and think pure, chaste thoughts.

It took her several dry-throated seconds to get on top of her steamy, impure thoughts.

'I take it you were working on the theory that more is better,' she remarked hoarsely.

'I was making a point.'

'If the point was you have no taste, congratulations—it worked.'

'I'm a changed man. I'm not running any more—not from anything.'

The same couldn't be said of Darcy, whose wary glance finally strayed to his face and refused to budge. 'Could you make that any more oblique if you tried…?' she croaked. If he wanted to say something, why didn't he just say it?

'I could have made it more tasteless, only they didn't have a Santa costume to fit me, which was a pity because they had this one number with strategically placed Velcro.

One quick flick and the whole thing was off.' He inscribed a sweeping motion with his hand.

The image his words and action conjured up reduced her to a stuttering wreck. 'That's d-disgusting!' she choked, going a deeper shade of pink.

'Ingenious, I thought.' He moved towards her, but his stride was lacking the flowing animal grace she realised she associated with him. It was then she saw what she'd been too self-absorbed to notice earlier—the screaming tension behind his mocking grin. 'So you came.' His eyes were acting very hungry as they moved restlessly over her slender figure.

'Clare can be very persuasive,' she croaked drily.

'Nice girl.'

'*Beautiful* girl.'

'Really…? I hadn't noticed.' His grin invited her to share the joke. It was an invitation she tried very hard to refuse. Reece sighed noisily. 'Listen, Darcy, I'm not interested in beautiful girls, I'm interested in *you*!' he announced forcibly. *'Oh, God!'* He struck his forehead with the heel of his hand.

Reece's relief was palpable when she started to laugh. The laughter didn't remove the high tension between them but it did reduce it slightly.

'Can we start again?'

She gave a jerky little nod and shot a covetous peek at his profile—it was perfect, but then she hadn't expected it not to be.

'Thanks. The thing is, I'm so damned nervous I don't know what I'm saying.'

'*You're* nervous!' The sneaky peek was in danger of turning into a transfixed stare.

'You look shocked.'

Darcy was shocked. 'I just never thought of *you* as….'

It wasn't the fact he was vulnerable that shocked her, it was the fact he was letting her see it!

'Human?' A surge of colour travelled along the slashing crests of his slanted cheekbones and his ironic gaze drilled into her. 'The rest of my life is hanging on my getting this right, Darcy. I think under the circumstances I've got every right to be nervous.' He dragged an unsteady hand through his hair, his raw frustration clearly evident in his voice and tense stance.

She raised her eyes slowly to his, and her heart began banging noisily against her ribs. 'Perhaps you ought to get on with it,' she suggested gruffly.

Darcy had the sort of optimism that wouldn't lie down and play dead for long. It was making a spectacular comeback at that precise moment and she was trying hard not to show it.

Reece nodded. He folded his long frame down onto the bed, and patted the spot beside him. 'Sit…?'

Darcy shook her head emphatically—if she did as he suggested they'd never get any talking done.

'You're probably right,' he conceded, apparently arriving pretty swiftly at the same conclusion she had. 'You said you loved me, and I ran away. I said I loved you, and you ran away. Have you wondered what would happen if we both said it at the same time…?'

Her throat was so dry she could hardly form the words. 'I don't waste my time on pointless speculation…'

He smiled; it wasn't a safe kind of smile.

'Neither do I, sweetheart.' There was a very predatory look in his eyes as he explained this—the sort of look which should have offended her sense of political correctness; hormones being what they were, it actually sent a surge of sexual excitement so intense through her that she felt dizzy.

'I reacted badly when you said you loved me, so any

scepticism on your part when I announce I feel the same way is kind of understandable—up to a point…'

'What point is that?'

'The point where you ruin both our lives, Darcy.' He paused as if he expected her to protest. 'I won't let you do that,' he warned forcefully.

'Then what are you waiting for? Talk. I'm listening.'

'I did come back because I got it into my head that you were pregnant…'

'Which I'm not…'

'…but that only speeded things up; I'd have come back eventually—how could I not…?' The wondering expression in his eyes as they came to rest on her made her eyes widen…she hardly dared believe what she was seeing was real. 'It just speeded the process up.'

'What process…?'

'The one that made me see that if you're a lucky sod you do get to be in love twice in one lifetime. Joanna died…' His head dropped so she could no longer see his expression, but she could see the strong muscles of his throat work.

'I know how she died, Reece,' Darcy cut in quietly. It was an awful feeling, standing there seeing how much he was hurting and being utterly impotent to help.

'Then you'll know she died and I couldn't do a damned thing—I was standing there and I…' At that moment he lifted his head, his expression more composed than she'd expected—as if he was telling a story and not reliving it, something she instinctively knew he'd done many times before. 'She was so damned happy about the baby—I couldn't do a thing to help her, Darcy.'

'I know,' she cried, dropping down onto the floor at his feet and taking his big hands in hers. She spread her small fingers out against his and she sealed their palms together.

'I was her husband; I was meant to protect her and I

didn't. There wasn't a scratch on me.' While staring at their conjoined hands, hers so ridiculously small by comparison with his, he experienced a great surge of protectiveness that was primitive in its intensity.

Darcy closed her eyes and a single tear slipped out between her tightly closed lids. Reece had scars—they just weren't the sort that showed.

'I never wanted to be in a position to let down someone I loved ever again. Can you understand that?'

Darcy opened her eyes; her lashes were wet but her gaze was clear and composed. She nodded.

'It was arrogance, really,' he conceded with a self-derisive sneer, 'that emotional-control thing. I was remote from all that messy emotional crap. Then you came along and you challenged all that just by being there—then to add insult to injury you used the L word; I was mad as hell with you about that!'

'I was mad as hell with myself about that,' she confided huskily.

'I didn't want to believe what was happening. But even I couldn't ignore what had happened to me for long, and I squirmed out of that by telling myself you deserved something better than an emotional cripple. I know I was brutal.' There was an expression of bitter self-recrimination on his face as he recalled the events. 'And I'm desperately sorry for it, but at the time it felt like the right thing to do.

'The truth is, Darcy, running away gets to be a habit after a while. In a way thinking you were pregnant suited me—gave me an excuse; I didn't need to think too much about why I needed to be with you. Didn't need to face up to my own feelings. I never believed in love at first sight—lust at first sight, sure, but not love.'

He hadn't known then that love came in many guises and not just in the form of a gentle, slowly growing bond. He'd finally come to accept that sometimes the strongest bonds were forged in fire. He just prayed he hadn't left it too late.

'It wasn't like that with…Jo…*sorry*.'

The man had just said he'd fallen in love her with on sight and he was *apologising*!

'I'm all right with your past, Reece—I've got one myself. It's your future I might get a bit possessive about.'

During the stark, shocked silence that followed Darcy felt his big body stiffen.

'Does that mean…?' he asked, his darkened eyes searching her face with unconcealed urgency.

Her fingers curled tight against his and the pressure he offered in return was so emphatic she almost winced. She only broke the contact in order to press her splayed fingers to either side of his strong face. He did the same thing to her, his own long fingers curling round the softly rounded outline of her jaw.

Darcy blinked rapidly, her head still reeling from his impassioned confessions. 'When you open up, lover, you *really* open up.'

'Pretty disillusioning stuff, I suppose…?'

His eyes didn't leave hers for an instant. Darcy could almost physically feel the waves of tension emanating from his lean frame.

'I suppose it might be for someone who has put the man she loves on some sort of pedestal. In case you're wondering—I didn't and I don't.' He continued to look blankly at her. 'Stupid,' she crooned lovingly. 'I'm saying I love you—not,' she added drily, 'for the first time, and I'm warning you, if you do what you did last time I'll…'

She never did get the chance to tell him what she'd do because the tight control he'd had on his emotions slipped. Darcy saw the fierce glitter of his emerald eyes just before his mouth came down hard and hungry on hers.

Darcy's arms snaked up around his neck as he lifted her

onto the ridiculously opulent bed and plunged deeper into the sweet, welcoming darkness of her mouth. For long moments they kissed and touched with frantic urgency.

'God, but I love you.' He continued to nuzzle her neck.

Darcy nodded in languid agreement; his hand was under her sweater, running over the warm skin of her stomach, and the other was fiddling with the zip on her skirt.

Thinking skin on skin made her dizzy and hot, but blissfully happy. In fact it was possible, she reflected dreamily, that this much happiness was illegal.

'Say you love me, Darcy,' he insisted.

'I...' His fingers chose that moment to correctly locate one shamelessly engorged nipple, and Darcy let out a long sibilant sigh of pleasure and threw one arm over her head.

Reece's eyes darkened as he studied the enraptured expression on her aroused face. 'You were saying...?' he prompted throatily.

'Was I...?' she asked languidly, forcing her heavy eyelids open.

He brushed the silvery strands of hair back from her forehead before kissing the tip of her nose. Their eyes collided and Darcy smiled a slow, languorous smile that oozed satisfaction—he loved her, he really loved her!

'I remember now. I love you, Reece.'

'Too right you do!' her forceful lover gritted back, a smile of triumph curving his sensual mouth. 'And don't you ever forget it.'

Somehow Darcy didn't think that was likely.

'What,' she asked, shooting a flirtatious little look at him through the spiky fringe of her eyelashes, 'would you do if I did have some problem remembering...?'

'I'd do this.' She let out a startled shriek as he lifted her jumper over her head and impatiently flung it aside. 'And this.' Her bra swiftly followed suit.

Breathing hard, he gazed, transfixed momentarily by the

spectacle of her heaving, pink-tipped breasts. The warmth low in her belly sizzled into a full-scale conflagration.

'Isn't that a bit…excessive…?' she wondered huskily.

'No,' he contradicted confidently. '*This* is excessive, and this, and this…'

'Menace me some more,' she whispered brokenly as he divested her of her last stitch of clothing.

'Like this?' he asked, settling between her parted thighs and thrusting up hard.

Darcy expelled her breath very slowly and turned her hot cheek against the cool pillow. 'Exactly like that,' she moaned feverishly. To feel him inside, all the way inside her, filling her so perfectly. 'Is there more?' She managed to force the husky question past her parched vocal chords.

She felt the laughter rumble deep in his powerful chest.

'As much as you can take,' he boasted—actually, it didn't turn out to be a boast at all.

'You know,' Darcy said some time later, 'I should be going.'

Reece's hand, which was stroking her hair, stilled.

She lifted her head from his chest. 'I don't want to.' She felt him relax.

'Then don't.'

'I wish I could stay, but there's loads to do for tomorrow and I should get back. Mum is quite likely to get an attack of superwomanitis, and it's important she doesn't overexert herself.

'In that case,' Reece remarked, throwing aside the covers and exposing her toasty warm body to a blast of cooler air, 'you'd better move your lovely little butt.'

Darcy rolled onto her side and propped herself up on one elbow. 'You're kicking me out of bed?' she asked indignantly.

'You'd prefer a display of unreasonable possessiveness…?'

She laid a loving hand on his chest and tweaked a curly strand of dark hair. 'Well, a sign or two that you'd miss me wouldn't go amiss,' she responded tartly.

'I won't miss you.' The extra-hard tweak she gave made him wince. 'Because I'm coming with you.'

'You are?' she echoed, her eyes growing round with wonder.

'Unless you have any objections.'

'Are you quite sure?' she wondered doubtfully.

'A man could get to feel unwanted…'

'Oh, no,' she purred lazily, 'you're wanted all right,' she assured him, allowing her wickedly lascivious stare to wander over his sleek, powerful body. Her smile grew smugly content as he responded instantly and pretty blatantly to her teasing. 'I just wasn't sure you'd be into our full-on, no-holds-barred, traditional sort of Christmas.'

'I just want to be with you,' he responded simply.

There was such naked, unconditional love in his face that Darcy's eyes filled with tears of sheer happiness. 'And I want to be with you,' she sniffed.

'Then let's get moving before we catch pneumonia.' Darcy let out a startled shriek as he tipped her off the bed. All thoughts of retaliation faded from her mind as she lifted her head in time to see Reece, completely at ease with his naked state, strut panther-like across the room.

Reece caught her looking and grinned. 'If you really want to go, Darcy, don't do that.'

'I'm only looking,' she complained.

'There's looking and then there's what you're doing…'

'If you don't like it, put some clothes on.'

'I will, but not because I don't like it…'

It took them longer to get dressed than expected because several items of essential clothing had gone missing. The silky pair of pink knickers were eventually discovered draped over a branch of the Christmas tree.

'It seems a pity to remove them,' Reece remarked indelicately as she snatched them free. 'You have to admit they'd be a talking point.'

'I know exactly what I'm going to buy you for Christmas,' Darcy confided as he slid her jacket over her shoulders. 'It'll be a bit late, of course, but you won't mind,' she predicted confidently.

'Is it a secret?' he asked, watching the play of emotions on her face with indulgent pleasure.

'No, it's a dress.'

He laughed low in his throat. 'Is it in my size?'

'No, it's in mine,' she giggled.

'It sounds promising.'

'You'll love it,' she promised.

The laughter died from his eyes. *'I love you.'*

The memory of the lonely ache in her heart receded even further.

He bent his head down towards her and Darcy stroked the strong edge of his jaw. 'You know,' she sighed, 'I'm going to miss this place.' She leaned backwards into his body and gave a contented sigh as his arms drew her closer still.

'You won't have to.'

'How's that...?' she murmured absently as she rubbed her cheek lovingly against his sleeve.

'I spent so much cash on the place that I thought I might as well buy it,' he explained casually.

'You what?' Darcy twisted out of his arms and gazed up at him, a stupefied expression in her wide eyes.

'Well, I'm as flexible as the next man, but I don't fancy sharing a bedroom with the twins every time we come to visit your parents.'

'And are we likely to be doing that often?' she enquired

wonderingly. It sounded as if Reece had been giving the matter a lot of thought.

'Well, obviously we will be after we're married, and, as fond as I am of your brothers, can you imagine trying to get a baby to sleep with them in the house?'

'Do you mind backtracking a bit there...?' Darcy pleaded hoarsely. 'You did say *married*?'

'I know we haven't discussed it, but *obviously*... What did you think I wanted from you, Darcy?' he demanded, looking mightily offended by her response.

'A baby...?'

'Naturally I'll cut back on my work commitments for the first year or so.'

'Do I have any say in this...?' she felt impelled to ask.

'You don't want a baby?' He accepted the news stoically. 'That's not a problem.'

'Of course I want babies!' she exclaimed.

'Whose?' he came back, quick as a flash.

Darcy blinked. 'Whose what?'

'Babies.'

'Yours, of course.'

'Then you'll have to marry me!' he responded with a smugly complacent smile.

'People get married for that reason but not me!' Her words carried the cool ring of total conviction.

The warm laughter fled his eyes, leaving a defiant wariness. 'What would make you want to get married?' He thrust his hands deep into his pockets and gave the impression of a man ready to argue her into submission.

'Finding a man I didn't want to live without, a man I wanted to share everything with, a man...'

'Like me.'

'Was that a statement or a question?'

'You little witch—you really had me going there for a minute!'

Still holding his eyes, she thrust out one slender hand. 'Shake on it…?'

'Don't be silly, woman,' he cried, hauling her into his arms. 'We'll kiss on it.'

'We don't have any mistletoe.'

'Who needs it…?' he growled, tilting her head back.

Who indeed? Darcy thought, melting with a blissful sigh into his masterful embrace.

CHRISTMAS IN THE BILLIONAIRE'S BED

JANICE MAYNARD

For all the wonderful authors who paved the way at Mills & Boon. I read your stories growing up, took trips around the world, and dreamed of writing my own romantic heroes one day...

USA TODAY bestselling author **Janice Maynard** loved books and writing even as a child. But it took multiple rejections before she sold her first manuscript. Since 2002, she has written over forty-five books and novellas. Janice lives in east Tennessee with her husband, Charles. They love hiking, travelling and spending time with family.

You can connect with Janice at
janicemaynard.com,
Twitter.com/janicemaynard,
Facebook.com/janicemaynardreaderpage,
Facebook.com/janicesmaynard and
Instagram.com/janicemaynard.

One

Mrs. Maeve Kavanagh
and
Mr. and Mrs. W. H. Larin
request the honor of your presence
at the marriage of their children
Dylan Edward and Mia Elaina
on Saturday, December 20th
The Chapel in Silver Glen

Aidan Kavanagh stared at the cream vellum card edged with tiny holly leaves and berries and shook his head in reluctant admiration.

Game. Set. Match.

His mother had won the war without firing a single shot. The last thing Aidan wanted to do was visit Silver Glen, North Carolina, during the holidays, but Maeve knew he wouldn't miss his own brother's wedding.

The first of his siblings, Liam, had tied the knot recently as well. That event had been a huge, splashy society affair at Zoe's home in Connecticut—a hop, skip and a jump from New York City. This time Aidan wouldn't be so lucky.

It wasn't that he didn't love Silver Glen. He did. But

going home for Christmas brought back too many ugly memories. So, he chose to visit his large, close-knit family at other times of the year: Easter, Mother's Day, the Fourth of July…and October, when the fall foliage in the mountains was at its peak.

But December? No. In the last decade, he had managed it only once and only then because one of his brothers had been in the hospital. Aidan would have felt like a total jerk if he had let his family down.

That visit had been both uncomfortable and unpleasant. His mother and brothers had walked on eggshells around him, everyone far too aware that Aidan carried the weight of past tragedy. He'd done his damnedest to prove to them he was fine…that he had moved on.

Unfortunately, no one had been convinced by his deliberate facade of Christmas cheer. Least of all Aidan himself. Because the truth was, December sucked. He was fine. His life was good. He was content. But not even his family knew the worst of what had happened so long ago.

He stood and stretched, tossing the offending invitation on his desk. The view from his office window stretched from the Statue of Liberty all the way to the George Washington Bridge. Aidan loved New York City. The constant pulse of life. The fact that he could stop for lox and bagels at three in the morning and no one batted an eye.

Most of all, he loved the anonymity. No one here cared about his past or even his future. The emotional breathing room had become as essential to him as food or water.

Growing up in Silver Glen provided an idyllic childhood—at least until his father's death when Aidan was a young teen. The little alpine-like town would always be home. But living in a fishbowl where everyone knew his business became unbearable when he was twenty-one and his entire world crumbled around him.

Moving to New York had been his salvation. With a hefty nest egg of Kavanagh money—long since repaid—he'd started a high-end real estate company. The lessons he'd learned as a youth working in his family's swank hotel stood him in good stead. Although the Kavanaghs were very wealthy, the crème de la crème here in the city took that definition to a far greater level. Aidan enjoyed the challenge of matching socialites and business magnates with their perfect homes on the rooftops of Manhattan.

His phone pinged, reminding him of an upcoming appointment. Once more he sat down, then picked up his favorite pen and rolled the heavy gold cylinder between his fingers. He had inked his first real estate deal with this pen. Beyond the leather blotter, the wedding invitation lay innocently. He read it a second time, finding its elegant cursive font no less stomach tightening than he had before.

December 20th. That meant Aidan would need to be in Silver Glen no later than the weekend before. Knowing his mother, she would undoubtedly have planned a series of social events to fill the days leading up to the wedding. And then he would be expected to hang around until the family celebrated Christmas together on the 25th. Almost two weeks. Might as well be a lifetime.

He glanced at the paper calendar his assistant kept updated on the corner of his desk. She was as tech savvy as the next person, but she had discovered that Aidan liked to keep tabs on his schedule in more than one medium. The month of December was notably blank.

No one, with very few exceptions, shopped for high-dollar real estate during December. His clients were too busy hosting parties, overspending on their spoiled children and taking trips to exotic locations. Which meant, unfortunately, that Aidan was free to do as he pleased.

Or in this instance as he did *not* please.

For a moment, he flashed back, his vision blinded to the present but very aware of the past. Two young women. Both beautiful. Both charming. Both full of life and fun. And he had lost each of them.

The familiar burning sensation in his gut was more than a mix of guilt and regret. It was a longing for what he would never have. Absolution. A woman and a family to call his own.

Spending Christmas at Silver Glen would undoubtedly resurrect a host of old memories that he'd rather not face. But if he were honest, the memories lived with him everywhere. The painful part of going home was having other people *share* the memories. The empathy and concern on the faces of his siblings and his mother would be his downfall.

He didn't want their love to heal him. He didn't deserve that. And he didn't want to *feel* anything. Family knew his weak spots. Family refused to let him cling to the cloak of indifference that made it possible to live from day to day.

Aidan Kavanagh was a charming shell of a man, interested only in closing a deal or cashing a check. Ask anyone. The persona was one he had crafted carefully to keep people away. After loving and losing three times in his life, he was through with emotion…with caring.

In Silver Glen, especially at the holidays, he would have to be himself—the young man who had enjoyed life and reached for happiness with the careless naïveté of the innocent. He would be forced to open himself up to the warmth of family celebrations that would make him terribly vulnerable.

Could he do that and still survive?

Doggedly, he reached for the peace he had created here in the city. Emotional anonymity. A pleasant shield that kept other people from inflicting hurt.

He didn't hurt. He *wouldn't* hurt. Loving his family was a given. But beyond that, he had nothing to offer. Loving and losing meant vicious, unrelenting pain. Only a fool would walk that path again.

Emma Braithwaite leaned into the bay window, perched precariously on a stepladder that had seen better days. Creating the shop's storefront display was usually the highlight of her workweek. Today's theme, not exactly original, was teapots. Twitching the edge of a lace drape into place, she tried to visualize what her handiwork looked like from the street.

On the other side of the glass, a woman stopped and waved madly. Emma smiled. Even through the reverse gold lettering that spelled out Silver Memories, she recognized her visitor. Maeve Kavanagh, matriarch of the Kavanagh family—mother to seven sexy, über-masculine, wildly attractive grown men, and heir to the Kavanagh fortune.

Maeve's husband's ancestors had literally created the town after discovering a rich vein of silver deep in the mountain. The family story took a tragic turn when Maeve's feckless husband, Reggie, became obsessed with finding the remnants of the mine. One day he climbed into the hills and never returned.

But that bit of local color was from long ago. Maeve was now a vibrant woman in her early sixties who managed to keep tabs on her brood and run a thriving business up at the Silver Beeches Lodge. A little bell tinkled over the door as Maeve entered. Her dark auburn hair—with only slight traces of silver—was done up in a stylish bun.

Emma climbed down from the ladder and straightened her skirt.

Maeve waved an envelope at her. "I know etiquette dictates I mail this to you, but I couldn't wait. Here. Take it."

Emma accepted the cream-colored envelope with a grin. The missive was thick, the paper expensive. When she opened it and examined the contents, she understood the older woman's enthusiasm. "Another wedding?"

Maeve's smug smile said everything. "Indeed. And this time right here in Silver Glen. I know it seems hurried, but Dylan's adoption of Cora will be final on the day after Christmas. He and Mia want to be married and have their family complete."

Emma tucked everything back in the envelope. "I'm honored to be invited."

Emma and Mia had met several months ago at a coffee shop around the corner from Silver Memories. Since then they had become friends. Emma knew Maeve had been extremely kind in including Mia's parents as hosts for the wedding. The Larins had given birth to Mia late in life and now lived in Florida on a fixed income.

Maeve waved a hand. "Don't be silly. You're practically part of my family now. Mia raves about you, and I've enjoyed getting to know you these last few months."

Not long after Emma opened her store, Maeve had dropped by to shop for a set of occasional tables to use in a lounge at the Silver Beeches. It was thanks to Maeve that word had spread and the small shop had become a success so quickly.

"May I ask you something personal, Maeve?"

"Of course."

"Is the baby's father in the picture? Mia never speaks of him, and I didn't want to upset her by asking."

Maeve shook her head. "Dear Mia chose to have a baby via a sperm donor. When she and Dylan got together, he fell in love with little Cora. They make a beautiful family, don't you think?"

Emma smiled wistfully. "They certainly do." She had often seen Dylan and Mia and the baby out walking on afternoons when the weather was still warm.

Silver Glen was a small, cozy town, even though it boasted a strong tourist economy. Movie stars shooting on location often took up residence, as well as wealthy travelers who loved the peace of the mountains. The town's alpine flavor reminded Emma of a Swiss village.

"There's one more thing," Maeve said, her expression cajoling. "Mia told me you're not going home to England for Christmas, is that right?"

"Yes. I spent two weeks in September with my mother for her birthday. She's handling the loss of my father better than I expected. And she has plans to tour the Greek Isles during the latter part of December with a group of her friends."

"Then I want you to spend the holidays with us. Mia's parents are coming only for the wedding itself. So I know Mia would enjoy having you around. We're gathering for several occasions at Dylan and Mia's home. My older son and his wife are still building their new house. And of course, we'll have some special events up at the lodge, too. What do you think?"

Emma didn't know what to say. She wasn't afraid to be alone. In fact, her childhood had been solitary more times than not. She enjoyed the peace and tranquility of her own thoughts. And she was not a Kavanagh. Surely her presence would be awkward.

Maeve spotted a silver rattle and a matching small cup from the 1950s. "I knew I remembered seeing these," she said triumphantly. "One of my college sorority sisters just became a grandma for the first time. This will be the perfect gift."

As Emma rang up the purchase and took Maeve's credit card, she wondered how large a wedding the Kavanaghs were planning. And then another thought struck. One that made her heart race.

"Will all of your family be able to attend on such short notice?" Emma had never actually confessed to Maeve that she knew one of her sons very well.

For the first time, Maeve lost a bit of her excitement. "I hope so. My third son, Aidan, lives in New York. We don't see him all that often. And besides..."

She trailed off, her expression indicating that she had traveled somewhere unpleasant in her mind.

Emma wanted to know badly. "Besides what?"

Maeve's lips twisted, her eyes shadowed. "Aidan had a very bad experience some years ago. It happened at Christmas. He comes home to visit, but not at the holidays."

"And this wedding?"

"We hope he'll make the effort, but who knows..."

What would Aidan think if he saw Emma ensconced in the bosom of his family? She hadn't set eyes on him in a decade. Her original intent in coming to Silver Glen during the late summer had been to speak with him and bring some closure to what had been a painful time in their lives. She had hurt him badly, and she wanted to explain and make amends. But she discovered he no longer lived in the town of his birth.

Her recent birthday had brought home the fact that life passed quickly. Regret was an emotion fraught with negativity. After healing a decade-long rift with her father back in the spring, she had realized she wanted to move forward and to make better decisions than she had in her early twenties.

It was entirely possible that Aidan had not clung to the memories the way Emma had. She might be nothing more than a footnote in his past life. According to Maeve, he sounded like an entirely different person than the boy Emma had known.

The fact that Emma had chosen to settle in Silver Glen permanently had more to do with the town's charm than it did with Aidan. But her initial motive remained. Even if her apology meant nothing to him, it would clear her own soul of lingering regret.

She couldn't control his response. In fact, he might not even show up. But if he did, she was determined to do the mature, responsible thing and own up to her mistakes.

Emma wanted to grill her visitor, but she had already overstepped the bounds of polite curiosity. "I'm sure he realizes how important it is."

Maeve gathered herself visibly. "You haven't given me an answer. And I warn you in advance that I'll only accept a yes."

"Then I will say yes with pleasure." And a healthy dose of trepidation.

"That's wonderful, Emma dear. My invitation is selfish actually. Everything you say in that delightful British accent makes me want to listen to you for hours, but I have to fly."

"I'd say *you're* the one who has the accent," Emma teased. "You, and the rest of Silver Glen. I've practiced my drawl, but it never seems to come out right."

Heading out the door, Maeve shook her head, laughing. "Let's face it, Emma. You're the quintessential blue-blooded Englishwoman. Fit to marry a prince if Kate hadn't snatched him up first. If you had a slow-as-molasses speech pattern, no one would ever believe you were an aristocrat."

In the sudden silence created by the departure of her vivacious guest, Emma felt her stomach curl. She had known this day would come eventually. It was a major reason she had chosen to roost in Silver Glen. That, and the fact that the town reminded her of the cheery Cotswolds village where she had grown up.

Sooner or later, Aidan would appear. If not at Christmas, then in the spring. The thought of seeing him face-to-face both elated and terrified her. She knew they were far beyond second chances. Too much time had passed. His life experiences had no doubt changed him, especially the tragedy to which Maeve alluded. Too many turns in the road. But Emma wanted to speak her piece. And she would make him listen.

He deserved to know that she had loved him beyond reason and sanity. That his leaving had nearly destroyed her.

Perhaps she was kidding herself. Aidan might not even remember her. Maybe she had magnified the importance of their university romance. Aidan had come to Oxford the fall semester of his senior year for a term-abroad experience. He had literally bumped into Emma on the street in front of a pub frequented by students.

They had both laughed and picked up their books and papers. Aidan offered to buy her dinner, and that was that.

Her heart actually clenched in her chest, the pain of

the memories still fresh after all this time. Would he look the same? Would he think she had changed?

And what was she going to say to Aidan Kavanagh when she saw him again?

Two

Aidan braked carefully and rolled to a stop in front of the courthouse that reigned over the town square. Darkness had fallen swiftly, proof that they were nearing the shortest day of the year. All around him, buildings were decorated in lights…some twinkling white, some a rainbow of colors.

New York City loved to deck itself out for Christmas. But nothing about Christmas in the city was as disturbing as this. As if it were yesterday, he remembered Danielle's delight when he first brought her home to spend the holidays with his family. She had loved the decorations, the town itself and the fresh snow that had fallen.

At least this year the roads were dry. Even so, the image of a long-ago snowball fight brought a small smile to his lips. Danielle had approached everything about her life with the enthusiasm of a puppy.

He was surprised and grateful to find that at least a few memories of their last days together were good ones.

Glancing at his watch, he knew he had lingered long enough. Though Dylan and Mia had invited him to stay with them, Aidan preferred the privacy of a hotel room up at the lodge. Then, it was nobody's business if he couldn't sleep.

His mother had a nice condo in town, though his oldest sibling, Liam, still had a suite with his wife, Zoe, at the Silver Beeches Lodge. They were in the process of designing and building their dream home, but it wouldn't be finished until the following summer.

Liam would be sleeping with one eye open, waiting to make sure that Aidan showed up safely, even if it *was* almost 3:00 a.m. *Why can't you fly down here like a normal person?* he had complained.

Aidan wondered that himself. The grueling hours on the road were supposed to have prepared him for his upcoming ordeal. Well, hell, that was a little too melodramatic. It wasn't as if he hadn't been back to Silver Glen time and again after Danielle was gone. But only once at Christmas. And then only to see his brother in the hospital and make sure he was okay. A little fruitcake, a few packages and as quickly as he could manage, he had returned to his home in New York.

This trip, however, there would be no reprieve. Maeve had already warned him that she expected his presence at an assortment of events and activities. Her third son had strayed beyond her reach, and since she had wrangled his presence via the unexpected wedding invitation, she planned to make the most of it.

Aidan put the car in gear again and cruised around town slowly, expecting at any moment for a cop to pull him over and demand an explanation for his nocturnal prowl. Things looked much the same as they had during his last visit. Except that his brother Dylan's pride and joy, the Silver Dollar Saloon, was once again open for business.

When Aidan had come home for the long 4th of July weekend, the Silver Dollar was still being repaired and renovated after a fire in June. Fortunately, no one had been injured, but he'd heard more than one person bemoaning the fact that the town's most popular watering hole was closed indefinitely.

He looped back toward the square, passing Silver Screen, the community's one and only movie theater. Way back in the forties and fifties, someone had decided all the stores in Silver Glen should be named with the theme of silver. As a marketing ploy, it was brilliant.

The town had grown and prospered, drawing visitors and business from all over the country. Despite his unease, Aidan found himself feeling distinctly nostalgic for this charming valley that had been his home for twenty-plus years.

As he turned the car one last time and headed for the narrow road that would take him up the mountain to the lodge, his headlights flashed across a darkened storefront that didn't look familiar. Silver Memories. From what he could see of the window display, the merchandise appeared to be antiques.

He frowned, almost positive that the last time he'd visited, this particular spot had been a leather shop. Operated by an ornery old guy who made saddles and guitar straps to order.

Odd. But then again, at Thanksgiving, he'd been in town barely twenty-four hours.

When he made it up the mountain, he pulled onto the flagstone apron in front of the Silver Beeches Lodge. After grabbing his bag and handing off his keys to a sleepy parking attendant, he sent a text to his brother. *I'm here. Go to bed, old man. See you tomorrow.*

A neatly uniformed employee checked him in. After that, it was a matter of minutes to make it onto the elevator, up to the top floor, down the hall and into his quiet, dark, pleasantly scented room.

He kicked off his shoes, plugged in his phone and

fell facedown across the bed, prepared to sleep until someone forced him to get up.

Emma kept one eye on her customer and the other on her laptop. The elderly woman came in a couple of times a month, mostly to window-shop. She actually sold Emma a few items from time to time, clearly in need of cash to supplement her social security check.

Since the white-haired lady seemed content to browse, Emma refocused her attention on the website she'd been perusing. Catriona's Closet was a designer boutique in London that had been Emma's go-to spot for special occasion clothes when she still lived in England. Fortunately for Emma, the shop now boasted a strong online retail presence.

Trying to decide between a cream lace duster over a burgundy long-sleeved jersey dress, or a more traditional green velvet cocktail number with a low, scooped neck, was impossible. With a few quick clicks, she bought them both, with express shipping. If she were going to see Aidan face-to-face, she needed armor. Lots of it. From the cradle, she had been taught the finer points of social etiquette. Mingling socially with the well-regarded and diverse Kavanagh family would pose no threat to her confidence.

But seeing Aidan again? That was another matter.

Finally, the customer left without buying so much as an embroidered hankie. Emma sighed. Her father, if he had lived, would have been horrified at his only daughter stooping to something as bourgeois as *trade*.

The Braithwaites were solicitors and clergymen and physicians, at least the menfolk. The females generally presided over tea, rode to hounds and threw dinner parties, leaving their offspring to be raised by nannies.

Emma had been eight years old before she understood that her dear Baba was not a member of the family.

Shaking off the bittersweet memories, she prepared to close the shop. This time of year, business fell off in the afternoons despite the holidays, so she rarely stayed open past four o'clock.

Outside, people hurried about their errands, braced against the stiff wind and the swirling flurries of snow. Emma would have much preferred to go upstairs to her cozy apartment and snuggle under an afghan, but she was completely out of milk, and she couldn't abide her tea without it.

Bundling into her heavy, raspberry-pink wool coat, she wrapped a black-and-pink scarf around her head, tucked her billfold and keys into her pocket and walked quickly down the street.

At the next block she shivered, impatient for the light to turn green so she could cross the street. So intent was she on making it to the other side that she didn't notice the silver Accord running the light until it was too late.

Her heart beat sluggishly, everything easing into slow motion as she hopped back. But not before the reckless driver clipped her hip, sending her tumbling airborne for several long seconds and then crashing into unforgiving pavement.

Though she was aware of people crowding around her, she lost herself somewhere internally as she catalogued all the places that hurt madly. Teeth chattering, she forced herself to sit up. Nothing appeared to be broken. A man crouched beside her, his scent a mix of warm male, cold air and an oddly familiar cologne.

"Don't move," he said, his honey-toned voice sharp with command.

She was glad to accept his support behind her shoulders. The world swam dizzily. Vaguely, she heard the wail of sirens.

Shortly after that, brisk strangers loaded her onto a gurney and lifted her into an ambulance. Though she protested as much as she was able, no one seemed prepared to listen to her. Her scarf had slid halfway over one eye. She was fairly certain her leg was bleeding.

The EMTs wasted no time. The vehicle moved swiftly, cutting in and out of traffic. Closing her eyes, Emma winced as a pothole caused fresh discomfort. Fortunately, the hospital was not far away. Before she knew it, she had been whisked inside and tucked into an emergency room cubicle. The dizziness was getting worse. She had enough presence of mind remaining to wonder if she was in any kind of serious danger.

A nurse came in to get vitals. Suddenly, the same deep voice with the bark of command sounded nearby. "How is she?"

"She's conscious. We'll have to get her up to X ray."

"I'm fine," Emma stated, her determination diluted somewhat by the high, wavering condition of her voice.

The nurse left. Though Emma's eyes were closed, she sensed the man standing nearby. His presence had a narcotic effect. She felt safe…as if he were keeping an eye on things.

"Don't go to sleep," he snapped. "Let's get this damned scarf out of your face."

She felt him untie it and draw it free. And then he cursed. "What the hell? Emma?"

She struggled up on one elbow and stared at her white knight. Instantly, shock flooded her already compromised nervous system. *Oh, God.* "Aidan. I didn't realize it was you. Thanks for helping me. I'm sure everything is okay.

You can leave now." The words tripped over each other as her limbs began to shake.

He'd gone white, his eyes wide with what appeared to be a combination of disbelief and horror. "What are you doing here?"

A smile was beyond her. Tears threatened to fall, but she blinked them back. This was not how she'd imagined seeing him again. Not like this. Not without warning. She swallowed hard. "I live here," she whispered.

"The hell you say. Is this some kind of a joke?"

The outrage in his voice and on his face might have been tinged with a hint of panic.

His fury was one blow too many. With a whimper of surrender, she fell back onto the exam table as the world went black…

Aidan strode out of the hospital at a pace little less than full-blown retreat. His heart slugged in his chest and his hands were ice-cold. Of course, that might have been the weather. He'd left his gloves in the car.

Emma was here. And Danielle was not. *Emma.* He repeated her name in his head, still seeing the look of dazed comprehension that filled her wide-set gentian-blue eyes. He was very familiar with those beautiful eyes. Not to mention the porcelain skin, the perfectly curved pink lips, the patrician features, and the silky, fine blond hair that fell past her shoulders. Emma…Good Lord.

The buzzing in his ears was probably a factor of the wind. But then again, his blood pressure might be in the danger zone. His emotions were all over the map. And how ironic was that? He'd made a science of becoming the superficial guy with *no* real emotions.

The lie had been practiced so deeply and so well, he'd begun to believe it himself. But a chance encounter on the street had cut to the heart of his charade. He was injured, bleeding deep in his gut, raw with pain.

Yet Emma was the one in the hospital.

He had no obligation to go back inside. He'd done his part. She was in the hands of professionals.

Standing beside his car, he slammed a fist on the hood…hard enough to bruise his fingers. He'd known that coming home at Christmas would be a test of how well he had healed from the past. But never in a million years had he imagined a confrontation with Emma Braithwaite. She was supposed to be in England, happily married to Viscount Supercilious. Raising upper-crust rug rats with Harry Potter accents and carelessly chic clothes.

Damn, damn, damn…

What would happen if he merely walked away? If he didn't ask for explanations? Could he pretend that the last two hours were a dream? Or a nightmare?

Another ambulance zipped into the admitting area. The flashing lights and ear-piercing siren shocked him back to sanity. He'd left Emma passed out on the exam table. True, he'd notified a nurse immediately, but after that he had fled. What would his brothers think if they could see him now?

They already teased him about his city polish and his propensity for take-out every night of the week. Even Liam, who dressed as befitted his position as co-owner of the prestigious Silver Beeches Lodge, was most at home clambering about in the mountains. He'd already taken Zoe camping and made a new convert.

The Kavanagh brothers, out of necessity, were physically and mentally tough. You didn't grow up with six same-sex siblings and not learn how to handle yourself in a fight. But as much as Aidan loved his brothers, he had always felt a bit out of step with them. He'd wanted to travel the world. He'd been strangled by the small-town lifestyle.

Regardless of the differences in personality and temperament, though, Maeve Kavanagh had taught her sons about responsibility and honor. Perhaps because their father had been lacking in that area, the lessons had stuck. Only the worst kind of cad would leave a woman alone in a hospital with no one to look after her.

Cursing beneath his breath, Aidan gulped in a lungful of icy air. This couldn't be happening. What terrible sins had he committed in the past that karma was so very ready now to kick his ass?

Minutes passed. All around him, people came and went. Hospital staff heading home for the night. Visitors walking toward the doors with worried faces. Aidan barely noted their presence.

Though it shamed him to admit it, he was actually terrified to go back inside. What if Emma were badly hurt? What if even now she was slipping into a coma?

As if it were yesterday he remembered pacing the halls of this very same hospital while Danielle struggled to live. It was a lifetime ago, but the agony was fresh and real. As if it were happening all over again.

He wouldn't allow that. Not on his watch. He had no clue why Emma was in Silver Glen. It didn't matter. He would make sure she was okay, and then he would walk away.

Just like he'd been forced to do ten years ago…

Three

Emma moved her shoulders and moaned. “My head hurts,” she whispered. When she tried to focus her eyes, rectangular ceiling tiles above her bed marched from one side of the room to the other. For some reason, that drunken motion made her think of the intricately plastered frieze in her childhood bedroom. She remembered trying to count the individual roses on days when she was ill in bed and stuck at home.

Sadly, this generic space was not nearly as beautiful.

At some point, an unknown set of hands had replaced her clothing with a standard issue hospital gown. The warm blanket tucked up around her shoulders should have felt comforting, but instead, she found it claustrophobic.

Despite her discomfort, she shifted until both arms were free.

An older nurse with kind eyes patted her hand. “You have a concussion. Try not to upset yourself. The pain meds will be kicking in any moment now.”

“How long was I out?” She could swear she had only closed her eyes for a moment.

“Not terribly long. But enough for us to get a couple of X rays. They were concerned about your leg, but nothing is broken. You’ll have to have a few stitches on your cheek and shin, but that's not too bad considering what might have happened."

"Oh...good..." Someone must have pumped wonderful drugs into her IV, because even with the pain, she was floating on a cloud of worry-free lassitude. Something important nagged at the corners of her mind, but she didn't have the clarity to summon it.

Time passed. Perhaps minutes or hours. She had no clue. She was aware of drifting in and out. Surely it must be dinnertime by now, but she had no appetite.

At one point she was startled by a loud crash in the hallway. Turning her head toward the window, she noted that it was dark. How odd. She remembered heading toward the supermarket for milk. And though the details were fuzzy, she recalled the accident.

But after that things blurred.

When she awoke the next time, her body rebelled. Turning her head, she gagged and reached for the button to summon help. The woman came instantly, offered a basin and spoke soothingly as Emma emptied the contents of her stomach.

The nurse's scrubs were covered in Christmas trees and snowmen. "It's normal, I'm afraid," she said. "The medicine helps the pain, but some people don't tolerate it very well. Try to sleep."

She lowered the lights again and the door swished shut. Feeling dreadfully alone and miserable, Emma was no longer able to stem the flow of tears. She sobbed quietly.

A warm hand stroked her hair. "Hush, Emma. Don't cry. Go back to sleep."

Her eyelids felt weighted down. But she forced them open for long enough to make out the shape of a man seated in a chair beside her bed. “Aidan? I thought I dreamed you.”

His laugh sounded rusty, as if he hadn’t used it in a while. “I’m afraid not.”

“Why are you here?” The syllables slurred together. She was so very tired.

Still he stroked her hair. “It doesn’t matter. You’re going to be okay. Go to sleep.”

When she awoke toward morning, her brain was clearer, but her body felt as if she had gone three rounds with a professional boxer. Maybe the medicine was worth it after all.

In one surreptitious glance, she ascertained that the room was empty. The taste of disappointment filled her mouth. Perhaps Aidan had been a dream after all.

An aide came in with breakfast. Emma’s stomach flopped sickeningly at the scent of scrambled eggs, but the tea bag on the tray caught her attention. When the woman arranged the rolling table across Emma’s lap and raised the head of the bed, Emma thought she might be sick again.

Breathing deeply, she closed her eyes and remained perfectly still until the feeling passed. At last, she summoned the energy to brew a life-saving cup of Earl Grey. With a dash of sugar, a squirt of lemon and a dollop of artificial creamer, the result was not entirely acceptable, but it was better than nothing.

She was poking at a lumpy biscuit when a female physician entered the room. “Ms. Braithwaite. How are you feeling?”

Emma shrugged. “Like I was hit by something big and hard?”

The doctor grinned. “Aptly put. We’ve patched you up,

and all your stats are good. Don't get me wrong. You're going to be in bad shape for a few days. But you were very lucky. It could have been a lot worse. I'm thinking of releasing you later today once I see how you do with your meals. Is there anyone at home who can look after you? So you don't have to be on your feet too much?"

Emma opened her mouth to speak, but before she could answer, a man stepped from the hallway into the room. "I'll get her settled and make sure she has help."

Aidan. She couldn't have been any more surprised if the Loch Ness Monster had paraded down the hall. Apparently the sexy phantom in her dreams was entirely real.

"That won't be necessary," she said firmly. Even as she spoke, she scrambled mentally for other alternatives.

Mia would be willing to lend a hand, but she had a baby to care for and a wedding to plan. And Emma definitely was not going to ask Aidan's mother for help. Which left Mrs. Correll, the retired lady who worked part-time at the antique store. But the older woman battled arthritis and couldn't climb stairs.

Emma hadn't lived in Silver Glen all that long. Certainly not long enough to have an extensive list of friends on hand to provide casseroles and sympathy soup.

Aidan ignored Emma's protest. He gave the white-coated physician a high-wattage smile that made her blink twice. "I'll make sure she follows your orders exactly, Doctor. You can count on me."

The doctor departed. Emma stared at the man who once upon a time had been her knight in shining armor. "I can explain," she said, eager to clear the air.

Aidan held up a hand, his gaze wintry. "I don't want to hear anything about the past or why you're here. I'm not interested, Emma. I'm going to take you home and sleep on your couch overnight. But that's it. I have no desire to hear anything you have to say. Are we clear?"

Her heart sank. She had hoped his animosity might have dwindled after all this time. But, no. She was an unwelcome obligation to him. Nothing more. Not even worth the effort of polite conversation.

Her throat tight, she nodded. Though it pained her to admit it, she didn't have the luxury of arguing with him. If Aidan's assurances of aid were enough to get her dismissed from the hospital, then she would swallow the words that wanted to tumble forth in a plea for understanding.

She watched him focus his gaze on the muted television as he feigned great interest in an infomercial for egg separators. His profile was dear and familiar, but the boy she had once known was gone, replaced by a man with even broader shoulders and a physique that was honed and strong.

His dark brown hair with a hint of red was expertly cut, his clothing masculine and expensive. The young university student she remembered had flaunted shaggy locks and a succession of rock-and-roll T-shirts that showcased his flat abdomen. Close-fitting denims had outlined long legs and a tight butt. His grin and American accent won over every girl in a ten-mile radius. But at the end of the day, he went home to Emma's off-campus apartment.

Shaking off the poignant memories, she stared at him. He'd said *no explanations*, so what else was there to talk about?

Abruptly, he turned to face her. "I'll ask the nurses' station to call me when they're ready to dismiss you. In the meantime, I have errands to run."

And with that, he was gone.

* * *

Emma ate and drank and did everything that was asked of her. For one panicked hour she contemplated faking a relapse to avoid being alone with the painfully distant man who looked so much like the Aidan Kavanagh she had once known. But as much as she dreaded being beholden to the glacial-eyed Aidan, she also wanted to get out of this noisy hospital and back into her own bed.

After a long afternoon of additional tests and X rays and blood work, a physician's assistant showed up and announced that Emma was free to go. Aidan appeared just as she tried standing beside the bed to dress in her sadly damaged street clothes.

He cursed quietly. "For God's sake. You're going to fall over." Her tights were badly torn. Aidan took one look at them and tossed them in the trash. "You'll have to go bare-legged on the way home," he said, "but I assume you live close?"

She nodded, humiliated by the way he tucked and pulled and fastened her bits and pieces as if she were a helpless child. Tension radiated from his large frame. Her head pounded, but she was damned if she would show weakness in front of this brusque stranger.

When her few belongings were gathered and in her lap, an orderly eased her into a wheelchair and gave Aidan a nod. "If you'll bring your car around to the front entrance, sir, I'll meet you there with Ms. Braithwaite."

Aidan nodded and vanished.

Emma wouldn't have minded a tour of the hospital, or a quick peek at the maternity ward with all the brand-new babies. Anything to postpone the moment of truth.

If she hadn't been in so much pain, physical and mental, the pun might have made her smile. Aidan didn't *want* to hear the truth. He'd already judged her and found her guilty. He believed that she had betrayed his trust. In his defense, the evidence had been pretty damning.

Outside, the wind was no less biting than it had been the day before. Only now it was dark as well. By the time she sank into the passenger seat of Aidan's fancy sports car with the heated leather seats, she was shivering. He grabbed a jacket from the backseat and handed it to her.

"Wrap that around your legs." He paused, staring out the windshield. His granite jaw flexed. "I need your address."

She sensed that having to ask for that one small piece of information pissed him off. Muttering the street and number, she leaned back and closed her eyes. The car smelled like him. Maybe he would let her sleep here. The prospect of making it all the way to her bed was daunting to say the least.

He parked at the curb in front of her business, his hands clenched on the wheel. "Here?" he asked, incredulity in his voice.

"I have an apartment upstairs. You don't need to stay. Really."

Ignoring her statement completely, he half turned in his seat and fixed her with a steady gaze that left her feeling naked…and not in a good way. The hazel eyes that had once twinkled with good humor were flat. It was difficult to believe that *anything* about this older, tougher Aidan twinkled.

His jaw worked. "Correct me if I'm wrong, but I was under the impression that Lady Emma Braithwaite was an heiress. To the tune of several million pounds. I can't fathom why she would be here in the mountains of North Carolina running an antiques shop when she grew up in a damned castle." He was practically shouting at the end.

"It wasn't a castle." His sarcasm cut deep, but it also made her angry. "You said you didn't want any explanations," she reminded him. "If you don't mind, I'm very tired and I need to take some medicine. If you'll help me up the stairs, you can go." She managed an even-toned, reasonable response until her voice broke on the last word. Biting down hard on her bottom lip, she swallowed and inhaled the moment of weakness.

After several long, pregnant seconds, Aidan muttered something inaudible and got out, slamming his door hard enough to rattle the window beside her. Before she could brace herself for what came next, he opened her side of the car and leaned in to scoop her into his arms.

She shrank back instinctively, unwilling to get any closer. He stumbled when her quick movement threw him off balance. "Put your arm around my neck, Emma. Before I drop you." Irritation accented every syllable.

"Are you always so grumpy?" she asked. If anyone had cause to be out of sorts, it was she.

He locked the car with the key fob and settled her more firmly into his embrace. "Don't push it."

To the left of her storefront, a single narrow door gave entrance to a steep flight of steps. The building dated back to the early days of Silver Glen. When Aidan took the key from her and let himself in, she wondered if his big frame would make it up the stairwell, especially carrying her.

But he was a natural athlete. She never even felt a jostle or a bump as he ascended to the second floor and her quaint apartment. His chest and his arms were hard, though he carried her carefully. If it were possible, she thought she might get drunk on the scent of his skin and the faint starchy smell of his crisp cotton shirt.

A second door at the top required a key as well. By

now, Aidan should have been breathing heavily. Emma was five-eight and not a slip of a woman. But he managed the final hurdle and kicked open the door, reaching with one hand to turn on the light.

She knew the exact moment he spotted her sofa. The red, velvet-covered Victorian settee was designed more for looks than for comfort. It was definitely not meant for sleeping. Fortunately, she owned a more traditional chair and ottoman that were tucked up close to her gas-log fireplace. If Aidan were determined to spend the night, he would be under no illusions as to his accommodations.

The apartment was fairly warm. When she'd left the day before, she had only been nipping out to grab the milk, intending to return in little more than a half hour. That was a blessing. If the rooms had been ice-cold as thcy somctimcs wcre, her misery would have been complete.

He set her on her feet in the bedroom, not even glancing at her large brass bed with its intensely feminine white lace sheets and comforter. "Can you get ready for the night on your own?" His hands remained on her shoulders, though it was clear he was lending physical support, nothing more.

"Of course." Her right leg felt as if someone had delved into it with an ax, and her head was a heartbeat away from a painful explosion, but she'd die before she would admit it. She had been brought up not to make a fuss. Her father hadn't liked female *histrionics*, as he called them.

Aidan stared down at her. For the first time, she saw something in his eyes that told her the past might be gone, but it was not forgotten. For the space of one brief, heart-stopping breath, she was sure she witnessed tenderness. But it vanished in an instant...perhaps never there to begin with. He unbuttoned her bedraggled coat and eased it from her shoulders.

"Where are your pajamas?" he asked.

She wrapped her arms around her waist. "I'll get them. Go fix yourself a cup of coffee."

One eyebrow lifted. "You have coffee?"

In England, she had done her best to wean him from the uncivilized beverage. "For guests," she said stiffly.

He nodded once and walked away. Sinking down onto the bed, she told herself she could manage to wash up and change clothes. It was a matter of pride and self-preservation. Having Aidan help was unthinkable. She was far too aware of him as it was. His physical presence dwarfed her cozy apartment.

In the bathroom she dared to glance in the mirror and groaned. Why had no one seen fit to give her a hairbrush? Moving as carefully as an old lady, she removed her rumpled and stained blouse and skirt and stripped off her undies and bra. Bruises already marked her skin in a dozen places. She had been given strict instructions not to get her stitches wet, so a shower was out. With a soft washcloth and a bar of her favorite lavender soap, she managed a quick cleanup.

When she was done, she realized that she had forgotten to get a nightgown from the bureau. Wrapping a towel around herself sarong-style, she opened the bathroom door and walked into the bedroom.

As she did so, she caught Aidan leaning down to put a cup of steaming hot tea on her bedside table.

Four

Aidan froze. If Emma's eyes grew any bigger, they would eclipse her face. Though it hurt to look at her, he forced himself to meet her gaze with dispassion. "Drink your tea while it's hot," he said. "I'll see what I can whip up for our dinner."

In her tiny kitchen, he put his hands on the table, palms flat, and bowed his head. So many feelings, so many memories…

Emma laughed up at him, her skin dappled by shadows from the willow tree that served as shelter for their impromptu picnic. "Why the serious look?" she asked.

She lay on her back, arms outstretched above her head, eyes ripe with happiness. They had borrowed an old quilt from her neighbor. The faded colors only made her more beautiful in comparison.

"I have to go home soon," he said, unable to comprehend the upcoming rift. "What will I do without you?" He sat upright, his back propped against the tree trunk, trying not to think about how much he wanted to make love to her at this moment. But the perfectly manicured English park was filled with adults and children eager to enjoy the warmth of a late fall afternoon.

Emma linked her fingers with his, pulling his hand to her lips. "Don't spoil it," she whispered, for a moment seeming as desperately dejected as he was. But immediately, her optimism returned, even if manufactured. "Remember—you'll graduate in the spring, and then we'll have all sorts of choices."

There was no acceptable choice if it didn't include her. He managed a grimace that was supposed to placate her. But from the expression on her face, he knew she saw through him. She had since the first day they met.

He lay down at her side, not caring if anyone raised an eyebrow. Propped on an elbow, he brushed the back of his hand down her cheek. "I can't leave you, Emma. I can't..."

But in the end, he had...

Inhaling sharply, he slammed the door on recollections that served no purpose. That day was so far in the past, it might as well be written up in the history books. Perhaps in a chapter labeled "youthful indiscretions."

Turning his attention to practical matters, he examined the contents of Emma's fridge. The woman lived on yogurt and granola and fancy cheese. His stomach rumbled in protest. But he'd have to make do with a gourmet grilled cheese sandwich.

He found a skillet and spooned a dollop of butter into it, listening to the sizzle as he strained to hear movement in Emma's room. Even now, the image of her half-naked body remained imprinted on his brain. All that creamy English skin. Long legs. Hair the color of spring sunshine.

He dropped a chunk of cheese on the burner and had to fish it out before he set off the smoke alarm. His final efforts were not visually pleasing, but the sandwiches would keep them both from starving.

Leaving his meal in the kitchen, he took Emma's plate to her door and knocked quietly. She would be dressed by now, but he didn't want any additional surprises. He knocked a second time and then opened the door a crack. "Emma?"

The lights were on, but Emma was in bed, fast asleep. Curled on her side, she slept like a child with a hand under her cheek. A neat row of stitches near her ear reminded him anew of how close she had come to disaster.

He glanced at his watch. He hated to wake her, but if she awoke later in pain, it would be worse. He put the plate on the dresser and crouched beside the bed. The instinct to touch her was one he had to ignore.

"Emma," he said quietly, not wanting to startle her.

She moved restlessly but didn't open her eyes.

"Emma."

This time her eyelids fluttered. A small smile curved her lips before she realized where she was and with whom. Immediately, a mask slipped over her features. "Aidan. I told you to go. I'll sleep 'til morning."

Fishing the bottle of pills out of his pocket, he shook a couple of tablets into his palm. "The doctor gave you enough pain meds to last until we can get your prescription filled tomorrow. You're an hour past due, so you'd better take them. And at least eat a few bites of food."

She took his offering with visible reluctance and washed it down with two sips of tea. When he brought the grilled cheese, she stared at it. "You cooked for me?"

He felt his face redden. His lack of expertise in the kitchen was well documented. "It's a sandwich," he said gruffly. "Don't get too excited. I'll be back in a minute with a glass of milk. That might help you sleep."

When he returned, she had managed to finish half of the meal. He held out the tumbler of milk and waited until she drained most of it. Already, the simple exertion of eating had taxed her strength. She was as pale as her bedding, and he saw her hands shake before she tucked them beneath the sheets and settled back into her original position.

"Do you want the lights off?" he asked.

"I suppose. Please leave, Aidan."

He flipped off all except the bathroom light. Leaving that door cracked an inch or so, he took one last look at the patient. "Go to sleep. Everything will be better in the morning."

The chair and ottoman were more comfortable than they appeared. With the gas logs flickering and a couple of woolen throws in lieu of blankets, he managed to fall asleep. His dreams were a mishmash of good and bad, past and present.

Somewhere in the middle of the night a crash jerked him out of his restless slumber. Leaping to his feet, he headed for Emma's room, almost sure the noise had emanated from that direction.

He found her in the bathroom surrounded by the broken remains of a small water glass she kept on the counter. "Don't move," he barked. Her feet were bare. Scooping her up, he avoided the worst of the mess and carried her back to bed. "Why didn't you call me?" he grumbled.

"I didn't need a witness for *that*," she snapped. Even drugged and injured, she had spunk.

Smothering a smile he knew she wouldn't appreciate, he tucked her in and straightened the covers. It was still another forty-five minutes before she could have anything for pain. "How do you feel?"

She shrugged, her expression mulish. "How do you think?"

Evidently, the ladylike manners were eroding in direct proportion to her unhappiness. "Sorry I asked," he said drolly, hoping to coax a smile.

But Emma turned her back on him. "Don't be here when I wake up," she ordered, the words pointed.

He shook his head though she couldn't see him. "Do you want me to bring in the medicine when it's time?"

"No." She burrowed her face into her arm. "I can take care of myself."

Emma had cause to regret her hasty words only a few hours later. When pale winter sunshine peeked into her room, she stirred and groaned. Today was worse than yesterday, and that was saying something. Of course, part of the problem was her stubborn pride. It was long past time for a pain pill, and she was paying the price.

She eased onto her back and listened. The apartment was silent and still. For a moment, she panicked about the shop, and then she remembered it was Sunday. Well, she wasn't going to get any relief until she took something, so she had to get out of this bed.

Cursing softly when pain shot up her thigh, she grabbed hold of the foot rail and found her balance. Her slippers were tucked beneath the edge of the bed, but if she bent to retrieve them, she was fairly certain her headache would ratchet upward about a million notches.

Tiptoeing on icy feet, she went in search of the elusive pill bottle. What she found was Aidan, sleeping soundly beside the hearth. Her shock was equal parts relief and dismay. His longs legs sprawled across her ottoman, his shoes in a jumble nearby. Though his neck was bent at an awkward angle, he snored softly, irrefutable evidence that he was actually slumbering.

She counted the breaths as his broad chest rose and fell. Though she couldn't see his eyes, she knew their color by heart. Hazel, beautiful irises that changed with his mood. Lately all she had seen was the dark glare of disapproval.

His thick hair was mussed. The top three buttons of his shirt were undone, revealing a dusting of hair below his collarbone. The intimacy of the scene curled her stomach with regret and sharp envy. No doubt there was a woman in New York who had laid claim to this beautiful man. But Emma had known him before…before he had acquired the spit and polish of a successful entrepreneur.

As he slumbered, she finally caught a glimpse of the boy she had known. After all, even at twenty-one she and Aidan had been little more than teenagers. They'd had no clue what forces could tear them apart, no way to understand that life seldom produced fairy-tale endings.

The old Emma would have curled into his embrace, not waiting for an invitation, confident of her welcome. Wistfully, she allowed herself a full minute to watch him sleep. But no more.

Easing past him, she spied the bottle on the end table, scooped it up and retreated before the lion awoke and caught her gawking at him. Her bravery extended only so far.

Though she would sell her soul for a cup of hot tea, that luxury would have to wait. The simple task was more than she could handle at the moment, and she had leaned on Aidan far too much already.

Thankfully, he never stirred as she retraced her steps. The partial glass of milk from the night before still sat beside her bed. It wouldn't have spoiled in this amount of time, and she needed something to coat her stomach. Wrinkling her nose at the taste, she swallowed the medicine with one big gulp of liquid.

Though she had heard Aidan clean up the mess in

the bathroom, she knew it was foolhardy to go in there again with bare feet. So she forced herself to slowly and carefully retrieve her footwear from its hiding place beneath the bed. When she straightened, she saw black spots dancing in front of her eyes and her forehead was clammy.

Even so, her immediate need was pressing. After a quick visit to the facilities, she washed her face, brushed her teeth and shuffled back to bed. She didn't even bother glancing at the clock. What did it matter? She had no place to go.

Aidan breathed a sigh of relief when he heard Emma's door shut. He'd heard her the moment she climbed out of bed. Feigning sleep had seemed the wisest course of action. But he hadn't anticipated how strongly her silent perusal would affect him.

What was she thinking as she stood there and stared at him? How did she reconcile the way they had left things between them years ago with her current choice to live in Silver Glen? She had to possess an agenda. There was no way she could call such a thing coincidence. She was far too intelligent to try that tactic.

The only explanation was that she had come here intentionally. But why?

He told himself it didn't matter. And he almost believed it.

Scraping his hands through his hair, he sat up and put on his shoes. As he rolled his neck trying to undo the kinks, he wondered how long it had been since he'd spent a platonic night on a woman's sofa.

Emma would probably sleep for a few hours now that she had taken her medicine. Which meant he had time to drop off her prescription, grab some breakfast and dash up to the hotel for clean clothes and a shower.

The first two items on his list were accomplished without incident. But when he tried to access the back stairs at the Silver Beeches to avoid any awkward questions, he ran in to Liam coming down as he was going up.

His older brother, dressed to the nines as always, lifted an eyebrow. "Look what the cat dragged in."

"Don't rag on me, Liam. I haven't slept worth a damn."

"At least not in your own bed. I thought all your lady friends were in New York."

Aidan counted to ten and then to twenty. Liam was not giving him any more grief than usual, but Aidan wasn't in the mood to be teased. Not today. His jaw clenched, he offered a simple explanation, knowing that Liam wouldn't let him pass without at least that. "I ran in to a friend who was having a bit of trouble. I helped out. That's all. Now if you don't mind, I'd like to go to my room and get cleaned up."

Liam leaned against the wall, his arms crossed over his chest. "This wouldn't have anything to do with the young woman who was hit by a car day before yesterday…downtown?"

Aidan stared at him. "Damn it. That's exactly why I don't live here anymore. Nobody has anything better to do than gossip."

"People were concerned. Silver Glen is a tight-knit place."

"Yeah. I got that."

Liam's face changed, all trace of amusement gone. "I know it's hard for you to be here this time of year. But I want you to know how glad we all are to have you home for the holidays."

The knot in Aidan's chest prevented him from answering—that and the sting of emotion that tightened his throat.

His sibling knew him too well to be fooled. "I'll let you go," Liam said, his eyes expressing the depth of their relationship. "If I can help with anything, let me know."

Five

By the time Aidan picked up the prescription and made it back to Emma's place, almost two hours had passed. He had taken her key with him, so he let himself in quietly and placed his packages on the table. Peeking into the bedroom, he saw that she still slept.

The extra rest was good for her. And besides, the sooner she was stable, the sooner he could leave.

He shoved the carryout bags he had picked up into the fridge. The greasy burgers and fries came from a mom-and-pop joint down the street. The Silver Shake Shack had been there since he was a kid. While Emma had converted Aidan to drinking proper English tea, he had been the one to teach her the joys of comfort food.

His immediate mission accomplished, he sprawled in the chair again and scrolled through his email. No big surprises there. Except for the one from his mother that said: Dinner at eight. S.B. dining room. Don't make me hunt you down.

He laughed softly, knowing that had been her intention. Everyone wanted Aidan to be in a good mood. To be happy. He understood their concern, but he was fine. He was here, wasn't he? They couldn't expect more than that.

Evidently the smell of his lunch offering permeated the apartment. Emma wandered out of her room wearing stretchy black knit pants and a hip-length cashmere sweater. She had done her hair up in a ponytail, and wore bunny slippers on her feet.

She gave him a diffident smile. "Hey."

"Hey, yourself. Doing any better?"

"Actually, yes. Was that food I smelled?"

"Some of the best. I put it in the fridge, but it hasn't been there long. We can zap it in the microwave. Are you hungry now?'

She nodded, heading for her small dining table. Her gait was halting, so he knew her leg was bothering her.

While Emma sat and rested her head in her hands, he managed to rustle up paper plates and condiments. "I ordered you one with mustard, mayo and tomato. I hope that's still the way you like it."

Her expression guarded, she nodded. "Sounds lovely."

The silent meal was half-awkward, half-familiar. Emma had changed very little over the years, though he did see a few fine lines at the corners of her eyes. She had always been more serious than he was, conscientious to a fault. The one thing he couldn't help noticing was that her breasts had filled out. The soft sweater emphasized them and her narrow waist.

When the food was gone, down to the last crumb, he cleared the table. "Do you feel like sitting up for a little while? I'll give you the seat by the fire."

"That would be nice."

So polite. Like a little girl minding her manners. Swallowing his irritation at her meekness, he hovered as she made her way across the room. He wouldn't touch her unless she showed signs of being lightheaded. When she was settled, he stood in the center of the room, hands in his pockets. "If you have an extra key," he said, "I can check on you later and you won't have to get up to answer the door. I have dinner plans, but I'll bring you something hot to eat before I go."

Staring into the fire, she nodded. Her profile, silhouetted against the flames, had the purity of an angel's. He felt something in his chest wrench and pull. The shaft of pain took his breath away. That wouldn't do. Not at all. He was way past dancing to Emma Braithwaite's tune.

He made a show of glancing at his watch. "Will you be okay for the afternoon on your own?"

"Of course." Her chin lifted with all the haughtiness of a duchess.

For all he knew, she might actually *be* a duchess. He hadn't kept up with the details of her life. Anything was possible.

She pointed. "The spare key is in the top drawer of that desk by the window. I think it's tied to a bit of green ribbon."

He rummaged as directed and found what he was looking for. As he pushed everything back into place, his gaze landed on a familiar-looking piece of paper. When he recognized what it was, he felt a mule-kick to the chest. "Emma?"

"Yes?"

He held up the offending card. "Would you care to explain why you have an invitation to my brother's wedding?"

Emma groaned inwardly. Could things get any worse? Aidan's original animosity had faded as he cared for her. Now his suspicions were back in full force. His expression was glacial, his demeanor that of judge and jury combined.

"Your mother gave it to me," she said, the words flat. Let him think what he wanted.

"My mother…"

Emma nodded. "I'm sure Mia asked her to. Mia and I became friends when I moved here a few months ago."

"How convenient."

As bad as she felt, her anger escalated. "I don't know what you're implying, and I don't care. I don't have to explain myself to you. Leave the key and go. I can manage by myself."

His face darkened with some strong emotion as he crushed the beautiful invitation in his fist. "You have no food in the house. I said I would bring your dinner. Now if you'll excuse me, I have things to do."

The way he slammed the door as he walked out was entirely unnecessary. She already knew he was furious. And that was just too damn bad. Emma had as much right to be in Silver Glen as he had. If he cared to listen, she would be happy to explain. But she had a sneaking suspicion that Aidan Kavanagh was too darned stubborn to hear her out.

Aidan wondered if he were losing his mind. Had the trauma of coming to Silver Glen at Christmas finally made him snap? When he left Emma's apartment, he sat downstairs in his car for several long minutes, trying to decide what to do. Finally, he drove out to Dylan's place for a visit. If he should happen to pump Mia for information in the meantime, that was *his* business.

Dylan answered the door, his face lighting up as he grabbed Aidan in a bear hug. "Thanks for coming home, baby brother. It means the world to Mia and me. I couldn't have a wedding without you."

Aidan shrugged, uncomfortable that everyone was making such a big deal of his visit. "Of course I'm here. Why wouldn't I be?"

The empathy in Dylan's steady gaze made Aidan feel raw and vulnerable, neither of which was the least bit appealing to a grown man.

Mia broke the awkward silence. "I'm glad you're here, too. And so is Cora."

Aidan took the child automatically as Mia handed her over. Cora gave him a sweet smile that exposed two tiny front teeth. He kissed her forehead. "Hey, darlin'. You want to go joyriding with Uncle Aidan? I'll show you where all the toddler boys live."

Mia rolled her eyes. "Why is it that no one in the Kavanagh family knows how to talk to girls?"

Dylan looked at her with mock outrage. "I might point out that *you* fell for some of my best lines."

Mia kissed her soon-to-be-husband on the cheek. "Whatever helps you sleep at night…"

Aidan grinned. He'd expected to be a little jealous of Dylan's storybook ending…and Liam's. And perhaps on some level, he was. But even so, he was happy for his older brothers. It was about time the Kavanaghs found something to celebrate.

Reggie Kavanagh had died when his boys were young. Liam, at sixteen, had been the only one close to adulthood. Truthfully, it wasn't exactly accurate to say that Reggie died. One day he simply went off into the mountains and never returned. Looking for the silver mine that had put his ancestors and the town of Silver Glen on the map.

Aidan tried to shake off the memory. He could still see his mother's face at the memorial service. She had been devastated, but resigned. Apparently, Reggie had never been the husband she deserved. But then again, life wasn't about getting what you were owed. It was more about dealing with what you were given.

In Aidan's case, that meant surviving loss. First his father. Then Emma. And finally, poor Danielle.

Cora's pudgy little body was warm and solid in his arms. A baby was such beautiful proof of life's goodness. Aidan needed that reminder now and again. He glanced at his brother, who apparently couldn't resist nibbling his wife's neck since Aidan was running interference with Cora.

Aidan complained. "In case it's escaped your notice, your innocent daughter is right here in front of you. How about a little decorum?"

"Decorum sucks." Dylan grabbed Mia for a quick smacking kiss on the lips. While Mia giggled and turned pink, Aidan put a hand over Cora's face. "Don't look," he whispered. "The adults are being inappropriate."

Laughing, but starry-eyed, Mia rescued her daughter and cuddled her close. "She'd better get used to it. Dylan wants at least two more."

Aidan lifted an eyebrow. "Seriously?" His brother had changed a lot in the last year. He was happier. More grounded. Less defensive about his place in the world.

"I like having kids around." Dylan's crooked grin said he recognized Aidan's astonishment and understood it. There had been a time when Dylan was the ultimate party animal. Now, however, he had embraced the role of family man with enthusiasm.

It didn't hurt that beautiful, quiet, smart-as-Einstein Mia shared his bed every night. They were an unlikely couple in many ways, but somehow the two of them together made it work.

Mia glanced at her watch. "Are you both going up to the lodge to eat with your mom and the rest of the clan?"

"You're not?" Aidan was surprised. His mother's command performances demanded proper deference.

Mia shook her head. "I've been given a dispensation. I want to get Cora to bed on her usual schedule, because we're going to Asheville tomorrow to find her a dress for the wedding."

"Cutting it a little close, aren't you?"

Mia shook her head. "Blame it on your brother. He's the one who decided we had to get married ASAP."

"Because?"

Dylan spoke up, his face a study in love and devotion as he eyed the two women in his house. "I'm adopting Cora," he said. "The papers are going to be finalized the day after Christmas. I want us to be a family before the New Year."

Conversation wandered in less serious directions after that. Dylan offered Aidan a beer while Mia sprawled on the floor to play with Cora. Aidan decided in that quiet half hour that he couldn't go back to Emma's. Not today. He had things to figure out, and he needed space and time to understand what her motives were.

When he and Dylan joined the two females on the floor, Aidan addressed Mia. "I need a favor, since you and Cora aren't going up the mountain for dinner."

She untangled Cora's fingers from her hair. "Name it. I need to build up all the family points I can get."

He chuckled. "It's nothing bad, I swear. But did you hear about the accident in town on Friday afternoon?"

Mia nodded, pausing to blow a raspberry on Cora's tummy. "Someone ran a red light and hit a pedestrian."

"Yes. I happened to be there at the time and followed the ambulance to the hospital. The woman's name is Emma Braithwaite. She says she's friends with you."

He felt a lick of shame at manipulating his sister-in-law. But he needed to know if Emma had disclosed the relationship she shared with Aidan.

Mia's gaze was anxious. "Is she okay?"

He nodded. "Home resting now. A concussion and some stitches. She didn't want to bother you because of the baby and the wedding. But it seems that she's fairly new in town… right? And doesn't know many people? I was hoping you and Cora could run over there and take her some dinner."

Dylan's eyes narrowed as though he sensed something was going on but wasn't sure what. "Who died and made you Clara Barton?"

"I watched the accident happen. All I had in mind was heading to the hospital and making sure she was okay. But when I found out she didn't have anyone to help out, I offered to get her home and settled when she was discharged."

"How convenient."

Hearing Dylan voice the same sarcastic response Aidan had used with Emma made him wince inwardly. "I don't know what you're talking about."

"Give me a break, Aidan. I've seen Emma. She's tall, blond and gorgeous…with a voice like an angel. You were smitten and decided to go all Galahad on her poor, helpless self."

Mia looked up with a frown. "I'm sitting *right* here," she said.

Dylan gave her a smoochy face. "Don't worry, my love. You know I'm into short, dark and cuddly."

"Oh, dear Lord," Aidan groused. "You two are embarrassing little Cora."

Cora, oblivious to the repartee, played with her toes.

Aidan weighed the facts. Clearly, Emma had made no mention to Mia of the fact that Emma and Aidan went way back. So if she wasn't using her past relationship with Aidan to ingratiate herself into the Kavanagh family, what was her deal?

* * *

He wrestled with his suspicions all evening, in the midst of a loud, argumentative, completely normal dinner with his siblings and his mother. To be honest, he'd forgotten how much fun it could be when they were all together. Usually when he came home to visit, at least one or two of the crew were missing…spread out here, there and yonder. It was increasingly difficult to corral all the Kavanaghs in the same place at the same time.

Maeve hadn't forgotten, though. It was at her insistence that they were all gathered under one roof tonight. And this was only the first of a series of holiday moments scripted by the matriarch of the family.

Liam's wife, Zoe—still with a new bride's glow—fit right in. Unlike the introverted Mia, Zoe loved a social gathering. She laughed and flirted and played the role of naive newcomer with verve, all under the indulgent eye of her besotted husband.

Aidan tipped a metaphorical hat to his mom. With Dylan's wedding, the whole Christmas season and a brand-new, soon-to-be-adopted Kavanagh kiddo, Maeve had scored a trifecta.

He left the Silver Beeches Lodge with a smile on his face. Though his room was upstairs, he was too wired to sleep. Instead, he climbed into his car and drove toward town. The closer he came to Emma's place of business, the less he smiled.

Parking at the curb below her windows, he stared up at the light. Why had she come to Silver Glen? He told himself he didn't care, but that was a lie. The Emma he had known in college was neither devious nor vengeful. Though, that was a very long time ago. Had she somehow decided to blame him for the meltdown of their relationship?

Only the most naive of assessments could attribute anything positive to her unexpected appearance in Silver Glen. His immediate reaction to finding her was suspicion and wariness. None of this made sense.

But even knowing that she had made the acquaintance of at least of two of his family members and that she had never once mentioned to either of them her connection to Aidan, he didn't want to believe the worst.

Truthfully, now that he had spent some time with her, it was impossible to hold back the flood of memories. Feelings he thought long dead pumped adrenaline into his bloodstream. She was like a drug in his system. He had detoxed after she nearly ruined his life. But the addiction was still there. Waiting to be resurrected.

If he had an ounce of self-preservation, he would stay the hell away. He'd crafted a decent life for himself—an even-keeled existence with no surprises, no regrets. No highs, no lows. It was safe…and financially remunerative. Even without his share of the family business, he had plenty of disposable income. And many friends of both sexes to help him fritter it away.

Emma's unexpected incursion into his life shouldn't even be a blip on his radar. Yet he had spent the night at her place. The same old Aidan, looking out for a woman who didn't want or need his protection.

He knew better.

But did he have the guts to turn his back on the one person who had taught him both the incredible rush of desire entwined with new love and also the soul-crushing agony of betrayal?

Six

December in the mountains of North Carolina was a capricious season. It could either be snowy and cold, balmy and sunny, or—as was the case this year—wet and gloomy.

Emma leaned against the windowsill, hands tucked in the pockets of her chenille robe, and watched water droplets track down the glass. Her view of the street below was distorted...like an image in a dream.

For four days she had expected Aidan to return, and for four days she had been disappointed. Now, there was no denying the truth. He was not coming back.

Having Mia show up on her doorstep Sunday evening had been the first sign. Though Emma was delighted to see her friend and little Cora, the fact that Aidan had promised to bring her dinner and then delegated that responsibility suggested he had been caring for Emma only out of a sense of duty.

She was the one who had wishfully attributed his emotions to feelings of affection. Which was ludicrous, really...she fully admitted that. Aidan had good reason to despise her. Only the honor and integrity instilled by Maeve Kavanagh into each and every one of her sons had compelled Aidan to come to Emma's aid.

Twitching the lace sheers back into place, she contemplated the outfit that lay draped across the red velvet settee. Tonight was the first of Maeve's holiday events—a fete for Dylan and Mia. Since the wedding plans had been thrown together so quickly, there hadn't been time for a more traditional bridal shower.

Because Dylan's home was fully outfitted, particularly with the addition of Mia's things, tonight's invitation had requested gifts to one of three charities in lieu of toasters and stemware. Emma had already written a large check and tucked it in her shimmery silver clutch. As a small thank-you gift to Mia and Dylan for their friendship, she had wrapped up a memento—an antique silver picture frame engraved on the lower edge with the words, *'til the end of time...*

In her imagination, she saw a young war bride tucking it into her soldier's pocket as he headed off to the other side of the world. Emma was a romantic. And a proud one. At one time, she had believed that every woman could find her soul mate. Now, older and wiser, she wasn't entirely sure. But she still hadn't given up on romance, even if it was mostly for other people.

Quite honestly, she didn't want to go tonight. Her leg still hurt, though it was much improved, and her head ached if she tried to do too much. But the doctor had cleared her to go back to work.

If she planned to open the shop tomorrow after a several-day absence, she could hardly expect Maeve to understand if Emma cried off tonight's festivities for health reasons. She was trapped by her affection for Mia and Maeve and the many kindnesses they had shown her as a newcomer to Silver Glen.

On the upside, if Aidan were avoiding her, it would make tonight more tolerable. Maybe they could sit on opposite sides of the room. She didn't have a problem with that, at all.

She sat down and stroked the fabric of her formal dress. Strapless and Grecian in design, the column of platinum silk was actually quite comfortable. A Christmas gift from her mother, the dress made the most of her height and her pale skin. Instead of washing her out, the color was surprisingly flattering.

Regrettably, because of her painful leg, she would have to forgo her favorite, sparkly three-inch heels. Silver ballet flats would have to do. In the meantime, she would practice not tripping since the skirt was bound to brush the floor.

Mia had insisted on sending a car to pick up Emma at her apartment. Though Emma thought it a wasteful luxury, she had to admit that *not* having to drive was a relief.

The hours of the afternoon crept by. The cleaning lady came and went, leaving the small rooms spotless. Afterward, Emma took a bath in the old-fashioned claw-footed tub, leaning her head back and closing her eyes as she escaped to a sweeter, less volatile time in her life…

Aidan met her at the library, his hushed greeting drawing disapproving stares. Perhaps because he dragged her against him and gave her an enthusiastic kiss. He was always doing that. The uninhibited American and the repressed Englishwoman.

"Did you get your paper turned in?" she asked, loving the way his eyes ate her up. Aidan made her feel like the world's sexiest woman. It was heady stuff for a girl who had spent much of her youth as a wallflower. Crooked teeth, a slight stammer and paralyzing shyness had made boarding school a nightmare. At home, things were not much better. The few village children who were her age were either intimidated by her title or openly

sullen, resenting the money that made her life easy in their estimation.

Aidan stroked her hair, his eyes lit with humor and lust. "My paper on the wives of Henry the Eighth? Yes. Barely. All I could think about was getting you naked again."

They had been lovers for a week. Seven glorious days that had changed her life. "Aidan," she said urgently. "Hush. I don't want to get tossed out of here."

"Won't dear old Daddy take care of any demerits?"

"Don't joke about that," she said, shivering as if a ghost had walked over her grave. "He would kill me if he knew that I—"

"Let your virginal self be ravaged?"

Her grin was reluctant. "You are such a scoundrel."

He slapped a hand over his heart. "Me? You must have me confused with someone else. I'm the man who loves you, body and soul..."

From the living room, she heard the chiming of the hour on her mantel clock. It was five-thirty already. Her pumpkin coach would be arriving in little more than an hour.

Climbing out of the tub, she dried herself with a thick Turkish towel and sat in front of the mirror to twist her hair into a complicated style befitting the dress. When that was done, she applied makeup with a light hand. A bit of blush, a hint of glittery powder at her cleavage. Mascara to darken her too-pale lashes, and finally, a spritz of her favorite perfume and a quick slick of lip gloss.

Hobbling into the bedroom at a much slower pace than usual, she dragged open her lingerie drawer and selected a matching set of silk undies in pale celery green. Since it was too cold and damp to go bare legged, she added a lacy garter belt and cobweb-thin stockings with a naughty seam up the back.

She might be dateless tonight, but that was no reason to let her spirits drag. It was Christmas, damn it. And she intended to squeeze every last bit of ho-ho-ho cheer out of the occasion. Aidan and his judgmental attitude could take a hike to the North Pole and stay there for all she cared.

It was becoming increasingly clear that her move to Silver Glen might have been ill-advised, at least when it came to Aidan. He didn't want to hear anything she had to say. But fortunately, he would be gone soon—back to the big city where he could wine and dine every woman in Manhattan if he wanted to.

Emma had finally found a place where she felt at home. After so many years in Boston, she was out of step with her English roots. And city living in Massachusetts really hadn't suited her, despite enjoying her job. She was really a small-town girl when all was said and done.

Here, in Silver Glen, she had a future. Her business was off to a good start. She had the opportunity to meet new people. Even if Aidan never gave her a chance to make things right between them, his charming hometown offered a cozy place to create her nest.

At twenty 'til seven, she realized that since her accident she had never actually tried negotiating the steps to the street. Slipping into her winter dress coat and adding a filmy scarf that would serve as a shawl later, she grabbed her purse, locked the apartment door and slowly made her way downstairs.

Apparently, she had taken her pre-accident fitness for granted, bounding up and down the steep staircase several times a day. Tonight, by the time she made it to street level, her leg throbbed and she trembled. Fortunately, the uniformed driver was early and immediately opened the car door when he saw her appear.

Emma sank into the comfortable backseat and folded her hands in her lap, her heart racing. Like Cinderella being escorted to the ball, she wondered what lay ahead. No Prince Charming, that's for sure. More likely a grumpy beast. Aidan had made his feelings clear.

Pulling onto the large flagstone apron that led to sweeping steps accessing the doors of the Silver Beeches Lodge, the driver halted the car and jumped out to come around and open Emma's door. The scene that awaited her was magnificent. Two huge Fraser firs, adorned with white lights and silvery stars, flanked the hotel's entrance. On the porch, a dozen more trees, each decked out as one of the twelve days of Christmas, cast a glow against the night sky.

Though the rain had stopped, the air was misty and cold, much too chilly to linger outside. Stepping into the lobby was equally impressive. Here, a Victorian holiday theme had overtaken the large public area. On a huge round table that normally supported a lavish flower arrangement in an ornate urn, poinsettias had been stacked in tiers to form the shape of a crimson-and-green tree.

Much of the traditional décor reminded Emma of her childhood during the month of December. All she needed was a mince pie and some plum pudding and she would feel right at home.

A formal doorman took her coat and greeted her, directing her toward the ballroom at the rear of the main floor. Emma hesitated in the doorway, feeling abashed at the swirl of light and color and conversation. Gold and green festoons draped the room along the ceiling. Bunches of real mistletoe hung from curling red ropes.

Twined in the quartet of chandeliers were narrow red-and-green-plaid ribbons.

Everywhere, the air carried the scent from great boughs of evergreens that adorned the massive fireplaces on either end of the room. Before Emma could turn tail and run, Mia spotted her and hurried across the floor, her smile infectious. "I'm so glad you're here," she said. "Come let me introduce you to some of our friends."

Dylan and Mia were well liked. Emma lost count of the townspeople she met. Fortunately, there were no seats at the family tables, so Emma courted invisibility by seating herself with a couple of business owners she had met soon after she'd moved in to her storefront.

Maeve had planned the evening to the last detail. First was a sumptuous four-course dinner, beginning with cranberry salad, then butternut squash soup, and finally, the entrée consisting of squab, asparagus with Hollandaise sauce, twice-baked potatoes and yeast rolls. The china, crystal, silver and napkins were impeccable.

By the time the sweet carts rolled out, Emma was stuffed, but not so much that she couldn't enjoy a piece of pecan pie.

Her tablemates were chatty and kind, including Emma in their conversations. She found herself smiling for no particular reason except that she was happy to be there.

As the dessert course wrapped up, Dylan stood and, on behalf of Mia and himself, thanked the crowd for their gift donations. He named a total that made Emma blink. Not that she wasn't accustomed to moving in social circles where fundraising dinners were de rigueur, but many of the Kavanagh party attendees seemed like ordinary people.

After Dylan's brief speech, several people toasted the bride-and-groom-to-be, and then it was time for dancing.

A small orchestra set up shop in one corner of the room. The lights dimmed. Music filled the air. Holiday songs and romantic ballads and even a smattering of classical pieces coaxed brave couples onto the floor in the center of the room.

Emma watched wistfully. She should probably slip out. This was not the time to be without a date.

Before she could make her excuses to her tablemates and head unobtrusively to the exit, Mia appeared unexpectedly with Aidan in tow. "Emma…" Her smile was conspiratorial. "I told my future brother-in-law you were feeling much better. I know you met under odd circumstances, but we should celebrate, don't you think? You could have been badly hurt. And since neither of you has a date tonight…"

One look at Aidan's face told Emma this was not his idea. "I'm sure Aidan has lots of people he wants to chat with since he lives out of town. I'll just sit and listen to the music." She tried to back out gracefully, but though Mia was quiet by nature, she was a woman of strong opinions.

Mia tugged Emma to her feet. "Don't be silly. Aidan *wants* to dance, don't you?" She looked up at her fiancé's brother with a cajoling smile.

Aidan nodded stiffly. "Of course. If Emma's up to it."

He was giving her an out…perhaps giving *both* of them an out. Perversely, his patent reluctance made her want to irritate him. "I'd love to dance," she said, draping her scarf across the back of her chair. The room was plenty warm. With two large-scale fires blazing and the body heat from a hundred guests, she was definitely not going to get a chill.

Mia, her job done, waved a hand and went to reclaim Dylan for the next dance. Emma and Aidan stood in a small cocoon of awkward silence. He wore a tux, as did most of the men in the room. Only in Aidan's case, the formal attire fit him so comfortably and so well, he seemed in his element. A man who, no doubt, had a closet full of such clothes back in New York.

He was bigger than the boy she remembered. His shoulders—barely contained by the expensive fabric of his jacket—were broad, his belly flat. When he took her hand and pulled her into a traditional embrace, she felt a little giddy.

Was it wrong to be glad that Mia was bossy and that Aidan was too much of a gentleman to make a scene? Emma bit her lip, looking anywhere but at his face. One of his hands, fingers splayed, rested against the back of her gown just below the place where bare skin met soft fabric.

She had intended to make light conversation, but her throat dried up. A wave of nostalgia and sexual yearning swept over her with such force that she stumbled once. Aidan righted her effortlessly, his strong legs moving them with ease across the crowded dance floor.

When Aidan spoke, she actually jumped.

"Relax," he said, his tone frustrated. "I'm not going to out you to the room. No one needs to know our dirty secrets."

Her spine locked straight. "We don't have any dirty secrets," she said, enunciating carefully.

"Then why haven't you told my family who you really are?"

Finally, she allowed her gaze to meet his. If she had expected to see tumultuous emotion, she was way off base. His face was a pleasant mask, only a tic in his cheek betraying any hint of agitation. "Who am I?" she asked pointedly. "An old girlfriend? That hardly seems worth mentioning. We were little more than children playing at being grown-ups."

Finally, she stirred the sleeping dragon. Fire shot from his eyes, searing her nerves and making her tremble. "Don't you dare," he said, the words forced from between clenched teeth. "It may have been a long time ago, but I won't let you rewrite history so you can whitewash the truth."

"The truth?" She stared up at him, confused and upset. "I don't know what you mean."

"You screwed me over, Emma. Though I must admit that your prissy English manners almost made it seem like a privilege. I was a young fool. But I learned my lesson. When I told you I didn't want to talk about the past, I meant it. But apparently, it's not so easy to overlook."

"I didn't ask you to dance with me," she said, the words bitter in her mouth.

"You didn't put up much of a fight, either."

To any onlookers, it must have appeared that Aidan and Emma were conversing politely in the midst of a dance.

Suddenly, she couldn't bear to have him touching her. Not when she knew how much he despised her.

"I will *not* cause a scene and ruin Mia's party." Her tone was soft but vehement. "But I am leaving this dance floor—now."

"Not without me." The fake smile he plastered on his face was in direct counterpoint to the unrelenting grip of his fingers around her wrist as he walked casually away from the dancers, pulling Emma in his wake.

If she struggled, everyone would see.

She waited until they reached the relative privacy of the hallway until trying to jerk free. "Let go of me, damn it."

But Aidan wasn't done. He stared down at her, a slash of red on each of his cheekbones. The glitter in his eyes could have been anger—or something far more volatile.

"We're going upstairs," he said. "And we're going to hash out a few things.

"My scarf and purse are at the table."

"I'll call and ask them to hold your things at the front desk."

"Oh, good," she said, glaring at him. "At least someone will know I've gone missing."

Seven

Aidan knew the moment they stepped into the elevator that he had made a strategic mistake. The mirrored walls reflected Emma's cool, English beauty no matter where he turned his gaze. The swanlike grace of her neck. The perfect features…even the vulnerable spot at her nape that he had unfortunately fantasized about all evening.

She carried herself with the poise of a Grecian goddess who might have worn such a dress once upon a time. The only flaw he could see was the slight limp caused by the injury to her leg. She had used makeup to cover the stitches near her ear. They were barely noticeable.

From the first moment he saw her tonight with her hair intricately woven around her head, he had wanted nothing more than to remove each pin, one by one, and watch all that golden silk tumble down around her bare shoulders.

They reached his floor in a matter of seconds. Emma made no move to elude him. Perhaps she knew they had been heading for this moment all along.

When he opened the door of his suite and ushered her inside, she glanced around curiously but did not comment. The accommodations were luxurious, but for a woman of Emma's background, the antique furnishings and Oriental rugs were old hat.

"Would you like a drink?" he asked.

She perched on the edge of a chair, her hands folded in her lap. "Whiskey. Neat."

He raised an eyebrow. The girl he had known rarely drank anything stronger than wine. Perhaps she was more nervous that he realized. It was petty of him to be glad. But he was.

When he handed her the heavy crystal tumbler, she eyed him over the rim, tossed back her head and swallowed the shot in one gulp. She might be nervous, but she was defiant as hell.

Taking a sip of his own drink, he rested a hip against the arm of the sofa, too antsy to sit down.

Emma finally relaxed enough to lean back in her chair. Kicking off her small shoes, she curled her legs beneath her. For a moment he caught a glimpse of slim ankles and berry-painted toes before she twitched her skirt to cover the view.

"I find myself at a loss," he said. "I know you're up to something, but since my sister and my mother have taken you to their bosom, I can hardly toss you out on your ear."

"I live here now," she said, her gaze daring him to disagree.

"And why is that?"

"You didn't want any explanations," she reminded him, the words tart.

"Perhaps I was too hasty." He offered the conciliatory olive branch, but Emma stomped on it.

"The information window is closed." Her ironic smile and visible satisfaction at thwarting him made his temper spark, but he was determined to keep the upper hand.

"What if we agree to an exchange? One piece of info for another."

"I don't need to know anything about you. I don't care."

If the way her breasts heaved was any indication—threatening their containment—she cared far more than she was letting on.

He poured her another drink. "I forgot to ask if you were still taking pain pills."

She took the second shot and treated it like the first. Though her face turned red and her eyes watered, she never wavered. "Of course not. I'm not stupid."

"I never said you were. Everyone at Oxford was quick to point out to me that you were one of the smartest women on campus."

"Not too smart, apparently."

"What does that mean?"

"Oh, never mind." She seemed crestfallen suddenly, her lower lip trembling, her expression lost.

"I own a very lavish penthouse apartment in the heart of New York City. I deal in high-end real estate."

"Believe me, Aidan. That's not exactly news. Your mother has been singing your praises in great detail. She misses you."

"I'm here now."

"Yes, you are."

"Look at me."

He strode to where she sat, pulled her to her feet, and settled them both on the sofa. Finishing his own drink, he placed his glass on the coffee table. "Actually, there's only one thing I really need to know."

She half turned to face him, her wide-eyed gaze curious. The platinum silk molded to her body with mesmerizing results. "What's that?"

"I'll show you." Capturing her mouth beneath his, he kissed her slowly, allowing her every opportunity to resist. Nowhere did their bodies touch except for the breathless press of lips on lips.

Her scent was familiar—sweet English roses with a hint of dewy spring. He'd been down this road a hundred times…heard the same angel choirs…seen the land of milk and honey.

His heart slugged in his chest, struggling to keep up with the need for oxygen. His circulatory system was taxed to the limit, as if his blood had become thick molasses.

In his head he heard the raucous sound submarines make when diving. Something was pulling him under. Something dangerous.

Emma made no move to put her hands on him. He was the one to crack first. Helpless, desperate, he slid both hands alongside her neck and angled her chin with his thumbs.

The room was silent except for their harsh breathing. He felt as if he were floating on the ceiling, watching himself fall through the same rabbit hole. At one time, Emma's kisses had been the magic elixir that made his days in England as bright and sweet as a dream.

He was losing control. His brain knew it. His body fought the truth. Shuddering with a desire that shredded his resolve, he used one hand to tug at the bodice of her dress. The thin fabric yielded easily, as did the filmy lace of her bra. In moments his fingertips caressed the puckered tip of one breast, then the other.

Emma groaned. "Aidan…" The word was barely a whisper.

He leaned over her warm, curvy body stretched out on the sofa. Abandoning her lips with no small amount of regret, he moved lower to kiss her more intimately, using his teeth to scrape furled nipples.

So lost was he in the feast that was her body, it took several long seconds for him to recognize the moment when she rebelled. Small hands beat at his shoulders. "No more, Aidan. No more."

Groggy with shock and confusion, he sat up, moving away from her with haste. In her face he saw what they had done. In her eyes he saw the woman he had loved more than was sane.

"God help me," he muttered, unable to look away as Emma tugged her dress into place. Several strands of her hair had come loose to dangle onto her shoulders. She looked rumpled and well loved.

She sat up as well, her complexion paler than the night he'd brought her home from the hospital.

Rage and fear consumed him. He stared at her in silence, his chest roiling with emotions to which he dared not give a name. Self-preservation kicked in. He wiped his mouth with the back of his hand, removing traces of lip color. "Amazing," he said, his heart as cold as his hands. "How can you look like a princess, kiss like a siren and have the duplicitous heart of a cheat and a liar?"

Emma blinked. He saw the moment she processed his deliberate insult. Dark color flooded her face. She smacked him hard with an open palm. The sound echoed. "How dare you," she cried, as moisture brightened her eyes. "You don't even know me. Apparently you never did."

He shrugged, insolent and furious, as much at himself as at her. "I know enough. I won't be wrapped around your finger again, Lady Emma. I learned my lesson."

She lifted her chin, as though daring the teardrops to fall. "You're a miserable, hardened, shallow man. You've let your prejudices and your grudges and your righteous indignation blind you. I can't believe I ever thought I was in love with you."

"But you never really were. It was all a charade.

Though for the life of me I can't understand why you bothered. Was having a fling with an American something on your bucket list? Or did you simply want to defy your father and prove your independence?"

Emma stared at him, her lips pressed together in a thin line. If there were a prize for dignity, she would win it every time. He *knew* she was in the wrong, and she knew it as well. Yet somehow, she managed to look like the injured innocent. Making him the villain.

"I'm going home," she said, the words flat. "You've made your point. Do us both a favor and keep your distance."

She jumped to her feet abruptly, obviously intending to reach for her shoes. But she tripped on the hem of her dress and slammed into the coffee table. Her cry of pain made him wince. Blood colored the skirt of her dress, no doubt from the stitches on her leg.

"Good Lord," he said. "What have you done to yourself?"

Not waiting for permission, he scooped her up and took her to his bedroom. Flipping back the covers to protect the expensive duvet, he set her down and unceremoniously lifted her dress.

"Don't touch me." She batted his hands away. The tears she had held at bay earlier fell now. Silent wet tracks that dripped onto her bosom.

"Settle down," he muttered. "Let me see what you've done." He took her ankle in his hand and bent to get a closer look. The bones beneath her skin seemed impossibly fragile. Touching her hastened his own defeat. But he had no defense. The feel of her skin beneath rough fingertips did something terrible to his resolve not to get sucked in again. He would have to keep up his guard.

He didn't care about her. Of course he didn't. It had

been a decade. Only his libido had any interest in pursuing this inconveniently persistent attraction. Emma Braithwaite was a stunning woman. It was normal for him, or any man, to react to her sexuality. In fact, if he *weren't* affected by her allure, he would be worried.

The carefully worded but unspoken argument did little to settle the churning in his stomach.

The wound on her leg had been healing nicely, but the blow to her shin evidently had landed in exactly the wrong place. One end of the reddened seam had pulled apart maybe an eighth of an inch and was bleeding profusely. "We need to go back to the emergency room," he said.

"No. I don't want to. I have butterfly bandages at home. That will take care of it."

She tried to pull her skirt down, but he held the cloth firmly. Her bare thighs were slim and supple. *Damn it...* He cleared his throat. "You don't want a nasty scar."

"The worst scars are the ones you can't see."

Her eyes met his. Their gazes clung. Something hovered in the air. Memory. Regret.

He almost kissed her again. The urge was overpowering, his need vital and pressing. "Don't move," he said. "I have some Band-Aids in my shaving kit. That will cover it until you get home."

His miscalculation cost him. Perhaps he had misunderstood the import of their kiss, because he had been in the bathroom no longer than thirty seconds when he heard the door to his room slam shut. Rushing out to stop her, he saw the empty bed. The bed that already figured prominently in his dreams at night—only in the dreams, he was not alone...

Emma's skin glowed like pearls in the shaft of moonlight that fell through her window. The bed was narrow, the sheets unexceptional. For a student apartment, the two-room space was above average. Aidan barely noticed his surroundings. How could he with a naked Emma on her back waiting to love him?

Ripping off the last of his clothes and donning a condom, he gave her a quick grin. "Scoot over. There's no place for me."

She bent one knee, placing her foot flat against the mattress. The sight of her feminine secrets made his hands shake.

"I suppose you'll have to climb on top," she said, her smile droll and mischievous.

The sex was still new. He felt like a fumbling peasant in the presence of royalty. Not that Emma gave herself airs. But because she was so damned perfect. He was hard and ready. But still he waited.

Emma seemed to read his mind. "I won't break," she said softly. "I love it that you want me so much. It's the same for me."

It couldn't be. No one could feel what he felt in that moment...

He sat on the edge of the bed and put his head in his hands, his elbows on his knees. How ironic that he had been so worried about recollections of Danielle during the holidays, when in fact, the worst memories of all were the ones about him and Emma that had blindsided him.

The urge to jump in his car almost won. He could be back in New York by morning if he managed to stay awake. Emma would understand, once and for all, that her ploy hadn't worked...whatever it was.

But his mother would never forgive him. And he wouldn't forgive himself. It would be unbearably selfish to let his problems ruin Dylan and Mia's wedding day. Equally as bad would be abandoning his family at Christmas. They were all so wretchedly glad to see him. As if he were the prodigal son returning after a long absence.

He came home to Silver Glen all the time, damn it.

But not in December. And now he was paying the price.

Since he had no choice in the matter, he would have to take Emma's suggestion and stay as far away as possible. Otherwise, he couldn't trust himself not to beg. That was the bitterest pill of all to swallow. Despite the fact that she had humiliated and betrayed him, given half a chance, he would willingly forget the past for one more night in her bed.

It was laughable now to think he had taught himself not to feel. Of course he felt. He felt it all. Everything from the purifying blaze of well-founded anger to the crazed urge to let his lust dictate the course of the next ten days.

The choice was his. All he had to do was let Emma speak her piece. Presumably, she had some explanation for lying to him. He could pretend to believe her and they could wallow in erotic excess until it was time for him to go home to New York. The hunger that turned him inside out would be appeased.

The idea had a certain wicked appeal. But like making a deal with the devil, if he gave in to temptation, his soul would never be his own again. If he bedded her, skin-to-skin, nothing between them but the air they breathed, he might decide he could live with the past.

When whatever game she was playing ended, there was the reality that she would lie to him again. Women didn't change. He hadn't been enough for her once before and she had crushed him with her betrayal.

Could he do it for the sex? Could he draw a line in the sand and take only what he wanted? He'd sealed off his heart long ago. No woman since Emma had managed to tempt him. Except for his family, he cared about no one. He was a hollow man.

Pain came with relationships. His father had abandoned him by putting his obsessions ahead of his family. Danielle had abandoned him by dying. But in Emma's case, Aidan had been the one to leave. As soon as he learned the truth, he didn't hang around to be kicked in the teeth again. Even so, that pain had been the worst of all.

Eight

Emma cleaned blood off her leg and pondered all the ways she could murder Aidan Kavanagh in his sleep. He was infuriating and stubborn and his masculine arrogance made her want to hurl things at his head.

He still felt something for her. Even if it was only lust. But no way in heck was she going to tumble into bed with him when he thought so little of her. Perhaps she should have insisted on clearing the air immediately when he first recognized her. After all, the reason she'd come to Silver Glen, in part, was to make amends for the way she'd handled things in the past. She had hurt both Aidan *and* herself, though he bore some responsibility as well.

Maybe her stubborn pride was as bad as his, because she didn't want to make her apologies to a man who said he didn't care enough to hear what she had to say. There were a lot of things they could talk about. Important things. In her personal version of a twelve-step program, making amends was high up on the list. But it was hard to do that when the person you injured wouldn't let you do what you needed to do.

It was probably just as well. Look at what happened tonight. It was a really bad idea for the two of them to relive their college infatuation. Sex would introduce a whole extra layer of entanglement, because Aidan's family had no idea that Emma and Aidan shared a past.

Still, when she thought about his kiss, it was difficult not to imagine what would have come next. Feeling his hands on her body had kindled a fire, a yearning to experience his possession one more time. No man in the last ten years had made her feel a fraction of what Aidan could, not that many had tried.

Americans attributed her standoffishness to British reserve. But it wasn't that. Not really. She wasn't shy. She had simply learned to protect herself. Meeting Aidan at Oxford was a chance encounter. She'd been freer back then, more apt to take a chance on love.

Now, she was mostly happy on her own. Men complicated life. She had girlfriends back in Boston. And here in Silver Glen, she was already building a circle of support. She wanted to make things right with Aidan. But if that never happened, at least she had found a place to call home.

She glanced at the clock on the wall, realizing that the hour was really not that late. Even so, she was beat. Her first outing since her accident had required more energy than she realized. Suddenly, the idea of curling up in bed for an early night was impossible to resist.

After brewing a cup of herbal tea, she set it on her dresser while she changed into a comfy flannel nightgown. Then, moving the tea to the bedside table, she sat down on the mattress, plumped the pillows behind her back and picked up the novel she was in the midst of reading. She managed to finish her tea, but just barely. After her eyelids drifted shut for the third time, she gave up, climbed under the covers and turned out the light.

* * *

Sometime later, an insistent noise woke her. In the dark, she listened carefully, her heartbeat syncopated. It took only a moment to process that the sound she heard was the street-level buzzer. It rang upstairs whenever she had a visitor.

Leaning up on one elbow, she hit the button on her phone and gazed at the time blearily. Good grief.

Since the person at the other end of the buzzer didn't appear to be dissuaded by her lack of response, she got up, shoved her feet into slippers and reached for her fleecy robe. Her wound was still tender, but the Band-Aid had stopped the bleeding.

In the living room, she pushed aside the sheers and looked down at the street. There were no cars in sight except for her neighbor's familiar sedan. But even from this angle she could see the figure of a man.

As if he could feel her watching him, he stepped back, looked toward her window and made a familiar let-me-in motion.

Clearly, she should ignore him. He would go away soon.

Even as she lectured herself, her feet carried her down the steep stairs. Her hand on the doorknob, she called out, "Who is it?"

With only a couple of inches of wood separating them, she could hear the response distinctly. "You know who it is. Open the door, Emma."

Her toes curled inside her slippers. "Why?"

"Do you really want the whole town to know our business?" he muttered.

The man had a point. She jerked open the door and stared at him. He was bareheaded despite the fact that it was frigid outside. "Do you have any idea what time it is?" she asked, trying to sound irritated instead of excited. There was only one reason a man came calling at this hour. The intensity of his shadowy gaze made her pulse jump and dance.

"No. I don't. But I'm freezing out here. May I please come in?"

She stepped back to allow the door to close, and suddenly the two of them were practically mashed together in the handkerchief-sized space. "Where is your car, Aidan?"

He shrugged, his clothes smelling like the outdoors. It was a nice fragrance, a combination of cold air and evergreen. "I walked," he said bluntly. "We'd had a few drinks, if you remember."

"That's at least five miles." She gaped, unable to comprehend such a crazy thing in the middle of the night.

"Why do you think it took me so long to get here?"

"Oh, for goodness' sakes. Come on up. I'll make you a hot drink. Can you deal with coffee at this hour?"

He followed on her heels. "I'll take some of your famous herbal tea."

In the kitchen, he took off his wool overcoat and tossed it over a chair. The light was too bright. She felt exposed, though she was covered from head to toe. His sharp gaze took in her decidedly unseductive attire. Though his lips twitched, he made no comment.

He still wore his tux pants and white shirt, but he'd left his jacket behind. The shirt was unbuttoned partway down his chest. A partial night's beard shadowed his firm jaw. He looked sexy and dangerous, like a man who was about to throw caution to the wind.

What did it say about her that his rakish air stirred her? That his undiluted masculinity was both mesmerizing and exciting?

He sat down in one of her spindly wooden chairs, his weight making the joints creak. For the first time she recognized his fatigue. Was it because of the hour or because of his nighttime prowl or because he had been wrestling with himself? The third option was one she understood all too well. Why else had she opened her door?

Without speaking, she handed him a cup of tea and poured one for herself. Instead of joining him at the table, she leaned against the fridge, keeping a safe distance between them.

"Why are you here, Aidan?"

The satirical look he gave her questioned her intelligence. "Don't be coy."

She shrugged. "Does this mean you're ready to listen to my explanations?"

"I told you before. I don't want to hear anything about the past or why you're here in Silver Glen."

"What else is there?"

He stood abruptly and plucked the china cup out of her hand. "This."

Dragging her flush against his big frame, he dove in for a hard, punishing kiss, one arm tight across her back. His lips moved on hers with confidence…as if he remembered in exquisite detail exactly what she liked.

The old Aidan had never been this sure of himself. But darned if she didn't like it. Without shoes, she was at a distinct disadvantage, though. She stood on her tiptoes, straining to align her mouth with his. Everything about him was warm and wonderful. Despite his gruff refusal to let her plead for absolution, there was tenderness in his kiss.

She shivered, even though in Aidan's embrace she was perfectly warm. Too warm, maybe. She felt dizzy. As if all the air had been sucked out of the room.

"I want you, Emma," he muttered. "Tell me you want me, too."

It was a hard thing to deny when her arms were twined around his neck in a stranglehold. "Yes," she said. "I do, but—"

He put his hand over her mouth, stilling her words. "No buts," he said firmly. He paused for a moment, the look on his face impossible to decipher. "There's only one question I need answered." His Adam's apple bobbed as he swallowed. "Are you married?"

Shock immobilized her. She twisted out of his embrace, staring at him wide-eyed. "No. *No.*" She answered more forcefully the second time.

"Good." He picked up her left hand and lifted it to his lips. "Then, Lady Emma Braithwaite, will you do me the honor of taking me to your bed?" His droll smile was at odds with the intensity of his gaze. A tiny muscle ticked in his granite jaw as though her answer was far more important than he was letting on.

Emma had come to that moment in life when plans had gone awry and the road ahead was no longer clear. "Do you hate me?" she asked bluntly. "For what happened?"

Aidan was unable to hide his wince. "Does it look like I hate you? I'm practically eating out of your hand, damn it."

It wasn't really an answer to her question. "Please, Aidan. Tell me the truth."

His broad shoulders lifted and fell. Full, masculine lips twisted. "No. I don't hate you." He paced the confines of her small kitchen. "There was a time when I *wanted* to hate you, but no more. Life is short. I'll be leaving soon. I think we can chalk up tonight to what-might-have-been. It's Christmas. I'm feeling an odd, sentimental need to be somebody else tonight. Somebody that I used to know. A boy, not quite a man. An idealistic, heart-on-his-sleeve kid. Too naïve to be let loose in the wild."

For the first time, she understood that he was telling her the God's honest truth.

"I loved that boy," she whispered. "He was amazing and kind and perfect in every way."

"He was a fool." The blunt exclamation held a trace of bitterness and anger, despite his professed lack of enmity.

"I won't let you say that." Her tone was firm. Though Aidan Kavanagh was a mature, successful man, she saw in painful clarity the many ways she had damaged him. "If you don't want to rehash the past, then so be it. We'll make tonight all about the present. Come to bed with me."

He paled beneath his tan. "No regrets when the cold light of day dawns, Emma. From either of us. I need your promise. I won't be accused of taking advantage of you."

Crossing her fingers left and right over her heart, she lifted her chin and eyed him steadily, even though her chest jumped and wiggled with fizzy shards of happiness. "No regrets."

Quietly, he switched off the kitchen light and followed her to her bedroom. The sheets and comforter were tumbled where she had leapt up quickly to answer the door. Stopping beside the bed, she battled a sudden attack of shyness.

Aidan had no such problem. He removed her robe with gentle motions, and then touched the button at her collarbone, unfastening it along with three more. "Lift your arms," he commanded.

When she obeyed, he pulled the gown over her head. She wore not a stitch beneath it. He had her naked in less than five seconds.

The look on his face was gratifying. He brushed his thumb over her navel. Gooseflesh broke out all over her body.

"You're cold," he said.

She shook her head slowly. "Not cold. Just ready."

When he lifted her into his arms, she was confused. They were both at the bed already. But as she rested her cheek against his chest and looked up at him, her heart twisted. For a split second, she saw the young man who had loved her with such reckless generosity and passion.

He stared down at her for long seconds. She could almost feel his turmoil. "No one needs to know about this," he said.

Though the words hurt, she nodded. "I understand."

"Birth control?" His communication had been reduced to simple phrases, as though he barely retained the capacity to speak.

"I'm on the pill. And no health problems to worry about."

"Nor I." He shook his head as if to clear it. "I'm not sure I can wait any longer."

She cupped his cheek with her hand. "Why would you? We're both on the same page tonight, Aidan. Make love to me."

Hesitating, he stared at her with stormy eyes. "This is sex. No more, no less."

Not love. Message received.

"Whatever you want to call it is fine by me. Now if you'll excuse me, I need to freshen up."

Fleeing to the bathroom, she leaned her hands on the counter and stared into the mirror. Her cheeks were flushed, her pupils dilated. Was she making a monumental mistake? Was it wrong to share her bed with Aidan when there were so many things left unsaid?

A slight noise in the bedroom reminded her that there was no time for dithering. Either she wanted him, or she didn't. When you put it that way, there was only one clear answer.

She took two minutes to prepare. Then she opened the door, squared her bare shoulders and returned to the bedroom.

Nine

Aidan couldn't believe this was happening. How many times over the years had he imagined this very scenario? Or dreamed it, vividly erotic in his head?

As he stripped off his pants and boxers, socks and shoes, he was painfully aware that he had been hard for the better part of the evening. Dancing with Emma was a particularly wicked kind of torture. Now, naked and lovely, she stared at him, her nervousness impossible to hide. He wanted to reassure her, but in truth, he had no reassurances to give. What they were about to do was either self-destructive, or at the very least unwise. Even knowing that, he couldn't work up any enthusiasm for the idea of being sensible.

"You're beautiful," he said. It seemed a trite thing to mention. Surely the men in her life had been telling her as much since she was an innocent sweet sixteen.

Her hands twisted at her waist as though she wanted to cover herself. She was clean-shaven between her legs except for a tiny strip of blond fluff that proved her hair color was natural. Her legs were long and shapely, her waist narrow, her breasts high and firm.

If he were strictly impartial, he might note that her forehead was too high for classic beauty…and her nose a tad too sharp. But those minor flaws were balanced out by the heart-shaped face, full pink lips and eyes the color of an October sky.

He took one of her hands in his, finding it icy. Chafing it carefully, he cocked his head toward the pile of covers. “I think in December the preliminaries should probably be carried out in bed. I don’t want you to catch pneumonia.”

“This feels awkward,” she said with blunt honesty and a crooked smile of apology.

He nodded. “It will get better.”

They moved, one at a time, into the relative warmth of the bed. The sheets seemed chilled, but heated rapidly.

Emma reclined on her side facing him, head propped on a feather pillow. She watched him with fascination and reserve. “You must have lots of experience,” she said, the words hinting at dissatisfaction.

He mirrored her position, though he propped his head on his hand. “I doubt we want to compare notes on our sexual histories. Do we?”

“No. I suppose not.”

In her pose and in her gaze he saw the same thing that had drawn him to her when he was at university. There was no other way to describe it than *goodness*. It radiated from her. No woman he’d ever met appeared to be so unsullied, so open and warm.

Yet, he knew for a fact that it was only a facade. Emma had a capacity for deception, as indeed did most humans. Aidan made no assumptions about her. He had not listened to malicious lies. He’d gone straight to the source, had asked Emma for the truth. Even now, recalling that moment stabbed his heart with disillusionment.

Shaking off the unpleasant memory, he concentrated on the woman who was so close, her breath mingling with his. Reaching out, he stroked her hair, sifting the strands through his fingertips. "We were so young," he said. "But I thought you were the most exquisite thing I had ever seen."

"And you were brash and handsome and charmingly affable. A young Hugh Grant. Except with that adorable American accent."

Aidan chuckled. "Perhaps it's true that opposites attract. I was mortifyingly intimidated by your pedigree and your finishing school manners." He moved a fingertip lazily from her cheek to her collarbone to her cleavage. Emma's sharp intake of breath told him that the simple touch affected her as strongly as it did him.

Gently, he pressed her shoulder, urging her onto her back. As he shifted positions to lean over her on one elbow, he mapped her body with his palm. Plump, curvy breasts. Smooth rib cage. Almost concave belly. And then—the mother lode.

Keeping his gaze fixed on hers, he traced the folds of her sex with gentle persuasion. Her legs moved restlessly, her thighs widening in unspoken invitation. It would be so easy to pounce and take. But since his plan was to allow himself only a single night of delirium, he had to go slowly. Make it last. Wring every drop of pleasure from the hushed minutes when he had her to himself.

Emma's hands roved over his scalp, her fingers sweeping across his forehead, stroking his neck, playing with his ears. It was embarrassing that such chaste touches made him rigid with need. His erection was full and hard and throbbing with eagerness.

Do it. Take her. Now.

Every masculine impulse leaned toward plunder. Only the mitigating tenderness of their past reined him in.

Emma exhaled in a shuddering sigh. "When you touch me, I melt inside. It was always that way, Aidan."

Perhaps that much was the truth. He would never really know. But she couldn't fake her body's response at the moment. The warm, soft welcome at her center was slick and moist and scented with her need.

He had intended to tease them both with long minutes of foreplay. But why? He couldn't want her more. No hunger could be as gut-wrenching. He was primed and ready.

Moving over her on shaking arms, he positioned the head of his sex at her entrance and pushed with a groan that betrayed his need. Her excitement eased his passage, taking him to the hilt with oxygen-stealing speed. *Holy hell.* Either his memories were faulty or she had slipped some kind of aphrodisiac into his tea.

"Damn, Emma."

She arched her back, taking him deeper still. Her legs wrapped around his waist, her heels locking in the small of his back. "Don't stop," she begged, the words ragged.

Cursing and laughing, he moved in her with what little control he had left. "Not a problem."

To say they were good together was like saying the horizon was infinite. He'd had plenty of sex in his adult life. But whatever happened when he joined his body with Emma's defied description.

A sappy English poet might talk about roses and hearts afire and the purity of true love. Aidan took a more visceral approach. When he screwed Emma, his body went berserk. Fireworks, explosions, searing heat...incandescent pleasure.

And all that was before he climaxed.

He buried his hot face in her neck. "Once won't be enough."

She bit the side of his neck. "I never said it would."

Feeling her teeth on him was all it took. Light flashed behind his eyelids. He pistoned his hips. In some dim corner of his brain, he tried to make sure he gave her what she needed. If her wild cries were any indication, he was succeeding.

Then he went rigid as the world went black and he lost himself in the flash fire of completion.

Emma trembled uncontrollably. Most of Aidan's weight pressed her into the bed. His breathing was harsh and uneven. She had no idea if he were awake or asleep. She was hoping for the latter, because she hadn't a clue what she was supposed to say.

Wow, Aidan. That was awesome. Let's do it again.

Or...*you rocked my world. And I'm pretty sure I never stopped loving you.*

Hysteria bubbled in her chest. She was in so much trouble. How had she blinded herself to the truth? She hadn't come to Silver Glen to find Aidan and make amends for their past...or at least not only that. She wanted to win him back.

Since the chances of that happening were about as good as the possibility of the Queen dancing naked beside the Thames, Emma had a choice to make. She could slink away quietly and go home to England—forgetting she ever knew Aidan Kavanagh—*or* she could fight for him. But the emotional barriers he had built were formidable.

Confrontation was not Emma's strong suit. Aidan didn't want to hear her version of the past. Anytime she tried to bring it up, he stonewalled her. But tonight, he had given her a powerful weapon. He had shown her clearly that at least one thing hadn't changed over the years. He and Emma were still magic between the sheets.

That had to count for something, right?

She smoothed his hair with her hand, relishing the opportunity to touch him as she wished. How different her life might have been if she'd had more gumption at twenty-one…if she hadn't been under her father's thumb…if she'd had the confidence to accept that the handsome American really loved her.

But deep in her heart, she had doubted Aidan. It shamed her to admit it. And it had taken her a long time to face the truth. One reason their relationship had ended so abruptly and with such devastating finality was that she hadn't really believed a man could want her for herself.

The preteen wallflower had grown up to be a self-conscious academic. Her degree in art history was achieved with highest honors, but no one had ever expected her to use it, least of all her family. Emma's purpose in life was to marry well and continue the Braithwaite legacy.

Perhaps to someone of Aidan's background, such a notion was antiquated. But Emma had grown up circumscribed by the expectations of her rank and position in society. Her parents adhered rigidly to the tenets of their social code. As their only child, Emma's path in life had been well defined. Even so, she'd certainly had the freedom to fall in love…as long as the man of her choice passed muster in the pages of Debrett's *Peerage & Baronetage*.

Now, holding the mature, sexy Aidan Kavanagh in her arms, she couldn't fathom that she had been so foolish. His advent into her young life had seemed like such a fairy tale, she'd lived the fantasy and refused to think about the future. Which meant that when disaster struck, she hadn't been prepared. Neither had she possessed the confidence to fight back. A mistake she bitterly regretted.

Her cowardice had hurt Aidan and destroyed their fragile, beautiful relationship. Even though she had tried her best to fix things in the aftermath, the damage had been done.

Already, she wanted him again. Hesitantly, she ran her hands down the taut planes of his back, as far as she could reach. He was a beautiful man. Naked, he seemed both more powerful and more approachable.

Moving slowly and carefully so as not to wake him, she eased him onto his back. His broad, hair-dusted chest rose and fell with his steady breathing. The flat belly, muscled thighs and surprisingly sexy feet caught her eye. But it was his quiescent sex that made her sigh with appreciation. Even at rest, it shouted his masculinity.

Men were so wonderfully different from women. In her art history classes she had studied hundreds of famous nudes—painted on canvas, chiseled in marble, sculpted in bronze. But no matter how impressive the subject, there was nothing to compare to a living, breathing man.

Resting her hand on his thigh, she bent to examine a small white scar on his right hip, probably a childhood injury. He and his brothers had been wild rascals growing up, particularly after their father died. She could only imagine how Maeve Kavanagh managed to wrangle them all into becoming upright citizens of the community.

"Em, are you window-shopping or trying to get something started?"

She sat up abruptly, shocked to the core. Apparently, Aidan was a better actor than she realized. Clearing her throat, she sat back on her heels. "How long have you been awake?"

"Long enough." He linked his hands behind his head, smiling slightly, clearly enjoying her discomfiture.

She couldn't think of an excuse that would explain her intense interest in his body. So she changed the subject.

"Sorry I woke you," she said, not quite able to meet his knowing gaze. "We should both probably get some sleep. The next three days are going to be busy."

He took her hand and tugged her down beside him. "Hush, Em. Don't be embarrassed. I want to look at you, too."

But she wasn't as blasé as he was about her nude body. Dragging the sheet to her chin, she bit her lip. "I thought you might want to go back to the hotel now."

"It's the middle of the night." He chuckled. "And I don't have a car. As far as I can tell, staying right here in your bed is a damned good plan. Do you have any objections?"

Lord, no, she thought. Why did it matter if they were sleep-deprived? It was about time some of her other physical needs took center stage for a change. She could sleep when she was old.

"You called me *Em*," she said.

His smile faded. "Don't make a big deal out of that. It slipped out. That's all. Old habits."

She hoped it was more than that. *Em* was the nickname he'd sometimes used for her when they were in college. Often he would whisper it in the midst of sex. A tender, affectionate means of address that always sounded indulgent and proprietary.

She nodded, unsure what was going to happen next. While they talked, his erection had flexed to attention again. A thing like that was hard to ignore. But the expression on Aidan's face was serious.

Touching her cheek gently, he grimaced. "Tell me why you moved from England to Silver Glen."

Her heart leapt. It was a chink in the wall, though a small one. "I didn't," she said. "I've lived in Boston for the last nine years."

"Doing what?" She had startled him, no question.

"I was an art appraiser at the Sotheby's branch there."

"Why work at all?"

"You're rich. And *you* work. We all need a reason to get up in the morning."

"Why did you leave England?"

She wanted to be a smart-ass and remind him that he wasn't interested in having information or explanations. But it would be foolish to bypass this opportunity. "I had a falling out with my father. We're both stubborn people, so neither side wanted to concede. I refused to go home for eight and a half years. My mother visited me often in Boston, but until this past spring I had not seen my father for a very long time."

"And why last spring?" He seemed genuinely curious.

The reasons for her voluntary exile to the States involved Aidan, but she didn't think he was ready to hear that. Not yet. Maybe not ever. So she told him the bare bones.

"My father was an old-school autocrat. He ruled our family with an iron fist, expecting absolute obedience. When it became clear that he and I were never going to see eye-to-eye about several very important topics, I knew I had to strike out on my own."

"Must have been scary."

"It was...but exciting, too. Even so, I missed home. When my father was diagnosed with pancreatic cancer in April, the doctors told my mother he had only weeks to live. I flew back immediately, and thankfully, I was able to reconcile with him before he left us. That experience taught me it's never too late to heal old wounds."

The personal story was about as blunt as she was prepared to be. Aidan was an intelligent man. Surely he could read between the lines. It had taken until today for Emma to acknowledge to herself that her reasons for coming to Silver Glen were more convoluted that she had been willing to admit.

She wasn't committed to any man at the moment. And unless Aidan was not the man she once knew, he was not attached either, or he would not be in bed with her. If she could convince him that what tore them apart was no longer relevant—if he would accept her apologies—then surely there was no reason they couldn't make a new start.

That was a big pile of assumptions. Built mostly on fantasy and dreams. But he was in her bed, so that was a start.

Ten

Aidan tried to find his anger and his righteous indignation, but it seemed to have disappeared along with his pants. It was difficult for a man to hold a grudge while a woman's naked body was pressed against his. He stroked Emma's hip. "Enough chitchat," he said. But he smiled to let her know he wasn't making light of her revelations.

Her hair was rumpled. Dark shadows smudged beneath her eyes spoke of exhaustion. Perhaps another man would have been content to hold her. But not Aidan. Not after waiting a decade to be with her again.

Difficulties lurked outside this room. And reality. Not to mention his vivid, painful memories of the past. For the moment, however, he was content to overlook the negatives. Probably because his brain was not in control. That function had been ceded to his baser anatomy.

He kissed her softly, one hand balanced on the pillow, his fingers tangled in her hair. "I want you again," he said. His lips moved to her eyelids, her cute nose, her perfect earlobes.

When Emma squirmed, her hand brushed his erection. Accidentally, or no? He sucked in a sharp breath. "Don't stop there." The gruff command worked. Perhaps because it sounded more like a plea. When her slender fingers closed around his firm shaft, stroking up and down, he shuddered and gasped, totally unable to hide his excitement.

Emma might have seen his reaction as proof of her power over him. But instead, her gaze was one of fascination. “I don’t remember what you liked,” she said quietly, as if confessing a wretched secret.

“No complaints here.” He forced the words between clenched teeth. She was adorable. But then she always had been. He refused to think about any other men who might have been part of her life. He didn’t want to know. If he could keep his mind on the present and nothing else, everything would be okay.

“Aidan?” She abandoned her activity and put both hands on his cheeks lightly.

He turned his face and kissed one soft palm. “What?”

Big eyes searched his as if seeking answers to questions they hadn’t even spoken aloud. “I’ve missed you.”

She paused before she said those last three words, giving him the impression that she might have changed what she was going to say at the last minute.

What did she expect from him? He felt a lick of anger and shoved it away. “I’m here now. Roll over, Emma.”

Suddenly, he couldn’t bear to look her in the face, couldn’t stand to see the gaze that made *him* feel guilty… as if he had been the one to break her heart and not the other way around.

Rubbing her firm, round bottom, he leaned over her, tucking her hair across one shoulder and kissing the nape of her neck. When they were together in the past, he had never taken her like this. She had seemed too much the lady for a naughty position.

Or so he had thought. Maybe she had seen his naïveté as comical.

"Are you okay?" he asked, cursing inwardly that he felt the need to check.

She turned her head to smile at him with a mischievous look. "I won't break, Aidan. I swear."

He took her at her word. Checking her readiness with two fingers, he found her sex slick with moisture. She squirmed at his touch. Entering her slowly, he cursed. The fit was different from this angle, but no less stimulating. Sweat broke out on his forehead as he tried to pace his thrusts. The visual wasn't helping.

Emma's pale skin was luminous. Streetlights below cast a gentle glow through the thin curtains, so the room was never truly dark. He could see the curve where her waist dipped in and her hips flared.

Reaching beneath her, he palmed one breast, then the other. The flesh was full and firm. She wriggled backward, seating him more fully inside her. He was so close to coming every inch of skin all over his body was taut with expectation.

Suddenly, he knew it had to be different. If he and Emma had been long-time lovers, nothing would have been out of line. But they were neither lovers nor long-time. They were reconnecting with a tentative passion that left too much unspoken. She deserved to know he wanted *her*, not merely a faceless hookup.

Disengaging their bodies carefully, he moved her onto her back, lifted her leg over his hip and slid home again. She cried out and stared at him with a hazy expression, her lips parted, her breath coming quickly. Pleasure was the only emotion he recognized without question. And truly, he didn't want to examine the others too closely. Pleasure was fine. Pleasure was good. He didn't need to know what was going on inside her head.

Exhaustion lay heavy on his shoulders. If he had the

energy, he would move inside her forever. Feeling the butterfly caress when her sex squeezed his. Watching the way her breasts lifted and fell as her excitement grew. Touching her intimately, stimulating her little nerve center.

But the night had waned and he and Emma were half-sated from their earlier coupling. Even still, he managed to hold off for one more minute. "You enchant me," he said.

Emma frowned slightly. His statement held a hint of accusation, even to his own ears.

"I don't need you to talk, Aidan. Take us both where we want to go."

Closing his eyes, he heaved a deep breath and did just that…

When Emma awoke the next time, morning light filtered into her small bedroom. Aidan stood beside the bed, almost fully dressed. As she watched, he finished buttoning his shirt and tucked it into his pants.

She reared up on her elbows. "Are you leaving?"

He shot her a glance, nodding. "I promised Dylan and Mia that I would help them today out at the house. The whole crew is coming over for dinner tonight."

"Mia invited me, too."

She saw him go still, witnessed the rigid set of his shoulders. His reaction hurt, but she wasn't surprised.

No one needs to know about this.

Sitting up, she clutched her knees to her chest, the sheet protecting her modesty. "If you don't want me there tonight, I'll stay home."

He shrugged, still not meeting her eyes as he fastened his cuff links. "Go. Don't go. It's up to you."

"You don't have anything to worry about, Aidan. I won't embarrass you."

He slipped into his overcoat and buttoned it. "It's not a question of embarrassment. But my mother and Zoe and Mia get a real charge out of matchmaking. I don't want to get their hopes up."

"What does that mean?"

"I never bring women to Silver Glen. If they think you and I are an item, they'll hound me without mercy."

"Surely you've introduced them to women in the past."

"No."

She waited for him to continue, but that was all she was going to get.

He sat down on the edge of the bed and touched her cheek. "Thank you for last night. It was pretty damned incredible." Finally, she was able to see past his reserve to the genuine warmth and affection in his eyes.

Her face heated. "That must have been all you. My sexual prowess ranks one notch above old-maid schoolteacher."

Curling a hand behind her neck, he pulled her close for a long, sweet kiss. "Don't underestimate your appeal, Emma."

His tongue stroked hers gently, raising gooseflesh on her arms. What would he do if she threw herself into his embrace and begged him to stay? She mimicked his caress, no longer shy about letting him see what he did to her. When she bit his lip gently, teasing him with the sharp nip of her teeth, he rested his forehead on hers.

"Don't start something," he muttered.

She winnowed her fingers through the silky hair at the back of his head. "Why not? It's still early."

"You have a store to open, and I have to get home and take a shower."

"I have a shower," she pointed out.

"I'm wearing a tux, Emma. If I have to do the walk of shame, I'd rather get it over with before there are too many witnesses out and about."

"Ah." She pondered that. "You don't have a vehicle."

"I'll call Liam to come get me at the coffee shop down the street. He'll give me hell, but at least I won't have to walk back."

"It's not the walking that's a problem, is it? You don't want people to know you spent the night in town."

He shrugged. "Small communities thrive on gossip. I'd prefer to keep my affairs private."

"Is that what this is?" she snapped. "An affair?"

"I wasn't using that context, and you know it."

"Honestly, I don't understand much about you at all. You're an enigma, Aidan. My own personal sphinx. Once upon a time I thought I knew you inside and out. But no more."

"And whose fault is that?"

They had gone from hot kisses to bickering at warp speed.

"I take it the suspension of hostilities is over?" Stubborn, stubborn man. Why wouldn't he listen? "In case you forgot, *you* were the one who came to my bed, not the other way around."

"I don't want to fight with you," he said, shoulders slumped, his tone rough with fatigue.

"Fine. Then leave. And don't worry. When we see each other tonight, I'll act as if I barely know you. After all, it's the truth."

For long, heated seconds their gazes dueled. Hers angry and defiant, his stony with indifference or bitterness or both. When the standoff seemed at a stalemate and there were no more words to be said, he turned on his heel and strode out of the bedroom. Slamming the apartment door behind him, he left her, his rapid steps loud on the staircase down to the street.

She bowed her head, raking her hands through her hair. That certainly wasn't how she'd planned to end one of the best nights of her adult life. Why did she have to provoke him? Why couldn't she be satisfied with the knowledge that he had wanted her enough to show up in the middle of the night despite his better judgment?

The pillow beside her still carried the imprint of his head. She picked it up and sniffed the crisp cotton pillowcase, inhaling his scent…warm male and expensive cologne. For a brief time, it appeared that his enmity had vanished in the mist. Reconciliation had seemed possible.

Truthfully, she was spinning dreams out of thin air. Aidan was a man. He wanted sex. She was available.

There was no more to it than that. Maybe before he went back to New York he would relent and let her clear her conscience. But based on tonight, she wouldn't bet on it.

Aidan had to endure a merciless ribbing from his older brother in exchange for a ride up the mountain. Though Liam poked and prodded and did his best to ferret out information, Aidan wouldn't be moved. It was bad enough that he had caved to temptation and ended up in Emma's bed. He wouldn't compound his mistake by letting his family know the history he shared with one of Silver Glen's newest residents.

Fortunately, by the time he cleaned up and changed clothes and headed out to Dylan's place, Dylan and Mia were more than happy to see him. Cora was not in the best of moods. The housekeeper was in the kitchen cooking all the side dishes that would accompany the meal.

Dylan was still insisting on barbecuing despite the outside temperature.

"I'll bring it all inside," he said. "When everything is done. It's no big deal."

Mia glared at him, the baby on her hip. "You're the *host* tonight, Dylan. And this party was your idea. Just because it's family doesn't mean you can hide out by the grill."

Aidan inserted himself as peacemaker, raising his eyebrows. "I thought you were the party animal among us, bro," he said. "What's with this burning desire to play chef?"

Dylan snickered. "Burning. Get it? Maybe no one trusts me with raw meat. Is that the problem?"

Mia put her foot down. "I am your *almost*-bride, Dylan. And I'd really like a bubble bath, a glass of wine and some downtime, not necessarily in that order. Instead of dragging out the grill, why can't you let Aidan handle the barbecuing later so that you can entertain Cora for a little while?"

Aidan shrugged. "She has a point. I'm here to help. Why not take advantage of my culinary skills and kick back?"

"I've seen you cook," Dylan pointed out. "You have a tendency to burn water."

Mia wasn't impressed. She hugged Aidan. "Thanks for offering. And we accept." She handed a cranky Cora over to the baby's adoptive father. "Don't disturb me unless the house is on fire."

Aidan chuckled as he followed his brother back to the sunroom. "That woman of yours is a firecracker. Plain paper wrapper on the outside, but when you get her ticked off...*boom*."

"Are you saying my wife is plain?"

"God, no," Aidan said, backpedalling. "She's amazing, of course. I only meant that she seems quiet and shy until you get to know her."

Dylan made a sound something like a harrumph. In the middle of the cozy, sun-warmed den, he reclined on the floor with the baby, letting her climb over him like a play gym.

Aidan sprawled in a recliner, telling himself he wasn't envious. He didn't want kids. Though they were cute as hell. He had almost dozed off when Dylan's voice snapped him back to attention.

"So how long are you going to grieve, Aidan? Danielle has been gone a long time. She wouldn't want you to wear sackcloth and ashes forever. You've honored her memory. It's time to move on, don't you think?"

Aidan swung a foot lazily, his leg draped over the arm of the chair. "What I *think* is that my whole damned family can't mind their own business. Do I look like I need help with my love life?"

"Who knows? Whenever any of us visits you in New York, you pretend to be living like a monk in that fancy-ass apartment of yours."

"I didn't know I needed to introduce the occasional female guest to my extended family."

Dylan tickled Cora's tummy. "Is there really no one you can see yourself settling down with?"

Aidan shook his head in amazement. "I can't believe it. You and Liam get hitched and suddenly you're handing out advice to the lovelorn. I'm okay, I swear. My life is perfect. And if it's ever not perfect, you'll be the first to know. Now, can we drop it?"

His brother eyed him suspiciously. "There's something to be said for getting laid every night."

"Hell, Dylan. You're impossible. I'll have you know

I did have sex last night." As soon as the words left his mouth, he realized what he had done. *Crap.*

Dylan perked up like a retriever spotting a quail. "Say what?"

"Nothing. Forget I mentioned it."

Dylan rolled to his feet, holding Cora like a football. "Now I get it."

"Get what?"

"You look like you've been up all night. Liam told me he had to pick you up in town this morning. And that you had given him some lame excuse about an early morning walk."

"The two of you gossip more than a couple of old biddies. Have you checked your testosterone lately? I think you may be a quart low."

"Do we get to hear about her? Is it anyone I know?"

"Nothing happened. Nothing at all."

Eleven

Fortunately for Emma, her day was full. With the sun shining, Christmas shoppers were out in force. She and Mrs. Correll barely had time to take a breath in between customers.

Mia called midafternoon. “I wanted to make sure you were still coming to my house this evening,” she said. “You left the party early last night, and I was afraid you were feeling bad.”

Emma blushed, even though her friend couldn’t see her. “I’m fine, honestly. I’ve been trying to pace myself.” Except for the several hours last night she spent making love to Aidan instead of sleeping. “Do you need me to bring anything?”

“We’ve got enough food to feed half of North Carolina, but if you wouldn’t mind coming an hour early, I’d love some help with my hair and makeup. Would that rush you too much?”

“Not at all. Mrs. Correll has offered to close up the shop today, so I can be there whenever you want me.”

Emma had been to Dylan and Mia’s house once before when she babysat little Cora. Even during this cold winter, she had to marvel at the home Dylan had built before he met Mia. The approach was a narrow lane flanked by weeping willows that in summer would create a foliage-lined tunnel. Today, though, the trees were sparse and bare.

As the house came into view, she sighed in envy. Dylan and his architect had created a magical, fairy tale of a place. The structure, built of mountain stone, dark timbers and copper, nestled amidst the grove of hardwood trees as if it had been there forever.

She parked in the area that had been roped off for cars and took one last look in the visor mirror. Coming face-to-face with Aidan was inevitable this evening, but even if they were going to ignore each other, she wanted to look her best.

The jersey dress she had ordered from England was comfortable and fit like a dream. The lace duster dressed it up and made the form-fitting fabric a bit more modest for a family dinner.

As she walked toward the front door, the unmistakable smell of meat cooking teased her nose, making her stomach growl. She'd grabbed a cup of yogurt for lunch, but that was a long time ago.

Mia answered the door herself. "Thank God you're here. Look what I've done to myself." She whipped the towel off her head.

Emma did her best to cover her shock, but it was bad. "Oh, dear..." She managed a smile. "We'll fix it. What did you do?"

"I was sick of having boring hair, and I didn't have time to make it to the salon, so I tried a home color—highlights actually. But all I got was this."

Emma winced inwardly. "Not to worry. But let's get started. We don't have much time."

Fortunately, the orangey red was mostly on the ends

of Mia's dark brown hair. Even so, this intervention was going to require desperate measures.

Aidan carried a tray of bison burgers into the kitchen and snagged a handful of potato chips before he went back out into the cold. Playing chef wasn't a bad gig, though. The down jacket he wore was plenty thick, and standing so close to the grill, even his hands were warm.

It wouldn't be long until his entire family came roaring down the lane. The momentary peace and quiet of a beautiful winter afternoon would get lost in the chaos. Even Cora was napping at the moment. And Dylan...who knew what Dylan was doing?

Seasoning and flipping meat didn't require much concentration. Aidan had plenty of time to think...and plenty to think about. Was Emma going to show up? Or had he been such an ass that she would decide to make an excuse to Mia and skip the whole thing?

He'd tried to speak to her before he came out to Dylan's. But when he parked in front of the antique shop, he could see through the window that her small business was packed with customers. Since he certainly didn't need an audience for a conciliatory conversation, he had put the car in gear and driven away.

After all, it wasn't as if anything he said to her last night wasn't true. But he felt bad for making her question her right to come to the party. She was Mia's friend, and Dylan and Mia could invite whomever they pleased to their dinner.

Aidan was the one with the problem, not Emma. Now, he had complicated his life even more by sleeping with the woman who had dropped back into his life so unexpectedly. Did he still wonder why she came to Silver Glen? Yes. Did he still want her? Yes.

The question was, what was he going to do about it? Already he felt himself softening toward her. Seeing her, talking to her, sleeping with her...all of that was dangerous. Clearly, Emma regretted the past. But he couldn't open himself up like that again.

Losing his father had left him to flounder in a world with too many temptations for a young boy. He'd missed his dad fiercely, but at the same time resented him for dying.

Aidan found Danielle in college and had latched on to her as if he had found his life's mate. But the magic had faded. That relationship ended in tragedy.

And then, there was Emma. Losing her had been the worst of all. He had learned his lesson. Emotional distance was key to his survival. Hats off to Liam and Dylan for committing to a future that held no guarantees. Aidan couldn't do it. Wouldn't do it. He'd had enough loss and suffering to last a lifetime.

He wanted Emma more than he wanted his next breath, but sharing her bed came with too many dangerous side effects. Emotions. Yearning. Hope. Hope for a different outcome this time.

If he had to go cold turkey to keep away from her, he'd simply have to do it. Last night had shown him a disturbing truth. He would never stop wanting Emma. And because being with her permanently was not in the cards, he had to protect himself. Even if Emma had some notion of getting back together—and that was a long shot—he was not interested.

He had to guard his impulses where she was concerned. Their interactions would take place only in public or amidst a crowd. That way he could avoid the temptation to share her bed again. He was a grown man, not a kid. Self-control was a product of maturity. Until it was time to go back to New York, celibacy was his friend.

The trouble was, everywhere he looked he could see her. In his mind's eye. Smiling at him. Flushed with pleasure. Arms outstretched to welcome him into her embrace. Her scent was in his head, the feel of her skin imprinted on his fingertips.

He poked at a half-done burger, scowling at it blindly. There was nothing special about Emma, other than her accent. If he still carried baggage from the past, it was only because he'd been an impressionable college kid, and she had made him feel like a man.

But he was smarter now. The sex last night was nothing out of the ordinary. No reason to think he was at risk for doing something stupid. He had enjoyed it, but it was over.

By the time Aidan finished his assigned task and carried the last of the main course into the kitchen, Dylan had come out of hiding and was talking to the housekeeper in between stealing bites of the appetizers. He took the heavy tray of meat from his brother. "Thanks, man. These look great."

"I guess we've got, what, twenty minutes until everyone shows up?"

"Maybe less. You know our crew. They can smell food from a mile away."

Before Aidan could respond, Emma appeared in the doorway. "I need to see you both in the living room, please."

Aidan frowned. "What's wrong?"

"Just come."

They followed her into the empty room. Emma, as always, looked effortlessly stylish. The form-fitting wine-colored dress she wore hugged her shape lovingly. If Aidan had his way, she would remove the lacy overdress thing so he could get a better look at her curves.

Dylan looked puzzled. "Where's Mia? I thought you were helping her get ready."

Emma wrinkled her nose and grimaced. "Mia had a little accident with some hair color." She fixed Dylan with a determined gaze. "You can't tease her about this, okay?"

"About what?"

"The color was dreadful, a cross between tomato-red and jack-o'-lantern-orange. We had no choice but to cut it off."

Aidan blanched. "You cut her hair?"

She shot him a look. "Not to worry. In boarding school we weren't allowed to go to the salon without our parents' permission. So anytime one of the girls wanted a new cut, I was the stylist."

Dylan firmed his jaw. "Is she crying? I want to see her."

Emma put a hand on his arm. "She's okay now. But the new 'do' is short. She wants you to see it before your guests arrive. But don't make a big deal, okay?" She turned to Aidan. "And when your family begins to show up, it would be nice if you could give them the same message."

"Of course."

Emma walked toward the bedrooms. "Hang on. I'll go get her."

Moments later a hesitant Mia appeared from around the corner. Her eyes went immediately to Dylan. "I feel like a fool." Her bottom lip trembled visibly.

Dylan put a hand over his heart. "Holy hell, woman. That is so hot." He went to her and feathered his fingers lightly over the ends of the pixie cut. "We may have to cancel the party," he said in a stage whisper, kissing the side of her neck.

Though Mia's eyes were pink-rimmed, she smiled and threw her arms around his neck. "I love you, Dylan."

He lifted her off her feet in a bear hug. "And I adore you, my sexy little fairy. Your hair is beautiful."

She pulled back, her gaze dubious. "You really think so?"

"I'll show you later," he muttered.

Aidan watched Emma, who was watching Mia and Dylan. On Emma's face was a wistful look that said she found the bridal couple's byplay romantic. Of course, that was a woman for you. Always suckers for a happy ending. Too bad those same women didn't realize life was seldom so tidy.

He glanced out the front window. "Car number one. Looks like Mom's. I'll go meet everybody if you two want a moment alone."

Mia smiled at him. "Thank you, Aidan, but I'm fine." She smoothed the skirt of her black dress, looking up at the man who would soon be placing a wedding ring on her finger. "Dylan and I are the hosts tonight. We should go greet our guests."

The two of them hurried away, arm in arm, leaving Aidan alone with Emma for the first time since he'd left her bed early that morning. "I stopped by to see you this afternoon," he said, "but the shop was really busy, so I didn't go in."

She perched on the arm of a chair. "I'm sorry I wasn't available."

"How's your head?"

"I'm still taking over-the-counter stuff for the headache, but it's not bad."

The stilted conversation was almost painful. Only hours ago they had been naked together. The mental image made his skin heat. "Last night was amazing, but it can't happen again."

"Why not?" She was pale, her expression mutinous.

"I'll be leaving soon. There's no future for us, Emma."

"Because you've decreed it?"

"Is that why you came here?" he asked. "To start over with me?"

"Not in the beginning. I was telling you the truth. I wanted to make my peace with you. To explain the past. But now that I've seen you again…now that we've made love…well, I have to wonder if there's something left between us. Something that never died."

"There isn't."

"Liar." She said it calmly, as if she could see inside the tortured recesses of his soul. "If you can kiss me and prove to me that you feel nothing at all for me, I'll leave you alone."

He held out his arms. "Do your best. It's sex, Emma. That's all. And I can get that from any woman. The young man you remember so fondly doesn't exist anymore."

"You're trying to make me angry by acting like a pig."

"Is it working?"

When she stood, the skin at his nape tingled. Emma on a mission was a formidable opponent. But he knew something she didn't. He knew that resisting temptation was not a choice. It was his only defense.

She crossed to where he stood and went nose-to-nose with him, although her nose was admittedly a few inches lower…almost at his collarbone, in fact.

He stared straight ahead, trying not to inhale her scent.

"This isn't fair," she complained. "I can't reach you. Sit down." She poked him in the chest until he took a step backward and sat down hard, hands behind him, on the edge of a beautiful oak table behind the sofa.

Now, their heights were much closer. The dress she wore had a scooped neck that revealed modest amounts of cleavage…but only if he let his gaze fall. His fingers gripped wood until pain shot up his wrists.

"Do your worst," he said, staring at her chin. His throat was so dry the words came out hoarse.

Emma leaned in. "You are a ridiculously handsome man," she murmured. "Gorgeous lips. Masculine. Sexy. Here goes…"

She pressed her mouth to his. Nothing happened except for his blood pressure shooting up about twenty points. *Focus. Focus.*

The first few seconds were barely a challenge. Her kiss was chaste, almost sweet. Nothing he couldn't handle.

Then she curled a hand behind his neck, her fingertips slipping inside the collar of his shirt to scrape deliberately across the bump at the top of his spine. *Sweet mother of God.*

Warm breath ticked his ear when she whispered. "How am I doing so far?"

He shrugged, his jaw so tight his head ached. "I've had better."

Emma's low chuckle was intensely sexual. He found himself getting hard despite his fierce concentration.

She came back to the kiss and put her all into it. When she nipped his bottom lip with sharp teeth, he gasped, giving her an opening to slide her tongue against his. Her taste went to his gut like raw liquor on an empty stomach. Hell, this was a pointless game.

He grabbed her close and angled her chin with one hand. The shock in her blue eyes gave him an enormous jolt of satisfaction. "You're an amateur," he said. "But I give you points for enthusiasm."

Then it was his turn. If he were going to admit defeat, he would drag her down with him. Pulling her fully into the V of his legs, he simply snapped. Everything he had tried to keep to himself, every needy, greedy urge to plunder, was unleashed.

Ten years of memories, of wondering, of futile anger and grief, coalesced into a white-hot need to make Lady Emma Braithwaite his. "Don't think you've won," he croaked. "This means nothing."

Her eyes brimmed with moisture, the look on her face a mixture of tenderness and wonder. "I understand," she said quietly. "Whatever you say, Aidan. Whatever you want."

Cupping her breast in his hand, he stroked the nipple through its soft covering. "I want you. Now."

Before Emma could say a word in denial or consent, a loud noise nearby shattered the mood, the one sound guaranteed to stifle a man's ardor.

Maeve's Kavanagh's cheerful greeting…"We're all here. Let the party begin."

Twelve

For Emma, the next two hours took on a surreal quality. The mood in the house was joyful and rowdy, rightly so. The Kavanaghs en masse created a special kind of magic. One of their own was tying the knot, and in true Irish fashion, they were prepared to party all night.

Despite Emma's efforts to stay in the background, Mia insisted on making sure she met everyone individually. The festive gathering at the hotel had been much larger and more formal. Tonight, however, was a time for one-on-one conversations, sibling jokes and eating.

Emma had been taken aback at the amount of food laid out buffet-style, sure they would never consume half of it. But she had underestimated the appetite of a full-grown Kavanagh male. Amidst much good-natured jostling and name-calling everyone filled his or her plate and found a seat.

Dylan's mission-style dining room table, with leaves inserted, was big enough to handle the whole crew in one sitting. Emma took a spot at the far end and across the table from Aidan. She had promised not to embarrass him, and despite what had happened moments before the party began, she was determined not to give anyone cause to think she and Aidan were a couple.

Her interactions with him were complicated enough

already without other people butting in and offering their opinions. Apparently Aidan had come to the same conclusion, because he barely acknowledged Emma's presence. It was Mia who offered her a seat, Mia who involved her in the conversations that bounced back and forth during the meal.

Cora sat in a high chair at one corner, her chubby cheeks red with excitement. It was probably too much stimulation for a little one near bedtime, but Dylan and Mia had wanted to include her.

Each of the younger Kavanagh men had brought a date. As far as Emma could tell, the females in question were casual connections at best, because all four of them had to be introduced to the group.

The only unattached members of the dinner party were Maeve and Cora, Aidan and Emma. At first, Emma was on edge. But when she realized that no one was inclined to ask awkward questions, she relaxed.

It was almost unbelievable that every single one of Aidan's siblings was tall, broad-shouldered and dangerously attractive. The deceased Mr. Kavanagh must have been a fine figure of a man. Only the youngest, James, looked more like his mother.

Emma had been reared in *polite* society. By the time she was ten, she knew how to comport herself at an afternoon tea or a grown-up dinner party. Although tonight's gathering was much less stuffy, the Kavanaghs were a sophisticated lot, well traveled, well read and comfortable with the trappings of wealth.

The discussions of books, movies, politics and the world in general were stimulating. After a while, Emma felt comfortable enough to jump in and be a part of the occasional debate. Aidan, on the other hand, remained oddly silent. He nodded and answered when asked a direct question, but he was content to nurse a beer and observe the proceedings with a small smile on his face. From where Emma sat, his little grin seemed to encompass love for his family and an enjoyment of their eccentricities.

When the housekeeper took Cora, ready to put her to bed, Liam held up a hand. "One moment please, Gertie." He stood and picked up his wineglass. "We're gathered here tonight to celebrate the upcoming marriage of my brother Dylan to the beautiful and much-too-good-for-him Mia."

A wave of laughter greeted his statement.

He carried on, looking at Mia with warmth and affection. "Mia…when my brothers and I asked Dylan what kind of bachelor party he wanted tonight, his answer was *none*."

Dylan's face turned red. He ducked his chin.

Liam shook his head, smiling. "He told us everything in the world he wanted was under this very roof. And that the two days when you and Cora become official Kavanaghs will be the happiest of his life."

Every female around the table, Emma included, gave an audible sigh…*awwww*. For the first time during the meal, Aidan looked straight at Emma and rolled his eyes with a humorous expression. She shrugged, not about to apologize for appreciating romance.

"To Mia and Dylan." Liam held his glass toward the happy couple. The toast echoed around the table.

"To Mia and Dylan."

Maeve had tears in her eyes as she gave Cora a quick kiss. When the housekeeper departed with the baby, Maeve remained standing. "This is a party," she said. "So I won't belabor the point. But I want to say that I have the most wonderful sons in the world. And adding

Zoe and Mia to our family has been a joy." She paused, moving her gaze from Aidan to Gavin, Patrick, Conor and James. "But the rest of you..."

The men all groaned, as if they knew what was coming next.

Maeve ignored their response. "I'm not getting any younger," she said, managing to look frail and needy despite the fact that she was a vibrant woman in perfect health. "You young women be careful. The Kavanagh male is a slippery species. I'd love to have half a dozen grandchildren while I'm still able to enjoy them."

Catcalls and hoots and hollers ended her pseudo-pitiful speech. Laughter erupted again as she was forced to sit down in defeat. But the broad smile on her face told Emma she was perfectly happy to sit back and watch her sons find worthy matches.

Emma wondered if she understood exactly how unlikely that was in Aidan's case.

By unanimous consent, the group moved to the large, comfortable living room. A roaring fire warmed the space and cast a circle of intimacy. Again, Emma stayed far away from Aidan.

This time the conversation turned to less personal topics. Gavin's date mentioned spending Christmas in Zurich with her family. Emma, seated beside her, sighed. "It sounds like a wonderful trip. I've heard the skiing there is awesome. Actually, now that I've moved to Silver Glen, I was hoping to learn how to ski myself."

Without warning, a dead hush fell over the group. Like Sleeping Beauty's castle under a wicked spell, everyone in the room froze. What had Emma said? She replayed her innocent statements in her head. They hardly seemed the kind of words to provoke such a response. Though the women who sat with Aidan's younger brothers appeared confused, no one could miss the uneasy silence. The expressions on Kavanagh faces ranged from dismay to outright alarm.

Maeve suddenly looked her age, and Mia's distress was palpable. *What did I do?* Emma wondered frantically. In desperation, she looked to Aidan for help. He stood up, never once looking her way, his face carved in granite. "If you'll excuse me..."

No one said a word as he left the room. Thirty seconds later, the front door of the house opened and closed quietly.

Emma swallowed. "I'm sorry," she said. "But what just happened?"

Liam heaved a sigh, his expression a combination of resignation and worry. "Come with me to the kitchen, Emma."

She followed him out of the room with her heart thumping like mad. When they were out of earshot, she leaned against the sink. "What in the heck is going on? What's wrong with Aidan?"

"It's not your fault." Liam ran both hands through his hair. "You stepped on an emotional land mine."

"I don't understand."

"Aidan never comes home at Christmas. When he was younger, he brought his fiancée to Silver Glen at the holidays to meet the family. While they were here, she and Aidan went skiing. Danielle fell and hit her head. She died forty-eight hours later without ever waking up from a coma."

"Oh, my God." Emma's stomach heaved. "I'm so sorry."

"You had no way of knowing. He's been on edge since he left New York. Coming here...in December...has been a strain. But he wouldn't miss Dylan's wedding."

"I'm going to go talk to him."

"Probably not a good idea. When a man is hurting, he wants to hide and lick his wounds."

"I've ruined the party, Liam. I should go."

Liam touched her shoulder. "Nothing is ruined, Emma. Aidan will be okay. He needs a little time to regroup, that's all."

Mia wandered into the kitchen, her face troubled. "Did Liam tell you?"

Emma nodded, her throat too tight to answer.

Mia hugged her and then stepped back. "I should have warned you, I guess. Dylan told me how bad it was back then. My heart breaks for Aidan. He's never been serious about anyone since."

"I see." Emma swallowed hard, on the verge of tears. "Thank you for inviting me tonight," she whispered. "I'm going to see if I can find him and apologize."

"It might make things worse," Liam said.

He was probably right, but Emma couldn't bear the thought of Aidan wandering cold and alone on a night that was supposed to be a celebration. "Maybe," she said. "But I have to try."

Mia nodded. "I'd want to do the same."

"Please tell Dylan I'm sorry," Emma said.

"Don't be ridiculous. I'm so glad you were here. Mom and Dad and my friends from Raleigh aren't arriving until a few hours before the ceremony tomorrow, so it's been nice having some emotional backup."

"Hey," said Liam, his tone aggrieved. "*We* love you."

Mia kissed his cheek. "I know you do. But sometimes a woman needs a break from all that testosterone."

Emma walked to where her vehicle was parked, her feet crunching on the frost-covered grass. The truth was, she had no good plan to look for Aidan…none at all. When she made it back to town, she cruised the darkened streets, trying to spot his fancy sports car. She even made a pass through the parking lot of the Silver Dollar Saloon. But no Aidan.

Driving up the mountain was her last shot. Aidan was staying at the lodge, true, but there was at least a possibility that he had left town. When she handed her keys to the valet and stepped out, she shivered. The wind had picked up, making the night seem even colder. She bundled her coat around her, hurrying up the steps of the hotel.

In the lobby, she paused. Aidan might be outside, though it was unlikely. The young man working the desk tonight was an employee she didn't recognize, so that might be to her advantage.

She approached him casually, removing her coat and straightening her dress and duster. "Hello," she said, beaming him a bright smile. "I'm trying to catch up with Mr. Kavanagh, Aidan Kavanagh," she clarified. "Did you happen to see him go up to his room earlier?"

The barely twenty-something blinked, seeming dazzled by her deliberately cozy manner. "Yes, ma'am," he said. "About an hour ago. May I ring his room for you?"

Emma reached in her purse and pressed a large bill into his hand. "No, thank you. He's expecting me."

Leaving the flustered clerk to ponder the fact that he might have been indiscreet, Emma headed for the elevator. She had no clue what she was going to say to Aidan or how she could make things better, but she had to try. The memory of his face as he left the party hurt her deeply.

Stepping out of the elevator, she paused a moment. The elegant hallway was quiet. It was possible that some guests had retired for the night, though unlikely. Even still, she didn't have the luxury of making a scene.

At Aidan's door, she knocked softly and listened for any sound inside his room. Nothing. Knocking harder, she held her breath, praying that he wouldn't ignore her.

At last, she was pretty sure she heard him on the other side of the door. She knocked a third time. "I know you're in there, Aidan. Let me come in. Please."

Thirteen

Aidan unlocked the door with a sense of fatalism and swung it open, stepping back to allow Emma to enter. She would not leave until she was satisfied that he was okay. It was his own damned fault for reacting so viscerally to her innocent observations. But somehow, the thought of Emma on a ski slope had made his heart stop and his stomach revolt.

No surprise, really, given his past with her. But she didn't need to know that. His job now was to convince her that he was fine…that he'd had a momentary crisis, but it had passed.

He saw her glance at the whiskey decanter. "I'm not drowning my sorrows," he said, leaning heavy on the sarcasm.

"I didn't say that."

"But you were thinking it."

She removed her coat and tossed it on a chair. Only hours before he had been holding her, his body taut with need. What he wouldn't give to rewind the clock and pretend this evening had never happened.

"I'm so sorry, Aidan."

He shrugged, her sympathy about as comfortable to him as a hair shirt. "It's no big deal. I was caught off guard, that's all."

And stunned at the thought that you could die...just like poor Danielle.

"It was more than that, and you know it." She cupped his face in her hands, her eyes filled with tears. "I can't imagine how horrible it must have been for you...losing someone you loved that way. No wonder Christmas is a bad time."

He couldn't bear her touch. Not now. He was raw inside. "Feel free to go," he said, pushing her hands away along with her gentle empathy. "As you can see, I'm neither drunk nor high and I have no plans to harm myself in a dramatic show of grief."

Turning his back, he paced the room, wondering how long it would take to get rid of her. The longer she stayed, the more he wanted her. And he'd done enough stupid things for one night.

Emma curled up in a chair. "Tell me about Danielle," she said softly. "What was she like?"

He continued to traverse the room, in danger of wearing a path in the carpet. Talking to Emma about Danielle was both ironic and terribly sad. "She was delightful," he said, casting back for memories. "A good person in every sense of the word. She threw herself into life with abandon—charming, funny, always kind to those who were out of step with the world."

"She sounds like a lovely woman."

"She was. I never heard her say an unkind word about anyone."

"How long had the two of you been together?"

"Four years."

Emma winced visibly. "And the accident?"

He didn't want to go there. But that moment was as vivid in his mind as if it had happened yesterday. Some days he thought he would never be able to erase the recollection. So why did it matter if he told Emma at least part of the truth?

"Liam told you, I guess, that I brought Danielle home to meet my family. It was December, and the town was decked out for the holidays. Danielle fell in love with Silver Glen."

"That doesn't surprise me. Who could resist?"

"True. At any rate, we had been here a couple of days when we got a surprise. An early snowfall, almost six inches. Conor and I were jazzed. We made plans to go skiing and took Danielle with us."

"Had she skied before?"

"She knew *how* to ski, but she wasn't very good at it, and it had been a long time. So we kept to the easy runs, not quite the bunny slopes, but close. She regained her confidence finally, and we decided to tackle something a little more challenging. Conor went first. Then Danielle. I brought up the rear. About halfway down, she lost her balance and careened off the course, headed for a clump of trees. I heard her laughing, and then she screamed, and then she crumpled in a broken heap on the ground."

He wasn't looking at Emma as he struggled through the dark tale. So he was startled when he felt her arms come around him.

She pressed her cheek to his chest. "I can't even imagine what you went through. How dreadful."

"We got her down the mountain with the help of the ski patrol, but she was unconscious. At the hospital, they determined that the blow to her head had caused a massive brain bleed. She never woke up. Two days later, she was dead."

Emma hugged him so tightly he thought his ribs would crack. He rested his chin on the top of her head. He knew Emma was crying…for him. He wished he could cry, too. But he had buried his wounds and his emotions so deeply they were fossilized.

"There's more," he said, the two words hoarse.

She took him by the hand and drew him to the sofa. He sprawled in the corner and draped an arm around her shoulders when she nestled close.

"You don't have to do this," she said. "I've heard enough."

"But not the worst part. There's something I've never told anyone."

"You can trust me with your secret." She squeezed his hand.

"I was the one who thought Danielle should come with us. I'll never forget asking her. She was curled up by the fire—wrapped in a cozy afghan, reading. I told her the plan, but she said for me to go on with my brother…that she was perfectly happy to sit with her book and enjoy a quiet morning."

Emma moved restlessly, perhaps sensing what was to come. But she didn't speak.

"I'm to blame," he said, shuddering inwardly. "I begged her to go with us. Told her how much fun it would be. And in the end, I won her over."

"Oh, Aidan."

He ignored the loaded comment.

"It was my fault she died. I have to live with that."

Emma sat in silence, her world in ashes. Aidan hadn't lied to her after all. When he told her the sex was only sex, it had been the truth. Because he was still in love with his dead fiancée.

He might not realize it. But she heard the emotional pain in his words…heard him describe Danielle with such love and affection. And because his grief was so all-encompassing and so deep, he had been unable to move on.

Clearly, coming to Silver Glen at Christmas for his brother's wedding was a decision he had made at great personal cost. Every Christmas tree and wreath and sprig of holly must be a bitter reminder of all he had lost.

His reaction, more than anything, told Emma she'd never had a chance at rekindling their old romance. There was nothing to rekindle. She was the only one who had kept the glow of a youthful relationship alive. For a man to love so faithfully and so well that he still grieved years later and continued to carry a load of guilt, meant that his heart was not his own. He had buried it with Danielle.

She cleared her throat. "Thank you for telling me. She must have been a very special woman."

Suddenly, everything seemed awkward. Should she go…leave him to his own devices? Or should she stay to give him comfort…any kind of comfort she could offer?

Aidan sat up and rested his elbows on his knees, his head in his hands. "Did I upset Dylan and Mia?"

Emma chose her words carefully. "If you're asking was the party ruined…no. But of course your family is worried about you. We could go back if you want."

"God, no." His rough laugh held no humor at all. "I did enough damage earlier. I'm sure they don't need me throwing a damper on things. I'll have an early night, and tomorrow I'll make it up to them somehow. I feel like an idiot."

She touched his arm. "You're a man who cares deeply. Nothing wrong with that." Since she still had not resolved her inner struggle, she rose to her feet. "I should go now. I'll see you at the wedding tomorrow." She put a hand on his shoulder. "I'm really sorry. About Danielle, I mean."

He stood and faced her. "Will you think it incredibly crass if I ask you to stay tonight?"

She searched his eyes, looking for any indication that he truly wanted her. Was it enough to know that she would be giving him comfort in a way no one else could at the moment? "I thought you said physical intimacy between the two of us was a bad idea."

"It's been a hell of an evening. Being rational is not high on my list at the moment. But you're free to say no. I would say no to me if I were you."

The humor was weak, but it was there. He had turned a corner. "I don't believe saying *no* to you is my strong suit."

He curled a strand of her hair around his finger. "I want to make one thing clear before we go any further..."

"Okay." She braced inwardly.

"When I went all psycho tonight, it wasn't only because I was remembering Danielle's accident. It was also a gut-deep reaction to the idea that you could get hurt. You mean something to me, Emma. Maybe it's not what it was in the past, and maybe it's not what you deserve, but I do have feelings, despite my efforts to the contrary."

Her heart warmed more than it should have. His eyes were filled with *something*. Affection? Attraction? What self-respecting female went to bed with a man who was in love with another woman? Was she a masochist?

"You mean something to me as well. But you should know that I don't expect anything beyond tonight. I want to be with you. If that brings us both pleasure, that's reason enough."

Fourteen

Aidan was so deeply enmeshed in his lies of omission that he couldn't even *reach* the moral high ground, much less stand on it. He was too busy protecting himself from Emma. And now…tonight…with deliberate intent, he was going to take what she was offering and damn the consequences.

When Emma mentioned skiing earlier, it *did* bring back the past and Danielle's accident. But what had really prompted his abrupt departure was a vicious jolt of panic at the thought that the world could lose Emma as well.

For the last ten years, in the midst of anger and grief and frustration with himself for still caring about her, at least he had known that somewhere on the planet she was alive and well.

He hadn't truly realized until this evening that if she were to die, he couldn't bear it. Emma married to another man and happy with babies? That, he could wrap his head around. But dead? Like Danielle? The notion was unfathomable.

Gripping one of her wrists, he reeled her into his embrace. "I have fantasies about your hair," he muttered.

"My hair?" A little squiggle of a frown appeared between her brows. "Surely you can do better than that."

"Oh, no," he said, drawing her toward the bedroom

before she could change her mind. "It's a guy thing. The more you pin and twist and tuck it, the more I want to muss you up."

She laughed softly. "Be my guest. This fancy updo is giving me a headache anyway."

Once they crossed the threshold into the inner room of the suite, he closed the door and leaned against it. A single small lamp cast an intimate circle of light. Emma eyed him warily, perhaps wondering if he were in his right mind. Maybe he was and maybe he wasn't. Ever since the moment he came face-to-face with her in the emergency room, he had questioned his sanity.

Ten years ago she had betrayed him and made a fool of him, and yet at the same time she had been the center of his world for three amazing months. Now, the good memories battled the bad, as if trying to convince him that the past was the past…that the future held endless possibilities.

Emma had asked again and again for the chance to explain her actions. To make amends. To request absolution. He had shut her down every time she tried.

Should he let her speak of that terrible day? Let her attempt to make sense of it? Or did it even matter from the vantage point of a decade in time? He was a man. He understood that life included disappointments. The blessings of family and friends were balanced with the inevitable struggles of living. Not that all struggles were as tragic as Danielle's death.

Shaking his head slightly, he decided such questions could wait. Emma wasn't going anywhere. Maybe he would let her open the door to the past. But not here. And not now.

"Come closer, my English rose," he muttered, unbuttoning his shirt and pulling it free of his pants. When he shrugged out of it and tossed it toward the closet, Emma's eyes widened.

She sighed, lips parted, as she obeyed his command. Placing her hands flat on his chest, she flicked his flat, copper-colored nipples with sharp fingernails. The tiny stings of pain arrowed to his groin and joined the rush of arousal that already had his sex lifting to attention.

"I won't regret this," she said softly. "I'm glad we had this chance to see each other again. Maybe we both needed closure."

He didn't like the finality in her description, even though he'd been the one to say they had no future. "You talk too much," he said, only half-joking. He didn't want to *think* tonight. All he wanted was to feel her body straining against his.

Without asking, he pulled the pins from her hair one at a time and dropped them into a crystal dish. Each small *clink* was quiet music to his ears. When he was done, he used both hands to winnow through her hair, separating the strands and smoothing the wavy tresses. "That's better," he said softly.

The prelude to sex was easier this time, more natural. Removing Emma's clothes was a reverent task not to be rushed. When he had her down to a set of ultrafeminine undies and bra, he finished his own disrobing. Lowering the zipper on his slacks was tricky. His erection bobbed thick and eager as he eased it free of confinement.

Together, they climbed into the enormous hedonistic bed. The Silver Beeches Lodge spared no expense when it came to their guests' comfort. Whether for sleep or more intimate pursuits, the bedding and mattress provided an island of physical bliss.

He leaned over Emma on one elbow, studying the dewy perfection of her skin. Maybe something about the air and water in the British Isles produced this exquisite variety of female.

"Tell me one of *your* fantasies," he said. "Something naughty you've always wanted to do but never had the chance."

Her instant, cheeky grin made him shiver. She sighed. "I've always wanted to have sex in a lift."

"A lift?" All the blood in his head had rushed south, making him slow to comprehend.

"You know…an elevator. Preferably one with glass on the top half. So people watching might have a clue as to what's happening, but wouldn't know for sure."

He gaped at her. "Emma. You wicked girl."

Her shrug was epic. "You asked."

"So I did." And now all he could think about was where such an elevator might exist. Certainly not in the town of Silver Glen. "I'm going to forget you said that," he muttered. "Although getting the image out of my head will be hard."

"You said *hard*." She snickered. "Is that a Freudian slip?"

He touched her smooth thigh, running his hand from her knee to the crevice where leg joined torso. Her underwear was tiny and sexy. Twisting a finger in the side band, he snapped it deliberately. "Freud might want to study my caveman tendencies." Tugging the small piece of fabric to uncover her secrets, he nudged her hip. "Lift your butt."

Now she was completely bare from the waist down. He took the opportunity to tease her with kisses that ranged from playful to deliberately sexual.

Emma moved restlessly, her hands gripping his head. "Aidan."

"Hmmm…?" Her taste was exquisite.

"I want to do something."

"Pretty sure we're already doing it."

"I'm serious."

He winced when she pulled his hair. "Okay, okay." Rolling to his back, he turned his head to look at her. "You have my attention."

Emma, in turn, surprised the hell out of him by moving agilely and straddling his waist. "I want to take care of you tonight," she said. "Will you let me?"

Her body was a pleasant weight at his hips. "I'm not sure what you mean."

She leaned forward, her lace-covered breasts in kissing distance, and took his wrists in her hands. "I want you to grab hold of the spindles in the headboard. We don't have anything to tie you with, so you'll have to promise not to let go."

A fresh current of arousal flooded his veins. "Please don't tell me being a dominatrix is on your bucket list. I'll never believe it." People often made jokes in tense situations. This definitely counted. "A lady never acts out of character," he said. "I think you've been reading too many erotic novels."

"I'm not always a lady, Aidan. Perhaps you don't know me as well as you think."

Well, hell's bells. That shut him up. With her small hands guiding his wrists, he found the slender pieces of wood and wrapped his fingers around two of them. The stretch in his shoulders was pleasant. So far.

"What next?" he asked, trying to gauge her mood.

Emma shifted her weight back to his hips again. Her expression defied analysis. Not uncertainty. More like assessment. He wasn't sure if that aroused him or worried him. In all honesty, a bit of both.

"Are you comfortable?" she asked, her hands flat on

her thighs. Considering that her lady parts were tantalizingly close to his rigid sex, it was a loaded question.

"Yes."

She nodded once. "Good. Now close your eyes."

"Um..." He flexed his feet, his toes cold.

"Are you afraid of me, Aidan?" Her question could have been flirtatious, but the tone suggested she was serious.

"Should I be?" he asked, dodging the truth.

"I want to make you feel good...that's all. No need for alarm. You can trust me."

He wondered if this were some kind of test. To prove to him that she had changed. "I'm in your hands. Be gentle with me."

His half-hearted teasing didn't even coax a smile from her. "I'm waiting for you to close your eyes." She said it patiently in the tone of someone dealing with a stubborn toddler.

"Are you going to ditch the bra?" he asked hopefully. The pastel lace was mostly transparent, but that didn't mean he didn't want to uncover what was underneath. He simply hadn't gotten to it when she turned the tables so unexpectedly.

Emma shrugged. "It won't matter," she said softly. "You won't be able to see."

The simple statement struck him as a threat, even though there was nothing of menace in the words. Apparently, his trust issues went deeper than he realized. Now that he thought about it, he'd never allowed any woman this kind of physical control.

He'd played naughty games with females in the past, but Aidan had always wielded the power. From this side of the metaphorical whip, he felt distinctly uneasy. But he wasn't about to reveal his reservations. Not at this particular moment.

Inhaling a deep gulp of air that lifted his chest, he let it out slowly as he closed his eyes and tightened his grip.

Fifteen

Aidan Kavanagh was an extraordinarily masculine and beautiful man. Though he had complied with her orders, Emma sat motionless for a moment, enjoying the tableau. His skin was lightly tanned, the hair on his torso and beneath his arms a shade darker than his deep brown locks with the hint of fire in them.

With his arms extended above his head, she could see the tendons and muscles that delineated his strength. Broad shoulders and a hair-dusted chest tapered to a trim waist, flat stomach and below...*Oh, lordy...*

His sex, though still somewhat turgid, lay against his thigh. Perhaps her offer to make him feel good was ambiguous enough to make it difficult for him to relax.

"I'm going to start with a massage," she said quietly.

Aidan made no response, but he muttered something inaudible.

Scooting up onto his chest, she leaned forward until she could reach his wrists. Pressing her thumbs to his pulse, she dug into his flesh and ran a path all the way to the crook of his elbows. Then, using both hands on one arm at a time, she worked her way from his elbow to his upper arm.

Perhaps because of the posture she insisted he adopt, his shoulder muscles were tight. She spent some time there, finding knots and working them out. It might have been easier if he had been on his stomach, but she wanted to watch his face.

At one point, he flinched. "Too hard?" she asked. One of her college friends had studied sports medicine, and Emma had picked up tips from her. But sometimes people couldn't take too firm a pressure.

"Your *assets* are in my face."

"Ah." She blushed, though he couldn't see her. "Almost done with this part." She moved on to his neck and behind his ears. As her hands warmed his skin, she inhaled the smell of him…the yummy *guy* aroma that made a girl's knees weak and led to all sorts of improper thoughts.

The next bit was very personal. Letting her fingertips glide gently, she feathered her way across his forehead, down his nose and cheeks, along his chin and over his firm jaw to his throat.

Aidan's Adam's apple bobbed visibly when she pressed lightly where his pulse beat in the side of his neck. Moving to his collarbone, she stroked it slowly. As she shifted back a couple of inches so she could reach his chest, she realized that his sex was no longer at rest. It was firm and erect and bumped her bottom eagerly.

From this particular angle, she could have joined their bodies easily. But there was time for that later. She concentrated on rubbing his chest, tracing his rib cage, following the line of his sternum.

She saw his tongue come out to wet his lips. It seemed as if his breathing had picked up in tempo. At one time, she'd had the freedom to touch Aidan however and whenever she wanted, knowing that every brush of skin made them both drunk with happiness and arousal.

For one painful moment, the stab of grief consumed

her. Even if Aidan eventually forgave her for the past, they would never be the same two people. What they had shared at Oxford was exhilarating. They had been young and in love and frightfully full of themselves.

Determined to forget the past, she moved quickly, avoiding Aidan's straining erection and settling in between his legs. She heard him curse, possibly because he thought she had been preparing to join their bodies by sliding down onto his shaft.

She crouched on her knees. Avoiding his groin area, she rubbed his hipbones. His thighs were next, then his bony knees, his calves, his ankles and finally his big feet. When she slid her fingers between his toes, his back arched off the bed.

"Enough," he wheezed.

"I'm trying to relax you. These are standard massage techniques."

"Screw that." He sat up, raking his hands through his hair. His eyes glittered with desire. "Either your technique sucks, or when you touch me I go insane. I'm betting on the latter."

"Oh." She'd been trying to calm him, to make him feel good after a crappy evening. "I didn't even touch your..."

"My penis?" he offered helpfully.

Frowning at him, she eased back onto her bottom and pretzeled her legs. "I don't like that word."

"It's a perfectly good word...unless you prefer di—"

She slapped a hand across his mouth. "I prefer not to talk about it at all. I'm more into *doing*."

One side of his mouth kicked up in a grin. "Happy to oblige." He mimicked her position, then took her hands and tucked them around his shaft. "Feel free to massage this poor neglected body part."

It was her turn to swallow. His sex was proportionally large, the shaft veined and strong, the head weeping for her. "I don't think they covered this in the manuals," she muttered.

When she ran her thumb beneath the flange and used her other hand to squeeze, Aidan's eyes rolled back in his head. Well, they might have. She didn't exactly know since his face was scrunched up and his lashes fanned out against his cheeks.

So far, so good. "You really are tense," she breathed.

Despite his advanced state of arousal, Aidan laughed, opening his eyes to look at her with a glazed expression. "*Tense* doesn't even begin to describe it. You have an unfair advantage with that upper crust British accent. Everything out of your mouth sounds like a sexual come-on."

"Close your eyes, naughty boy," she said, channeling her old headmistress. "I'm not done yet."

Emma might not be done, but Aidan was almost there. His skin was so sensitive to the touch that it hurt. He took her hand and removed it from the trigger. "Not like this, Emma. I want to be inside you."

Her lower lip pouted the tiniest bit. "I wanted to make you feel good," she said.

He groaned, shaking his head in bemusement. "Mission accomplished. Now turn around."

"Why?"

"Don't you trust me?"

"Not funny, Kavanagh."

"Don't be so prissy. I'm only going to undo you." When she gave him her back, he unfastened the band of her bra carefully and slid the straps down her shoulders. "There. Now was that so bad?"

She faced him again, her breasts high and firm and

beautiful. Although she had been bold when his eyes were closed, now she seemed hesitant…even shy. He cupped one breast in his hand. "You don't have to stay. I'm fine." Why he was giving her the chance to leave, he wasn't sure. But it seemed somehow important.

She took his free hand and held it to her cheek. "I don't want to leave, Aidan."

"Are you staying because you feel sorry for me?" The thought of her sympathy chafed.

But she shook her head vigorously. "I'd be lying if I said yes. I really did want to make you feel better, but the real reason is selfish."

He cocked his head. "Tell me. Please."

Pale, narrow shoulders lifted and fell. "I want to feel it again."

"It?"

"The high. At the risk of giving you a swelled ego, you're very good at satisfying a woman sexually."

Her explanation was not what he expected to hear. It seemed impersonal and cold. Though paradoxically, he and Emma were anything but at the moment. Hunger sizzled between them. It seemed, however, as if they were reading from a script, both of them afraid to speak the truth.

Refusing to acknowledge her confession, bogus or not, he took her with him under the covers. Their arms and legs tangled. "I want you, Emma. You have no idea how much."

She nestled against him. "I want you, too, Aidan."

Still, he felt dissatisfied. Perhaps this was payback for the way he had insisted that anything physical between them was *only* sex. Who had he been trying to convince?

Emma had asked him if there was still a spark. He had

denied it. But with her here in his bed, he seemed like the worst kind of liar.

He ran his hands over her back, tracing her spine, feeling the press of her breasts against his chest. If he closed his eyes, he could pretend he was twenty-one again. Eager. Painfully naive about women. Standing on the precipice of a moment that would change his life forever.

How could he have made such a wrong choice? Such a desperately wrong choice? He'd been hurt, true. But he liked to think he was wiser now. Even in the face of Emma's betrayal, he should have fought for her.

Her cheek rested trustingly against his chest. Could she feel his heart thump? To him, it felt like a runaway train. Beating out a rhythm on the tracks.

Last chance. Last chance. Last chance.

Confusion and lust were poor bedfellows. Lust won every time, even in the absence of clear thinking. He moved over her and kissed her roughly. She arched into his embrace, giving him everything. Her softness. Her kindness. Her capacity for loving.

Love. The word was so damned dangerous. As he entered her with one hard thrust, he felt the syllable reverberate in his head, in his heart, in his loins. He did not love her. He wouldn't allow it. Never again.

But as his body stroked into hers, as her arms linked around his neck, binding him to her, he felt his will crumble. How could this be wrong? How could anything this good be wrong?

They loved wildly, passionately, battling almost to see who could give the other more pleasure. He lost the ability to speak, to reason, to keep her at bay.

He wanted everything she was, everything *he* was when he was with her. Emotions he had denied for years washed over him, drowning every one of his stupid life rules. His need for release bore down on him, but he didn't want this to end. He wanted to love her all night long.

When Emma cried out his name, though, shuddering beneath him, he had no choice but to follow her. The intensity of his climax tore him apart and rebuilt him cell by cell.

Eons later, he clutched her close and slept. But it was a fitful slumber. He jerked awake, time and again, dreaming that he had lost her. In his nightmares, he stood inside a train car, watching her wave to him as some immoveable force carried him away.

After the third time when he awoke sweating and trembling, he eased from the bed and went in search of a drink of water. He stood naked in the living room area of the suite and peered out at the night between a crack in the drapes. The world was still and dark.

Today was his brother's wedding day. Dylan was gaining a wife and a daughter in one fell swoop. What must it be like to know that people depended on you? That their health and well-being directly impacted your own happiness?

In Dylan's shoes, Aidan would be scared to death. That was a hell of a thing for a grown man to admit. Even now, with Emma asleep in the other room, Aidan had to resist the urge to run. He remembered his early twenties all too well. He'd been a mess. Drinking too much. Sleeping with too many women. Teaching himself not to feel.

All because Emma Braithwaite's betrayal had crushed him. The pain had made it hard to breathe. And it had made him stupid. Unfortunately, Danielle had borne the brunt of that.

His breath fogged the glass. Rubbing his thumb across the condensation, he told himself to let go of the memories. But what was the old saying? He who forgets the past is doomed to repeat it?

Aidan couldn't live through such a cataclysm again. He wouldn't. He'd been as vulnerable as a newborn pup, no defenses at all.

This time he was smarter.

When he was chilled to the bone, he returned to the bedroom. The small lamp still burned. Emma looked like a painting, her golden hair strewn across the pillow, her ivory breasts rising and falling with each breath.

He climbed beneath the covers, his heart catching sharply in his chest when she murmured and curled into his embrace.

"You're so cold," she said. She didn't open her eyes, but her face scrunched up in dismay.

"Sorry." Her skin felt like velvet—warm, supple and soft.

Even half-asleep, she tried to protect him. She patted his thigh. "Stay close to me." The words were slurred. "I'll warm you up."

For the remainder of the early morning, he listened to her gentle breathing, his body wrapped around hers. It was too important a moment to be lost in sleep. He loved her.

I love you.

No one was there to hear when he whispered the admission, dry-eyed. He loved Emma Braithwaite. Perhaps he had never stopped. But now was all there was. Come daybreak he had to let her go.

Though he closed his eyes, he kept slumber at bay. Around seven-thirty, she stirred. He feigned sleep, giving her the chance to make a trip to the bathroom, to find her clothes and to dress.

When she was ready, he pretended to wake up, rearing up on one elbow to gaze at her sleepily. "You're leaving?"

Emma's smile was shy. "I have to go home and shower and open the shop. Mrs. Correll is coming at two so I can get ready for the wedding, but I'll be on my own until then."

She sat down on the side of the bed and touched his arm. "I wanted to ask you one more thing. If you don't mind."

He tensed inwardly. "What is it?"

Emma glanced down, her expression troubled. When she looked up at him again, he felt as if he could see into her soul. "How long ago was it that Danielle died?" she asked, the words barely audible.

Here it was. This was his chance. All he had to do was tell the truth and he'd be free of Emma forever. She would be hurt, but she deserved to suffer a little. It was only fair.

Feeling cold to his bones, even though the bed still carried the warmth of their two bodies, he looked at her grimly. "Ten years." When the words left his mouth, it was too late to change his mind.

As he watched, Emma's forehead creased. He saw her do the math. "But you left England ten years ago… the first week in December. And you were engaged by Christmas?" Her voice broke on the last word as she stumbled to her feet. "You and Danielle were together before you came to England, weren't you?" Her tone was less accusatory than grief-stricken. She had gone so white, he feared for a moment she would faint.

"I guess you weren't the only one with secrets, Emma. Perhaps no one is ever who they seem."

Sixteen

Emma didn't react outwardly. Not even a single tear. She couldn't. Not with him watching. The hurt ran too deep. It was all she could do to breathe and move one foot in front of the other. She was perfectly calm as she walked out of Aidan's suite and rode the elevator down to the lobby. In the early morning there were few people around other than employees. She was not a hotel guest. Anyone could draw a conclusion from that. But what did it matter?

Perhaps she shouldn't have gotten behind the wheel of a car. But the choking need to put distance between herself and Aidan won out. She kept her speed ten miles under the limit. The mountain road was tricky.

By the time she made it to her apartment, she hovered on the brink of an ugly crying jag. Her chest felt as if someone had ripped it open with a dull blade. Her eyes burned. Her stomach revolted.

Upstairs, she glanced at the clock. In barely an hour she had to open the store for one of the biggest shopping days of the year. What was she going to do? She lay across her bed, utterly lost. Aidan was lying. He had to be. He could never have spent time with her at Oxford, adoring her, having sex with her, making plans with her…if he had been in love with another woman. It was impossible. She refused to believe it.

But then she saw his face as it had been when she walked out of his bedroom. She remembered his dark-eyed stare. And she realized he was right. She didn't know him at all.

Raw, brokenhearted sobs wet her pillow and left her feeling hollow and sick to her stomach. Somehow she had to make it through this day. Somehow she had to survive seeing him one more time. Tonight was Dylan and Mia's wedding. Neither Emma nor Aidan had the luxury of avoiding one another.

Though the thought of it was beyond comprehension, she knew she had no choice. She gave herself twenty minutes to cry out her misery and pain. It wasn't enough. It would never be enough. The empty cavity where her heart normally resided was frightening…like a black hole waiting to swallow her until she was nothing but a spot of darkness.

She dragged herself to her feet and undressed, ashamed that she had no underwear. What had seemed sexy and fun the night before now carried the tawdry feel of regret. A blistering hot shower did nothing to warm her soul. She dried her hair, applied light makeup with trembling hands, and dressed in a wool sweater and pants.

In a very real sense, Silver Memories became her salvation during the day. The heavy flow of customers, the constant *ching* of the cash register…all of it anesthetized her so that she could function.

When Mrs. Correll arrived midafternoon, the older woman didn't appear to notice anything amiss in her boss's demeanor. They exchanged a few words, Emma handed over the keys and fled upstairs.

For the longest time she sat huddled in her chair by

the fire, remembering how Aidan had looked sleeping in this very spot. She wanted to wail and throw things and smash bits of glass, but she was very afraid if she gave in to the emotions tearing her apart, she would never regain control.

The afternoon ticked away until it was far past time to prepare. She forced herself to heat a can of soup and eat it. She had skipped lunch. Though hunger was the last thing on her mind, she knew she needed the sustenance.

At last, she went to her tiny closet and reached for the green velvet dress. It was as beautiful as when she had first opened the box and lifted it out. The style was reminiscent of the 1940s, nipped in at the waist, full-skirted and cut low at the bodice with a sweetheart neckline. Trying it on had made her feel like a movie star.

Now, looking at herself in the mirror, all she saw was the ghost of a woman with sad eyes and a barely beating heart.

The skies had been clear all day, which meant that by five, the temperatures started to plummet. Emma was to be at the church at five thirty for pictures. Although she was only in charge of the guestbook, Mia had insisted she be included.

The small chapel where Mia and Dylan had chosen to have their ceremony was one of the oldest structures in Silver Glen. In lean, hard times, the early townspeople had erected a place of worship, nondenominational, welcoming all who wanted to come.

Only two blocks from Emma's apartment, the historic building was a favorite stop for tourists in the summertime. Tonight, even though Emma walked quickly in her high heels, the wind cut through her thick wool coat as if she were naked.

Breathless when she arrived, she paused at the doors

to the church, drawing on the faith taught to her as a child for strength to face the night ahead. Then lifting her chin, she turned the polished tin knob and let herself in.

The well-worn pews were original wood, as was the floor. Etched windows had been a later addition. Instead of stained glass, they were clear, affording grand views of the mountains in the daytime.

Candles in hurricane globes flickered softly on the high windowsills. Someone, Maeve perhaps, had surrounded them with fresh evergreens and red bows. The scent took Emma back to England, when her rambling, drafty home was decked out in holiday array.

A small group of people milled at the front of the chapel. Mia had refused to give credence to silly superstitions, as she called them, so all the pictures were to be taken with bride and groom together. Dylan couldn't take his eyes off her. His pride and happiness wrapped his woman in a romantic glow. Cora was passed from arm to arm, everyone fighting for the privilege of holding her.

Emma and Aidan stayed on opposite sides of the group, never making eye contact. No one seemed to notice. The photographer was talented and socially adept. He managed to get what he wanted without making anyone feel rushed or stressed. By a quarter 'til seven, it was all done.

Mia disappeared into a small room at the back, where she would wait until it was time for the ceremony. Her parents took a seat on the front row, left-hand side. Four of Mia's friends from Raleigh sat behind them. The Kavanagh boys, resplendent in formal wear, settled beside and behind their mother on the opposite side of the church.

The guest list was relatively small. Over the next half hour, thirty or so people drifted in, all of them longtime friends of the Kavanaghs. Emma offered the book and pen as each couple appeared. Standing so near the door, she shivered, but at least she was as far away from Aidan as possible.

At seven twenty-five, a violinist began to play softly. Emma made sure the old paneled door was firmly latched before taking a seat in the back row. Moments later, the musician began playing an evocative piece that echoed Mia's Russian heritage.

The bride appeared and stood in the center of the aisle. Her eye caught Emma's for a split second. The two women exchanged a smile. Then as the music swelled and danced, Mia walked slowly toward Dylan carrying a bouquet of red roses and eucalyptus tied with gold braid.

Her traditional wedding gown suited her small frame. White satin with long transparent sleeves, the dress's simplicity was a perfect foil for the antique lace that covered the bride's head and reached the floor in back. The veil and pearl-studded headpiece had belonged to Mia's Russian great-grandmother.

The bridal couple had chosen not to have attendants. Only the robed minister stood with them at the chancel rail.

Dearly beloved...

At that moment, Emma lost her composure. Tears rolled, one after the other, down her cheeks. If she had not made such foolish mistakes when she was younger, she and Aidan might have been married a long time by now...perhaps even had children.

Extracting an embroidered handkerchief that had belonged to her grandmother from her clutch purse, she dabbed her cheeks. This was why she felt so much passion for preserving the past. Tangible objects carried the memories of loved ones. They recalled the beauty of earlier times.

Silver Glen had made a point of preserving its heritage, of telling the town's story. And on virtually every street, some evidence of Kavanagh influence could be seen. Aidan was a part of that, though he chose to live elsewhere. Would he ever want to come home for good?

All she could see of him at the moment was the back of his head. She was grateful for that. If he had stood beside his brother, Emma would have been hard-pressed to look away.

She refocused her attention on the minister, who was guiding his charges in repeating wedding vows to each other. Dylan, sensitive to his struggles with the written word, had wanted to use the traditional liturgy. *To have and to hold, in sickness and in health, 'til death do us part.*

The words resonated, beautiful and timeless.

Even in profile, holding hands, Dylan and Mia looked so happy. The tenderness on his face was almost too personal to witness.

When Aidan became part of Emma's life in Oxford, he had looked at her much the same way. She had felt his love to the marrow of her bones. Had never doubted him for a minute. Despite what he told her this morning about the timing of his engagement, she knew he had loved her once upon a time.

Maybe she was blind…or ridiculously naive, but she refused to believe that the Aidan Kavanagh she knew in England was that good an actor.

The minister gave the pronouncement. Dylan and Mia faced their guests, arm in arm, beaming. Someone handed Cora to them. Cheers broke out in the small chapel.

There was no recessional. Everyone stood in the aisle,

talking and laughing. Emma made her way to the front, hugged Dylan and Mia, and prepared to make her escape.

But she hadn't counted on Maeve Kavanagh. Emma was four rows away from the back door and a clean getaway when Aidan's mother hailed her. "Slow down, Emma, for heaven's sake. You don't want to be the first one at the reception."

It didn't seem polite to say that Emma had planned to avoid the post-ceremony soiree all together. "Did I forget something? I put the guestbook in Mia's tote bag like she asked me to…"

Maeve shook her head. "This isn't about the guestbook. I wanted to let you know that I booked a room at the hotel for you tonight."

"Why would you do that? I live here."

"We Kavanaghs know how to throw a party. And though this group tonight will be small, don't underestimate their enthusiasm. We're going to give Dylan and Mia the send-off they deserve. Which means a late night. Grab a toothbrush and whatever else you need and don't argue with the mother of the groom."

"Seriously, Maeve. I'm touched that you want me there, but I don't know any of your guests."

"You know Aidan." Something about the other woman's sly glance told Emma that Maeve was perhaps a bit too perceptive when it came to her sons. "And here he is now."

Emma's stomach flipped hard. Maeve had crooked a finger, and her son, clearly not willing to spoil a family occasion, had come as commanded. But the cold, closed look on his face when he looked at Emma said he was not happy about the situation.

Maeve ignored any tension. "Aidan…I need you to give Emma a ride to her apartment so she can pack a few things. Then bring her up the mountain. I've promised her a room."

"Why?"

Even Maeve faltered at the incredulity in that one syllable. "Well," she said, soldiering on despite the awkward moment, "she will want to have some wine, at least, and no one should drive that mountain road on a dark winter night when she's been drinking."

Aidan shoved the heels of his hands in his eyes. "Mother, you're meddling...and not very subtly. Emma has a perfectly fine vehicle and impeccable driving skills. If she wants to come to the party, she can come on her own."

Maeve bristled. "Watch your tongue, Aidan. You might be a grown man, but you're still my little boy. And I raised you better than that. Apologize to Emma."

Aidan glanced at Emma, his jaw tight. "I'm sorry. I'll be happy to give you a ride up the mountain. Let me get my coat and keys." The bitter sarcasm in his tone was barely veiled, yet Maeve seemed oblivious.

When Aidan strode away, Maeve touched Emma's arm. "Be patient with him, my dear."

"I don't know what you mean." Emma shifted from one foot to the other, uncomfortable and embarrassed.

Maeve shook her head slightly, her eyes filled with a mix of emotions, the clearest of which was determination. "I saw you leave the hotel this morning, Emma."

Bloody hell. "Oh, but I—"

Aidan's mother stopped her with an upheld hand. "It's none of my business. And I don't want or need explanations. But I love my son. And I want to see him happy."

Emma looked toward the front of the church, where Aidan stood talking to James and Conor. She bit her lip.

"I think you've misunderstood. Aidan doesn't have feelings for me. At least not the good kind."

"He's angry with you right now." It wasn't a question.

"Yes, ma'am."

"And you knew each other before you came here."

Emma nodded. She wasn't a very good liar. "We did."

"That's all I need to know. If you have a past with my son, I'm asking you to not give up on whatever this is between you. He can be bullheaded and emotionally distant, but I swear to you that he feels things deeply. Like the silver mines in these hills, sometimes you have to dig through the layers to find what's worth keeping."

Aidan was on his way back down the aisle.

"I understand," Emma whispered. "But there's a lot you don't know."

Maeve patted her arm. "And I don't need to know. Just remember what I said." She touched the skirt of Emma's dress as Aidan joined them. "Doesn't Emma look gorgeous in this shade of green, Aidan?"

"Stop it, Mother."

His parent lifted both eyebrows with an innocent expression. "I don't know what you mean."

"Matchmaking. You're embarrassing Emma."

"Am I?" She looked at Emma beseechingly.

With Aidan standing there like judge and jury, Emma had no choice but to tell the truth. "Yes, ma'am. A little bit."

Maeve waved a hand, dismissing their concerns. "Very well. I'll leave you two alone. But don't be long. We don't want to start the party without you."

Seventeen

Aidan strode around the corner, retrieved his car and turned the heater on full blast as he approached the church and idled at the curb. The door of the old building opened a crack. Emma spotted him and hurried outside, bundled to the chin as she slid into the passenger seat.

"Thank you," she said quietly. "I could have walked back, but I appreciate the lift. It's colder now than it was when I came. And don't worry. I'll drive myself up the mountain."

"Oh, no," he said. "My mother has spoken. My life wouldn't be worth two cents if she found out I didn't follow her directive."

The brief drive was silent after that. Aidan parked in front of Silver Memories. "I'll wait here." He didn't want to see Emma's cozy apartment again. Nor did he want to remember the first time they had made love. Damn his mother for interfering.

He could have told Maeve to go to the devil, but given all that she had sacrificed over the years for Aidan's sorry hide, he didn't have it in him to treat her so shabbily. She was simply trying to help in the only way she knew how.

When Emma reappeared carrying a small suitcase, he hopped out of the car, took it from her and placed it carefully in the trunk. After that, neither of them spoke as they made their way up the winding mountain road. Despite the silence, however, he was stingingly aware of everything about his passenger.

Her scent. Her body language. The way her soft velvet skirt spread across the seat, nearly touching his thigh.

This morning he had been so sure about everything. But tonight, seated in a hundred-year-old church, watching his brother marry the love of his life amidst the romantic glow of candlelight, even Aidan's calcified heart had begun to quiver and crack.

When all was said and done, did it matter that Emma had betrayed him once upon a time? Could he put the past behind him?

His introspection was short-lived. Soon, the magnificent hotel, ablaze with lights, welcomed them. Though all the family benefitted materially from the hotel's success, Liam and Maeve were the forces behind the day-to-day operations.

As Aidan exited the car and handed over the keys, Emma walked on ahead of him. To any onlooker, it might have seemed as if she were trying to get in out of the cold. But Aidan knew the truth. She didn't want him to touch her…even something as innocuous as holding her elbow as they ascended the steps.

The elegant lobby was festive and crowded. The longtime concierge, Pierre, directed them to a private room at the back of the hotel. Aidan and Emma were the last to arrive. Only Cora was missing. Dylan's housekeeper had taken the baby home to put her to bed.

Aidan grabbed a beer and some food and made a beeline for an unoccupied seat near Gavin. His brother shot him a look rife with curiosity. "You not hanging with your girlfriend?"

Stabbing a canapé with a silver fork, Aidan shook his head. “Not my girlfriend.”

“Mom seems to think differently.”

“Mom is a busybody.”

Maeve appeared out of nowhere to thump him on the back of his head. “I heard that.”

Aidan gave her a measured look. “If the shoe fits…”

She bent to kiss his cheek. “My job is to see my children settled happily.”

Gavin blanched. “Don’t get any ideas about me. Two out of seven isn’t bad, Mom.”

“Don’t worry,” she said. “When the right woman comes along, I won’t have to do a thing. I love seeing my big strong boys give in to love.” She didn’t pause to sit down. “Pay attention now. Mia and Dylan are about to cut the cake.”

Aidan turned his gaze to the appropriate spot in the room, but he couldn’t help tracking Emma. So far tonight, she had been introduced to Mia’s Raleigh friends, and she had danced with at least three of Aidan’s brothers, including the groom.

As far as he could tell, she was having a wonderful time.

The more Emma glowed, the more Aidan glowered. He’d told her today that he had lied to her and cheated on her. Did she not believe him? Or did his confession not matter at all?

He couldn’t understand her. That infuriated him more than anything. He was accustomed to sizing up a man or a woman at first meeting. Such people skills made him successful in his work.

But Emma remained an enigma. When he was in bed with her, it was easy to pretend she was the girl he knew in England, the young woman who made his life complete.

With a bit of emotional distance, though, his cynicism returned in full force. People didn't change. If Emma had betrayed him before, it was in her DNA to do it again. No matter how good the sex—and even he would admit that it was pretty damn spectacular—he would be a fool to set himself up for disappointment and loss a second time.

It was bad enough that he loved her. But he would get over that. He had to. He also had to make it clear to her and to himself that whatever her reasons for coming to Silver Glen…he wasn't interested.

The hours passed slowly. Never once did Emma glance his way. In her deep emerald pin-up-girl dress, she laughed and chatted and danced and partied the night away. He studied her for long chunks of time, trying to decide what it was about her that called to him. Was it the classic features? The golden hair? The female chuckle that went straight to his gut and ignited a slow burn? Seeing Conor pull her out onto the floor a second time made Aidan clench his jaw. But he kept his seat.

Emma could dance with every man in Silver Glen for all he cared.

Only for Mia did Aidan make an exception. His new sister-in-law sparkled with happiness. "I've danced with everyone but you," she said, taking him by the hand and pulling him to his feet. "You're acting like Scrooge over here in your corner. Don't make me beg."

"I wouldn't dream of it," he said, smiling at her with affection. "You've made my brother a very happy man."

Mia returned the smile. "Your whole family has welcomed me so sweetly. It's a novelty to have brothers after all this time. But I think I like it." He steered her around the floor, responding to her happy chatter when appropriate. Mia was an exceptional woman in every way. But never once had he felt anything for her other than fondness and admiration.

Even if Dylan hadn't been in the picture, Aidan wouldn't have made a play for Mia. Because no matter how foolish and self-destructive it was, the only female who gave him sleepless nights and unfulfilled sexual dreams was Emma Braithwaite.

At the song's end, he delivered Mia back to her new groom. Then, trying not to be obvious about it, he scouted the room for Emma's location. She was nowhere to be seen.

He couldn't ask about her, or he'd risk setting off his mother's radar. After half an hour, when it was clear Emma hadn't merely slipped out to the restroom, Aidan gave the bridal couple and his mother one last set of hugs and said his goodbyes. If they were suspicious, they gave no sign.

In the lobby, he hesitated. Everyone on staff knew him. It wasn't as if he could make an inquiry on the sly. So he might as well sin and sin boldly.

He approached the check-in area, giving Marjorie, the desk clerk who had known him since he was a boy, his best winsome smile.

Lowering his voice, he leaned an elbow on the granite counter. "Can you please give me Emma Braithwaite's room number? She slipped out before I had a chance to tell her good-night."

Marjorie eyed him with a wry twist of her lips. "Is this going to get me in trouble, Aidan?"

He held up his hands. "Not at all. I swear."

Shaking her head, she jotted the number on a slip of paper and pushed it toward him. "Don't make me regret this."

"I'm on my best behavior."

She snorted. "When it comes to Kavanagh men, that definition has all sorts of interpretations. Good luck."

"With what?" He lifted an eyebrow.

"The pretty English lady. You could do a lot worse."

"Forget that," he chuckled, though his throat was tight. "I haven't caught wedding fever, despite all the festivities. This confirmed bachelor is completely content with his lot."

Emma unpinned her hair and brushed it out. After taking off her stockings and shoes, she curled up on the sofa. Though this room was nowhere near as large as Aidan's suite, it was nevertheless extremely luxurious. More for company than anything else, she turned on the television and muted it.

Two different channels were showing the classic holiday movie *White Christmas*. She paused on one, but it was late in the film. Rosemary Clooney and Bing Crosby had argued and were in the midst of a party, trying to ignore each other. The similarities between the fictional couple and Aidan and Emma were hard to miss.

Even Rosemary's clothing struck a chord, perhaps the reason Emma had ordered this particular style and color for Mia's wedding. She couldn't bring herself to take off the dress yet. The soft green velvet buoyed her spirits and made her feel feminine, despite her sad mood.

When the knock sounded at her door, she couldn't even say she was surprised. But her heart skipped a few beats anyway.

After glancing through the peephole, she unlocked the dead bolt and opened it. Aidan lingered in the hallway, his expression hard to read.

"May I come in?" he asked, his formal tone at odds with the turbulence in his gaze.

"Of course." She stepped back to allow him to enter.

He prowled the confines of her room, hands shoved in his pockets. "I thought you would be angry," he said.

"About what?"

"Don't play dumb. About what I told you this morning. The timing of my engagement."

She debated how to answer him. "We both made mistakes, Aidan. I'm hardly one to criticize."

"Are you even human?" he snapped. "Why aren't you calling me names? Why aren't you throwing things at me?"

"For the same reason that you're in my room right now," she said quietly, her heart breaking. "We don't know how to be together because we ruined the past, but there's something between us that we haven't managed to kill."

He ripped off his tie and ran a hand behind his neck. "I'm leaving in the morning." The dark-eyed gaze dared her to protest.

Emma shook her head vehemently. "Your mother will be crushed, Aidan. She's so looking forward to having her whole family together on Christmas Day. And the special events this week, the children's party, the caroling—please don't leave. I'll go instead. You won't have to see me again."

"Where would you go?"

"Back to England, I suppose."

"But your mother is traveling. That's why Mia and my mom have included you as part of our family this past week."

"It doesn't matter. I'm not a Kavanagh. But you *are*, Aidan. You can't forsake your family this year. If you do, they'll realize that you've never gotten over losing Danielle. And somehow, I think you don't want them to know that."

"What makes you think I've never gotten over Danielle?" Hostility crackled in the words.

"I heard it in your voice this morning. You loved her. And you lost her in a tragic accident. Being here in Silver Glen at Christmas has revived those terrible memories."

Aidan felt as if were being ripped apart. He knew exactly what kind of ass he would be to abandon his family now. But God knows, it seemed like his only choice at the moment.

Allowing Emma to leave Silver Glen would accomplish nothing. He was deliberately fostering the lie that Danielle was his long-lost love…that he had kept an emotional vigil for her all these years.

If that lie was supposed to be a punishment for Emma, then why was *he* the one who felt like hell?

"I can't stay," he said bluntly. "I don't want to."

Emma wrung her hands. "But you have to," she cried. In her bare feet, and with her hair loose around her face, she looked more like the girl he had loved in Oxford.

"Perhaps you could convince me," he said slowly. *Bastard.* His mind was made up, and yet he was willing to use Emma's concern as a bargaining chip. In his defense, if he were never going to see her again, surely it wasn't such a terrible crime to steal one more night in her arms.

She stared at him in silence. Even disheveled and upset, her dignity was unassailable. Inevitably, he felt like a peasant begging for crumbs.

"Say something," he growled. "Yes or no?"

He watched her chest rise and fall. Blue eyes, tinged

with some painful emotion, judged him and found him wanting.

"Yes."

The exultation that swept through his veins was at odds with Emma's expression. Her misery infuriated him. "You don't have to look like a condemned woman on her way to the guillotine. If you don't want me, say so. I'm done playing games."

Her quiet laugh held no amusement at all. "It's not a game, Aidan, believe me."

When she turned on her heel and left him standing alone in the sitting area, he gaped. The bathroom door opened and closed. He heard water running.

Grim-faced, he pounded on the wood. "Quit hiding from me, damn it. And don't undress. That's my job."

She swung open the barrier between them so quickly he almost pitched forward. Her eyes flashed blue fire. "Fine. Have it your way." She stalked toward the bed and stood beside it, her back to him. She had swept her hair over one shoulder, baring the nape of her neck.

A pulse, low and sweet, began to thrum in his veins. He closed the distance between them. "I'm not a big fan of angry sex," he whispered, kissing the top of her spine. "Let's forget everything tonight except for the way we make each other feel."

Glancing at him over her shoulder, she gave him a mocking smile. "You mean the way we want to strangle each other?"

Eighteen

How could she make him want to laugh at the oddest moments? He shook his head. “I don’t want to strangle you, Emma. At least not most of the time.” He was forced to add that last bit in the interest of honesty.

She sighed and bowed her head, her posture submissive despite her sarcasm. “We seem to make better enemies than we do friends.”

The phrasing bothered him. “I don’t want to be your friend.” These feelings he had were too strong for friendship and too complicated for anything else.

When she turned to face him, he held her by the shoulders…suddenly afraid she would bolt.

Emma was smaller and more vulnerable in her bare feet. She tilted her face up to his and studied him intently, as if trying to see inside his soul. “We were friends once upon a time.”

“No.” He shook his head, the word vehement. “We were lovers. I never had time to be your friend, because the first day I met you I fell head over heels in lust with you.”

“Lust? Not love?”

He had no doubt he was hurting her now. “Lust, Emma,” he said flatly, “a young man’s physical passion for a beautiful woman. Love lasts. Lust fades. That’s how you know the difference. If we ever had a shot at love, it ended before it began."

"And yet you still want me."

Only then did he see the trap he had set for himself. *Damn.* He backtracked quickly. "But only because we've been thrown together in this Christmas-wedding, romantic atmosphere. It's not real. *We're* not real. I wasn't kidding when I said I'm leaving in the morning. And no matter what I intimated, you can't change my mind."

Her small smile was wistful. "Final answer?"

He steeled himself against her charm. "Final answer. Now, do you want me under those conditions, or not?"

Two soft hands cupped his face. Feminine fingers slid cool against his overheated skin. Her eyes searched his. "I love you, Aidan. I know you'd rather not hear it. Perhaps you don't believe it. Or maybe our history discredits what I say. But before you leave, I want you to understand how I feel. I don't know what Danielle has to do with all of this, but she's gone and I'm here. I can't change what happened in England. I'm sorry for that. But please, Aidan. Don't live in the past."

Every word she spoke was a shard of glass, piercing his skin and finding its way to his heart. *Emma loved him.* He wanted to crow with masculine triumph. Beat his chest. Shout it from the rooftops.

Yet in the midst of all that rose a terrible pain. He'd believed her once upon a time. Had handed over his heart with the carelessness of youth, not realizing what he risked.

Three times he'd been betrayed by love. His father had not loved his sons enough to put them before his obsession with finding a lost silver mine. Danielle had died, leaving Aidan with the guilt of knowing he hadn't loved her enough. And Emma…Emma had made him *believe* in love. That was the cruelest blow of all.

His heart encased in ice, he removed her hands from his face and forced her arms behind her back, manacling her wrists with one hand. Her bones, delicate in his grasp, struck him as feminine and helpless. "I don't want you to love me," he said. He crushed his mouth over hers taking the kiss he wanted, feeling the way her lips quivered against his. "All I want is you."

Emma felt the sting of hot tears and blinked them back. She had gambled her all on one roll of the dice and lost. Gasping, she struggled to free her arms. "I want you, too," she whispered. "But I don't like angry sex, either. Come to bed with me, Aidan."

He let her go instantly and stood stone faced as she reached behind her to lower the zipper. When she faltered, he finished the task, holding her hand as she stepped out of a sea of velvet. Carefully, he draped the dress over a nearby chair.

She saw Aidan's eyes burn as he took in the matching bra, undies and garter belt she wore. Her nipples tightened in helpless pleasure. His hot gaze raked her from head to toe, leaving no doubt about his desire for her. A less pragmatic woman might have told herself that love was there buried somewhere under that brusque facade.

But she had come too far to fool herself now. Aidan wanted her body—not her soul, not her heart, not her whispered confession of devotion. And because she loved him enough for two, she would give him everything. If that left her with nothing, she would not cry.

Taking his hand, she climbed into the bed. He was on her instantly, his face flushed, the bulge in his trousers impossible to miss. They kissed wildly. He tasted of coffee and wedding cake.

"God, you drive me insane," he muttered, sucking one nipple through a covering of ecru lace. "Tell me you want me."

She unbuttoned his shirt with fumbling fingers. "I do, Aidan. I do."

The juxtaposition of those five words so close to tonight's wedding ceremony made him wince. Emma saw his involuntary response. Though she hadn't meant to make the connection—obviously, he had.

He rolled away from her long enough to toe off his shoes and unfasten his trousers. When he freed his sex, it was dark red and rigid. "Can't wait," he groaned. "Not this time."

The fact that he didn't bother to finish undressing either of them was as arousing as the touch of his big warm hands on her body. "Then don't," she said, tugging him closer.

He took two seconds to move aside the narrow fabric between her legs. Then he positioned himself and shoved to the hilt in one forceful thrust that smacked the headboard against the wall.

A ragged laugh shook his chest. "Please tell me I didn't bust a hole in the wall. I'd never live it down."

"Do you really care?" She linked her ankles at the small of his back. Neither of them was naked. Yet this was the most intimate time she had shared with him since he'd arrived in Silver Glen.

For a flash—a split second—he looked down at her with the face of the young man who had stolen her heart. Carefree. Happy. Determined to make her his. "No. I suppose not," he muttered.

Keeping his gaze locked on her face, he moved inside her. One steady push after another. His skin heated. So did hers. The pace was lazy, but the look in his eyes was anything but.

"Tell me what you're thinking," she said, the words tumbling out impulsively.

It was a mistake. Instantly, his expression shuttered. His jaw rigid, he closed his eyes and closed her out.

Beneath her fingertips, his hair was soft and springy. Her thighs ached from the effort of clinging to him. He overwhelmed her suddenly, so much a man that she could almost forget the boy.

But even as he stroked her intimately, she felt echoes of sweetness from the past. Almost everything had changed. The world. Their lives. Their bodies. Yet when she closed her eyes and gave herself over to the intense pleasure of the moment, she could pretend she was back in England. Back with a young Aidan. Back under the influence of a love that was innocent and perfect.

Without warning, he shifted suddenly, putting pressure where her body craved his touch. She shivered, so close to her climax that she felt little flutters of anticipation in her sex.

Aidan nipped her earlobe with sharp teeth. "I'll stay 'til morning." The promise was hoarse.

"Yes." It was all she could manage. He took her with him then to a place that held a poignant mixture of regret and physical bliss.

"Emma..."

She couldn't answer him in words. Her throat was too tight. Instead, she rained kisses across his face and canted her hips to take him deeper. He groaned as if he were in pain when he came. And she followed him. But the pleasure was hollow and the end incomplete.

Because what he gave her was not enough. And it never would be.

Nineteen

Aidan huddled into his wool overcoat, turning up the collar in a vain attempt to escape the howling wind from the arctic front that had blasted through New York that morning. Snow fell, but it was dry and icy…nothing to hamper shoppers on the next-to-last shopping day before Christmas.

He'd been walking the streets of Manhattan for hours, his hands and his feet numb. The physical discomfort was some kind of punishment, though he didn't know exactly what for or why. All he knew was that he'd been compelled to leave his apartment in search of relief from his pain.

Booze hadn't done it. Nor back-to-back movies at the closest theater. Not even an impulsive volunteer shift at a local soup kitchen…though that last stint had at least reminded him that holiday misery took on a far more serious face in many corners and back alleys of the city.

Everywhere he went he faced incessant, relentless good cheer. Even the poor and downtrodden found something to smile about in the presence of an artificial tree and modest gifts from local charities.

Aidan was so lost he couldn't even begin to find the path. The life he'd been so pleased with before he decided to spend Christmas at Silver Glen was gone, eradicated by the memories of Emma.

He saw her in every window display, in every shiny package carried by smiling passersby. Everything good and joyful and meaningful about Christmas conspired to remind him that true love meant forgiveness. It was that simple. And that impossible.

He could forgive Emma for just about anything, if the truth were told. But what if he had her and lost her again?

Imagining such a thing made him shudder with a biting chill that was far worse than any winter weather he could conjure. He wanted his old life back...the one where he didn't *have* to feel anything. A satisfying job. A pleasant social life. And plenty of his own company.

Where was *that* Aidan Kavanagh?

At last, when his face was in danger of frostbite, he headed for home. Leftover pizza in the fridge would be his companion tonight. Hopefully, none of his family would ring him up again. He'd already fielded one tearful phone call from his mother that left him feeling like the worst kind of vermin on the planet.

Hell, Dylan had even texted Aidan from his honeymoon and called him a handful of choice names that were spot on. Without even trying, Aidan had become something worse than a Scrooge...if there was such a thing.

When he reached his building, he gave the doorman a fifty-dollar tip and a muttered "Merry Christmas." But he never made it to his apartment. When he stepped off the elevator, Mr. Shapiro, his across-the-hall neighbor, appeared, wild-eyed.

"Help me, Aidan," he cried. "Mrs. S. fell in the kitchen and she's out cold."

Aidan dashed into the apartment with him. "Have you called 911?"

The old man wrung his hands. "Yes. But how long will it take?"

As Aidan knelt beside the white-haired lady, he thought he heard sirens in the distance. "Hang on, Mr. Shapiro. She's breathing." That was a relief. Surely things couldn't be too bad. Had she passed out and fallen, or had she fallen and passed out after she hit her head? "Grab me a pillow and something to cover her with. We don't want her to get cold here on the floor."

Aidan was not a trained medic, but even he could see that the poor guy needed something to do.

Fortunately, the EMTs made it upstairs in the next ten minutes. They loaded the elderly woman onto a gurney and rolled her out into the hall. Mr. Shapiro looked pale enough to pass out himself.

A uniformed kid who looked all of twenty smiled encouragingly. "We're taking her to Lenox Hospital. Don't worry. She seems to be stable."

Suddenly, the professionals were gone. Mr. Shapiro seemed at a loss. He had to be ninety if he were a day. And the poor guy was shaking all over. "Let me get you something to drink," Aidan said. "I think you need to sit down."

Suddenly the man's spine snapped straight. "I'm fine. Take me to see her. Please?"

The naked entreaty in his wrinkled face was impossible to resist, even if Aidan had possessed a heart of stone. "Of course." Aidan pulled out his phone and summoned a cab. When he turned around, Mr. Shapiro was standing in front of a menorah, his lips moving in a quiet prayer.

"Are you ready?" Aidan asked quietly.

The man nodded, plucking his jacket from an antique coat tree. "What should I take for her?" he asked suddenly, the agitation returning to his face.

"If she needs anything later, I'll bring you back here," Aidan promised.

Aidan's apartment was only three blocks from the hospital, but the old man was in no condition to walk, especially not on a night that was as wickedly cold as this one.

The cab ride took no time at all. Aidan paid the fare and jumped out to help Mr. Shapiro. They didn't need a broken bone to add to the evening's trauma.

Inside the hospital, the emergency room admitting nurse was kind but firm. "No one can go back yet. Give them time to assess her condition and make sure she's stable. I'll keep you posted."

Aidan found a couple of chairs, and the two of them sat down. Moments later, Mr. Shapiro's chin rested on his chest. He was either sleeping or praying again.

When he lifted his head and spoke suddenly, it startled Aidan. His gaze was clear and sharp in a face that was worn with time. "We've been married seventy-one years. Came over during the Second World War as newlyweds. Our families pooled money for our passage. We lost them all in the holocaust. Esther is all I have in the world."

"No children?" Aidan asked quietly.

"We couldn't have any."

The silence lengthened after that. Aidan felt the story in his bones. Love and loss. The fabric of life.

At last, when the summons came, Mr. Shapiro jumped to his feet like a young lad.

Aidan touched his arm. "Do you want me to go back with you?"

"I'd like that. You're a good boy."

It had been many years since Aidan had considered himself a boy, but from Mr. Shapiro's perspective, the reference made sense.

They made their way back to a tiny exam room. "I'll

stay in the hall for now," Aidan said. "You tell me if you need me."

The door was open and stayed open, so Aidan hovered just out of sight. When he took a quick peek, he saw Mrs. Shapiro's arms go up to embrace her husband. The look on the old woman's face made something hurt in Aidan's chest. The moment was intensely personal, yet he couldn't look away. For a split second he could see the couple as twenty-somethings, walking the streets of New York arm in arm.

Forcing himself to back up, he leaned against the wall in the corridor and shut his eyes. Five minutes passed, maybe ten, before Mr. Shapiro touched his arm. Though stooped and shuffling, the devoted husband smiled with relief. "It was a mild heart attack," he said. "But she's going to be okay. They're keeping her overnight. She wants me to go home and get some rest."

Aidan nodded. "Sounds good."

In Mr. Shapiro's apartment, Aidan prepared to say his goodbyes. But his neighbor sank into a chair, his gnarled hands gripping the arms white-knuckled. "I'll sit here tonight," he said.

"Why on earth would you do that?"

Mr. Shapiro grimaced. "My hearing's gone. I don't want to miss the phone if the hospital calls. She might need me."

"What if I sleep on your sofa?" Aidan said. "You need to keep up your strength so you can take care of your wife. If the hospital contacts you, I'll make sure to wake you up."

The old man sniffed and wiped his nose with the back of his hand. His rheumy eyes held a wealth of gratitude. "God bless you, Mr. Kavanagh."

"Call me Aidan...please."

"And I'm Howard."

The two men stared at each other, opposites in every way. One young, one old. Two different faiths. One with more family than he knew what to do with. The other alone in the world.

Aidan knew in that moment that something had changed. No longer would he be able to hide behind the anonymity of the city. From the first moment he set eyes on Emma again and realized he still wanted her, the painful process of metamorphosis had begun. The man he had been was gone. But who would surface in his place?

Twenty

Emma locked the door to Silver Memories at four o'clock and pulled the shade over the glass. Fastened to the other side was a notice that said: Closed until January 3rd. It had been a good holiday season for her fledgling business. Though financially it wouldn't have mattered one way or another, she took quiet pride in knowing she had pulled it off.

It was Christmas Eve. Maeve had offered numerous invitations to join the Kavanagh clan for the evening and the next day, but Emma declined them all. Holidays were a family time. If that weren't reason enough, Emma bore the guilt of feeling responsible for Aidan's absence.

Maeve hadn't said much on that subject, but Emma knew the Kavanagh matriarch was deeply disappointed not to have her whole clan together. Dylan and Mia had chosen to take a brief honeymoon with a longer trip planned for later. They had returned midday today and were looking forward to spending Christmas Eve with their daughter and the rest of the family.

Mia hadn't called Emma this afternoon. But she was undoubtedly busy. Perhaps she, too, blamed Emma for Aidan's return to New York. Unless Aidan had made any explanations—and that didn't sound like him at all—none of the Kavanaghs could know for sure what was going on. If, however, Maeve had shared what she knew about seeing Emma at the hotel in the early morning hours, then speculation might have filled in the details.

When the shop was set to rights and the till counted, Emma grabbed her coat and the day's deposit in hopes of making a dash to the bank before it closed. The weather was far balmier today than it had been a week ago. She didn't even need gloves or a hat.

People on the street bustled happily. Some of the die-hard shoppers made last-minute purchases, though like Emma, most business owners were closing up for the long weekend.

With her errand done, Emma found herself walking aimlessly, enjoying the waning sunshine and the scent of wood smoke and evergreen in the air. Even though she felt very much alone, she drew comfort from the cheerful "busy"-ness of small-town life.

She recognized many faces now that she had been around for a few months. Silver Glen was a close-knit community and would be a wonderful spot to put down permanent roots. Emma's mother was already talking about coming over for a visit in the New Year.

And as for Aidan…well, that situation would resolve itself. He didn't come home to visit very often, and when he did, Emma planned to make herself scarce.

Without conscious thought, she found herself in front of the chapel where Dylan and Mia had exchanged vows. The town council had decided long ago to leave the little church unlocked at all times, not only for tourists' benefit, but so that the people of Silver Glen could also stop by and say a prayer or light a candle.

Emma opened the door and closed it behind her. It was cold inside the small sanctuary. With the sun going down, shadows spread long and dark across the wooden pews.

In one corner, a simply decorated tree stood ready for the late night service. Candles burned on the altar already. The evergreen boughs from the wedding still adorned the windows.

She sat down on the second row and ran her hand over the velvet cushion. Several generations of Silver Glen's families had worshipped here. Emma felt an unseen connection to the little abbey back home in the Cotswolds.

Breathing slowly, she took stock of her disappointment and grief. Aidan was not hers. He didn't want anything *from* her. She had been so sure she could convince him they deserved a second chance. But in the end, she was forced to recognize the futility of her hopes and dreams.

Whatever Aidan had felt for her once upon a time didn't matter. All that was important now was for Emma to move on.

Even with all that grown-up reasoning, surely a girl deserved a moment to indulge in self-pity. Resting her arms on the pew in front of her, she buried her face and let the tears fall.

But her catharsis was short.

"Emma..."

When a voice sounded behind her, she jerked upright and wiped her cheeks with trembling fingers before turning around. The shadows were deeper now. Even so, she recognized the figure standing tall and still in the center aisle.

"Aidan?"

"Yep."

He sounded resigned. Or mildly amused. Or maybe both.

"What are you doing here?"

"Here, where? In Silver Glen? Or in this church?"

"Either. Both." She felt dizzy—hot one minute and cold the next.

"It's Christmas Eve."

He said it calmly as if it were perfectly normal for him to be in the one place that held so many dark memories.

When he took two steps in her direction, she held up both hands. "Stop. Don't come any closer."

He obeyed, but he cocked his head. "Are you scared of me, Emma?" Now, he was near enough for the candles on the altar to illuminate his face. In his dear, familiar features she saw fatigue…but something else as well. Light. Steadiness. Contentment. As if someone had wiped away his customary air of cynicism.

"Please don't say whatever you're going to say," she cried. "I can't bear it. I've made my peace with this whole mess. I need you to go away." Ruthlessly, she stomped on the hope that tried to gain a tiny foothold in the hushed atmosphere.

"I can't, Emma. I owe you an apology and an explanation."

"I don't want it. It's too late. Your family is waiting for you up on the mountain. Go."

He took two more steps, his posture confident and relaxed. "I've made you miserable, Emma. I'm so sorry."

Literally backed into a corner because of the closed-in pew, she inhaled sharply. "I need you to respect my wishes." Unfortunately, the words came out quavering and tearful instead of firm and demanding.

Aidan must have made his own interpretation. He crowded her, his scent and the warmth of his body making her pulse jump. "I love you, Emma."

She put her hands over her ears. "No. Don't say things you think I want to hear. You're in a sacred place. Lightning will strike."

He ran his hands down her arms and tugged her by the wrists until she landed firmly against his chest. One of his thighs lodged between hers. His gray sweater was soft against her cheek. If she listened hard enough, she could hear his heart beating in time with hers.

"Neither of us can dance around the facts beneath this roof, can we? It has to be the truth and nothing but the truth." He stroked her hair. "Sit down with me, Emma."

He didn't give her much choice. Tucking her in the crook of the arm, he cuddled her close.

But she couldn't bear it. Jerking away and standing abruptly, she kept him at bay. "Let me out."

"No."

Emma started to shake. "We've come to the end of the road, Aidan. Don't make things worse."

"I was a free agent when I came to England," he said. "Danielle and I had been dating for a long time. But we weren't sure if what we had was merely comfortable. The decision was mutual. We agreed to see other people while I was gone."

"And at Christmas, you went home and realized that you had loved her all along." It seemed petty and wrong to be jealous of a dead woman, but however unpleasant, the reality was clear.

Their intense conversation was interrupted momentarily when the minister came in and turned on the lights. He halted abruptly when he saw them. "Sorry to interrupt. Just getting ready for tonight. Merry Christmas." He departed as quickly as he had come.

The fixtures were original to the building and could only handle low-wattage bulbs, so even now the room was softly lit. Emma wasn't sure if it were better or worse that she could see Aidan's face more clearly. He remained seated, but she sensed his determination.

"When I left England," he said, "I was a mess. But I was a guy, so I wasn't about to let anyone know how I felt."

"I called you and sent emails for weeks, but you didn't answer."

"In case you haven't noticed, I'm a stubborn man. Even worse, back then I was too young to know that few situations in life are entirely black or white. You had betrayed me. That was all I knew. I got back to campus and saw Danielle. She represented everything uncomplicated and easy. Without thinking about the consequences, I proposed."

"And she accepted."

"Yes. It was something we had thought about for a long time, so the proposal was almost anticlimactic. We made plans to go to Silver Glen and spend Christmas with my family. But by the time we made it to North Carolina, I realized I had made a mistake."

"What kind of mistake?"

"I *loved* her, but I wasn't *in* love with her. I knew I couldn't drag things out, so as soon as the holidays were over, I planned to tell her the truth and to apologize."

"But she died."

After all this time, his face reflected a pain that was still deep. "I failed her on so many levels."

"But you made her happy, too."

"God, I hope so." He raked his hands through his hair, leaning forward with his elbows on his knees. "As soon as I broke things off with Danielle, I planned to go back to England and confront you…to fight for what we had."

"But you didn't…"

"I couldn't." He sat back against the pew, his expression bleak as he stared at her. "How was it fair for me to reach for happiness when her life was over?"

Hearing that Aidan had wanted to come back to England healed some of the raw places in Emma's heart. "I'm so sorry."

He shrugged. "It all happened a long time ago."

"Is it my turn now?" she asked quietly. "Will you let me tell you my story?"

He stood up and took her in his arms a second time, smoothing the hair from her face. "It doesn't matter, Emma. Whatever mistakes you made back then were no better or worse than mine. It's over." She saw the love in his eyes, but she couldn't let him believe that she had betrayed him.

It was her turn to pull him down onto the pew. She half turned to face him, taking his hands in hers. "Richard lied to you."

Aidan frowned. "He introduced himself to me as your fiancé. And when I looked at you to ask if it was true, you hesitated. I saw in your face that you knew who he was and you weren't surprised."

"I wasn't surprised, because my father had been telling Richard for two years that if he only waited for me to finish college, my father was sure that I would consent to an engagement."

"And would you have? Had it not been for me?"

"No," she said firmly. "I'd made that clear to my father, but Richard's estate adjoined ours, and my father had visions of joining two great families, even though Richard was a decade older than I was. Poor Richard was not a malicious man, but he let himself be manipulated by my father. When Daddy got wind of my romance with you, he sent Richard to London to stake a claim."

Aidan closed his eyes momentarily as a pained look crossed his face. "So none of it was true..."

"No. But I handled things poorly. When you asked me

if Richard was my fiancé, I should have denied it immediately. I'd been brought up to keep the peace whenever possible, though. I didn't want to hurt Richard's feelings, because he hadn't really done anything wrong except for letting my father fill his head with nonsense. But in my naïveté, I hurt the one person I loved more than anything else in the world."

"Was that incident what caused the rift with your father?"

"Yes. I was furious and distraught and completely at a loss as to what to do. He ruined my life."

"Or maybe you and I ruined our lives together."

She grimaced, nodding. "A decade lost."

Aidan cupped her face in his hands. "That decade taught me some important lessons, my love. I've come to understand that forgiveness has to be unconditional. And it's finally been pounded into my hard skull that the people who love me don't deserve to be shut out…that our connection and commitment to one another make life rich." He paused, his throat working. "I won't ever let you go again."

Emma trembled, afraid to assume too much. "Meaning what, Aidan?"

He kissed her softly on the lips, a reverent, sweet caress. When he pulled back, his eyes gleamed. "It means that you're going to marry me. The sooner, the better. My work, your antique business—we can handle those details as we go along."

Joy welled in her chest. "Don't I get a say in the matter?"

"Not at all. This is nonnegotiable. But I think we'd better get out of here quickly."

"Why?"

"Because the thoughts I'm having about you right now are definitely not appropriate in this setting."

Outside, he took her in his arms again, and kissing her deeply, backed her up against the door of the church and sealed his vow. He had come so close to losing her a second time, it terrified him. "I love you, Em. Body and soul. I never stopped. I've lied to myself for years, living on the surface of life, never willing to admit that there was more."

Her smile was radiant, warming him even as the chill of night swirled around him. "You're the best Christmas present I've ever received. I love you, too, Aidan. My apartment is close. What if we go there and I show you exactly how much?"

He shuddered, already imagining the feel of her body pressed against his. "Hold that thought, my little tease. There's one thing we have to do first."

Her eyes widened in comprehension. "Of course…"

The Silver Beeches Lodge was booked to capacity. Aidan held Emma's hand as they walked up the steps. As the doorman welcomed then into the lobby, Emma hung back.

"I'm nervous," she whispered.

"Why, my love? You've already met everyone."

"But it's Christmas. And I'm the reason you almost missed it."

"You're also the reason I came back."

Emma's brow furrowed as they headed back toward the small dining room that had been set aside for the Kavanagh celebration. "I forgot to ask. Did you have some kind of epiphany about us?"

He stood in the doorway, his arm around her waist

and surveyed his loud, wonderful family before they had a chance to notice him. The remnants of dinner littered the large table. In the far corner, a mountain of brightly wrapped gifts waited to be opened.

Pressing a kiss to the top of Emma's head, Aidan paused to savor the incredible feeling of happiness and joy that swept over him. "Let's just say that I did the math, and I realized if we start right now, we can still make it to our fiftieth wedding anniversary."

Emma leaned into him, the woman he'd always loved and needed. "Merry Christmas, Aidan," she said.

"Merry Christmas, my English rose..."

* * * * *

THE BOSS'S MISTLETOE MANOEUVRES

LINDA THOMAS-SUNDSTROM

Linda Thomas-Sundstrom writes contemporary and paranormal romance novels. A teacher by day and a writer by night, Linda lives in the West, juggling teaching, writing with family and caring for a big stretch of land. She swears she has a resident muse who sings so loudly, she often wears earplugs in order to get anything else done. But she has big plans to eventually get to all those ideas. Visit Linda at lindathomas-sundstrom.com or on Facebook.

One

Chaz Monroe knew a great female backside when he saw one. And the blonde with the swinging ponytail walking down the hallway in front of him was damn near a ten.

Lean, rounded, firm and feminine, her admirable backside swayed from side to side as she moved, above the short hemline of a tight black skirt that did little to hide a great pair of legs. Long, shapely legs, encased in paper-thin black tights and ending in a pair of perfectly sensible black leather pumps.

The sensible pumps were a disappointment and a slight hiccup in his rating overall, given the sexiness of the rest of her. She was red stilettos all the way, Chaz decided. Satin shoes maybe, or suede. Still, though the woman was a visual sensory delight, now wasn't the time or place for an indulgence of that kind. Not with an employee. Never with an employee.

She wore a blue fuzzy sweater that molded to her slender torso and was on the tall side of small. Her stride was purposeful, businesslike and almost arrogant in the way she maneuvered through the narrow hallway, skillfully avoiding chairs, unused consoles and the watercooler. Her heels made soft clicking sounds that didn't echo much.

Chaz followed her until she turned right, heading for Cubicle City. At that junction, as he hooked a left toward his new office, he caught a whiff of scent that lingered in her wake. Not a typical floral fragrance, either. Something subtle, almost sweet, that would have decided her fate right then and there if he'd been another kind of guy, with a different sort of agenda.

This guy had to think and behave like the new owner of an advertising agency in the heart of Manhattan.

Taking over a new business required the kind of time that ruled out relationships, including dates and dalliances. In the past two months he'd become a freaking monk, since there wasn't one extra hour in his schedule for distractions if he was to turn this company around in a decent amount of time. That was the priority. All of his money was riding on this company making it. He'd spent every cent he had to buy this advertising firm.

Whistling, Chaz strolled past Alice Brody, his newly inherited pert, big-eyed, middle-aged, fluffy-haired executive secretary. He entered his office through a set of glass doors still bearing the name of the vice president he'd already had to let go for allowing the company to slowly slide from the top of the heap to the mediocre middle. Lackluster management was unacceptable in a company where nothing seemed to be wrong with the work of the rest of the staff.

"There is one more person to see today," Alice called after him.

"Need a few minutes to go over some things first," Chaz said over his shoulder. "Can you bring in the file I asked for?"

"I'll get on it right away."

Something in Alice's tone made him wonder what she might be thinking. He could feel her eyes on him. When he glanced back at her, she smiled.

Chaz shrugged off the thought, used to women liking his looks. But his older brother Rory was the real catch. As the first self-made millionaire in the family, his brother made headlines and left trails of women in his wake.

Chaz had a lot of catching up to do to match his brother's magic with a floundering company. So there were, at the moment, bigger fish to fry.

First up, he had to finish dealing with old contract issues

and get everyone up to speed with the new company plan. He had to decide how to speak to one person in particular. Kim McKinley, the woman highly recommended by everyone here for an immediate promotion. The woman in line for the VP job before he had temporarily taken over that office, going undercover in this new business as an employee.

More to the point, he had to find out why Kim McKinley had a clause in her contract that excluded her from working on the biggest advertising campaign of the year. *Christmas.*

He couldn't see how an employee headed for upper management could be exempt from dealing with Christmas campaigns, when it was obvious she was a player, otherwise.

He'd done his homework and had made it a priority to find out about Kim, who spearheaded four of the company's largest accounts. Her clients seemed to love her. They threw money at her, and this was a good thing.

He could use someone like this by his side, and was confident that he could make her see reason about the Christmas campaigns. Intelligent people had to be flexible. It would be a shame to issue an ultimatum, if it came to that, for Kim to lose what she had worked so hard for because of his new rules on management and contracts.

Chaz picked up a pencil and tucked it behind his ear, knowing by the way it stuck there easily that he needed a haircut, and that haircuts were a luxury when business came first.

He was sure that his upcoming appointment with Kim McKinley would turn out well. Handling people was what he usually did best when he took over a new company in his family's name. Juggling this agency's problems and getting more revenue moving in the right direction was the reason he had bought this particular firm for himself. That, and the greedy little need to show his big brother what he could do on his own.

The agency's bottom line wasn't bad; it just needed some TLC. Which was why he had gone undercover as the new VP. He figured it would be easier for other employees to deal with a fellow employee, rather than an owner. Even an employee in management. Pretending to be one of them for a while would give him a leg up on the internal workings of the business.

He would be good to Kim McKinley and all of the others who wanted to work and liked it here, if they played ball.

Did they have to love him? *No.*

But he'd hopefully earn their respect.

Chaz turned when the door opened, and Alice breezed in without knocking. She handed over a manila file folder held together with a thick rubber band. Thanking her, he waited until she left before sitting down. Centering the file on his desk, he read the name on it.

Kimberly McKinley.

He removed the rubber band, opened the folder and read the top page. She was twenty-four years old, had graduated from NYU with honors.

He already knew most of that.

He skimmed through the accolades. She was described as a hard worker. An honest, inventive, intelligent, creative self-starter with a good client base. An excellent earner recommended for advancement to a position in upper management.

A handwritten scribble in the margins added, *Lots of bang for the buck.*

There was one more thing he wished he could check in the file, for no other reason than a passing interest. Her marital status. Single people were known for their work ethics and the extra hours they could put in. McKinley's quick rise in the company was probably due not only to her ability to reel in business and keep it, but also to her availability.

What could be better than that?

He stole a glance at the empty seat across from him then looked again at the overstuffed folder. He tapped his fingers on the desk. "How badly do you want a promotion, Kim?" he might ask her. The truth was that if she were to get that promotion, she'd be one of the youngest female vice presidents in the history of advertising.

And that was fine with him. Young minds were good minds, and McKinley truly sounded like the embodiment of the name her coworkers had given her. *Wonder Woman.*

Although he was already familiar with her tally of clients, he checked over the list.

Those four clients that he'd classify as the Big Four, refused to work with anyone else, and it was a sure bet McKinley knew this, too, and would possibly use it as leverage if push came to shove about her taking on holiday-themed campaigns that didn't suit her. Would those clients turn away if he accidentally pushed McKinley too hard, and she walked? Rumor had it that three of them had been hoping she'd add Christmas to her list and stop farming those holiday accounts out.

He looked up to find Alice again in the doorway, as if the woman had psychically picked up on his need to ask questions.

"What will Kim have to say about believing she has been passed over in favor of me in this office?" was his first one.

Alice, through highly glossed ruby lips, said, "Kim had been promised the job by the last guy behind that desk. She'll be disappointed."

"How disappointed?"

"Very. She's an asset to this company. It would be a shame to lose her."

Chaz nodded thoughtfully. "You think she might leave?"

Alice shrugged. "It's a possibility. I can name a few other agencies in the city that would like to have her onboard."

Chaz glanced at the file, supposing he was going to have

to wear kid gloves when he met McKinley. If everyone else in town wanted her, how would pressure tactics work in getting her to stay put and take on more work?

He nodded to Alice, the only staff member who knew what his real agenda was for playing at being the new VP, and that he now owned everything from the twelfth to the fourteenth floor.

"Why doesn't she do Christmas campaigns?" he asked.

"I have no idea. It must be something personal," Alice replied. "She'll attend meetings when necessary, but doesn't handle the actual work."

"Why do you think it might be personal?" Chaz pressed.

"Take a look at her cubicle."

"Is something wrong with it?"

"There's nothing Christmasy about it. It's fifteen days until the big holiday, and she doesn't possess so much as a red and green pen," Alice said.

An image of the blonde in the hallway crowded his mind as if tattooed there. He wondered if Kim McKinley would be anything like that. He tended to picture McKinley as a stern, no-nonsense kind of a gal. Glasses, maybe, and a tweed suit to make her seem older than her actual age and give her some street cred.

"Thanks, Alice."

"My pleasure," Alice said, closing the door as she exited.

Chaz leaned back in his chair and scanned the office, thinking he'd like to be anywhere but there, undercover. Pretending wasn't his forte. To his credit, he had been a pretty decent young advertising exec himself a few years back, before entering the family business of buying up companies. In the time since then, he'd made more than one flustered employee cry.

He was responsible for the decisions regarding the upper echelon of this agency. But once he revealed he was the new owner, the future occupant of the VP's office would require more than a rave review on paper and a few happy clients. He found it inconceivable that anyone considered for such a promotion would avoid working on campaigns that brought in big revenue for the company. What was Kim McKinley thinking?

Chaz swiveled toward the window, where he had a bird's-eye view of the street below. Though it was already dark outside, he got to his feet and peered out, counting four Santas on street corners collecting for charity in a city that was draped in holiday trappings.

When the knock came on his door, Chaz looked around. He wasn't expecting anyone for another hour, and Alice never bothered to announce her own entrance. The thought that someone could bypass Alice seemed ludicrous.

The knock came again. After one more sharp rap, the doorknob moved. It seemed that his visitor wasn't going to wait for permission to come in.

The door swung open. A woman, her outline exaggerated by the lights behind her, straddled the threshold in a slightly imperious stance.

"You wanted to see me?" the woman said.

Chaz figured this could only be the notorious McKinley, since she was the only person left on his list to see that day.

After realizing she wasn't actually going to take a single step into the room, he blew out a long, low breath without realizing he'd been holding it, and squelched the urge to laugh out loud.

Had he wished too hard for this, maybe, and someone had been listening?

The woman in his doorway was none other than the delicious blonde.

Yep, *that* one.

"*The* Kim McKinley?" the man by the window said.

Kim was so angry, she could barely control herself. Her hand on the doorknob shook with irritation.

"You wanted to see me?" she repeated.

"Yes. Please come in," he said from behind the desk that should have been hers. "Have a seat."

She shook her head. "I doubt if I'll be here long enough to get comfortable."

This was an unfortunate double entendre. Chaz Monroe was either going to praise her or hand her a pink slip for being his closest competition.

With a familiar dread knotting her stomach, she added, "I have a pressing appointment that might last for some time."

"I won't keep you long. Please, Miss McKinley, come in."

She stood her ground. "I have a tight schedule to maintain today, Mr. Monroe, and I came here to ask if we can have our sit-down appointment at a later time?"

She had been expecting this talk from the new guy, but truly hadn't expected *this*. His looks. The shock of seeing the usurper in the flesh held her in place, and kept her at a slight disadvantage. At the moment, she couldn't have moved from the doorway if she'd tried.

For once, rumors hadn't lied. Chaz Monroe was a hunk. Not only was he younger than she had imagined, he was also incredibly handsome…though he was, she reminded herself, in *her* office.

This newcomer had been handed the job she had been promised, and he'd summoned her as if she were a minion. He stood behind the mahogany desk like a king, impeccably dressed, perfectly gorgeous and not at all as rigid as she had anticipated he would be.

In fact, he looked downright at home. Already.

She stared openly at him.

Shaggy dark hair, deep brown, almost black, surrounded an angular face. Light eyes—blue maybe, she couldn't be sure—complemented his long-sleeved, light blue shirt. He flashed a sensual smile full of enviable white teeth, but the smile had to be phony. They both knew he was going to gloss over the fact that he'd gotten this job, in her place, if he'd done any research at all. He no doubt would also ask about the Christmas clause in her contract, first thing, without knowing anything about her. He'd try to put her in her place, and on the defensive. She felt this in her bones.

A shiver of annoyance passed through her.

She was willing to bet that this guy was good at lording over people. He had that kind of air. Monroe was a devil in a dashing disguise, and if she didn't behave, if she said what was really on her mind, she'd be jobless in less than ten minutes.

"Did you want something in particular?" she asked.

"I wanted to get acquainted. I've heard a lot about you, and I have a few questions about your file," Monroe said, his eyes moving over her intently as he spoke. He was studying her, too. Maybe he searched for a chink in her armor.

She'd be damned if she'd let him find it.

A trickle of perspiration dripped between Kim's shoulder blades, caused by the dichotomy of weighing Monroe's looks against what he was going to do to her when she refused to play nice with him. Maybe it wasn't his fault that she'd been passed over for the promotion, but did he have to look so damn content?

And if he were to push her about her contract?

Monroe had only been in this building for two days, while her guilt about Christmas was years-old and remained depressingly fresh. Her mother had died only six months ago; it hadn't been long enough for Kim to get over the years of darkness about the Christmas holidays that had prevailed in the McKinley household.

Kim shut her eyes briefly to regroup and felt awkward seconds ticking by.

"Please come in. If you're in a hurry, let's talk briefly about the Christmas stuff," he said, verifying her worst fears.

"If it's the Christmas files you want, you'll need to see Brenda Chang," she said coolly. "Brenda's the one down the hall with the decorated cubicle. Red paper, garlands, tinsel, and holiday carols on CD. You can't miss it. Brenda oversees some of the December holiday ads."

She watched Monroe circle to the front of the desk, where he sat on the edge and indicated the vacant chair beside him with a wave of his hand. *Just a friendly little chat...*

Refusing to oblige his regal fantasies, Kim stubbornly remained in the doorway, anxiously screwing the heel of one shoe into the costly beige Berber carpet.

He maintained eye contact in a way that made her slightly dizzy from the intensity of his stare. "And you don't have any Christmas accounts, why, exactly? If you're one of the best we've got, shouldn't you be overseeing our biggest source of revenue?"

"Thanks for the compliment, but I don't do this particular holiday. I'm sure it's all there in my file. I can help Alice locate my contract before I go, if you'd like."

Monroe's calm, professional expression didn't falter. "Perhaps you can explain why you don't *do* Christmas? I'd honestly like to know."

"It's personal. Plus, I'm very busy doing other work here." Kim held up a hand. "Look, I'd love to have this get-acquainted chat." The words squeezed through tight lips. "But I'll have to beg off right now. I'm sorry. I really am expected somewhere."

"It's almost five. Do you have a work-related appointment?" Monroe asked.

Kim started to ask what business it was of his, then thought better of voicing such a thing because like it or not, he was her boss, and it was his business. She had agreed to meet some friends for a quick drink in the bar downstairs, and it was important that she got home right after that, before the beautiful holiday lights made her think again and more seriously about dishonoring her mother's memory.

Lately, she'd been having second thoughts about what she'd experienced growing up, and what she'd been taught, both about the insensitivity of men and the pain of the holidays.

Her mother hadn't approved of anything to do with Christmas. For the McKinleys, Christmas meant sorrow and the extremes of loss. It meant sad memories of a husband and father who had deserted his wife and five-year-old daughter on Christmas Eve to be with another family.

Kim looked at Monroe levelly. No way she was going to tell him any of that, and she shouldn't have to dredge up the details of something that had already been hammered out a year ago when she negotiated her contract with somebody else on this floor.

"Sure, meeting later would be fine," Monroe said. "Maybe around eight?"

"I'm usually in by seven, so yes, I can return first thing in the morning if that's what you'd like," Kim said.

"Actually, I meant tonight. 8:00 p.m.," he clarified, enunciating clearly. "If it wouldn't be too terribly inconvenient, that is, and you're still around. We can keep it casual and meet in the bar downstairs. That's not too much out of the way, right?"

"The bar?" Kim heard the slip in her tone.

"In the bar, yes," he said, without losing the charming, almost boyish smile.

Damn him. It was a really nice smile.

"I'm told it's a regular meeting place after hours for employees," he continued. "Maybe we can snag a quiet table?"

So they could do what? Have a friendly drink before the ax fell? Before the arguments began?

Don't think so.

"Will you be finished with your appointment by then?" Monroe pressed.

Realizing that she couldn't lie, and since others from the agency were going to be in that same bar, and still might be hanging around at eight, she said, "Yes," adding in another job-related double entendre, "I'll be finished."

With those last three words dangling between them, Chaz Monroe got to his feet and walked right up to her.

She had to wince to keep from backing up.

He came very close. Obviously, he had no intention of preserving her tiny circle of personal space.

Then he invaded it.

And hell…

Up close, he was even better.

"Your appointment isn't a date?" he asked in a husky tone that wasn't at all businesslike.

Kim felt breathless so close to this incredibly gorgeous guy who was her new boss, and chastised herself for being affected by him in such a physical way. Monroe was a time bomb comprised of every woman's sexual addictions, from his shaggy hair to his loafered feet. In order to become desensitized to this kind of personal frontal attack, she'd have had to experience quite a few near misses in the past with men of Monroe's caliber.

No such thing was in her dating history.

Her feet inched forward to close the distance to him before she could stop them. Her breasts strained at her sweater with a reaction so unacceptable, she wanted to scream. But she heard herself say, "Not tonight. No date."

The words *wrong* and *harassment* sailed through her mind. He was close enough to touch. Why?

He was also near enough to punch, but she didn't take a swing.

Chaz Monroe was a head taller than she was and smelled like *man,* in a really good way. He radiated sex appeal and an easy, unattended elegance. He didn't wear a coat or a tie, yet what he did wear was confidence, in an unintimidating manner. His casualness was reflected in the fact that his shirt was open at the neck, revealing a triangle of bare, lightly tanned skin. That taut, masculine flesh captured her attention for what seemed like several long minutes before she glanced up....

To meet his blue eyes.

That's when she heard music.

She shook her head, not quite believing it, but the music didn't go away. It was Christmas music, she finally realized, coming from the lobby and signaling the nearness of closing time for most of the staff. She had to get out of there and was caught between a rock and...a hard body.

"Good. I'll see you at eight," Monroe said, breaking the standoff.

The sensation of his warm breath on her face gave Kim a ridiculously flushed and tingly few seconds. The look in his eyes doubled that. What kind of boss was he? The kind that wouldn't mind breaking a few laws in order to get his way? The kind with a casting couch?

Had her mother been right about overly attractive men being saps, after all?

She broke eye contact. Her lashes fluttered.

"Eight o'clock. In the bar," he said in a tone that gave her an electrical jolt and made her clothing feel completely inadequate as a barrier against the sleek, seductive hoodoo he had going on.

Excuses for her reaction beat at her from the inside. The air around her visibly trembled with the need to shout "Go to hell!" Yet she stood there, helpless to get out of this, speechless for once, before backing up and turning abruptly.

She left Chaz Monroe, knowing that he stared after her, feeling his heated gaze. That scrutiny was so hot, she had an absurd longing to run back to him and get it over with. Just press her mouth to his in a brief goodbye kiss, then laugh maniacally as she headed back to her cubicle to clear out her things.

The strangest bit of intuition told her that he wanted that same thing. In those insane moments of confrontation and unacceptable closeness, her senses screamed that Chaz Monroe had wanted to kiss her.

She knew something else, as well. Because of the fire in her nerve endings and the way her heart thundered, meeting Chaz Monroe at the bar tonight was a very...bad...idea.

Two

Chaz faced the distinct possibility of being in serious trouble before Kim McKinley had left him standing in the open doorway. He had very nearly just breached every rule of decorum in the book. Well, he had thought about it, anyway.

She hadn't helped any.

Resisting the urge to loosen his collar, which was already loosened, he cleared his throat and looked to Alice, who was watching him with a raised eyebrow. Only practice allowed him to keep his expression neutral when he felt an annoying shudder in the abs he had worked so hard on in the gym before his takeover of this company shot down his regular routine.

Nodding to Alice, he stepped back into his office.

"Damn."

He had gotten up close and personal with an employee. His idea to dish some of that haughty attitude of McKinley's right back at her had backfired, big-time.

Not only were her body and her sexy scent tantalizing as hell, Kim's face and voice were undeniably appetizing. She had an accent, a slight Southern drawl that resulted in a slow drawing out of syllables. Her voice was deep, sultry and a lot like whispered vibrations passing through overheated air.

As for her face…

It was the face of an angel. The pale, silky-smooth, slightly babyish oval wasn't in any way indicative of her crisp attitude.

He could feel the residual intensity of her expressive hazel eyes, and didn't even want to think about her lips.

Pink lips, moist, slick and slightly parted, as if just waiting to be kissed.

Chaz touched his forehead absently. Hell, if he didn't have a bone to pick with her over the Christmas stuff, and if he actually relied on first impressions of a physical nature, he'd have been tempted to throw in the towel and give her the office right then and there—anything to get closer to her.

Anything to taste those lips.

Man. His mind had taken an inconvenient slip, a sudden, unexpected detour, and he wanted to laugh at the situation and at himself. However, there was more to be considered here. If he was going to be around Kim McKinley on a regular basis, he'd have to be able to keep his mind on business; a real feat, given the outline of the world-class breasts he'd seen through the thin layer of cloud-blue cashmere.

Damn it, why hadn't anyone told him about *that?*

Returning to the desk, pulling the pencil from behind his ear, Chaz scratched *Personnel files should contain all pertinent information in the future* on a yellow notepad.

Tapping the pencil on McKinley's file, he vowed not to debate with himself about what a pouty mouth like hers might do, other than kissing, while realizing that X-rated thoughts had no place in contract negotiations or the boardroom.

He shook his head. In spite of the untimely, if temporary, dilemma, Chaz didn't lose the smile when he looked again to the doorway where Kim had just stood, cute as a bug from the neck up and devilishly delicious from the neck down, while she made a decent attempt at blowing him off.

Can we talk later?

I have a schedule to keep to.

Kim McKinley, it seemed, wasn't going to take losing this office well. She was angry and trying to deal. It was possible that as long as she remained on his payroll, thinking he had the job she coveted, she might do everything in her power to either avoid him or bust his chops.

True, he had pushed her a little, and hadn't explained what he was doing here, undercover—which would have defeated the purpose of being undercover.

Could she really be so good at her job? She might be decent at what she did for this agency and damn nice to look at, but no one was so indispensable that they could afford to anger the new man in charge within the first sixty seconds of meeting him.

Yet that's just what she had done. Sort of.

Reopening her file, Chaz pondered the question of whether she had actually just offered up a challenge. Had McKinley meant to wave a flag in front of the bull, a flag bearing the legend *Leave me alone, or lose me?*

The back of Chaz's neck prickled the way it usually did when the anticipation of a good challenge set in. This particular tickle was similar to the feelings he'd had when he had handed over ten million dollars for a company he had every intention of making more successful than it was before he stepped in. The tickle was also similar to the one brought about by thoughts of the self-imposed challenge of tackling his brother's track record of successful takeovers, and proving his own business acumen.

Testy employees had no place in either of those particular goals, except for doing the jobs assigned to them. He really could not afford to be distracted right now.

Chaz stared at the door, where Kim McKinley had drawn an invisible battle line on several levels. His mind buzzed with possibilities. Maybe she used her looks to get what she wanted, and that was part of her success. It could be that she believed herself to be so valuable that he wouldn't mess with her if she resisted his logical suggestions.

Or if she resisted his advances.

What? Damn. He hadn't just thought that. *Advances* were totally out of the question.

Sitting down in his chair, Chaz placed both hands on the desk, disgusted that he'd been waylaid by this surprise. Kim McKinley just wasn't what he had expected, that's all. And the firm could always find someone to replace her if her attitude got out of hand.

Was that a fair assessment of the situation?

As he tapped his pencil on her file, he mulled over the fact that she had avoided their first sit-down appointment. Did she consider that a point for her side? Would she believe she had racked up another point for failing to give him any of the information he had been seeking, or meeting his demands on that Christmas clause head-on?

Was she the type to keep score?

Chaz rubbed the back of his neck where the darn prickle of interest just wouldn't ease up. Buttoning the collar of his shirt, he firmed up his resolve to get to the bottom of the McKinley mystery. Wonder Woman would be wrong if she thought him a fool. He was a master at compartmentalizing when he had to. He hadn't gotten to where he was in business by tossing employees on the carpet according to whim, or dumping their sorry backsides in the street without real cause. He was bigger than that, and he always played fair.

He would meet Kim McKinley tonight and set things straight. He'd give her the benefit of the doubt about adhering to his company plan, and get her onboard, whatever it took to do so.

"Your contract. No question marks. Not up for negotiation."

He practiced those words aloud, repeated them less forcefully and set his mental agenda.

The bar, in three hours.

They'd have a friendly chat and get to the specifics of the deal. McKinley might turn out to be a good ally.

As for the bedroom dreams...

He let out a bark of self-deprecating laughter over the time he was spending on this one issue, a sure sign that truly, and admittedly, he hadn't been prepared for the likes of this woman.

He really would have to be more cautious in the future, because, man-oh-man, what he needed right that minute, in Kim McKinley's saucy Southern wake, and in preparation for meeting her again was…

…a very long, very cold shower.

Kim tumbled into her chair and laid her head down on her desk. She turned just far enough to eye the golden plaque perched next to her pencil sharpener that had been a gift from her friend Brenda.

Kim McKinley, VP of Advertising.

"Some joke." She backhanded the plaque, sending it sailing. Who had she been kidding, anyway? Vice president? A twenty-four-year-old *woman?*

There would be no big office with floor-to-ceiling windows in her immediate future. No maple shelving for potted plants, and no opportunity to implement her plans and ideas for the company. So didn't she feel exactly like that jettisoned plaque—shot into space, only to land with a dismal thud right back in her own six-by-six cubicle?

Could the moisture welling up in her eyes be *tears?* As in about to *cry* tears?

Unacceptable.

Twenty-four-year-old professionals didn't blubber away when they were royally disappointed, or when they were overlooked and underappreciated at the office.

No tears. No way. No how.

She was mad, that's all, with no way to express how sad she was going to be if she had to leave this building and everything she had built here in the past five years.

"Why does everyone want to push me about the damn contract?" she grumbled, figuring that Brenda, in the next cubicle, would be listening. "Haven't I worked extremely hard on every other blasted campaign all year long? I've all but slept in this cubicle. I keep clothes in my desk drawers. Would it be fair to dock me over one single previously negotiated item?"

Inhaling damp desk blotter and the odor of evergreen that now pervaded the building, Kim reviewed the proverbial question on the table.

Was there another person on earth who could say that Christmas had been their downfall?

Plunking her head again on the desk, she muttered a weak "ouch." Rustling up some anger didn't seem to be working at the moment. It was obvious that she needed more work on self-defense.

"You okay?" a voice queried from somewhere behind her. "I heard a squeak."

Kim blinked.

"Kim? Are you, or are you not okay?"

"Nope. Not okay." She didn't bother to sit up.

"Are you in need of medical attention?"

Moving her mouth with difficulty because it was stuck to some paper, Kim said, "Intravenous Success Serum would be helpful. Got any?"

"No, but I've got something even better."

"Valium? Hemlock? A place with cheap rent?"

"An invitation to have drinks with the new boss tonight in the bar just arrived by email."

Kim muffled a scream. What had Brenda just said? They were both to have drinks with *Monroe?* The bastard had invited a crowd to witness her third degree and possible dismissal?

"Now's not a good time, Bren," she said. Having a coworker for her best friend sometimes had its drawbacks.

Like their close proximity when she wanted to pout by herself.

"I think now would be a good time, actually," Brenda countered. "We can find out what the new guy is like, en masse."

"I'll tell you what he's like in one word. *Brutus!*"

Brenda stuck her head over the partition separating their cubicles. "I'm guessing your meeting didn't go well?"

Kim pried her cheek from the desk, narrowed her eyes and turned to face Brenda.

"So not afraid of that look," Brenda said.

"That's the problem. Neither was he."

"Yes, well, didn't you just know that the damn Christmas clause was going to jump up and bite you again someday? I mean how could they understand when they don't know…."

Kim held up a hand that suggested if Brenda said one more word along those lines, she might regret it.

"I've probably just lost my dream job, Bren. For all intents and purposes, this agency considers me an ancestor of old mister Scrooge. And by the way, aren't best friends supposed to offer sympathy in times of crisis, without lengthy lectures tacked on?"

Not much taller than the five foot partition in her bare feet, Brenda, who went shoeless in her space, was barely visible. All that showed was a perfectly straight center part halving a swath of shiny black hair, and a pair of kohl-lined, almond-shaped eyes. The eyes were shining merrily. There might have been a piece of tinsel entwined in a few ebony strands near Brenda's forehead.

What Brenda lacked in stature, however, she made up for in persistence. "I might suggest that nobody will believe that anyone actually hates Christmas, Kim. Not for real."

Brenda didn't stop there. "That's what the new guy will be thinking. So maybe you can come up with an alternate reason for holding back on the holiday stuff that he will buy into. Like...religious reasons."

"Seriously?" Sarcasm returned to Kim's tone as she offered Brenda what she thought was a decent rendition of a go-away-and-leave-me-alone-or-else look.

Brenda performed a glossy hair flip. "Still not afraid," she said. "Or discouraged."

Kim got to her feet and smoothed her skirt over her hips. "I think it's already too late for help of any kind."

"Tell me about it," Brenda said. "But first you have to dish about whether Monroe really does have a nice ass."

Kim kneaded the space between her eyes with shaky fingers, trying to pinpoint the ache building there.

"You didn't think he was hot?" Brenda continued. "That's the word going around. H-o-t, as in *fan yourself*."

"Yeah? Did you hear anything about the man being an arrogant idiot?" Kim asked.

"No. My sources might have left that part out."

"I don't actually care about the nice ass part, Bren. I prefer not to notice an area that I won't be kissing."

"Don't be absurd, Kim. No one expects you to kiss anyone's backside. It isn't professional. What happened?"

"I'll have to start over somewhere else, that's what. Monroe won't let me off the hook. He expects me to explain everything. He'll expect me to cave." She waved both hands in the air. "I can't tell him about my background. I can barely talk about it to myself."

"You told me."

"That's different. Best friends are best friends. How I grew up isn't any of his business."

"What about the fact that you've been wanting to forget about this issue with your family for some time now, anyway?" Brenda asked. "Maybe it's the right time to take that next step."

Kim couldn't find the words to address Brenda's remark. She wondered if anyone really knew how bad guilt trips felt and how deep some family issues went, if they hadn't experienced it.

She had a hole inside her that hadn't completely closed over and was filled with heartaches that had had plenty of time to fester at a cellular level. Her mother had constantly reminded her of how they'd been wronged by a man, and about the dishonest things all men do for utterly selfish reasons.

Her mom wouldn't listen to advice about getting help in order to emerge from under the dark clouds surrounding her traumatic marital disappointment. Instead, she had spread those dark clouds over Kim.

The guilt about wanting to be rid of the deep-seated feelings of abandonment was sharp-edged, and nearly as painful now as the old heartaches. The warnings her mother had given her had calloused several times over.

Kim had thought long and hard about this since her mother's death. What she had needed was a little more leeway to get used to the fact that with her mother gone, she could embrace change without angering or hurting anyone else. Still, did that entail capitulating on the Christmas issue so soon? Was she ready for that, when this particular holiday had played such a negative role in her life?

Brenda hurried on. "If you don't want to tell Monroe the truth, you have about an hour to formulate a reason he'll accept in lieu of the truth. Fabricating illusions is what we do on a daily basis, right? We make people want to buy things."

After letting a beat of time go by for that to sink in, Brenda spoke again. "Call me selfish, Kim, but I'd like to keep you here and happy, and so would a whole host of other people. I doubt if the new guy would actually fire you, anyway. He'd have no real reason to. You can work this out. Also, you could try the truth. Talking about it might be cathartic."

Kim shook her head. Brenda hadn't witnessed Monroe's show of personalized aggression in his office doorway. Monroe had used the physical card to get her to back down, intending to intimidate her with his stockpile of charisma. And it had worked. There was no way she'd talk to a complete stranger about complicated and painful personal details and have him laugh them off as childish. Or worse, have him wave them away as being inconsequential.

"If the truth is still too painful, maybe you can spin the issue another way." Brenda snorted delicately. "You could tell Monroe that you have a Santa fetish."

Kim gave her a look.

"You can tell him a therapist explained that your Santa fetish means that you're looking for a father figure to replace yours, and you've attached yourself to a fantasy ideal. So much so, that it's embarrassing to discuss or work with."

Kim knew a ploy to lighten the mood when she heard one.

"Bren, you are usually so much better than that."

"The source of the idea wouldn't matter, Kim. Mention the word *therapist,* and Monroe would be afraid of a lawsuit if he were to ever fire you for mental health reasons."

Brenda had the audacity to giggle, despite the seriousness of the subject matter, because she was on a ludicrous roll. "You secretly long for the person who is supposed to possess magical powers that he uses for good, and this longing makes you crazy at this time of year."

"Bren, listen to yourself. You're suggesting that I tell my boss I have a secret hard-on for the guy whose belly shakes like a bowlful of jelly, and reindeer with dorky names."

"Humor aside, isn't that what you're actually waiting for? Haven't you been searching for a man with the ability to override your background issues by making dull things seem shiny and bright? You'd like to find an honest man who could disprove your mother's ideas about relationships."

Kim rubbed her forehead harder. Brenda was right. She did want a man with those quasi-magical qualities. Someone caring, understanding, strong and above all, loyal. She got breathless just thinking about it, and about separating herself from the dark spell her mother had woven.

The problem was, she seemed to only date men who had none of those things to offer. Every one of her companions so far had come up short of ideal. Maybe she'd made her poor choices to subconsciously confirm her mother's philosophy of relationship instability and injustice. She could see this. It made sense. Honestly though, she did not want to end up alone, and like her mother.

She sagged against the wall. "There's a fatal flaw in your reasoning, Bren. If I had a desire for Santa Claus and his magic, why would I be opposed to working on Christmas? I'd love Christmas. But you are partly right."

Kim pressed the hair back from her face and continued. "Secretly, I've always wanted to dump the darkness and embrace the holiday celebrations. I've wanted that for as long as I can remember. It's been my secret heartache."

More to the point, she couldn't stand anger and blame and insidious hatred, and had missed a good portion of her childhood fantasies because of her mother's take on those things. The idea of a real Santa Claus had been her one ongoing illicit passion from early on. A dream. A ray of light in the dark world she'd grown up in.

She had never disclosed this secret longing to anyone. What good would it do? What child didn't want to lighten the load and share celebrations with her friends, in spite of the fact that some things were forbidden?

Guilt was a desperate emotion. Its tentacles ran deep and clung hard. Nevertheless, contrary to her mother's feelings, she had never wanted to commit her father to the fires of Hades for making her mother's life miserable. For Kim, there had only been sadness, emptiness. Little girls needed their fathers.

She had grown up desiring the ability to absorb pain, table it and move on. She wished to fill the emptiness inside her with something better than loss. Creativity had done that for her. This job had done it. She made other peoples' fantasies come true on a regular basis. Just not hers.

Not that one specific fantasy, anyway.

"I want to participate in the holiday festivities and be really truly happy," she confessed. "I just don't know how to go about it, or where to start. I'm afraid my mother might roll over in her grave if I did."

As for the theory of cheating men, wrong men…that image seemed to fit the new boss, Chaz Monroe. Although she'd had tingly feelings in his presence, and her heart rate had skyrocketed, all that proved was that her pattern of choosing inappropriate males hadn't ended. She was attracted to flighty men caught up in their own needs. If she went down that particular path, led by Chaz Monroe, she'd regret it.

"I'm considering shock treatment," she said. "I don't rule it out."

"To my way of thinking, a little therapy now might save you a load of trouble in the long run," Brenda agreed. "Please don't be mad that I'm telling you this. Friends have obligations."

Way too much time had been spent on this. Kim could hear her watch ticking.

Brenda sighed. "There is always plan B. If you don't want to discuss this tonight, you could distract him. Throw Monroe a curveball. A sexy new outfit and some killer shoes worn as a talisman against unwanted negativity might work. At least it might give you another day or two to decide what to do."

"I didn't know shoes could repel negativity."

"They can if they're the red stilettos in the window of the shop next door."

"Those shoes cost more than my rent."

"Won't they be worth it if they work?" Brenda pointed out.

"If they don't, will you pay my bills?"

"I have a little cash saved up," Brenda admitted.

Kim tried not to choke on the Tree In A Can spray coming from Brenda's cubicle. She didn't want to bring Brenda down with her. The fact was that this new boss was likely going to create some havoc, and she'd have to wiggle her way out of the situation in order to prolong her employment. Chaz Monroe hadn't seemed like the kind of guy who was used to compromises.

Was Monroe a jerk? Maybe. He'd wanted to make her uncomfortable with all that forbidden closeness, and his method had scored. Worse yet, he had seen her squirm. If he got close to her again, though, she'd cry foul, in public, where she'd have witnesses to his behavior.

Oh yes, Chaz Monroe, playboy, would be trouble, all right.

"He has big blue eyes," she said wistfully, then looked to Brenda, hoping she hadn't just announced that out loud.

"Then there's nothing to worry about," Brenda concluded. "Because real demons have red eyes. And tails."

A chill trickled down Kim's spine, messing with the heat left over from her meeting with Monroe. Misplaced heat waves aside, the real question was whether she wanted to keep this job, and the answer was yes. No one wanted to find out how long the unemployment lines would be in December. Plus, she truly liked most of the people she worked with.

So…could she afford to allow Christmas to be a deal breaker, or was she willing to fight for what she wanted?

"A sexy dress and some shoes, huh?" she said.

Brenda nodded. "It's a bit aggressive, but it's been done for ages. Think Mata Hari."

Kim tilted her head in thought.

"Uh-oh," Brenda said, disappearing from behind the partition and appearing in the entrance to Kim's cubicle. "I don't think I like what I see in your eyes."

"I don't know what you mean."

"You wouldn't do anything stupid, right, like trying to seduce Monroe out of his title?" Brenda advanced. "You wouldn't play the harassment card, if it came to that? Seduce him and then blow the whistle to get him out of the way? That would be a terrible plan, Kim. It would be desperate, and unlike you."

Kim nodded. "In any case, I'm thinking I might have to get plastered before that meeting in the bar."

"You don't drink. You never drink."

"Exactly."

"Fine," Brenda said doubtfully. "But if it goes all haywire, please leave me the red shoes in your will for when this is all over, and the comfy chair by the window in your apartment."

Kim grabbed her purse and headed for the door. Brenda was right. Revenge wasn't like her. Not even remotely. However, if Chaz Monroe continued to play the intimidation card, and if he proved himself to be another unreliable male adversary, she'd have to find the strength to enact Plan C. Char his ass.

"Cover for me, Bren," she called over her shoulder. "I'm going shopping."

"May the force of Mata Hari be with you," Brenda called out conspiratorially as Kim headed for the door.

Three

Chaz had pegged the bar scene perfectly. Young people were expensively turned out. Women in chic attire carried neon martinis and threw air kisses. At thirty-two and in a sports coat, he felt like their slightly out-of-it older brother, though women eyed him up and down with avid interest and unspoken invitations in their eyes.

Half of these people probably worked for him in some capacity or another and didn't yet recognize him by sight. By the end of the month, he would know each and every name on his payroll, and all ten of the building's janitors. Just now, however, he needed to remain incognito and observe the scene while he waited. For her.

He chose a table in a dark corner and sat on a stool with his back to the wall and his eyes on the door.

"Big Brother is watching you," he said beneath his breath.

He didn't really like chic bars where the young and the restless gathered to prance and preen. He preferred quiet corners in coffee shops where actual conversation could take place. The bar would likely be neutral territory for Kim, though. There'd be no battle lines here, away from official turf. Nor would there be any one-on-one private time that might get him into trouble.

He ordered a draft beer from an auburn-haired server in a tight black dress, who had a small tattoo on one sleek upper arm. He kept his attention on the doorway Kim would soon walk through, wanting to witness her entrance and observe her for a minute before she saw him.

He had spent the last hour trying not to imagine what she would be like in action, and he now wondered which of the guys surrounding him might have dated her and known her intimately. The thought made him uncomfortable, as did the image of some other guy tasting the heat of her hot pink mouth.

He did know one thing for sure. He had put way too much emphasis on their brief meeting, and had given McKinley far too much credit as a femme fatale. Not long now, and he'd find out how ridiculous his fantasies had been, because nobody liked a diva who ruled from within the confines of a short, tight skirt, and a lot of people in this building liked Kim.

His beer arrived, along with a phone number scribbled on a napkin. Chaz looked around. A pretty brunette at another table raised her glass and smiled at him.

He smiled back.

Pocketing the napkin, he took a swig from his long-necked bottle and refocused on the door.

Business first.

Several people entered in a group, but Kim wasn't among them. The noise decibel was rising quickly as the crowd swelled and empty glasses piled up. Chaz could barely hear himself think—which might have been a good thing in this instance, since thoughts turned to *her* again.

Would she work this crowd or ignore it?

Had someone else been waiting for her before this meeting? That *appointment?*

His stomach tightened when he thought about it. He was beginning to feel damp around the collar in spite of the cold shower.

With the bottle hoisted halfway to his mouth, Chaz suddenly paused, feeling Kim's presence before he actually saw her.

Then there she was, at last, the sight of her like a dropkick to his underutilized libido.

Again.

For the third time that day, he absolutely could not take his eyes off her. Tonight, the reason was downright blatant. Kim McKinley was a carnal vision in an eye-popping red dress. Tight, short and silky, that dress pulsed with the word *sex.* Cut low enough at the neckline for a far too revealing peek at bare, glistening, ivory flesh, it caressed her body, hugging each curve.

Diva with a red dress on...

He stifled a chuckle as she moved through the crowd by the door like a tawny-haired hurricane. He wasn't the only person who stared.

She had let down her hair. Golden strands gleamed in the darkened room, floating an inch or two below her chin and giving the impression that she possessed a halo. But it was a fact that no angel would dare to dress like that.

Chaz's stomach twisted at the sight. But Kim wasn't alone. Another woman accompanied her, as dark as Kim was fair. Points went to him for inviting Brenda Chang, who hopefully might already have knocked some sense into Kim about her future job description.

Another good gulp of his draft seemed to settle him as Chaz waited to see if McKinley would come over, or if she would expect him to bend in her direction. Her beautiful features were set. She didn't smile.

When Kim finally sighted him with a gaze like a searchlight, Chaz did a quick head-shake and slapped his bottle down on the table. He stood up.

As she approached, his gaze traveled down her length, stopping at her ankles. She looked taller tonight because she was perched on dangerously high heels, the kind he'd imagined her wearing the first time he'd seen her. Shiny crimson stilettos.

Chaz whistled to himself. He couldn't help it.

Had she read his mind that afternoon?

So you really do know how to make an entrance. Well, okay. You have my full attention.

He raised his bottle in acknowledgment of her presence, and ditched the urge to clap his hands at the show she was providing, sure the sexy clothes were meant for some lucky bastard's sensory pleasure in taking them off. It was possible she had lied about not having a date.

"Mr. Monroe," she said in greeting.

"Ms. McKinley." Chaz gave her a nod.

The electrical current whizzing through the air between them from the distance of two feet felt strong enough to have burned the bar to the ground. He didn't imagine that. Their chemistry was undeniable, at least on his end.

Fine hairs at the nape of his neck were stirring. Fire roared through his muscles, causing a twitch. These reactions were a further indication of their instantaneous attraction, and also a hint about being so close to a sin-coated challenge.

"I've brought someone you should meet," she said in that seductive drawl. "This is Brenda Chang."

Chaz held out a hand to Brenda, who took it, though her eyes avoided his.

"I'm happy to meet you in person, Brenda," he said.

"Thanks for the invitation to join you," Brenda returned.

"I heard that you two work closely together, and that you're a good team," he said.

"Yes, that's true," Brenda agreed.

She was an attractive young woman with porcelain skin, dark eyes and a slender body encased in a tasteful blue suit.

Gesturing to the table, Chaz said, "Care to sit down?"

Would Wonder Woman act on any suggestion he made? Quite surprisingly, she did. She slid sideways onto a stool and crossed her legs, placing the heel of one dagger-sharp stiletto just inches from his right calf and making Chaz ponder the idea of what those heels would feel like if they were in bed together. It was a thought he had vowed not to have tonight.

"So," he began, once they all were in place around the little table. He avoided staring at the spot where Kim's shapely knee disappeared beneath the colorful silk. "Thanks for coming."

"Shall we get right to it?" she asked.

This, too, was unexpected. Chaz rallied with another nod.

"I believe you wanted to speak about the Christmas campaigns?" she said.

Brenda passed her pal a silent glance of interest.

"Yes," Chaz replied. "I've read the contract from front to back. But first, would you like something to drink?"

"I could use some Chardonnay," Brenda announced in a breathy outburst, smiling at him.

"Martini," Kim said.

"Oh, boy," Brenda muttered after hearing her friend's drink order. She flashed Chaz another pretty smile.

Of course Kim wanted a martini, the drink of choice for the young, pretty people these days. Still, Chaz, for reasons he didn't quite understand, had expected her order to be bottled water with a lemon wedge. He was a little disappointed to have been wrong about that as he flagged down the server.

"What kind of martini would you like?" he asked.

Oddly enough, the simple query seemed to stump her. She glanced to Brenda.

"You always like the appletinis here," Brenda prompted.

"Yes. That's what I'll have," Kim said. Turning to Chaz, she added, "Now, where were we?"

Was he wrong in his impression that she didn't know what an appletini was, and that there was something going on between Kim and Brenda that caused Brenda to show concern? He was pretty sure that Brenda had just fed Kim a line about the drink order.

"I'm aware of your rather unusual contract," he said. "What I'd like to do is ask politely that you ink it out. I'm hoping you can see this as a special favor to the agency and to our clients."

"Do you mean the clients who would like to continue working with me?" she asked, stressing her point of being well liked by those accounts.

Chaz shrugged. Kim's scarlet dress and her chilly vibe were at odds with each other, a dichotomy that did nothing to lessen the warmth searing through him each time she moved.

"A vice president has to oversee all accounts," he said.

"Yes, you do," she tossed back, emphasis on *you*.

"Being new, I'd like your help," he said. "Maybe we can start small on the help, and see how it goes?"

"I'm all ears, Mr. Monroe, as to what you might require." She did not glance at her watch, but added, "For the next ten minutes."

"It's Chaz. Please call me Chaz."

He was peripherally aware of how Kim's chest rose and fell laboriously with each new breath she took. Was that a sign of anger or anxiety? Outwardly, she looked calm enough. Cool, calm and collected. Yet she was electrically charged. He felt that charge pass through him. His heart beat a little faster.

"We've been asked to attend a special party for a potential new client, and I have volunteered to help make this an event. It's a very last-minute request, so with Ms. Chang already inundated, I'd need your help," he said.

He looked to Brenda, who passed the look on to Kim.

"Sorry." Kim carefully folded her hands around the stem of her glass when it arrived. "If you mean helping with something right now, that's impossible. I have the next two weeks off, starting tomorrow at noon."

"I'd be willing to double your holiday bonus for the extra time and effort," he said, applying a bit of preplanned pressure to see if money floated her boat. "We can talk about the clause afterward if you like."

Brenda took a sip of her wine and continued to gaze at Kim over the rim of her glass. Brenda appeared to be nervous about being in the middle of this conversation, and had started inching her glass sideways on the table as if she and the glass might make a quick getaway the first chance she got.

Good for her, for noticing where she wasn't needed. And to hell with the crowd. Chaz now wanted Kim all to himself. He wanted nothing more. They could hash this out, once and for all. If she remained stubborn, maybe they could arm wrestle a deal.

"I'm really sorry I can't help," Kim said, lush strands of gold brushing her face when she shook her head. "I've already made plans for my time off."

Chaz was actually starting to enjoy this game. He had always been good at chess. He did wonder, though, how far she'd go…and how far he'd go to stop her.

"Any way you might break those plans?" he asked.

"I'm pretty sure I can't at this late date."

"If I say please?"

She sat motionless for a minute, and then began to turn her glass in circles on the table without taking a drink. Chaz didn't fail to notice that she hadn't so much as placed her lips on the glass since it had arrived.

"As a favor to a potential client, then," Chaz said. "Not to me personally."

Another beat of time passed while he awaited her response.

"Didn't you just say that you read my contract?" she finally said with a subtle tone of disappointment underscoring her reply.

Chaz found himself fascinated with thoughts about how this would play out. He had said *please,* right? Surely she had to realize that this one decision could make or break the upward mobility of her career, at least with this agency.

He downed some beer and waited to see if she would explain herself.

"I truly am sorry," she said seconds later. "I'd be happy to help out any other time, with any other holiday. Really, I would help now if my situation were different."

"Different?" Chaz couldn't wait to hear this. If she was seriously involved in a relationship with some guy, and had *that* kind of plans for the next week, he'd have heard it from the people feeding him office gossip that afternoon. According to Alice, his agency bloodhound, Kim was pretty much a free agent in the serious relationship department.

"I'm…" she began.

"It's against her religion," Brenda said for her, and immediately flushed pink for having spoken out of turn.

Kim squirmed. He saw it. In the process, her left arm brushed his. Chaz's body responded with a jerk. The aftereffects of the surprise ignited a new and relatively irritating blaze of heat in his chest that robbed him of his next decent breath.

"Oh," he said. "That's what prevents you from working on all this holiday stuff?"

She recrossed her legs and blinked slowly. "Well…"

She didn't finish her excuse. A lovely flush crept up her neck, presenting a very seductive picture, for sure. The best he'd seen in a long time. But right then he wanted badly to throw her over his knee and give her a good spanking. *Bad little princess,* he'd say. *Why the white lies and the avoidance? Let's get right to the truth. You could do this if you wanted to.*

Or maybe he should just kiss her pouty mouth for all it was worth and see if that got a rise out of her. Maybe if they got that kiss out of the way, Kim might confess the real reasoning behind her ridiculous holiday reluctance.

On the other hand, she might slap his face and call it a night, and he'd be back to square one. Taking it further, she might take that walk, and take her clients with her.

Well, okay, there was a fine line between pushing her away and getting what he wanted, but he did owe her a shot at the title she coveted.

His inner musings on how this might go ceased abruptly when she leaned forward over the edge of the table. His eyes dipped to the sight of the dewy top of her rounded breasts and the fact that she wore nothing beneath the red dress. Nothing visible, anyway.

Although the sight doubled his heart rate, a thought occurred about this sudden closeness potentially being a purposeful move on her part to distract him, an enactment of the power of her all-too-obvious feminine wiles. Of which she had plenty.

Hell, maybe he just got turned on by the promise of a good fight. In his family, close as they were, fighting had become a sport.

The truth, though, was that he had grown tired of women who assumed they were owed something because of their looks. That aside, he had a short span of time to get this agency working better, and a Wonder Woman could help him do that.

Working this out would be the decent thing to do. The best outcome for everyone.

"Anyway, as I was saying, it's a special event," he continued. "If you'll hear me out, I'll explain."

She had no immediate reply to that, and continued to absently fondle the fragile stem of her glass in a way that he found extremely appealing.

At the same time, he was nearing his limit on patience. He noticed Brenda looking at him intently, and that look served to clear his mind.

"I'll find someone to help you," Kim finally offered. "I can find someone who will do a good job and is an ace at spur-of-the-moment stuff."

"Who would that person be?"

"Will you excuse me a minute?" Brenda broke in. "I have to, well, you know." Her exit was abrupt.

Kim didn't seem to notice her friend's departure. She didn't lean back or try to make her own escape.

"All right," she said. "I'll hear you out since I don't seem to have much choice in the matter, and then suggest somebody to help you. What is this special project?"

Chaz tried really hard not to grin. Kim had just given in, and an inch was better than nothing.

"It's a party. A Christmas party, and as much of an extravaganza as we can pull together this late. Nothing huge, really, and more indicative of a big family celebration. We'll need decorated trees, live music and a couple elves."

"Elves?" she repeated with a touch of sarcasm in her tone.

Chaz nodded. "Can't have Christmas without elves. Then we'll need packages. Large boxes, small boxes, all with big red bows. And snow."

"Snow?" Kim offered up an expression of surprise that overrode her former skepticism about elves.

"Sure. We can bring some snow inside a building, can't we? Aren't there snow machines? We can bring in some of the real stuff on trays and carts for the buffet table, as well as ice sculptures."

She winced, probably unwilling to tell him what an idiot he was for suggesting real snow inside a building. It likely cost her plenty to hold that chastisement in.

"We're not party planners," she said calmly. "You do know that we're a respected advertising agency?"

Chaz couldn't address that. He didn't dare. This was a test. A silly one, true, but he had to make it sound as if he needed her help. He couldn't say that it was his family's party he'd invade with all those Christmasy things if Kim actually agreed. In the meantime, he'd try to find out what irked her about the holiday stuff. He'd use all the holiday terms to push her buttons.

"Candy canes," he continued. "Mounds of them. Also anything and everything else that could make an indoor fantasy come true for the company and its top tier of stock-holders."

McKinley's lush lashes closed over her eyes. Her hand stopped caressing the glass. She seemed to have stopped breathing.

"This must be a big deal," she said at length.

"Indeed, it's very big. For you."

McKinley's expression changed lightning fast. She sat upright on her stool, taking most of her deliciously woodsy scent with her.

Chaz's grin dissolved. Had he accidentally put the wrong spin on that last remark, making it sound sexual? Hell, he hadn't even thought about it, and sure as heck hadn't meant it that way.

"It's a potentially huge contract," he rushed to say, thinking that if she would merely agree, this would be over. One little "yes" and she'd be on her way to the metaphorical Oval Office. She just had to be willing to circumvent that stubborn mind-set and get down to business.

She didn't have to set one red-hot foot in his apartment. She didn't have to breathe in his goddamned ear. Those were daydreams. Man stuff. Wishful thinking. Most men were wired with those kinds of thoughts. All she had to do was cave on one little point, encapsulated by a single paragraph on paper.

But again, and to her credit, Kim didn't run away.

"Who is offering the contract?" she asked politely.

"I'm not at liberty to say. Not until you agree to help out."

"I did mention that I'm on vacation next week?"

"I'll give you a longer vacation at another time."

"I can't help you," she declared. But contrary to sounding smug about this persistent refusal, Chaz heard in her voice something else. Sorrow? Wishfulness? A silent desire that she didn't have to be so stubborn and inflexible?

He looked at her thoughtfully. "Are you really of a religion that shuns this holiday?"

She shook her head. "Irish. Completely. Three generations back."

"Ah." Chaz's breath caught in his throat as one of her hands rested lightly on top of his hand on the table, flesh to naked flesh, and cool from her grip on the martini glass.

The urge to tug at his collar returned.

"I'd like to be honest with you." As her eyes met his, Chaz couldn't help but feel as if he were drowning. The look in her eyes made the crowd around them disappear.

"I'd appreciate it if you would," he said, slightly shaken by the intimacy of her touch and her sudden change of expression. Truly, it wasn't a normal occurrence for him to be affected by the antics of a woman. He wasn't sex starved. He didn't need to count on Kim for those fantasies when the pretty brunette at the next table continuously looked his way.

"It would be better for me if you didn't pressure me into this," she told him in a carefully modulated tone that deepened her accent.

"Explain, and maybe I won't. I am human, you know."

When she frowned, the delicate skin around her eyes creased.

"I have a problem," she said.

Her fingers moved on his as if trying to stress a point he didn't see. Chaz found himself listening especially diligently for whatever excuse she'd come up with next. He could hardly wait to hear what she had to say.

She moistened her lips with the tip of her tongue, a provocative, erotic action.

"It's embarrassing to speak of, so I don't," she began. "If you were to fire me because of sharing this very personal confidence, I don't know what I'd do."

She hadn't removed her hand from his. His gaze lingered on her mouth.

"I have a problem with Christmas." As she spoke, earrings buried somewhere in her fair blond hair tinkled with a sound like stardust falling.

"It's not the holiday itself that bothers me," she went on. "An objection to the commercialism of Christmas would be funny in our line of business, wouldn't it?"

Kim's wan smile lifted the edges of her lips. "That's not the source of my problems."

"I'd sincerely like to know what is," Chaz said.

In another surprising move, she slid closer to him, inching her stool sideways and leaning in so that she didn't have to shout. With her mouth all but touching his right ear, she said, "Santa is my problem."

When Chaz turned his head, their lips almost met. He felt the soft exhalation of her breath. "Santa?" he echoed, his abs shuddering annoyingly beneath his shirt. "As in Santa Claus? You have a problem with Santa Claus?"

"Yes." Her reply was devastatingly breathy.

Was she making fun of him?

"How can Santa Claus be a problem?" he asked.

"I want him," she whispered.

He waited for the meaning of this to hit. Then he began to laugh. She wanted Santa? This was so much better than her shunning the holiday for religious reasons, or thinking Christmas too commercial as an advertising executive, that it came off as completely unique. Kim McKinley deserved a crown for this excuse.

She had put him on, of course, and she'd had him going for a minute. Her acting skills were applause-worthy. This was another point for her, well played.

But she didn't look so well, all of a sudden. Her smile had faded. Her face paled. The hazel eyes gazing into his were glazed and moist, very much as if she had just disclosed a terrible secret and was awaiting a dreaded response. As if she'd been serious.

And he had laughed.

Sobering, rallying quickly, he said, "I'm sorry. Please forgive me. I must have misunderstood your meaning. In what way do you want Santa Claus, exactly?"

"I..."

"Yes?"

"Well, you see, I..."

Her eyes held a pleading, haunted cast. She didn't want to explain herself, couldn't find the words. As he watched her, she began to look less like a mistress of fire, and more like a young, lost waif.

Chaz was moved by the change. Without thinking, he reached up to cup her face with his hands in an automatic reaction of empathy, sensing real trouble in her past. She stared into his eyes, and he stared back, groping for what was going on here, and what she might mean.

When her lips parted, they trembled enough that he could see the quakes. She wasn't acting or kidding around. Kim had been deadly serious about needing to shun what was going on with this holiday.

Wanting to ease the pain reflected in her eyes, and needing to fix what he had set in motion, Chaz pressed his mouth to hers before even knowing what had happened. When realization hit, he kept very still with his mouth resting lightly on hers as he sized up what he had just done.

Her lips were soft, slick and completely, heartbreakingly tender. Way better than anything he could have imagined. Light-years beyond better. But the biggest surprise of all was that he hadn't gotten close to her out of lust or the lingering effects of the dress and the shoes. It had been an unconscious need to comfort her, protect her.

He had just glimpsed something sad curled up in McKinley's core beneath the glamour and efficiency. He had wanted a confession, and instead had stifled that confession with a kiss.

He didn't move, draw back or try to explain. Neither did she. His pressure on her lips remained slight but steady, in a connection he had desired from the first time he'd seen her. He supposed she might scream when he let her go, and he completely deserved the slap he'd receive, though in this circumstance, his intentions had been honorable.

Her lips, her breath, her taste, fascinated him and moved him further, stirring emotions tucked inside. Strands of her blond hair tickled his cheek in a way that suddenly seemed right and completely natural. And since it was too late, anyway, and the damage had already been done, he added more pressure.

As the illicit kiss deepened, Kim's lips parted beneath his. She let a sigh escape and didn't pull away. The slap Chaz expected never came. Their bodies remained motionless, inches apart, as their breath and mouths explored the parameters of this very public forbidden kiss.

Her breath was enticingly hot, deliciously scented and as seductive as anything imaginable. Reeling from the sensations and spurred on by those seductions, Chaz dared to draw his tongue slowly along the corners of her mouth.

As he breathed her in, tasted her lipstick, felt the moistness of her tongue meeting his, she joined him in this unexpected faux pas.

For a minute, for Chaz, they were no longer employer and employee, or adversaries; only a man and a woman acting on a primal attraction that they had tried unsuccessfully to ignore. Giving in, ruled by feeling, Chaz tossed away all thoughts about the possible consequences of such a public display, and went for broke.

Four

Kim gripped the table with both hands. She heard the sound of her glass tipping, rolling, and couldn't reach out to stop it from crashing to the floor. She was locked to her new boss in a battle of bodies and mouths and wills. In a bad way. A physical way.

And it was sublime.

It was...beyond words.

With her eyes closed, she could sense Chaz Monroe's body in relation to hers and knew it was too far away for the flames to be so hot and all-encompassing. After several seconds with her lips plastered to his, her hands left the table as if they had a mind of their own. She was only vaguely aware of curling her fingers into the front of his beautiful blue shirt.

He tasted like beer, desire and of plans gone south. They weren't supposed to be doing this, like this. They were enemies of a sort, which made their actions run contrary to everything she had planned. How could she actually like the kiss she was supposed to hold against him if the harassment case idea became necessary? And was that plan necessary now?

Then why didn't she run away?

She hardly thought of anything but Monroe's mouth, and the result had her floating in a sensory fog. The kiss seemed to go on forever. Some distant part of her mind warned that she had to get out of this situation. She had to get away right that instant. This kiss could prove her downfall as well as his.

Yet her breasts strained against the red silk, her nipples hard and aching. The dress seemed much too tight and restrictive. Between her legs, she quaked with a new awakening.

She wanted more than a kiss. Her body demanded more.

Damn. She really hated this guy!

As his tongue teased and taunted and his lips became more demanding, Kim struggled to think. She had to keep it together. Plans A and B had failed miserably in the very fact that they were a success, but she could still turn this around. She could use this. *Would* use this...as soon as he stopped doing whatever the hell he was doing that felt so good.

His tongue swept over her teeth and across her lower lip, urging more participation. She tore at his shirt, tugging him closer with treacherous fingers, seeking a way inside his clothes.

His warm hands remained on her face, holding her while she drowned in his essence, his heat and the intensity of what they were doing. Chaz Monroe really was the epitome of everything masculine and powerful, right down to his kissing talent. He didn't ravage her or threaten to overpower. The kiss had started off tender and exploratory, without being tentative, then quickly escalated.

These feelings were a first, and they were outrageous. She wanted Monroe to throw her on the table and slide his heated palms over her thighs. She had never felt this out of control, had never been attracted to a man in such a fierce, feral manner.

But other than his warm hands on her cheeks, he made no further move to touch her. No illicit fondling, nothing that would have earned him a shove and a sharp reprimand if she had been thinking properly.

Kissing was supposed to be like this, yet for her, never was. No man had ever moved her in this way, making her want to surrender her hard-won hold on control.

And just when she had started to weaken further, he

tugged lightly on her lower lip and withdrew. The pressure on her lips eased. He removed his hands from her face slowly, as if reluctant to do so, leaving chills in their wake.

He remained close. His eyes bored into hers questioningly, offering a hint of a new kind of understanding that was so foreign to Kim, she misread it as sympathy. He spoke from inches away.

"What about Santa? Exactly?"

She expected to see a flicker of amusement in his eyes. Her stomach seized up as she waited for it, wondering if Monroe had merely been proving a point about being an experienced playboy able to get whatever he wanted from his latest acquisition.

Bastard!

Her heart tanked. Her mouth formed a steely line. She had almost fallen for that kiss, and for him. She hadn't been the one to put a stop to it.

"Kim?" Monroe's tone was a silky caress with a startlingly direct link to her trembling lower regions.

"I'm sorry," she replied breathlessly. "I just can't."

The words were forced, pitched low, angry. Kim got to her feet. Her knees felt absurdly weak and unsupportive.

"Kim," Monroe said again, standing with her, using her first name as if the kiss had earned him the right to be familiar. "Help me here. Give me something."

"That's funny," she said. "I thought I just did."

It was too late for confessions and explanations. There would be no laughing this off as a simple mistake. Dread filled Kim, so heavy it made her stomach hurt. Following that came a round of embarrassment.

She had worn the dress and the shoes, and those things had worked their magic, just as Brenda had predicted they would. Going beyond distraction, they had seduced Monroe into unwarranted intimacy. And though she had liked that moment of intimacy, in the end, Monroe had successfully manipulated her. As her boss, he would continue to push for answers.

She steadied herself with a hand on the edge of the table. Telling the truth was out of the picture now for sure, as was remaining in Monroe's presence for one second longer.

The ridiculous harassment case idea wavered in front of her as if it were written in the air. They had made out in the bar, surrounded by people, some of which were her fellow employees. Hopefully, none of them had noticed that she hadn't shoved Monroe away, and also the fact that she could no longer breathe properly.

After a kiss like that, so completely mind-numbing and seductive, she saw no other way out of this mess but to play the damsel in distress in order to save her traitorous ruby-covered ass. She hated that; despised the thought. But Monroe was a master at games.

With the hazy lingering imprint of his mouth on hers, Kim lifted a hand. She slapped Monroe across the face, hard, and said loudly enough for others to hear, "What were you thinking, Mr. Monroe? That I'd jump at the chance to bed my boss?"

Pivoting gracefully on her absurdly expensive shoes, she headed for the door, feeling the burn of Monroe's inquisitive gaze on her back and thinking that if she'd wanted to cry in frustration before, she had just taken it to a whole new level.

Shell-shocked, and beginning to get a bad feeling about what had just happened, Chaz smiled at the people at the next table and shrugged his shoulders. He couldn't quite believe this, though. He'd been completely helpless in resisting Kim McKinley. Once again, his plan had backfired.

He had locked lips with her. In public.

And he knew what that meant.

Waiting out several agonizing seconds before throwing

down cash for the drinks, he started after her, deciding that he wouldn't apologize if he caught up with her, since she had provoked that damn lip-lock.

That dress…

Those shoes…

The sudden waifish expression in her eyes.

There was no time like the present to get to the bottom of this charade and find out what Kim had up her sleeve. Certainly she had something up there.

He had taken the bait in what might have been a ploy to catch him off guard. Possibly a public seduction had been her goal all along. If so, this made McKinley a real master at manipulation.

He had believed, with his mouth on hers, and with her throaty moan of encouragement, that she wanted closeness as much as he did. That she enjoyed the kiss as much as he had.

Bottom line—he had believed her. He'd fallen victim to the flash of pain in her eyes and the acceptance of her lush mouth. He thought those things were real, as was the sorrow that had overtaken her saucy demeanor. He'd been sure the real Kim McKinley was facing him for the first time.

And she had played him?

What a sucker he'd been. Only one reason came to mind for an objective like hers—either the threat of a harassment case against him, or out-and-out blackmail. *A kiss for a clause.*

He didn't like his new title, which was Chaz Monroe, fool. People in the bar were looking at him. The brunette who had handed over her phone number winked knowingly.

Did Kim have any earthly idea what he'd like to do to her, now that he knew the score?

How could he have been so completely wrong? Because he would have sworn, testifying with one hand in the air and another on the Bible, that she had kissed him back and meant it.

Oh yes, she was good. Damn good. It had been a great performance. Perfect, actually.

"But it isn't over," Chaz said through gritted teeth as he moved through the crowd.

Kim strode past the bar's doorway and into the corridor beyond that led to the building's marble lobby. When she reached the bank of elevators, she punched a button with her palm and stamped her feet a couple of times in disgust. The wrong plan had worked. She felt terrible, sick.

All that evocative talk had done her in. Snow. Elves. Presents and candy canes. She hated the slinky red dress and the shoes she couldn't return.

The fact that she'd almost blurted out the truth about her family simply added fuel to the fire of an already demented situation. Now there was no going back. She'd have to nail Monroe to the wall by using that very public mistake if he continued to bug her about the contract.

To hell with Chaz Monroe for making her feel guilty about having to force her to use bribery and revenge to get him off her back. She cursed him for bringing up her dark past and causing her to become someone else, someone who would do such a thing for their own personal gain.

Darkness bubbled up inside her, coating her insides.

Once upon a time, she had wanted to trust a man for his good and magical qualities. She had wished hard for Santa Claus to bring her father back. On each anniversary of her father's exit, she had prayed for something to stop her mother's crying jags and all those days when her mom couldn't get out of bed.

She had secretly written to Santa once, and mailed the letter. But Santa hadn't bothered to respond or grant her that wish. Her father never returned, and her mother's depression got progressively worse until relatives had threatened to take Kim away.

The emptiness in her past was riddled with fear and loneliness and a young girl's angst. Her mother's rants and monologues had followed Kim everywhere, and guilt had made her stay close. Her mother didn't need another disappointment; couldn't have withstood her daughter leaving, too.

There had been no escape until college, and even there, while testing her wings, guilt had been part of Kim's existence. She had fled some of that darkness, while her mother had not. She was okay, and her mother stayed sick.

Tonight that sickness had become hers. She had become a player, against her will, as if her mother had risen from the grave to goad her on. She had been willing to hurt someone, a man, so that her secrets could go on being secrets, and her hurt stayed tucked inside. She had wanted to trust, and had been shot down.

"Kim?"

The voice was close, deep and too familiar for comfort. A wave of chills pierced Kim's red dress. The elevator was too damn slow, and she hadn't expected Monroe to follow her.

Now what?

Wobbling on her weakened knees, Kim whirled to face Monroe in all his gorgeous male beauty. The persistent bastard wasn't going to let her off the hook, but he wouldn't touch her again if he knew what was good for him.

He leaned toward her before she could voice a protest, and placed both hands on the wall beside her. It took him several seconds to speak.

"There's no need to run away." His tone seemed too calm for the expression on his face. He pinned her in place, within the cage of his arms, as if knowing she'd bolt at the first opportunity. The front of his shirt showed creases from where she had greedily tugged at it in a moment of blissful mindlessness.

Kim didn't reply. She could not think of one appropriate word to say.

"I really don't see the need for an all-out war, or whatever you imagine this is," he said. "I asked to meet in good faith to discuss the problems facing us. I was trying to find a way out of this mess."

Kim tried to hit the elevator button with her elbow. Though there'd likely be a hint of snow on the ground outside tonight, the corridor felt stiflingly warm. Part of that heat came from Monroe, who acted as if he knew exactly what she had done, and what the outcome had to be. *Clever man.*

"I believed we could work something out," he said. "For a minute back there, I thought you might honestly want to."

She had to fight for a breath. Monroe's closeness was a reminder of how far she had strayed. That kiss, in public, would be career doom for her if rumor of it got around. She wasn't the one with the VP spot. He was.

She tried to touch her lips, to wipe away the feeling of him, but couldn't raise her arms. Monroe's inferno pummeled at her, overheating her from the inside out, rendering her excuses for her behavior useless.

"I tried to explain," she managed to say.

Maybe he hadn't gotten the picture, after all, about the blackmail. His mouth lurked a few millimeters away from hers. Dangerously close.

"But you didn't explain. Not really," he said. "None of that was the truth, right?"

"More than you know."

"There's still time to explain, Kim."

She shook her head.

"I wasn't the only one who wanted that kiss," Monroe remarked. "And it wasn't planned."

"How dare you presume to know what I want?"

"Well, at least one of us is honest. I'll admit that it wasn't the goal of tonight's discussion, but I will also confess that I liked it. I liked it a lot."

"It was business suicide for me, and you know it."

"So, you'll use the kiss against me?"

"Do I have a choice?"

"Well, if it's a lawsuit you want, we might as well make the best of it. There's no need to slap me this time. What good would it do if no one is watching?"

Each time Kim inhaled, his shirt rubbed against the red silk of her dress, sending pangs of longing through places she hadn't focused on in a long time. The closer he got, the more of his disarming scent she breathed in.

She wanted that kiss his lips were promising. Another kiss. A better one, if there was such a thing, especially given that no one, as he said, was there to witness it.

With that thought, Kim knew she was screwed. Chaz Monroe wasn't merely an intelligent bastard, his actions were highly suspicious. Was he a man ruled by what was in his pants, or did he have some nebulous plan of his own to humble her with?

When his mouth brushed across her right temple, Kim squirmed and glanced up to meet the directness of his gaze. She absorbed a jarring jolt of longing for the closeness she had to repel. Monroe was her boss. No one in the company could condone a relationship with him that might eventually lead to the promotion she already deserved. Rumors were a plague in business. If she were to get a promotion in the near future, some would now say she had slept her way to the top.

Several coworkers had witnessed what happened in the bar. Whereas it might have gone unnoticed if she'd kept quiet, in a moment of panic she had idiotically made sure it hadn't gone unnoticed. Plan C had been set in motion.

Damn him. Damn you, Monroe.

"Why can't you leave me alone?" she demanded.

His breath stirred her hair. "Obviously, that contract involves personal issues for you that I hadn't anticipated."

"Bravo for concluding that."

"I have no way of knowing what those issues are unless you tell me about them."

"They aren't your business. Not something so personal. Leave it, Monroe. I'm asking you to let it go."

"Or what? A bit of blackmail will back your request up?" He sighed. "I'm concerned, that's all. Neither of us has to be those people in the bar. We can be friends if you'd prefer that. I'm actually a good listener. We could go someplace quiet and talk things over."

"Like your apartment?"

He shook his head.

"But you'd like to take me to your apartment," she said.

"What fool wouldn't? But that's not the point here."

"I've asked you to back off."

He touched the cheek she had slapped. "Right. I got that."

"And you refuse to listen," Kim said.

"I don't tend to take no for an answer when a moment like the one in the bar told me otherwise."

"Then we can finish this tomorrow," Kim said. "After we've thought it over and had some distance."

"I'm fairly certain we should finish this now," Monroe countered. "I'd really like to know what upsets you. I thought you were going to cry."

His gaze was volcanic. He had nice eyes. Great eyes. Light blue, with flecks of gold. Those eyes wouldn't miss much, if anything. He would see her cave. Right then, his gaze sparkled with a need to understand what she had been thinking, beyond the possibility of blackmail. Or else maybe he just wanted to know more about the terms of their deal.

Letting Monroe strike a nerve is what had gotten her into this mess. He was too handsome, and too willing to get to know her better. Men like him often used women, her mother had preached. If you gave them your secrets, they'd betray those secrets at the drop of a hat. If you gave them your love, they'd easily destroy it.

Kim wanted desperately to stop hearing her mother's voice. She would have covered her ears if Monroe had let her.

"If you're going to fire me for slapping you, go ahead," she said a bit too breathlessly for the sternness she had been aiming for. "There's no need for us to further humiliate each other."

"Fire you? Humiliate you? I wanted to meet with you to avoid those things."

"Well, you didn't do a decent job of reaching that objective. Now you do want to fire me, right? You'll have to, unless I protect myself?"

"That was never the idea, Kim. You'll have to believe me."

"Then why can't you leave me alone? We were doing fine here until you arrived."

"Fine? This company was sliding, whether or not you knew about the bottom line. It was in serious decline. I came here to help the agency out of that decline. The company's success means a lot to me because I have a stake in it. I need everyone to work, including you. If you're one of the best people here, your help is needed in all areas."

"I've been doing more than my share."

"I know that, and yet I need more. I'd ask you to do things you don't necessarily want to do because the company requires it right now, and for no other reason."

"Not because you want to kiss me again?"

"Yes, damn it. I want to kiss you. But believe it or not, I do have some control."

He leaned closer as he spoke, so that Kim felt every muscle in his body from his shoulders to his thighs, and everywhere in between. Yet his mouth drew her focus: the sensuous, talented mouth that had nearly done her in.

"It's going to be yes or no," Monroe said. "You have it within your power to upgrade, maybe even to upper management someday. All you have to do is what I ask, or explain why you can't."

Kim shut her eyes.

"Look, Kim. Do this one thing for me, and we'll reevaluate your position here."

Kim stopped shaking just as she realized she was shaking. Like the last VP, Monroe was promising her the moon when he had no real capacity for giving it to her. He was the vice president. The only way for her to take over that job was for him to leave it.

"I'd like you to leave me alone," she repeated.

"The company needs you."

"Yes. With your body pressed against mine in a public hallway, I can feel how badly you need me."

That did it. Enough was enough. No more squirming. No more playing around. Chaz Monroe had finally done it. He had just buried himself.

Smiling grimly, Kim reached into the purse hanging at her side. She pushed Monroe away and drew out the small tape recorder she kept there. With a precise movement of her finger, she clicked the gadget off.

He glanced at her in surprise, then looked down at what she held in her hand as if not quite believing what he was seeing.

"My lawyer will be talking to your lawyer in the morning if there is any further mention of my contract," Kim said, slipping out from beneath his arm. "You have heard of sexual harassment, being number-one boss man and all?"

He was staring at her as though he'd just felt the arrow of doom pierce his heart dead-on, and also as if he had been betrayed. His arms dropped to his sides. His expression smoothed into something unreadable.

The elevator pinged as the door rolled open. Kim walked inside and turned, wearing a smile she had to struggle to maintain. Her insides were in knots. Both hands were shaking. She hid her sadness and the urge to throw the recorder at Monroe. She felt like sinking to the ground.

He just stood there. He didn't look angry, only disappointed. He had been bushwhacked, broadsided. Did he fear what would happen to him if this conversation were to fall into the wrong hands? Did he now fear for his job?

Monroe had a casting couch, pure and simple, and she'd nearly been flat out on top of it. So what if she had liked the kiss and his hard body pressed to hers? It was best not to think about those things now. The guy, gorgeous as he was, charming as he could be, shouldn't have taken such liberties. The vice president should have known better.

With a stern bite to her lower lip, Kim used her purse to snap the button inside the elevator that would close this case once and for all. Was she proud of how she'd accomplished this? *No.* Happy about it? *Absolutely not.* She felt dirty. Yet she had remembered the recorder at the last minute and done what had to be done.

Monroe wouldn't fight her. Nothing good ever came of a lawsuit. So, the hope she maintained right that minute was that he would realize this and stop bothering her to change the terms of her contract. Life as usual would be the result.

The dark clouds she had been trying so hard to shake off drifted over her. She pictured her mother smiling. In reaction, Kim felt her face blanch. She swayed on her feet, truly hating what she had done and the memories that wouldn't stop invading her mind, all because of her mother's far-reaching influence.

This night was over, and it was too late to take anything back. She had made her bed, but at least Monroe wasn't in it.

"Good night," she said to him with a catch in her throat.

He stood in the corridor, motionless, his eyes on her as the elevator doors finally closed.

Five

Well, well...

Kim had called his bluff. She thought she'd done pretty well in this game, and he had to hand it to her. She'd hung in there and had been fairly creative about it. Still, the result was a disappointment. He hadn't figured she would go so far in the wrong direction.

As the elevator doors closed between them, Chaz shrugged his shoulders. He knew that Kim had to be feeling a little guilty after hearing him state his case. She wasn't dense. The telling detail about her current state of mind was that aside from the tape recorder, she hadn't slapped him again.

Hearing the clink of rapidly approaching heels on the marble floor, Chaz turned and said, "That wasn't remotely close to what we had discussed."

Brenda Chang strode up to him wearing a frown. "I don't feel very well. I feel like I've just stabbed my best friend in the back because—oh wait—*I have.*"

"You left us alone out of the goodness of your heart," he pointed out.

"Yes, but you didn't pay me enough to betray her."

"I didn't pay you anything at all."

"That's what I mean."

"I had to try to reach her. I did try." Chaz shook his head, eyeing the elevator.

"You have no idea how much she'd like to capitulate. She's just not ready," Brenda said.

"There's no way to help with that? You won't tell me what her problem is?"

"Not for love or money. Wild horses couldn't drag Kim's secrets from me without her permission."

Chaz ventured another lingering look at the elevator.

Brenda's voice sounded small. "What next?"

"My hands are tied. She wants to be left alone."

"You already knew that."

Chaz shot her a look that indicated quite clearly that he wasn't in the mood to prolong this discussion.

"All right," Brenda said. "But you'd better turn out to be a good guy, that's all I can say, or you'll have problems added onto problems. That's a promise."

Chaz leaned back to read the numbers on the elevator panel above the door. "If she's going back to the office, will she stay up there long?"

Brenda shrugged.

"Does she need your shoulder to lean on?" he asked.

"I doubt it. Besides, she'll probably get out one floor up and use the stairs to leave the building, knowing she'd get past you that way."

Brenda's eyes widened when she realized she'd said too much.

"That shrewd, eh?" he asked.

She blew out a sigh. "Every woman knows how to do this, Monroe. Avoidance is coded into in our genes."

"So what will she do after that?"

"Simmer awhile, most likely, and then start thinking."

"She doesn't really have a case you know," he said. "There's no one to remove me or waggle a finger over a kiss."

Brenda nodded. "I know that, and who you really are. You might have changed your name if being undercover here is your game, because I just looked your family up online. Kim doesn't know yet because I didn't get to it until now."

"You looked me up?"

"The internet is a marvelous thing," Brenda said. "Your family's business dealings are plastered all over it."

"Then you know why I'm here?"

"Yep."

"You'll tell her?"

"I would have already, if you hadn't followed her to this hallway. Just so you know, friends don't usually allow each other to do anything they might regret."

"When she knows about me, and without her little blackmail scheme getting her the office she wants, will she leave the company?"

"I wouldn't put it past her. What would you do, in her place, if you found out that the man you were going to resort to blackmailing was in fact the owner of the agency?"

"I'd take the damn Christmas gig and get on with it," Chaz said.

"Yes, well you have millions of dollars to fall back on, and no female hormones. Kim has a tiny apartment she can barely afford as it is, close by because she's here working most of the time."

Chaz gave her a sober sideways glance. "Point taken."

"Is it?" Brenda countered.

"Quite."

"She's not putting you on, you know. She has been dealing with holiday stuff for years. Very real issues. Serious setbacks."

Chaz looked again to the elevator, which had indeed stopped two floors up. He then glanced to the revolving doors leading to the street. "I don't suppose you'll tell me where her apartment is?"

"The name is Chang, not Judas."

"I want to keep her, but I'm running out of options, Brenda. I'd like to tell her about my real position here, myself, before she does anything stupid."

"So you'll show up on her doorstep?"

"Do you have a better idea?"

"I think that might be going beyond the call of duty. Unless there's another reason you want to keep her here, other than her ability to work her tail off."

Chaz thought that over, deciding that Brenda was right. He was letting an employee dictate his actions, actions that might appear as desperate. As for a reason for wanting to keep Kim, beyond chaining her to her desk…his body had made it pretty clear that he was interested in more than her work ethic. The intensity of their attraction that had led to the kiss couldn't be ignored, and hadn't lessened one bit.

It was a double-edged sword. If he went out of his way to keep her at the agency, his actions tonight might hurt her reputation. If she walked out, taking those big clients with her, the agency might tank.

This was an impossible situation that he had to try to put right.

"You're right," he said to Brenda. "She has to decide for herself, without further interference, what she will do next. Feelings have no place here."

Brenda thought that over with her head tilted to the side. She searched his face. "Feelings, huh?"

He shrugged.

She sighed loudly and opened her purse. Removing a piece of paper and a pen, she scribbled something and handed the paper over.

"If you tell her I gave this to you, I'll tell her you lied. Three guesses as to whom she will believe."

After a hesitation, she handed him something else. It was a tiny tape recorder just like the one Kim had used to record their conversation.

Chaz glanced at her questioningly.

"I taped something in case Kim and I needed a laugh later," Brenda said. "You might want to listen to the tape before finding her. It might help with that lawsuit business and save everyone some serious damage."

Chaz pocketed the recorder. "Does this mean you'll trust me to set things straight?"

"Hell, no. It's bribery for you to leave me out of whatever happens from this point on."

Chaz decided right then that he really did like Brenda Chang.

"Will she shoot me if I show up at her place?" he asked.

"I would."

He smiled. "I suppose following her seems desperate."

"Completely."

"Okay then, wish me luck."

"Boss, you are so going to need it," Brenda declared as Chaz headed for the street.

Kim's feet were killing her. Stilettos required a lot of downtime and motionless posing, not trotting down New York sidewalks, contrary to what TV shows might have everyone think. The shoes were impossible, especially on the icy sidewalk.

She waved down an oncoming taxi, waited until it stopped, then ran in front of it to cross the road, assured of not getting hit when the taxi blocked traffic. The driver grumbled, and might have extended one finger in a rude gesture. She didn't wait to see.

Thankfully, her apartment was around the corner from the agency, at the end of the block. Though close in terms of actual distance, she'd still have to soak her feet when she got there, and also work with her fractured ego.

The heels made sharp pecking sounds on the sidewalk as she threaded her way between other pedestrians. She'd left the office without her coat, and the red dress garnered a few stares and catcalls from men she passed.

"Imbeciles." What kind of man gave a woman a whistle on the street that she could hear?

She was shivering, but she'd had to get out of the agency building. Since Monroe had followed her into the hallway, he might have continued to the office. If he had pushed his way into the elevator with her, filling the tiny, confined space with his musky, masculine maleness, there was no way to predict what might have happened. Plus, there were cameras.

Any more time spent in Chaz Monroe's sight would be bad, and how much worse could she feel?

She walked with her gaze lowered, having set up her mental block against the windows in the stores she passed that were decorated with December finery. Some of them presented animated holiday scenes. Others showcased giant trees decorated with everything under the sun that could fit on a branch. It was especially important she didn't view these things in entirety; not after dealing with Monroe.

She was already on edge.

With great relief, she made it down the block without seeing a single Santa suit on a street corner—a sight that would not only have filled her with the old regrets, but also reminded her of what she had told Monroe.

She wanted Santa….

Yes, she had told him that.

Well, okay. So she had been impulsive enough to use Brenda's ridiculous excuse in a moment of panic and extreme need. Therefore, could she really blame Monroe for thinking her an idiot?

She wanted Santa. *Jeez...*

Feeling sicker, Kim rushed on. She nodded to the doorman of her building and whisked by without the usual benign chitchat. Six floors up and down one long hallway, and she was home free. No one had followed her. No pink slip waited on the floor by her door.

Kim stood with her back to the wood as the door closed behind her, only then allowing herself a lungful of air. She really did feel sick. Tonight she had been possessed by her mother's teachings. She'd been set back a few years with the flick of a tape recorder switch.

"There's no going back. No taking it back," she muttered.

The guilt tripled with her second breath of air. Even from the small front room, not much larger than her cubicle at work, she smelled the cookies she had dared to bake the night before.

Christmas cookies.

Her first disloyal batch.

The damn cookies might have been some kind of terrible omen. She had looked up the recipe in secret, and baked them as her first baby step toward freedom. Now her new boss had whispered fantastical things in her ear without realizing how much she'd love to participate in Christmas festivities, and how much it hurt to think of actually doing so.

Elves. Snow. Packages in red ribbons. She might have given her right index fingernail to join in everything going on around her, and had been slowly inching in that direction.

Then she kissed Chaz Monroe.

She hung her head. Her apartment smelled like a sugar factory. Worse yet, she wanted her place to smell like *him*. Like Monroe, companionship, sex, holiday glitter and all the other things her mother had shunned so harshly. You'd think she'd know better. Someone looking in on her life might expect her to just wipe the slate clean and start over, now that her mother was no longer in the picture. Who from the outside would understand?

If she tossed the cookies, would things change? If she marched into the kitchen and got rid of the little doughy stars and trees, would time reset itself backward so that she'd have another chance to get things right?

Monroe was a jerk. He had to be. Because if he wasn't, then she was.

Tossing her purse to the floor, Kim staggered to the couch and threw herself onto it, face-first, listening to the side seam in her tight red dress tear.

Chaz glanced at the paper, then up at the tall brick building. This was it. McKinley lived here, and he was going to trespass on her space and privacy because tonight he felt greedy. He wanted a showdown to get this over with once and for all.

She lived in a place that was a lot like his on the outside. He didn't know her well enough to gauge her decorating skills, but figured martini glasses wouldn't be one of her prominent fixtures.

In truth, he didn't really know Kim at all and was relying on the concept of animal attraction to nudge him into doing what he'd never done before—plead his case a second time.

He offered a curt but friendly nod to the doorman and went inside. The doorman picked up the lobby phone and dialed apartment 612.

"Yes?" she answered after a couple of rings.

The doorman spoke briefly, then handed the phone over.

Hearing Kim's voice left him temporarily tongue-tied, something so unlike him that he almost hung up. He thought about the napkin with the brunette's number on it crumpled up in his pocket. Calling that number might have taken his mind off Kim McKinley for a few hours.

So, the fact that he was standing here meant he was either acting like a madman, or a man possessed. Maybe even like a sore loser refusing to give up on the outcome he wanted. Those flaws made him see red. And in the center of that puddle of red was Miss Kim McKinley, the cause of all this.

"Delivery for Kim McKinley, advertising queen," Chaz said to her over the line, managing to keep his voice neutral. "I can't be sure, but from the feel of the package, I think it contains an apology."

A short span of silence followed his remark. His heart beat faster. What was he doing here, anyway? Had he just uttered the word *apology?*

"This only adds to the harassment, you know," she eventually said. "I believe stalking might be a felony."

"Yes, well, what's one more year behind bars when there's so much at stake?"

"None of this is funny, Monroe."

"No, it isn't. At least we agree on something."

"You can't come up."

"Then maybe you'll come down."

"Sorry."

"Are you sorry?"

After another hesitation, she said, "No."

"Not very convincing," Chaz remarked. "It's that gap between what you say and what you don't say that keeps me wondering what you might really be thinking."

More silence. A full twenty seconds, by his calculation. Chaz lowered the phone to keep her from hearing his growl of disappointment, then thought better of it. With the phone so close to his heart, she might be able to hear how fast it raced. She'd know something was up.

"You just don't get the picture," she accused. "I don't know you at all."

"You know me well enough to want to prosecute me for minor indiscretions. Also, I did say I'm willing to take on an added year in the slammer if you think I need it after we hash this out."

"Can I have that in writing? About the slammer?"

"I'm fresh out of pens."

"How convenient."

"You do have a tape recorder, though," he reminded her. "It's possible you're using it now."

Silence.

"You don't know how persistent I can be, Kim. Lawsuit or not, blackmail or whatever, I still have to take care of business while the fate of that business rests in my hands. Don't you have a sympathetic bone in your body? Can't you put yourself in my place?"

"I was supposed to be in your place."

"Water under the bridge, Kim. How long can you hold that against me?"

Another silence ensued. Chaz held his breath.

"Let me speak to Sam," she said.

"Sam?"

"The doorman. He'll come if you call."

Chaz called out to the man, and he ambled over and took the phone.

"Yep," Sam said to the receiver, nodding. "Yep. I certainly will, Miss McKinley." Then Sam hung up the phone.

"What did she say?" Chaz asked.

"I'm to take something as collateral, then send you up."

"Excuse me?"

"Miss McKinley wants me to hold something as ransom, in order for you to visit her apartment. You can pick that item up again when you come back downstairs. I have instructions to call the police if you don't pick it up within the hour."

"Like what?" Chaz said. "My wallet?"

"The value of that as collateral depends on what's in it," Sam said without missing a beat.

"Who do I call if I come back and you're not here with my wallet?" Chaz asked.

Sam looked dramatically aghast at the suggestion. "I

have a drawer right here, and I'll lock it up, minus whatever you see fit to give me for keeping it safe. If you prefer, I can give the wallet to a neutral third party."

"What kind of doorman are you?"

Sam held out his hand, palm up. "The kind that cares about his wards."

Chaz fished for his wallet, took out a wad of cash and his credit cards, then handed a twenty-dollar bill and the wallet to McKinley's private watchdog.

He held up the rest of the cash. "Just in case I have to buy off anyone else between here and her apartment."

Sam grinned and pressed the elevator button for him. "Apartment 612. Have a nice night."

The elevator was slow and bumpy, but Chaz stepped out on the sixth floor. He found number 612 a few doors down, its oiled wood glowing in the light from the wall sconce beside it.

As he waited to knock, he pondered further what Kim's home would be like, half dreading finding out. Personalities were reflected in a person's surroundings. If she preferred chintz chairs, mounds of pillows and draperies with fringe, he wasn't sure what he'd do. Run away, maybe. After all, he didn't want to marry McKinley. He just wanted to...

Well, he wanted to...

God, would she have a cat?

He'd be a dog guy, himself, if he had any time or space for pets.

And it was perfectly clear that what he was doing with all this ridiculous speculation was trying to talk himself out of this next meeting with her after getting this far.

Fingering the tape recorder in his pocket, he knocked softly.

"Yes?" she called out.

"Monroe. Not completely broke, I might add, because

Sam showed a little mercy. I think he recognized your real intention, which was to put me in my place."

"Say what you wanted to say and then go away."

"From here, with the door between us? What would the neighbors think?"

The door opened a crack. Kim's face appeared behind a stretched brass chain. "Go away, Monroe. We have nothing further to say to each other tonight."

"Then why did you let me come up?"

"To tell you that to your face."

He noticed right away that she looked smaller. She had ditched the red shoes, but still wore the red dress that glowed like liquefied lava in the light from the sconce.

"If I let you in," she added, "it might ruin my lawsuit. So why are you here?"

"You're a challenge I have to take up."

"Is that supposed to be a compliment, or are you merely the type of person that needs to win at all cost?"

"Winning isn't everything," he countered. "The need to understand you is why I'm here."

"What part of *none of your business* don't you get?"

"You kissed me," he said, wondering why he'd brought that up again. He'd kissed other women, for heaven's sake.

"So?" she said.

"Was it me or the game you might be playing that made you do it?"

She closed the door. He heard it seal tight.

"Would you prefer I spoke about holiday clauses here? How about if I mention Santa, and how you made that sound in the bar?"

The door opened again, not quite as widely, showing off Kim's exquisitely creased expression. "That's not funny."

Chaz shrugged. "What more have I got to lose?"

"How about your job?"

"Okay, Kim. But remember, you forced me to do this."

From his pocket, Chaz pulled out the tape recorder Brenda had handed him. He had listened to it on the way over, and bookmarked a starting point in case of just such an instance as this, figuring Brenda wouldn't have handed the tape over if it wasn't something useful to his cause.

He hit Play. Brenda's voice came from the tiny speaker.

Tell me about it. But first you have to dish about whether Monroe really does have a nice ass. You didn't think he was hot? That's the word going around. H-o-t, as in fan yourself.

Yeah? Did you hear anything about the man being an arrogant idiot?

No. My sources might have left that part out.

I don't actually care about the nice ass part, Bren, preferring not to notice an area that I won't be kissing.

Don't be absurd, Kim. No one expects you to kiss anyone's backside. It isn't professional. What happened?

I'll have to start over somewhere else, that's what. Monroe won't let me off the hook. He expects me to explain everything. He'll expect me to cave.

As Chaz fast-forwarded slightly, he said, "I don't think Brenda knew she was recording that. She had been making notes for herself on a project."

He held the recorder up and pressed Play again.

If you don't want to tell Monroe the truth, you have about an hour to formulate a reason he'll accept in lieu of the truth. Fabricating illusions is what we do on a daily basis, right? We make people want to buy things.

Chaz pocketed the recorder. "Then there was something about shoes and therapy and a Santa fetish."

Kim stared at him through the crack.

"Also, I believe that seducing me was mentioned, which might tend to negate that harassment suit and the blackmail you might have planned on using to get me to back down."

Kim looked very pale, in stark contrast to her red dress.

"So, there is no Santa fetish?" he asked. "You made that up?"

Now she looked sick, and he felt bad. But he wanted her to let him in. He needed to get that far for reasons he did not want to contemplate.

"Why are you here?" she asked. "What do you want?"

"You and I tending to that Christmas party by working together."

"You have no idea what you're asking."

"That's the point. I want to understand. Until you can help me do that, we're back to square one."

"No. We're back to you filling my place at the agency, because I'm out of there as of right now."

Chaz shook his head. "Now you're being stubborn. No one wants you to go, myself included. I've come here personally to tell you so, at much risk to my ego, I might add. Can't that constitute a win on your part if you're keeping score?"

She paled further. Possibly she wasn't used to direct confrontations.

He held up the recorder. "How about if you get yours and we toss them both out the window?"

"We're six floors up."

"There's little chance of them surviving the fall, right?"

"They might hit somebody. Maybe Sam."

Chaz nodded thoughtfully. "Okay. You're right. It would probably be simpler if we exchanged tapes. Then no one would have the goods on anyone else."

"This is ridiculous," she said. "What do you want?"

"Talk and a holiday party," he said. "That's all I ask."

"Okay."

"Okay?" he repeated, surprised by her reply.

"When is this damn party?" she asked.

"In a week or so."

"That's only a few days before…"

"Christmas," Chaz supplied.

She looked hesitant. "I can make some calls."

"You will do this personally, Kim?"

"Yes."

"Thank you." Chaz wasn't sure about feeling relieved, because winning this round wasn't as satisfying as it should have been. Kim was going to pass the test after being shoved into it, but he might have pushed her too far. Her sudden acceptance reflected that. He had, he supposed, lost by winning, and he experienced an immediate pang of regret.

"It's the last thing I'll do for you," she said, confirming his diagnosis of the situation.

Chaz wanted to let it go at that. At the same time, he desired to tell her she really didn't have to work on the ridiculous and imaginary project, and that he was sorry for putting her through this. Breaking her would have hurt both of them, and that realization came as a further surprise, because he found that he liked Kim exactly the way she was.

"I know it might be true that you'll decide to leave, but I'm counting on convincing you otherwise. I am sorry we had to meet like this," he said.

How serious he had grown in saying what he truly meant. Chaz fought a strange impulse to break the little chain keeping them apart and wrap his arms around the pale version of McKinley facing him. Again, his instinct was to protect her, comfort her, though he had no idea why. She was Wonder Woman, after all.

Okay. Backtracking, maybe he did know why he wanted to hold her. He had started to like her more than was appropriate, in spite of her stunt in the bar.

"Where is the party?" Her voice sounded dry. Her accent was pronounced, and no less sultry than the first time he'd heard it.

"I'll give you the details tomorrow. Unless you'll let me in right now," he said.

"Good night, Monroe. I think we've said all there is to say for one night, don't you?"

He supposed they had. Besides, Brenda would tell Kim about him any minute now, and that would be that. Cat out of the bag.

"Tomorrow, then."

She closed the door.

Wishing he had another beer to chase away the thrill of being so close to the woman he didn't want to feel anything for, Chaz instead considered calling his brother for a stern reprimand about pleading with any woman for any reason, and for putting himself in such an awkward position.

Big bro Rory, his elder by four years, wouldn't beat around the bush. He'd just reach out and take what he wanted, perfectly willing to suffer the consequences. Then again, Rory at times seemed a little insane.

McKinley had agreed to help out. Soon she'd know that he wasn't only her boss, but the new owner of the agency. His actual title shouldn't make any difference, in theory. Still, she might take the undercover boss business badly.

He could knock again and tell her the truth about this being a test of her willingness to work with him, before Brenda called to tell her the truth of the situation.

What about when he sold the agency, flipping it for a profit, as he'd planned to do? What would happen to her then, if she didn't back down first?

By helping Kim now, he'd be doing a good deed. So how the hell did he turn this situation around? Seriously, was that impossible?

As Chaz headed for the elevator, he had to concede that he'd at least given this a shot. But he didn't make it to the elevator before hearing a door open. He turned to see Kim standing with her hands on her hips in the hallway, her pallor ghostly white, her lips parted for a speech she didn't make.

In that moment, he thought how magnificent she looked, even in anger.

Six

Fighting off a round of pure, livid anger, Kim faced Chaz Monroe with a distance of thirty feet separating them. Her pulse thudded annoyingly in her neck and wrists.

"You're a bastard," she said. "Is this a game for you? Tell me that much."

"It wasn't a game until you kissed me back and then pulled out that recorder," he replied.

The door to the apartment next to Kim's opened, and her neighbor looked out. Kim smiled wanly at the man. "Having a difference of opinion," she said, explaining the noise.

"A lover's spat," Monroe clarified.

"Please do it elsewhere," the old guy said, retreating back inside. "You're spoiling my dinner."

She pointed a finger at Monroe. "How did you get that tape recording? Did you plant bugs all over the building to keep an eye on things?"

"I did nothing of the sort," he said. "It just happened to fall into my possession."

"Like hell it did."

"Maybe I should come in," he suggested. "We're beyond lawsuits, don't you think? Unless…"

"Unless what?" she snapped.

"Unless you're afraid you'll do what you said on that recording."

"What are you talking about?"

"Seducing me."

"Get over yourself, Monroe. That wasn't a plan, it was girl talk."

"Yet you accomplished it," he pointed out, shaking his way-too-handsome head and dislodging a strand of shaggy hair that fell becomingly across his forehead. It didn't help her cause that he in no way looked like a monster.

Nor did Monroe look as smug as she had expected him to. Frankly, he didn't appear to be pleased with his behavior any more than she was. He didn't grin or let on what he might be thinking, though she did see something in his expression that left her short of breath.

"You didn't think—" Her voice faltered. She started over. "You didn't come here to—"

"As a matter of fact, I think I must have," he replied.

"Dream on." Kim placed a hand over her heart in disbelief as her body produced a quake of longing so intense for that very thing they were both thinking, she nearly gasped aloud.

Was it possible to despise a guy and want to bed him at the same time? Monroe had this ultrasexy thing going on that affected her as if it were magical. But he was clouding her judgment and preying on her attraction to him. Obviously, he knew about that weakness. He had heard her conversation with Brenda, where she had wistfully mentioned his looks.

And then again, there had been the kiss.

Kim widened her stance with a crisp show of authority she didn't actually feel. The red dress strained at the seams.

"Letting me in would be a fitting end to this stalemate," Monroe suggested.

Kim glanced down the hallway. Anytime now her nosy neighbor would be back in his doorway. She had to move this conversation out of the open, yet was afraid to get closer to the gorgeous guy who had mesmerized her into facing him again. This meeting went against every principle she had erected to protect herself.

"Letting you in would also be business blasphemy," she said.

"Fortunately, I'm no longer talking about the business, Kim. Neither are you, I'm thinking."

Monroe closed the distance between them with long strides. He was terribly seductive, even when he pleaded his case so crassly. His features and his body were damn near perfect. She hadn't found a single physical flaw in the entire package, except for the shirt, visible beneath his open jacket, which still bore the creases from when she'd grabbed him earlier.

He possessed a damnable, pit-bullish persistence. She wasn't at all sure about the state of his mind.

Or hers.

"Look, Kim," Monroe said, "I can hardly explain how much I want to put business aside for just this one night, call a truce and get to know you better. That's the truth."

Kim's mind sluggishly tripped through rules of negotiation. Should she toss caution to the wind and maul Monroe in the hallway? In the midst of thanking her lucky stars that he hadn't yet reached her, her traitorous body had started to sag. She leaned a shoulder against the doorjamb and considered the ramifications of taking Monroe up on his offer. What could it hurt to speak to him further if she was going to leave the agency, anyway?

It wasn't as if she *cared* for Monroe, beyond her acute physical craving for him. Allowing him inside might be a fitting end to all this infuriating heat and drama.

He stood before her wearing a questioning expression, one eyebrow raised.

"Monroe," she began. "I'm not sure what's going on."

Her neighbor's door opened. Kim tossed him a friendly wave. Sighing heavily in resignation, she wrapped her hands in Monroe's coat and hauled him inside her apartment, hoping she hadn't gone completely insane.

The first thing Chaz noticed was the sweet smell of her apartment. The second was how his body had ended up pressed tightly to Kim's against the wall beside the front door that slammed shut behind them.

They were body to body, without an inch of space between, and below his waist, pertinent body parts were already thankful. Tight against her like that, he couldn't think about business, what her home looked like or about mistrusting her. In fact, he'd just discovered that he was no longer able to trust himself. His body had the lead on this one, and his mind seemed curiously foggy about the future.

Kim's long-lashed hazel eyes, mostly green, remained fixed on him. Her expression was hard to read. Her soft lips finally parted, and sensing another excuse coming that might end the highly sensual, highly addictive position he found himself in, Chaz didn't let her voice a protest. He pressed his index finger to her mouth and shook his head. "Now's not the time," he whispered. "Backward is never the right direction."

She offered him an expression that fell precariously close to being a grimace, and at the same time eyed him warily. But Kim's mind, it seemed to him, had to be in the gutter, next to his.

Wonder Woman was in his grasp, and had welcomed it. Her lips weren't pouty, exactly, but close to it, and relatively ruby-tinted, though he had kissed some of the color away in the bar. Her chest, against his, strained at the confines of the red dress. She breathed shallowly, in shudders.

"What do you propose we do about this?" she asked, biting down on her lower lip hard enough to leave an imprint of teeth marks.

"Are any tape recorders running?" he said.

She glared at him in a way that did nothing to ruin the glorious beauty of her pert oval face. Her ivory neck pulsed with a racing heartbeat. Feeling the firmness of her breasts pressed to his chest, Chaz knew the time for talk was over.

In a smooth motion, he slid one arm around her waist.

The other arm followed. He stroked her slender back with his open palm in a gradual downward glide over the red silk that had been such an inspiration, and now seemed like an unnecessary barrier between them and their crazy, wayward desires.

He found the silk warm and fragrant, the texture exotic. Around them, the room felt cool, dim and distant. Between them, the fires of lustful attraction beat at the air.

Kim shivered as his fingers trailed down her spine. This time when her lips parted, a sigh of resignation emerged. Chaz watched her intently, holding on to his control with every ounce of willpower he possessed.

Just a little longer...

All he needed was one more little sign that she actually agreed to what was going to happen next.

He felt downright greedy now that he'd gotten this far. He wanted more of Kim McKinley, and getting closer than this wasn't possible unless it became acceptable for two objects to actually occupy the same space at the same time. He yearned to be inside her, and to enjoy all of her. He hoped they'd settle for nothing less.

She closed her eyes in a flutter of long lashes. Her body swayed as if, parallel to his reactions, she had moved beyond the point of no return. She placed her hands on his hips, but didn't push him away. She gave a slight tug, as though she shared his desire to relish the physicality of the moment.

This was the sign he had been waiting for.

He kissed her.

Not a soft, tender kiss, but a hungry devouring one. There was no hesitancy in McKinley's response. She allowed this mouth-to-mouth exploration and joined in, meeting him in a white-hot dance of lips and tongues and fire, giving as much as receiving.

The McKinley he had wished for in his wildest dreams

kissed him with a fury backed by her own level of greed. As his hands moved over her fine, sleek body, she rubbed up against him, fanning the flames of his raging desires.

Chaz could not recall ever feeling this way. Never this greedy, this needy, or this consumed.

The woman was driving him crazy….

And the damn dress was in the way.

Wanting to feel the smoothness of her skin beneath the slinky fabric, Chaz slowly began to raise the hem upward, over her thighs, toward her hips, listening to the rustle of the expensive silk. He couldn't see the lace he hoped would be underneath, though he located its delicate pattern with his fingers.

Lace...

Narrow strips of elastic crossed her hips, holding the dainty lingerie in place. His fingers slipped under, sliding down the cleft that led to her feminine heat from the back.

She groaned. Their mingling breath was volcanic. He breathed hard and fast, ready to explode, and hadn't even seen her naked. Kim was like catnip, with her mouth, her flawless skin and her inferno-like heat.

He desperately wanted all of her, and knew he couldn't take the time. His pulsating body wouldn't allow for the slowness of a proper bedding. Plus, no bedroom was in sight.

He shifted his hands to find the zipper at her back. The zipper made no sound as he eased it downward.

Dragging his mouth from hers, he took seconds to study her face, wondering if Kim was truly going to allow this, not quite believing his luck. He felt compelled to speak. "It will be worth it," he said. "All the best things are."

Her wide-eyed gaze unflinchingly met his. "Then why are you dallying?" Her voice was low-pitched and sensuously breathy.

"Is that what I'm doing?" he asked.

"Don't you know?"

"I'm afraid you'll change your mind. Should I give you that option?"

"Why, when you're so barbaric about everything else?"

Chaz's physical urges escalated with the flirty tone of their repartee. It was to be a fight to the very end between them if their minds got in the way.

One of his hands remained on the zipper. He tilted her head back with his other one, with his fingers under her chin. "Maybe we can pretend we're just two people enjoying each other."

"Maybe I should have chugged that martini."

"Was that your first?"

"Kiss?"

"Martini."

"It couldn't actually be the first if I didn't drink it."

Chaz tilted her head back farther, wanting to see deep into Kim's soul through the pools of green in her eyes.

"And the kiss?" he said.

"Are you now asking for an accounting of other things in my personal life?"

"I'm jealous just thinking about your personal life."

He eased the zipper the rest of the way down. Kim's hands, on his hips, hadn't moved again. Each turn of her head sent her lush scent scattering. Chaz inhaled her woodsy fragrance and felt it mix with the rising heat waves inside his chest. Talk couldn't really spoil this for him. Nothing could. The deepness of her voice was a vibration that made him want her more than ever.

He feathered his lips over her forehead and placed a series of kisses on her cheek in a trail that led back to her mouth—not entirely sure why she allowed this kind of liberty.

She had a small waist and delicate bones. Touching her gave him a thrill equal to being caught in a lightning storm.

This wasn't love, it was lust, he reminded himself. Love didn't leave a man breathless and overheated. He'd always figured love as a lukewarm emotional state that developed slowly over time between long-standing acquaintances. He and Kim didn't know each other. They had barely spoken a few hundred words, total, and were acting on instinct.

"This is a truce," he said, brushing her mouth with his. "A white flag."

In a replay of the kiss in the bar, he rested his lips on hers lightly before drawing back far enough to note her response. Her eyes were half-closed now. Her lashes were blackened by eye makeup she didn't need to enhance her appearance. Her skin gleamed as though their steamy encounter had moistened it. Up close, she really did look younger. She looked…delicious.

The red dress, he decided in a whirlwind of thought, probably wouldn't hold a candle to Kim in a baggy T-shirt and nothing else. Kim with her hair mussed, getting out of bed on a weekend morning, or emerging from a shower, wet and soapy.

Those thoughts turned him on.

He wedged his thigh between her legs and pressed her roughly to the wall. Her mouth molded to his, and her mouth was a marvel. She nipped at his lips, breathing sultry streams of air into him.

Her hands found their way underneath his coat, and tugged at his shirt. Finding bare skin, her fingers splayed, hot as pokers, and sent streaks of pleasure soaring through him.

Who needed control when faced with *this?*

What man wouldn't consider giving up a future for a night like this one?

Liking how light she felt in his arms, he lifted her up. Her legs encircled his thighs. The spot he achingly wanted to reach settled over his erection as he held her close, though there were still too many clothes in the way.

Backing up a step made things worse. Part of him wanted to hold her like this forever, culmination be damned. But he was also aware of how close they had come to losing the chance of working anything out after this ferocious sexual escapade.

His mind's chatter stopped abruptly when her mouth separated from his and moved to his ear. Her lips flitted over his lobe teasingly before she came back for more, her mouth hungrier this time, their kiss resembling the furor of anger in its intensity.

She was giving in, meeting him halfway as an aggressor. He had never desired anything so badly as to be inside her. Surely there was a place to finish this—a sofa or a rug?

He caressed her, devoured her, his elation escalating. Her fingers dipped under his waistband, searching, scorching, ensuring his hardness, driving him mad. The only sound in the room was the rasp of their breathing. The only sensation left to him was Kim McKinley in his arms.

And then the air shook with the shrill sound of a phone ringing. The sound echoed loudly throughout the room.

Chaz's heart missed a beat. His lips stalled. It was Kim's phone, and a bad omen, he just knew.

The click of an answering machine turning on followed the second ring.

"Kim?" a voice said, loud enough for Brenda Chang to have been in the room with them.

"Kim, are you there? Pick up the damn phone! Listen. Monroe isn't who we think he is. He isn't the VP. He's the new owner of the agency, and is occupying that office in order to spy on the masses. He owns the agency and us, lock, stock and barrel. Kim, please pick up! Monroe might be on his way over there. I wanted to catch you before he arrives and pass on that news. Kim? Oh, hell. Tell Sam. Don't answer the door. Where are you? Call me back."

By the time the machine turned off, Kim's tight hold on him had gone slack. She stiffened so fast, her actions didn't register until her legs loosened, and he had to press her against the wall to support her.

Some of her glorious heat slipped from his grasp. Her eyes were averted, her lids lowered. Once she had regained her feet, she got her hands up between them.

She couldn't seem to catch a breath. Her chest still strained against his. When she finally looked up, her big eyes met his as if searching for something. Her pallor brought a whole new meaning to the word pale, despite the splashes of pink in her cheeks.

"Kim," he said, addressing her accusatory gaze. "It's okay. I knew Brenda was going to tell you. My role at the agency is supposed to be a secret for now. I wanted to get to know the workings of the place and play catch up."

"You own the agency?" The words tumbled out between harsh breaths.

"Yes."

"You're not the vice president?"

"No."

Her eyes projected an expression of betrayal. She blinked slowly. When she spoke, her voice shook. "Get out. I think you'd better get out right now."

"Kim—"

"You can see the door. Use it," she directed. "Please."

He held up both hands in a placating gesture, and tried to find the right words to ease the tension. No words came. Kim didn't look angry about this, she looked ill.

"Now," she repeated.

He had to explain, had to make her see. "I bought the company to make it better, more successful. The position you want is still on the table. I'll make a decision once I get a grip on the rest of the agency's personnel needs and can move things forward. We already have a truce, you and I, so we're in the clear about the situation. Nothing has changed."

"Oh, we're far from clear about anything," she countered. "And everything has changed."

"That doesn't have to be the case."

"Doesn't it? You were going to sleep with me, withholding a secret like that. You let me think you took my job, and you were willing to let me hang myself and my profession by directing me toward a bed."

"A date with a bed has nothing to do with work or the issues there," he protested.

She sucked in a big breath of air and lowered her voice. "What was this all about then, for you? A test of my character? You wanted to see if I'd actually sleep my way up the ladder? Maybe you wondered if I'd done it before, and that's why I had been promised your office?"

Chaz stared at her, sensing she wasn't finished.

"Are you so naïve that you'd actually believe I could remain at the agency after sleeping with you? That being here with you, like this, wouldn't affect my reputation, or reach the ears of the other employees, and eventually my clients? Or that it would all go away if you were to promote me now?"

"Kim, listen—"

She shook her head. "Tell me this, Monroe—is there actually a holiday party to cater?"

"There could be," he said, hating the way that sounded.

She turned her face. "Please leave."

Chaz's stomach tightened with pangs of regret over the way he had approached this, understanding how it must look to Kim. In his defense, he'd been smitten, for lack of a better word to describe the immediacy of his attraction to her. Had certain parts of his anatomy made him come here, under the premise of testing her work ethic? Could he have slipped that far?

She had told him to get out. What other option did he have after a command like that, except to do as she asked? His explanation hadn't swayed her. She was angry. Her eyes blazed. Kim was hurt, half-naked and feeling the need to protect herself from further harm…and he'd been less than stellar in his approach to this whole situation.

It was obvious she took into consideration things he hadn't thought over before showing up here and placing his hands on her. Also clear now, after what she'd said, was the idea that she might have opened herself to him because she truly hadn't planned on returning to her job. In that case, a liaison to explore the sparks between them would have been okay for her.

That had been ruined by one simple withheld truth.

Damn it.

"I'm attracted to you." Chaz retreated a step. "I'll confess that here and mean it. I wanted to get to know you, and still do. But what you're thinking wasn't what brought me here. I wasn't going to use you for some sordid purpose."

Her eyes met his. "Here's the thing, Monroe. Some women probably do sleep their way to the top, and I'm telling you now that I'm not one of them. In fact, it looks as though I've just kissed my way to the bottom."

His hands remained suspended in the air. Chaz had prided himself on being decent at handling people, yet had botched the hell out of this situation. He supposed that's what came of mixing lust with work.

He had known better and ignored the signs, but he wasn't an idiot or completely ruled by what was in his pants. He did comprehend her take on this predicament, and it was a damn shame, because in her mind the damage had been done, and he wasn't going to allow himself to beg her to change her mind.

A man could only go so far.

"Okay," he conceded, reaching for the doorknob. "Though you might not believe this, I am sorry the news has upset you. My purpose was never to hurt or demean you. And from everything I've heard about your job performance, you've proven your talent and superior work ethic to justify being in line for the promotion."

He really did not want to leave, especially like this. He gave her one last lingering look before opening the door, hoping she might soften. "No one needs to know about this. I'm not a kiss-and-tell kind of guy, and you can trust me on that. I've apologized. I've confessed to liking you. I guess what you do with that is up to you."

With a frown of disappointment etched on his brow, Chaz closed the door on what might have turned out to be the hottest night in history.

In the hallway, he slapped the wall and uttered a choice four-letter oath. This night had not gone well. In fact, it couldn't have been worse.

McKinley wanted him. Of that there was no doubt. She had been willing to take him in and take him on. Perhaps, now that she knew the score, she would come around. They could pretend this never happened and start over.

Or maybe not.

Seeing her at work might bring on his feelings of lust for her all over again. He wouldn't be able to touch her, talk to her privately or smell her rich fragrance up close, if she returned to the job.

Things were truly messed up, yet he couldn't go back and demand to be let back in. It was too late for that.

Sighing in frustration, he walked to the waiting elevator and stepped inside. Kim didn't open her door and call after him this time. It was like a slap in the face—the second in two hours. He didn't have to take that lying down. He shouldn't have to. He would move on and forget her.

Staring blankly at her door, Chaz rolled his shoulders. Something was definitely wrong with him. Despite arguments to the contrary, he'd already started imagining a strategy for getting Kim back, if not at the office, where she ultimately belonged, then into that baggy T-shirt he'd envisioned—and the naughty red shoes.

At the very least, he had to know what this was about, what her dislike of the holiday work meant. Research would be the key to unlocking Kim McKinley's secrets, and he had plenty of know-how at his fingertips.

"Nobody hates Christmas," he muttered as the elevator descended. "Not even you, Kim. I'll just have to prove that to you."

Kim slid down the wall, staring at the door the devil had just used to make his exit. Chaz Monroe was a monster, and she had been foolish to believe anything else.

He had almost succeeded in making her forget the hovering darkness of the season, and about men being liars when given the chance. She had been willing to share tonight with him under the waving flag of truce and the lure of the laws of man-woman attraction. And look where that had landed her.

Monroe had spoiled things, in essence tromping over her mother's grave in motorcycle boots and kicking up clods of freshly turned earth. She could hear her mother shouting *I told you so.*

Head in her hands, knees drawn to her chest, Kim sat without moving for a long time before finding the strength to get up. She had wanted so badly to believe that her mother didn't have to be right.

She walked to the kitchen and removed aluminum foil from the top of a pan on the counter. Turning slowly, she hit a lever with her bare foot and dumped the entire batch of frosted Christmas cookies into the trash.

"Lesson learned the hard way," she said, slipping out of the red dress and leaving the puddle of silk discarded on the hardwood floor.

Seven

She was supposed to be on vacation starting at noon the next day, and debated whether to show up at the office at all. After spending a sleepless night thinking about it, she had decided to go in.

If she was lucky, she'd beat Monroe to the office and be able to pick up a few things. She also needed to put the finishing touch on a project before heading out to take the vacation time due to her. At least she'd get something in terms of a paycheck before finding out if she'd have to terminate her employment.

But she was angry enough at the moment to keep the job and drive Monroe crazy, just to spite him.

Entering the building quickly, Kim hustled into the first open elevator. She got off on her floor and sighed with relief to find the hallway empty that led to the little cubicle that had been her home away from home for the last few years.

Monroe had said the next step was hers, so she'd ignore him and get on with things more or less as usual, for as long as she could. Time away would be necessary, and would allow her to set up a barrier between herself and the agency's new owner until they both cooled off. If more bad news was to come her way, it would have to find her someplace else.

In order to get unemployment money, she needed to be fired.

At the entrance to her cubicle, she stopped short. Brenda sat in her chair with her arms and legs crossed.

"You did not, in fact, call me back," Brenda said. "I worried all night."

Kim leaned a hip against what couldn't really be called

a doorjamb. It seemed there was no escaping some of what she'd hoped to avoid.

"Did you get my message?" Brenda asked.

"I got it."

"Did he show up?"

Kim nodded.

"Did you let him in?"

Kim nodded.

"Is that why you don't look so good?" Brenda asked frankly.

"Trust me, I feel even worse."

"So, you aren't going to speak to me ever again?"

The question got Kim's attention. So did the tone. "Is there a reason I shouldn't?"

"No. Well, maybe. But he swore all he wanted to do was keep you here, like I do, so I was with him on that one."

Brenda had done something bad and felt regretful—and that was the reason for her early arrival—though Brenda wouldn't have done anything to hurt her on purpose.

Kim's thoughts returned to the dress, the shoes…and then to the tape recorder Monroe had in his possession last night and her idea that he might have bugged her office in order to have captured conversations on tape.

"He got the tape from you, Bren," she said.

"Oh, crap." Brenda covered her face with her hands. "Yes, he did."

"Because?"

"I believed him. He seemed sincere when he said he wants to keep you here. I know he likes you. The way he looked at you in the bar was…"

"Inappropriate?"

"No. I don't think so," Brenda said. "Not exactly. More like he was awed."

Kim's heart shuddered with the memory of how blind-sided by Monroe's sexual magnetism she had been as she stood against that wall in her apartment with Monroe's hands and mouth all over her. After anger, embarrassment sat high on her list of emotions to avoid at night when attempting to count sheep.

She nailed Brenda with her gaze. "Cough it up, Bren. What else don't I know?"

"In his email yesterday he asked if I'd attend the meeting in the bar, then let you two work things out if the meeting went well. That's why I left. Well, that and I was trying to avoid watching you two going for the other person's jugular. Honestly, though, I wasn't sure you noticed I had gone."

"Moot point. It didn't work out, anyway," Kim said. "Monroe's a barbarian when it comes to negotiation."

And also a sexual barbarian, Kim inwardly added. The moniker probably fit, due to all those Celtic genes behind a name like *Monroe* that conjured images of men with blue faces. Marauding Vikings. People with wooden clubs.

Brenda looked up. "You're not going to do that party?"

"There was no party, Bren. I think that was a sham to see if I'd bend over backward."

Brenda's eyes went wide with surprise. She echoed Kim's word for Monroe. "Barbarian!"

"I suppose you didn't know for sure if there actually was a spur-of-the-moment holiday project?" Kim pressed.

Brenda crossed her heart with her index finger. "I most certainly don't know anything about that. I'm so sorry for having anything to do with last night. Really sorry."

Kim sighed. "It's okay. I almost fell for his line, too."

That was the hard part, the unacceptable part of this mess. She had sort of fallen for Monroe, despite his antics. She liked the angles of his handsome, slightly rugged face, and the shaggy hair surrounding it that often fell across his forehead. She liked the way his wide shoulders stretched his shirt, and the warmth of his hands on the exposed skin of her lower back.

She liked his voice and the easy way it affected her.

Heck, she might have fallen far enough to have assumed she'd be working on a project dealing with the North Pole today. If Brenda hadn't left that warning message in time, she might have ended up naked on the floor next to the new owner of this place, with nothing to show for it but a bruised backside.

The thought of that...

"What happened after you let him in?" Brenda's voice seemed distant, drowned out by the sound of Kim's heartbeat, which suddenly seemed uncharacteristically loud. It had been a mistake to think about Monroe.

"I got your message, Bren," she said, "and he left."

Brenda looked relieved. "You're still here, then? You didn't quit?"

"Not for the next several days. I'm going to take my vacation."

"This would be the first time you did."

"It's time."

Her heartbeat refused to settle down. Why?

She inhaled a breath of—not Christmas In A Can, but something else. A masculine scent. One she recognized.

Oh.

She saw her fear confirmed in the look on Brenda's face.

"There's someone behind me, isn't there?" Kim said.

"Yep."

Turning slowly, Kim's gaze met with the top button of Chaz Monroe's perfectly pressed blue- and white-striped shirt.

"Miss McKinley," Chaz said, reverting to formality to get over the shock of seeing her in the building after last night's anticlimactic rebuff.

Here she was, and he felt slightly taken aback.

"Mr. Monroe," she said, refusing to glance up at him as she took a step back.

She was perfectly tidy, dressed in a knee-length black skirt and a lavender sweater that covered her hips and other notable curves. Her fair hair fell softly toward her shoulders in a sheet of gold. The lips that had mesmerized him were freshly stained pink.

She looked ravishing. No evidence of a sleepless night showed on her face. There were no dark circles under her eyes. Not one eyelash seemed out of place. Had she dismissed him and what had nearly transpired between them so quickly, when he hadn't slept a wink? When his thoughts never strayed from her, and what he might say if she showed her pretty face on this floor?

Chaz cleared his throat. "You're working today?"

She still hadn't glanced up, though Chaz sensed she wanted to meet his eyes as much as he wanted her to. The electricity crackling between them hadn't diminished because of what had happened the night before. If anything, it was worse.

His wish list hadn't changed, he realized. His lust for this woman was now the size of a bloated balloon. Office or no office, and decorum be damned, he desired Kim McKinley more than ever. He'd start to work on that mouth of hers if given the opportunity, and torture it into a grin. He would offer half his earnings to be able to earn her smile, her trust, and to hear her laugh.

"I'm only in for an hour, then I'm off on that vacation I mentioned," she said, her voice unreasonably calm.

"Are you going someplace nice?"

"I'm going home," she said.

Brenda got to her feet, as if that were her cue to jump in. "I'll help with those last-minute details, Kim, so that you can get out of here."

They were presenting a united front against him. For

a minute, he actually envied Brenda her closeness to the woman he had come near to bedding. Again, though, it was a new day, and he'd deal.

"Okay. Have a good time." His tone was commendably casual, reflecting professional interest and nothing more. "By the way, have you decided on whether you'll be returning after that vacation?"

"I'm thinking on it. I'll be sure to let you know."

Kim's tone suggested to him that she wasn't going to let him ruin a good thing if she could help it, and also that she expected him to mind his manners if she did decide to keep her job.

Checkmate.

"Great. I'm sorry the party didn't work out for you," he said. "Maybe next time."

Kim raised her chin defiantly. Their gazes connected. Chaz rode out the next jolt that came with the blaze of inquiry he saw in those greenish eyes. He didn't want to push her buttons. Not now. Research awaited him. He had been able to access a few things about her background in those sleepless hours of the night, though nothing personal enough to give him a leg up on her issues.

"Yes. Maybe next time," she said.

He inclined his head and muttered in parting, "Ladies."

When he turned, he felt Kim's eyes on him in a gaze intense enough to burn a hole in his back. She was angrier than ever, though she looked to be in control of her emotions this morning. They were continuing to play this strange game with each other, with the outcome unclear.

This wasn't over. Not by a long shot. If she returned after that vacation, he would probably desire her more. When she left, he'd miss the spark of whatever existed between them.

Did this make him a lust-sick idiot?

He shrugged.

Back in his office, Chaz picked up the phone and hit a

number on speed dial. He hated to make this call, since he'd been trying to beat big brother Rory at his own game for more than a year…and maybe all his life. Other than his own personal need to be successful, Rory was always in the background setting the gold standard as far as the family business was concerned. Those business dealings weren't actually supposed to achieve the status of a competitive sport, but things between the brothers had turned out that way.

However, this wasn't *all* about business.

A male voice on the line answered in a brisk tone. "It's early, bro."

"I need some help, Rory. As my elder, I'm sure you're obliged to listen, in spite of the hour."

"I've been at work for three hours already, Chaz. It's not like I just got up. I call this early-rising routine CEO Stamina. It does my heart good to see that you're getting with the program."

Chaz sat back in his chair. "I need some intel."

"On a company?"

"On a woman."

Rory chuckled without bothering to hide it. "Well, that's a first. But you do know how to use the internet?"

"Tried that, and nothing pertinent turned up. I'd like to use your information source."

"Must be an interesting woman," Rory remarked.

"She's an employee."

"Do you suspect agency espionage?"

"I suspect she might have an interesting background that forces the issue of a contractual dispute."

"Is this employee attractive?" Rory asked.

"Would that matter to your source?"

"Nope. Does it matter to you?" Rory countered.

"Nope. So do I have your permission to contact Sarah?"

"With my blessing. And bro?"

"Yeah?"

"What's your ETA for getting that agency ready to flip? I have another business you might be interested in when you get the money out of your first big acquisition."

Hell, he had only owned this agency for a week.

"Still working on it," he said. "It's too early to tell how long it might take."

"Well, it doesn't pay to hang on for too long. You might become vested and actually see yourself as the head of a firm. Buy, fix and sell is the key."

"The family mantra," Chaz agreed, unwilling to think about the ramifications of Kim finding out he had planned all along to sell the company once it was on its feet.

"Want some more unasked-for advice?" Rory said.

"I'm all ears."

"Mom would appreciate a call now and then. She says it's been two weeks."

"Wherever does time go?" Chaz muttered before disconnecting.

That hadn't gone too badly.

As for Kim, he didn't really owe her anything. He just wanted to play fair. In pursuit of fairness, he'd get the intel on her lined up. Sarah Summers was Rory's secret weapon for finding things out. A grad student at M.I.T., Sarah specialized in what amounted to cloak-and-dagger information trading. She might be considered a hacker for her rogue-like pursuits, but no one was quite sure how she did what she did, and the results were more than satisfying. Over the last couple years, her reports had added a lot of bucks to the Monroe family business coffers.

If Kim had anything in her background to find, Sarah would be the one to find it. Chaz didn't need any more office intrigue or rumors spreading about that casting couch Kim mentioned. The situation would be out of his hands until Sarah got back to him. In the meantime, Kim would be gone, and he'd be able to keep his mind where it belonged…on business. Definitely not on McKinley's ultra-hot body, or the look in her eyes when Brenda's call had come in last night—the look showcasing betrayal and pain.

Other than Kim and Brenda, not one person at the agency knew he had bought this company in order to turn a quick profit, and that he hadn't planned on remaining here for long. He sure as hell didn't plan on becoming too comfortable, or being overly involved with employees' personalities. He had just inadvertently gotten stuck on the issue of a very tempting blonde.

After the sale, and after he departed, Kim might gain access to the job she coveted. Win-win? He'd move on, and she'd move up. If she got her promotion with somebody else in charge, he'd be off the hook, and this would work in his favor in terms of the possibility of getting to know her better.

That scenario might, in fact, solve everything.

But, his annoying inner chatter reminded him, Kim would probably still have to capitulate on the holiday clause in her contract, or risk being overlooked for the promotion by the next owner. She'd be hurt all over again. She'd be crushed.

Interestingly enough, he couldn't stand the thought of Kim suffering.

He had gone soft.

It looked a lot like Chaz Monroe cared too much about his employees already. Some of them, anyway.

One of them.

Chaz rubbed his temple as he stared at the phone. Certainly it appeared as though big brother Rory didn't linger for long on those kinds of things. If he did, he never spoke about it, or let on. Then again, it was entirely possible that Rory wasn't human. Did Chaz actually want to emulate the successful business profile of an alien?

He absently tapped on the desk with his fingers. He had not lied to anyone here. Owners went undercover all the time to ferret out business details. With the agency running smoothly and well in the black, the next owner would be crazy not to keep things the way they were.

As for Kim, the best thing for her and his conscience both would be to help her in any way he could, and then back away. He'd have to shelve his feelings for her in order to make sure she got what she deserved. And okay, so he was way too addicted to her. He could hide that, get over that.

At least he could try.

Leaning forward, he punched another number into the phone and waited until someone picked up. "Mom," he said, "about that party..."

Eight

"She's gone," Brenda said when Chaz appeared in her cubicle an hour later. It was probably just as well, he decided, because he hadn't actually thought out what he'd say to her now that he was here.

In spite of the arguments and his sense of fairness where Kim was concerned, he wasn't ready to just let her go away, maybe for good, without dealing with her future at the agency. Until he heard back from his intel source, he was willing to try to change her mind on this holiday issue one more time. The Monroes never backed away from a good fight, especially if there was a reward at the end.

"Fine," he said to Brenda, reordering his thoughts on the new challenge and how he'd have to play it. "It's you I came to see, anyway. Can you help me in Kim's place with the party event?"

Brenda raised an eyebrow. "The party that is no party?"

"Oh, there's a party, all right. Did she tell you there wasn't?"

Brenda swiveled in her chair. "Now I'm confused. But just so you know, I won't do anything else that involves my best friend's feelings for you or her job."

Chaz withheld a grin. "She has feelings for me?"

"You don't want to know about the name-calling," Brenda replied. "From both of us."

"I suppose I deserved that for my behavior at her apartment, but there is a party, and I do need help. Can I count on you?"

Brenda blinked slowly. "Depends. Are you offering the same deal you gave Kim? Time off after the holidays and a nice bonus?"

"Yes. Okay. Same deal."

"You'll sign that in blood? Your blood?"

"Brenda, I might remind you that I'm the owner of this place and have something better than blood."

"Power?"

He smiled.

"And we're not supposed to know about you owning the agency, or let that get around, right?" Brenda said sheepishly. "Though a couple of us do know that?"

"You're a heartbreaker, Chang. I had no idea blackmail made the world go around."

"I believe I said *nice* bonus."

"To which I agreed."

"So, will you appear at my apartment if I refuse, and…?"

"Never. That's a promise."

"Darn." Brenda smiled back. "Oh well, with an offer like that, how can I refuse? I may have to use the bonus to help support my friend if she leaves the job."

"I'm not sure Kim would like our deal," he said.

"I'm positive she won't," Brenda agreed. And the really good part, Chaz knew, was that Brenda wouldn't be able to resist running to Kim with this bit of news. He only hoped that Kim might react the way he hoped she would, and face him down. Again. At least he'd get more time with her if that happened.

Fighting with her was better than not seeing her at all, he had just that minute decided. *At least in theory.*

Kim hustled to the floor beneath her office, where the art department had their space. Just one more detail to take care of, and Monroe would be out of her hair for at least seven days. She wouldn't have to think about him, dream about him or convince herself to despise him.

Going home to her mother's meant dealing with things she had been avoiding since her mother's death. She hadn't set foot in that house since, and had dreaded going there for ages before that.

Because Kim was an only child, the house and all of her mother's belongings were now hers. She should have relished combing through her mother's things for remembered treasures. The fact that she didn't look forward to it piled on more guilt.

She read somewhere that emotions can attach to objects, and she wanted nothing that might remind her of the problems they had shared. Had she loved her mother? Absolutely, and maybe too much. Witnessing the level of her mom's nearly constant self-inflicted pain and suffering had become too much for one daughter to bear. She hadn't been able to keep up with the treatments and the arguments and the ups and downs of her mother's diagnosis of clinical depression.

This was the season that had kicked off the whole thing in the first place. December. Christmas. Betrayal. Would those things be contagious with her mother gone? Did houses retain the sorrow and joys of the people who had lived in them, or would her mother's house be just a house, empty and waiting to be dealt with?

She had given that house six months to let loose of its old memories and feelings. It was high time she dealt with this.

The art department had been waiting for her, and took less time than she had anticipated to finish up what she needed. On her way out, someone stopped her with a painting on a piece of white cardboard and a question.

"Do you like this rendering?" Mark Ogilvie asked, showing her the board. "It was done super quickly, but I thought I'd run it by you before you left on vacation."

"Sorry, Mark?" Kim took the board.

"The special Christmas party you and Brenda are doing as a favor to Monroe."

"I'm not sure what you're talking about." Kim flipped

the board upright. It took her a minute to understand what she was seeing. Then it dawned. On that board was a watercolor rendering of the party Monroe had asked her to do. The party that she believed wasn't really a party, and a complete sham.

Decorated tables, wrapped packages, ice sculptures, servers dressed up like elves—all of this had been painted in sparkling detail from Mark's artistic point of view, and it was a beautiful, magical wonderland.

Her heart stuttered. She sucked in a breath. Closing her eyes briefly, Kim handed the painting back to Mark. "This has nothing to do with me. Sorry."

He looked perplexed. "Can you get it to Brenda then, if you're on your way back up? She requested it about twenty minutes ago as a top priority."

"I don't think Brenda..." Kim didn't finish the protest. "Twenty minutes ago, you said?"

"She told me to show it to you on your way out. She made me promise to catch you before you reached the elevator."

Kim forced a smile. "Okay. Thanks. This looks terrific, Mark. I'll take it right up to her. I'm sure Brenda will tell you the same thing."

It took every ounce of strength she possessed to walk toward the elevator with the painting in hand. Brenda had given her a heads-up on some new turn in the tide, and this painting said it all. Monroe was at it again, with Brenda this time.

Had Brenda somehow fallen for his line? After not getting his way with her, had Monroe moved on to her friend with hopes of luring Brenda into bed?

"Monster!"

When the elevator arrived, Kim got on, punched the floor button with the edge of the painting and clenched her teeth. Monroe's antics were so unacceptable they were the definition of ludicrous. She wasn't going to take this lying down. Neither would Brenda.

She wasn't going back to Cubicle City. She'd ram this painting down Chaz Monroe's throat for causing yet another hitch in her exit strategy.

"Monster," she repeated, causing two other employees occupying the elevator with her to glance her way. "Brute."

Surely Brenda wouldn't fall for his nonsense after their conversation on the matter of Monroe's lack of integrity and business ethics. Brenda wouldn't have provided this heads-up if Brenda hadn't known the score.

She stormed out of the elevator, strode briskly to the offices and past Monroe's secretary, Alice.

"Kim?" Alice said, standing up.

"Personal matter," Kim tossed back as she reached for the door handle of the office that should have been hers, but now kept the king of jerks tucked inside.

Monroe was there. He stood with his back to the window, watching her as she entered. He was looking more attractive than she had allowed herself to remember from only an hour ago.

Propelled by the thrashing heartbeat in her chest and an uncontrollable wish to see Monroe squirm, Kim crossed to the desk and tossed the painting on top of it.

"What do you think you're doing?" she demanded, sounding winded. "One partial conquest isn't enough for you? You'd suck my best friend into your web, too? What I want to know is if you're doing this to get back at me, or if you're some kind of fiend? Sex fiend, maybe? I'd truly like to understand your actions. I'd like to know how far your lies usually get you."

She saw her mistake as soon as she'd said those words. Monroe wasn't alone. A woman sat in the leather chair beside the desk.

A chill ran down the back of her neck as Kim looked at

the woman, who without standing up said, "You must be Kim McKinley. I'm Dana Monroe. Chaz's mother."

"I..." Words failed Kim. "Excuse me."

She was really damn glad that the door was still open when she turned to rush through.

Chaz steeled his determination not to go after Kim, though he very badly wanted to. The blonde whirlwind had made his heart double up on beats.

"Feisty," his mother said, eyeing him instead of the doorway Kim had fled through. "Witnessing that little tantrum was part of the reason you asked me to rush over here, I suppose?"

"No. Not exactly. But thanks for coming, Mom. Lucky for me you were headed across the street when I called."

"Sex fiend, Chaz?"

"It's a long story."

"You've known her for how long, and she already knows your secrets?"

Chaz grinned. "Those kinds of things might be Rory's secrets, but not mine."

She waved a hand. "That's the woman you'd like to keep?"

"She is good enough at what she does to occupy this office someday."

"Yes, well, I hope she doesn't talk to everyone like that, or I fear there won't be any clients left."

He shrugged. "She's mad at me for being here, in this office, on this floor."

"That's all she's angry about?"

"Possibly not. Again, long story. So, the party is still on?"

"Everyone loves a good party, Chaz, including me. Hand me that picture, and I'll make some calls. I won't be stepping on anyone's toes by putting this together myself?"

"No toes."

"This is all for her? For McKinley?"

Chaz lowered his voice. "I have a feeling it might be the first Christmas party she has ever attended. If I can get her there, that is. She has a sad spot that surfaces when the holiday is mentioned."

"This is a goodwill effort on your part, then?"

"You could say that, yes."

"All right." His mother stood up and waited for Chaz to give her a peck on the cheek. "My sons know I'd do anything for them, and if it's a goodwill mission, so much the better."

On her way out, she paused to get in a longer last word. "You should probably spend less time with Rory. Whatever he has might be starting to rub off on you."

Dressed as well as any woman of substance in New York, diamond earrings, fur-trimmed suit and all, his mother said her farewells and left. Alice filled the doorway soon afterward.

"I suppose you were eavesdropping?" Chaz said.

Alice made a zipping motion across her lips and tossed away an invisible key.

"I suppose you'll be expecting a nice bonus, too, to keep that zipper zipped?" Chaz asked.

Despite the drama of the mouth-closing routine, Alice was able to speak. "Not necessary, since I'm only doing my job."

"Well, that's a relief," Chaz muttered as the door closed, sealing him off from some of the most enigmatic women to ever cross an office threshold.

As a matter of fact, he was starting to feel a little funny about that.

Now, he thought, turning back to his desk, if Sarah would call with that intel report on Kim, he might actually have a leg to stand on.

Big reminder here: he had only been in this office for a few days, and his mind had been hijacked for the last two by a woman he wanted to help as much as he wanted to…

Well, until Sarah called, maybe he could get some official work done, and be of use.

Glancing out the window, he smiled. "Hopefully, it will be a merry Christmas, Kim," he whispered as the phone beside him rang and Sarah Summers's number lit up the screen.

Brenda was waiting for Kim in the elevator and pulled the red Stop button once she had entered.

"I've been riding these things up and down for the last twenty minutes, changing elevators every five," Brenda said.

"Thanks for the warning," Kim managed to say before resting her head against the gray metallic wall. "Shall I warn you about him in more detail, Bren?"

"You're kidding, right?"

"Actually, no."

"You imagine I was born yesterday, or that I can't read between the lines? I'm hurt that you'd think I could be a traitor to our friendship, which means more to me than this job."

Kim smiled weakly, thinking about the tape recorder Brenda had given to Monroe.

"So, you're going home?" Brenda asked. "To your mother's house? Would you like me to come with you?"

"Thanks, but no thanks. You said yourself that it's time I face my demons."

"It's the season for joy, Kim," Brenda said. "You could wait until next month to confront those buggers."

"I don't think I have an option. It's now or never, or this might never be behind me. I can see that now."

They were silent as the remark soaked in.

"I won't help him," Brenda said. "I had Mark do the work, and promised that he would get the bonus."

Kim nodded.

"They're not all scoundrels, no matter what you tend to believe," Brenda continued. "The fact that Monroe is attracted to you doesn't mean he's a creep or that he can help it."

"You're taking his side?"

"I'm presenting both sides of what's going on without addressing what's at the core of all this."

"Which is me facing or not facing this damn holiday."

"Yes, and it's good that you know it."

Brenda was right. She had gone along with this fear of Christmas for the past few years, always rallying for Kim and helping to protect her—until now, when the time for frankness and real concern had finally arrived.

"Possibly going home will help," Kim said.

"If you need me, call."

Kim pressed the button. Instead of the elevator moving, the door opened. Chaz Monroe stood there, a serious expression on his devastatingly fine, chiseled face.

Nine

"Jeez. You'd think there were only three of us in the entire building," Brenda quipped, looking back and forth from Kim to Monroe.

"Will you please excuse us for a minute, Brenda?" Monroe said.

Kim stood very still, afraid to say more of what was on her mind after doing so in his office, in front of one of his family members. In all honesty, she didn't feel angry anymore, anyway; she felt drained. Dealing with Monroe had already taken its toll, and it seemed that toll kept on climbing.

"Kim?" Brenda awaited word on what to do.

"It's okay, Bren. I've got this."

Without further protest, Brenda left the elevator.

The door closed.

Monroe faced her from a distance of two feet; close enough for her to reach out and touch if she dared to confront the feelings she had tamped down in an effort to retain her dignity and sense of self. If she lost that sense of self, she feared what might happen. Would the past bring up trouble or be left behind in favor of something worse?

"I'm sorry," Monroe said, out of the blue.

The apology surprised her. She hadn't expected him to be so frank and straightforward, and had to distrust him, still.

More questions surfaced, like bubbles rising to the top of water, all of them concerning the man across from her.

If she were to start over, to leave the darkness in the distance, would she be setting herself up for a fall?

If she confessed to liking Monroe more than she should

after knowing him for a mere two days—the same man that had teased her, kept things from her and then made her overheat with pleasure on more than one occasion—he might act upon that weakness and take further advantage.

If he realized how difficult it was for her to keep her hands off him, he might throw her against the wall and kiss everything from her lips to her berry-colored toes. Too much kissing, fondling and overheating sexually would mean that their relationship, however temporary, might fizzle equally as fast as it began. Flames this hot tended to burn out quickly. If that happened, her secret dread of ending up like her mother, holed up in a house and simmering in defeat, year after year, alone, would reappear as a possibility.

Tendencies for depression and mental instability sometimes ran in families, she had read. Though she had successfully avoided the symptoms, fear of them had more or less made her an emotional hermit.

The good thing—if there was a good thing to be found here—was that she knew how flawed she was.

"Sorry?" she echoed, wondering if Monroe was sorry for the pressure he was putting on her over her contract or the seductive heat he caused.

Did he regret last night?

"I know I have a problem," she admitted, though the confession was difficult. "I've been trying to work it out, but it hurts me to do so. You'll have to take my word that this isn't some game I'm playing, and that I've protested the change in my contract in earnest."

"Can we forget the blasted contract for a minute?" he said.

Kim glanced up at him from beneath her lashes.

"I'm not using you," he went on. "I didn't comprehend how serious this holiday thing was for you, and had to push for what the company needed. So I tested you, yes, but with good intentions, as I said last night."

His expression confirmed his seriousness. The angles of his face were shadowed. He looked as if he hadn't slept, as if he also had tossed and turned, going over the events that had transpired and regretting not being honest earlier.

Was the elevator to become a confessional booth for issues that could be addressed right then in the secluded space, with no one else present? Personal confessions?

"I need time to process problems in my past," she said. "You've helped to make that clear, though I've known it all along. But because I might be vulnerable in my personal life doesn't equate to weakness in my professional ethics. It's just one thing that I need to deal with. Don't you have something you'd like to leave behind, even though it might be tough?"

"Yes," he said then added, "I'm sure everyone has something like that to face."

"It's easier when you have a family to back you up, though," she said. "As well as enough money to buy a company where you can set your own rules."

He took his time before responding. "There is a lot of risk involved with these investments. Not to mention stress," he said. "This has been an extraordinary few days, and I'll say one more time that I don't want the company to lose you. Will you agree to stay after all is said and done? Will knowing you have your job help with whatever it is you're going to do this week?"

Kim shook her head to hide the fact that the rest of her shook, as well. She felt something for this man, but wasn't sure what. The sensations had come on too quickly, were too intense and all-consuming. Their relationship had started with anger and ended with heat.

Last night had been over the top, for as long as it lasted. Monroe's body, his attention and his talents had caught her up, making her forget everything else that stood between them. But those moments of free fall had been ruined, and now she felt unsettled. The simplicity of an emotion like anger no longer fit or covered the situation. She wasn't sure what did.

She lifted her gaze to the level of his chin. "I'm sorry I said those things in front of your mother. That was inexcusable."

"I think my mother liked you. She called you feisty."

Kim blinked slowly to block out the scene.

"We don't have to talk now," he said. "Do whatever you need to do to fix what you have going on. Just don't count me as another problem to face, okay?"

"Are you offering to forget about the contract?"

"I can't forget it in a potential vice president. I know you understand that, and that I have to do what's best for the agency."

"What is it you want, then? Friendship?"

"Yes, if that's what it takes to keep you here. And no if I'm being completely truthful."

Kim's gaze rose higher. She didn't want to be his friend, either, though that might not have been possible anyway, given the intensity of their connection. Despite trying to repress her feelings, she imagined what his hands would again feel like on her bare back, and how his lips might again sweep her away if she and Monroe dared to allow the sparks between them to dictate their future actions.

Kissing him last night had seemed right. In his arms nothing else had existed for a while, beyond two flames merging.

Now…

Now they were embarrassed and taken aback by their behavior, and he wanted to mend the situation.

"We are having the party," he said. "It's my family's holiday celebration. I thought you should know that we're going to utilize all the ideas you and I talked about in the bar, and more. You don't have to be a part of planning, Kim, but I'd like you to attend."

"As your disgruntled employee whose covert nickname is Scrooge?"

"As my guest."

"I can't commit to that right now."

"Then you can give me your answer later. Maybe after a couple days off, you'll accept."

"Besides, I couldn't possibly be welcome after your mother witnessed the drama in your office," Kim said.

"On the contrary, my family thrives on drama. Trust me, you'd fit right in."

Kim fisted her hands, ready to get away from him and the things still left unsaid. Confusion reigned. She wanted to take a step forward, yet she couldn't allow it. She wanted to forget the past, but that past remained tied to her by a few tenacious threads. Relationship avoidance was one of them.

People got hurt if they fell hard and heaped love on one another, only to eventually have that love lost. Depression sometimes took over a lovesick soul. She had seen it happen firsthand.

She might like Monroe if she allowed herself to. She might have been able to love him someday, had the situation been different and she met him elsewhere.

"I'll send you the details," he said, bringing her out of her thoughts.

"You have a habit of refusing to take no for an answer," she said softly.

"Only where it concerns me personally, and I feel as though I have a stake in the outcome."

Of course, by personal, he was talking about his business, not about her. She had to keep that in mind. Monroe had to do what was best for the agency. His agency. Inviting her to the party was a final parting shot before sending her back to her cubicle.

He added, "If keeping you means hands-off, then that's the way it will be. However, I'm not lying to you when I say that I'd like to kiss you right now. Hell, I'd like to do much more than that, and take up where we left off last night. I will also tell you this, Kim. I have never invited a woman to my parents' home. You'd be the first. My guest. Night of fun. Truce in place."

She didn't have time to reply, and wasn't sure how to, anyway. The door opened with a whooshing sound. A wave of cooler air swirled around them. Kim didn't move until the doors started to close again and Monroe stepped in the way, a move that brought him closer to her and ensured that she had to touch him when she left the elevator.

Kim's motionless body brimmed with longing for the man she should be wary of. He was the boss, and she fully comprehended his problem with her. If getting the most out of the agency meant having management that oversaw every aspect of it, she was not that candidate.

Because she understood that, she also realized that Chaz Monroe wasn't the bad guy here, after all. She was disappointed about the job, but her anger with him had been misplaced.

The doors started to close, pushing at Monroe's wide shoulders. As she brushed past him, her left arm touched his. The charge that careened through her was powerful enough to bring on a gasp. The urge to turn to him, get close to him, walk right into the circle of his arms, was so strong, she stiffened. And in her peripheral vision, she watched his hands mirror hers, fisting so that he wouldn't catch her, change his mind and throw her against the gleaming metal.

And how she wanted him to do that, in spite of everything.

She paused close enough to him to feel his breath on her

forehead. Close enough that all she had to do was look up, and her lips would be within reach of his. The sensations running through her were blatant reminders that she really did feel something for this man.

"It should be easy to agree." Her voice caught. She sought his eyes, her pulse thudding hard. "When doing so might solve everything for a while."

"Maybe you will come to the party as a start toward a mutually beneficial future," he said. "I'm rooting for that."

He didn't grab her or kiss her, though Kim felt the pressure of that imaginary kiss as if he had overpowered her completely. She nearly backpedaled into the tiny space to make sure he did; almost asked him for a repeat of the mindless hunger that every cell in her body craved.

But Monroe moved out of the way, holding the door with one hand so that she could leave the elevator without further contact that would have spoken volumes about what they wanted to do to each other.

She had no alternative but to go.

Once she had passed him, Monroe stepped back inside and smiled at her earnestly, devastatingly, tiredly, as the elevator doors closed and the contraption took him from her, leaving her standing in the hallway.

Dozens of employees went about their business all around her, doing their jobs, unaware of the turmoil roiling through Kim that for one more brief moment made her need a wall for support.

Ten

Kim stood on the sidewalk, staring at the house. In the late-afternoon sun, the two-story brick structure had a forlorn appearance. Not shabby, exactly, but uncared for, unkempt.

Dark windows punctuated the 1940s brick cottage. On the front porch sat a collection of empty clay pots that had once contained pink geraniums to brighten the place. The small lawn was neatly trimmed, and a concrete walkway had been swept clear of debris. She'd seen to that by hiring a neighbor kid, who had taken the job seriously, though not once in the past six months had she thought to check.

"Welcome home, Kim," she said to herself.

She picked up her small suitcase. Though the house in New Jersey was merely a half an hour's train ride from her apartment, she planned to stay during her vacation.

It was several minutes before she took the first step up that walkway. Kim had to consciously remember that times here hadn't always been dark, and that angst hadn't always ruled the space between those walls. There had been good times. Fun times. Lighter moments. She had loved her mother, doted on her mother, until very near to the end when others took over the daily routine. Her mother had loved her back, to the best of her ability. It was just that her mother must have loved the husband that had long ago disappeared, more.

The windows, devoid of holiday trappings, were not welcoming. The blinds were drawn to keep out the world, and possibly to keep the old darkness contained.

Kim set her shoulders. This trip home was about coming to terms with those moments of darkness and banishing them for good. Harboring guilt about the past was unreasonable, unhealthy and getting in the way of living her life the way she wanted to.

It wasn't Monroe's fault that this confrontation had come up. She had meant to take care of this ages ago.

She wished now that she'd taken Brenda up on her offer of company. Having a friend along would have been preferable to facing some ghosts solo. But she was a woman now, no longer an impressionable child. She'd inform this house and its ghosts of her plans to let in the light and dust away cobwebs. Her presence might reinforce the good times.

If Monroe wanted a hassle-free associate, he'll soon have one, she thought as she blinked slowly and gritted her teeth. Then she headed up the walkway, determined to see this housewarming through, trying hard to keep her thoughts from turning to charming Chaz Monroe, and finding that task way too difficult.

Chaz could not sit down. He paced his office, stopping now and then to gaze out the window. Each time he did, he noted as many holiday details on the street below as he could from this height, and also took stock of the clouds rolling in to ease the transition from evening to night.

Each detail brought Kim to mind with the heft of a full mental takeover.

He had picked up the phone twice in the past fifteen minutes to call her, or Brenda Chang, or damn it, anyone else who knew Kim. Deep down inside him was a feeling of emptiness, of being lost and cast adrift.

He had rudely passed Alice without a word on his way to the water cooler not half an hour ago, and that had not gone down well with Alice. She had ignored him ever since.

He knew all too well the word Rory would have used for this current agitated state. *Whipped.*

Did that describe him, at this point, and the sensation of being helpless to fix things in light of Kim's fast exit?

He was acting as if she had become an obsession, when there were plenty of other women in New York, and plenty of years to find them. McKinley, with her obstinate refusal to meet his terms, was a pain in his backside.

He kept telling himself that, over and over.

In all fairness, though, she had confessed to having problems and had spoken honestly about the possibility of facing them. So, what did that make him for wishing she'd hurry up and do so, when he now knew a few of the reasons that might have contributed to how messed up she felt this time of year? Sarah Summers had been thorough with the few details she dug up for him.

Kim was alone. He sympathized with her lack of family. The Monroes were a tight clan. His mother and father were together after forty years of marriage, with a loving relationship still going strong. His sister, Shannon, had found her guy after her first year at Harvard and settled down with a ring on her finger by the time of her graduation last year. Rory was…Rory.

His family life wasn't perfect. Whose was? Yet they were supportive in the fierceness of their loyalty to each other. Their time together, though rare these days, was always a welcome delight.

What if, like Kim, he had no family? No brothers or sisters. No mother and father to use for backup. Taking that further, what if after working hard to gain traction in his career, some newcomer suddenly threatened to derail that career?

He leaned against the windowsill, deep in thought. Kim's father was probably alive, but lost to her. The man had filed for divorce when she was a kid. Intel said that Kim's mother had gone in and out of hospitals after the divorce, until Deborah McKinley passed away earlier this year. Had those things—the divorce and being left by her husband—been the cause of Kim's mother's prolonged illness?

That would have been hard enough to take, but nothing he had found explained why this holiday in particular got to Kim, and how it got her down. He needed to know about this. He had to understand what lay at the root of her dislike for the season. If as an only child, things had been bad with her mother, had some of her mother's depression rubbed off on Kim in ways that continued to show up?

With a quick glance at his watch, Chaz hustled out of the office, grabbing his jacket from the chair by the door. There was only one person who could help him out by filling in a few more blanks. He had to persuade Brenda to talk, knowing her to be Kim's best friend, and that it wouldn't be easy.

Kim climbed the stairs to her old bedroom and dropped her bag on the floor. The room smelled stale. Dust covered every available surface. The really scary thing was how nothing else had changed. Her bedroom remained exactly the same after all this time, yet another example of her late mother's need for pattern and constancy.

"I refuse to feel bad about the state of the place. I do not live here anymore."

She heard no answering voice in the empty house, only silence. The place felt cold. Outside temperatures had plummeted, and the inside of the house matched.

"Next stop, the furnace." She spoke out loud to ward off the silence.

On her way downstairs, she passed her mother's room. The door was closed, and she left it that way, preferring comfort to memory at the moment, and believing her recent mental adjustments to be good signs of being on the road to recovery.

"Thermostat up. Check."

To her relief, the furnace kicked on. She took this as another good omen, and headed for the kitchen, which would have been in pristine condition, except for the layer of dust.

Glad now that she hadn't turned off the electricity or gas, Kim took one good glance at the room where she and her mother had cooked and then dined at the small square table against the wall, preferring the warm kitchen to the formal dining room.

She opened a few cupboards and the refrigerator then headed upstairs for her purse. Kitchens needed to be stocked, and her stomach hadn't stopped growling. She couldn't recall the last time she'd eaten, or sat down for a meal. The hours spent in her apartment always seemed rushed, with lots of takeout Chinese.

She used to like to cook. Her mother, during her good spells, had taught her. Baking became her favorite, though those cookies she dumped last night had been her first foray into trying out those skills in years. *Christmas cookies...*

Well, she had plenty of time now to explore her talents. With a few days off, she'd get back in the groove and whip up something good. A roast, maybe, with vegetables. She'd clean up the house and make it sparkle before putting it up for sale with the hope that some family might be happier here than she and her mother were. Like most people, she supposed houses needed love and attention in order to feel homey. She'd see to that.

But first, groceries.

She'd change her clothes, walk to the market a block over, and be back before dark if she hustled. There'd be time to thoroughly clean the kitchen after she got something in the oven. She would have to learn to slow down in measured increments. She felt all riled up. She wasn't used to off-time from work, though her plan to fix up the house would occupy her for a while.

Plus, she was happy to note, she hadn't thought about

Monroe much in the last ten minutes. That also meant headway.

Damn his handsome hide. She'd see to it that running away from Chaz Monroe would turn out to be productive....

"Brenda?"

She did a slow rotation in her chair and looked at Chaz warily.

"You're working late," he said.

"If this job was nine to five, Mr. Monroe, maybe I'd have time for a date."

Alice had been right about Brenda, who obviously shared none of Kim's abhorrence of the season. A miniature Christmas tree sat on her desk, wrapped with blinking lights and tiny ornaments. Tinsel garlands hung between two bookshelves. The cubicle retained a faint smell of evergreen.

Chaz waved a hand at the tree. "Does she come in here?"

"Not this time of year." Brenda did not pretend to misunderstand whom he was talking about.

"You don't push your ideas on her?"

"She's my friend and has a right to her own opinions."

Chaz sat on the edge of her desk, looking at the wall separating Kim's cubicle from this one.

"You seem to be worried about her," Brenda said.

"Aren't you?"

She eyed him as if sizing him up. "She's a big girl and will get on with her life as she sees fit."

"She's sad, I think."

Brenda did not respond to his diagnosis of Kim's state of mind.

"Do you know what problems she has with the holiday, Brenda?" he asked.

"Sorry, can't talk about that. I promised."

"Yet I get the impression you'd like to help her somehow."

Brenda sighed. "Of course I'd like to help her out of the current mess she's in. I'm not insensitive to what's going on."

"But you believe that nothing, other than her job here, is my business?"

"That's right. I'm sorry."

Chaz stood up. "Fair enough. Can you tell me something, though, that might help? Anything?"

"I doubt it. So will you fire me for protecting my friend's privacy?"

"Only if I was the monster everyone seems to think I am."

"Are you saying you're not?"

He smiled. "I'm pretty hopeful that Kim might be the only one who thinks so."

"Yet you want more information from me so that you can do what?"

"Whittle away at her resolve," he replied.

"Which part of that resolve? The contract, or staying away from you?"

"I like her," Chaz said. "More than I should."

Brenda took a beat to think that over. "What makes you think whittling can work?"

"Because of something I just recalled about her apartment last night that I can't forget."

"What?"

"Last night her apartment smelled like cookies."

Brenda waved a hand in the air to dismiss the remark. "That tells you something, how?"

"Sugar cookies hold a fragrance unique to this holiday in particular," he said. "I grew up with that smell. It's unmistakable and always makes my mouth water. Sugar cookies are a Christmas staple. Even old Claus himself can't resist them."

Brenda took another minute to reply. Chaz watched her mull that information over. "Could have been something else, and you are mistaken," she suggested. "Could have been chocolate chip."

"I'm not wrong about that one thing," he said. "She had baked those cookies pretty near to Christmas. My question for you is if that's usual, and if Kim bakes all the time?"

Brenda's brow creased. Chaz noted how much she hated answering that question.

"I've never known her to bake anything," she admitted.

He nodded and asked the other question plaguing him. "Then how is it that a person who shuns the season and all of its trappings would bake Christmas cookies, especially after having it out with her boss about a holiday clause in her contract?"

Brenda, Chaz realized, was not at a loss. Rebounding from the cookie inquisition, she said, "If you're right about the cookies, it means she's trying."

"Trying to what?"

"Move on."

"Regarding the holiday?"

"In regard to everything."

Chaz glanced again at the wall between the cubicles. "Thank you, Brenda. That's all I needed to know."

She stopped him with a hand on his arm. "It's not all you need to know, and I can't tell you the rest."

"I know about her mother," he said. "And also about her father leaving early on."

"Maybe you do, but the story goes much deeper than that for Kim."

"Yet you won't help me to understand what that story is."

"My lips are necessarily sealed."

"Nevertheless, it's possible that she might be attempting

to deal with change. In the elevator, she told me she wants to. You do think she is seriously open to trying?"

Brenda nodded tentatively. "I do. But you're pushing her, you know. There's a chance you'll push too far."

"I feel as though I need to get to the bottom of this. I'm not completely insensitive. I have feelings, too. I like her. I've admitted that. And I know how to sell a project."

"Kim's not a project. She's a person."

"Yes," he agreed. "A special one."

Brenda looked to the hallway. "I get that you like her, yet I'm not sure you should be poking around where you don't belong, or that your interest can speed things up."

"I can only try to make things better. I won't purposefully hurt her. That much I'll swear to you right now. Any time you want to jump in and help my cause, you'd be more than welcome."

Brenda dropped her hand.

"I suppose," Chaz said, "it might not be a good idea to tell Kim about this conversation. Knowing where your loyalty lies, I'm asking for your trust in the matter."

Brenda looked terribly conflicted when he left her. He heard her say behind him, "You have feelings, huh? I certainly hope you prove that."

Eleven

An hour and a half after getting back from the market, the kitchen had filled with the delicious smell of a roast cooking. Pile a few carrots on, a cut-up potato and some broth, and the atmosphere of the house had already changed for the better. The place had started to feel lived in.

Kim wore an apron, which she figured officially earned her the title of Miss Homebody for the next few days. She had already scrubbed away at the layer of dust piled everywhere in the kitchen and dining room, and mopped the floors. Keeping busy was the key to kicking off this hiatus from her daily routine. She was used to being busy all the time. In advertising, there was little if any downtime because the mind had to constantly be on the move.

Wasn't there an old saying about idle hands?

She set the table for one and opened a bottle of wine to let it breathe, as the woman in the market had recommended. With no wineglasses in the house, she washed out a teacup and tried to recall when she had last dated. Thanksgiving week? Maybe nearer to Halloween? Could it have been as far back as Valentine's Day? She never went out after Thanksgiving, and tended not to look at men at all until after the New Year had rung in. Being anti-holiday had always been difficult to explain.

Clearly though, meeting Chaz Monroe brought home the fact that she'd been alone for too long. Being so very physically connected to him likely was the result of having saved herself from any kind of personal contact for a while. That's why her body and her raging hormones had been perfectly willing to allow Monroe's talented hands and mouth to take her over.

She might be flawed, but she was a woman, with a woman's needs. Monroe had made that all too obvious.

The cup rattled on the table when she set it down. *Monroe.* There he was again, in her thoughts, seeping through the cracks of her determination not to think about him.

Merely the idea of him set off physical alarms. Her neck began to tingle as if his lips touched her there in a soft, seductive nuzzle. Her back muscles tightened with the memory of the red dress's zipper inching down slowly to grant him access to her naked, heated skin.

There was something so damn sexy about a zipper.

She took hold of the back of the chair and tossed her head to negate those memories, tired of feeling torn by them and believing she was a freak. She refused to let all the pent-up emotion she'd withheld for so long come to a head before she'd spent one night in her mother's home.

"Facing this house has to be the first step," she said aloud to set that objective in stone. "If I can do this, I can tackle anything."

She got to work. When she had finished cleaning the dining room, she moved to the living room. Dusting, vacuuming, plumping pillows, she worked up a sweat. Finally satisfied that she'd done all she could for the moment to make the place habitable, she saw to her dinner.

Seated at the small table in the kitchen, she poured the wine. Without the talent to discern if it was good wine or not, she took a sip. "Not too bad, I guess, if alcohol is your thing."

Hell, if there was no one to talk to, she'd continue to talk to herself.

Dishing up the roast took seconds. Digging in took a little longer. Without anyone real to talk to, the kitchen seemed way too quiet. The clock on the wall no longer worked. There had never been a radio in the kitchen for comforting background noise—which might have set a good atmosphere for dinnertime conversation, and had never really turned out that way.

In contrast to the busy hallways and thin walls of her apartment building, the two-story house felt like a fortress of solitude, exemplified by the empty chair next to her. As Kim sat there with her uneaten dinner a pang of loneliness hit, accompanied by a wave of deep-seated sadness.

She had the power to fix this. She had to fix it by looking back logically. Her mother's decline was a lesson in how not to behave. Kim might have tossed some good guys with potential to the wayside because of a few deeply ingrained and very silly ideas about relationships.

If she didn't face her problems head-on, she'd never have anyone in her life. Being good at her job was one thing, and satisfying, but coming home to an empty house or an empty apartment night after night forever was a nightmare she had feared to confront.

She pictured her mother here, cooking dinner for one and eating in the quiet. The image broke her heart. The guilt she'd harbored for growing up and being away, for leaving her mother for school and work, plagued her all over again. She just hadn't been able to cope year after year with her mother's mental illness.

Kim lifted her chin. Raising her cup to the empty chair, she spoke with more confidence than she felt. "If things are going to change, we're going to have to break the spell."

The cup was halfway to her lips when a bell rang. Startled by the sound, Kim jumped to her feet.

Doorbell?

Her city sensibilities kicked in. Single women didn't answer the door unless they knew who stood on the other side. Buildings had doormen for that reason.

Other than Brenda, no one knew she was here. But, she reminded herself, this wasn't the city. This was a family neighborhood. Things were different here. Maybe the kid down the street had seen the lights and wanted payment in person for mowing the lawn.

With a glance through the small glass panel in the front door, Kim flipped on the porch light. She saw no one on the steps. Cautiously, she opened the door. Nobody was there. Her gaze dropped to the large cardboard box on the doorstep.

There had been a delivery, but it had to have been a mistake.

Stepping outside, looking around, she again glanced at the box. Her name was written on it, but there was no return address.

She took the box inside and carefully tore it open, then drew back after viewing the contents. The box contained several smaller boxes with see-through lids and big red bows. All of the boxes contained cookies. By the looks of things, every kind of cookie under the sun, including decorated Christmas trees.

It took her a moment to remember to breathe. Forgetting her mother was no longer there, Kim waited for the rant against the holidays to begin. A Christmas gift had been delivered to a house that didn't take kindly to such things. *Who would dare to deliver such a thing?* her mother would have shouted. *Who would allow items like that in their house?*

Of course, no rants came. Her mother's tirades were over. The walls hadn't fallen down because of the box on the living room floor. Her mother hadn't been raised from the grave by the pretty sugar-coated shapes.

Kim let out a breath and went back to the door for a second look outside. Cars went by. Two kids rode skateboards down the middle of the road. There was no one else in sight.

"Okay, then. It's an anonymous gift. A surprise."

Leaving the box on the floor, she headed to the kitchen. At the table, she sat down and picked up her fork, though jumbled thoughts prevented her from taking a bite of the roast, which was getting cold. Brenda wouldn't have delivered a package like that, thinking to help Kim's vow along. Brenda probably would have presented the box in person if it was to be an offering to the House of Christmas Doom. Besides, Bren didn't know about the secretly baked sugar cookies she'd dumped the night before.

If not Brenda, who had sent them?

She felt a chill on the back of her neck. Kim sat up straighter, not liking the idea that sprang to mind.

Monroe?

No. It couldn't be him.

She wasn't sure why his name had come up with regard to this box. He had no idea where she'd gone. However, Monroe might do such a thing if he knew where she was. She wouldn't put it past him to send his own version of a peace offering.

The tingle at the base of her neck returned, along with a fair amount of heat that wasn't in any way reasonable. The telltale flush creeping up her throat wasn't reasonable, either.

She couldn't allow herself to go there, to think about him, when already her forehead felt damp, and her hands were shaking. But accepting his gift would amount to another step in the right direction in her plan to tackle each problem that came up, and deal.

There wasn't any reason to close the box back up and put it outside. Letting it remain there, on the floor, was okay, but it did press home the fact that she was no longer bothered by one objective, but by two: how to face the holiday positively, and what to do about her boss.

Her stomach tightened, but not in a bad way.

Leaving her dinner untouched in the kitchen, Kim stood up. There was only one way Monroe could have found her, if in fact, he had.

"I'll get you for this, Bren," she muttered, heading upstairs for her cell phone.

But she didn't call Brenda. Instead, she dialed the number of the VP's office, wondering if she'd hang up if someone answered this late, and what she planned to say if *he* picked up the phone.

He did.

"Monroe," he said in the way he had of making the simplest words sound provocative.

Kim didn't speak. She hadn't been prepared for her reaction to the deep richness of his voice. Her finger hovered over the button that would disconnect her from him even as her mind registered this kind of reaction as being silly. All she had to do was ask him if he'd sent the box, and the mystery would be over.

"You got the package?" he asked, somehow knowing she was on the line, obviously confident she'd respond positively to his gift.

For the first time in her life, Kim felt at a loss.

Hang up now, she told herself. *I don't need this.*

"I found your mother's address and wanted to send you something," he said, as if they weren't having a one-sided conversation. "Everybody likes cookies. And I'm still hoping that you'll be staying on at the agency."

"So you sent a bribe?" she managed to say, realizing only then that he'd have access to her files and her old address, and that Brenda might not have been a traitor.

"You do know they're Christmas cookies?" she added.

"I had them delivered to you by courier because I thought returning to your former home with your mother gone might make you sad, and that you might need cheering up."

That made Kim hesitate. He might or might not have known about the depth of her aversion to this holiday, but he did know about her mother's passing. He hadn't sent this package to distress her further, but with hopes of making her happy. The gift was kind of personal. He had chosen it himself.

Kim wasn't sure how to take that. She did feel a ridiculous amount of anxiety—or maybe it was excitement—over the thought of Monroe taking the time to buy her a gift and get that gift to her not long after their conversation in the elevator.

Uncertain, she said, slightly breathlessly, "Thank you."

It was his turn to hesitate. She heard him breathing, and she also fought for each breath taken. The electricity in their connection felt like tiny jabs of lightning piercing her skin. Their chemistry was palpable, even this far apart.

"Are you okay?" he asked, sounding concerned.

"I'm fine," she lied.

"The gift didn't offend you, I hope? I swear that wasn't my intention."

"Not anymore."

"Good." Relief lowered his voice. "The red bows made me think of you in the red dress. You caused quite a stir in that dress, you know."

"Are you going to talk dirty to me on the phone?" she asked, at a loss for keeping the conversation on a serious track.

He laughed, and the sound rippled through her like a warm, sunny breeze. She loved that laugh. It made her feel lighter and not so alone. It made her want to laugh with him, and at herself for being so serious.

Maybe Monroe wasn't so full of himself after all.

Maybe she was.

Chances were that they could at least be friends if she allowed it.

"Actually," he said, "it's not late, and I wondered if you'd invite me over to eat some of the cookies."

"I'm pretty sure that wouldn't be a good idea."

She was positive that having him over wouldn't be a good idea. With a connection this strong, being in the same room with Monroe might lead to another situation she'd regret. This was her mother's home. A man of interest had no place here until she got her act together and banished the multiple years of gloom.

"I can bring dinner," he said. "No strings, just dinner."

"Thanks, but I've made dinner."

"Made dinner?" he repeated. "You cook?"

The astonishment in his sexy voice ruffled her ego.

"As a matter of fact, I do a lot of things you don't know about, and rather well, I might add," she said.

"I don't get much home cooking these days. Of course, you've probably already eaten, and you're busy getting a start on that vacation. So, all right. I didn't mean to pry any further into your affairs."

"Of course you did," she said.

"Well, yes, I guess I did…though I respect your right to turn my company down."

"Not your company, necessarily. Just you."

"Ouch. Well then, enjoy your time off. I hope those cookies bring you some happiness, too. I'd like to think they could, anyway."

Not knowing how to respond to the attention, Kim muttered "Thank you" again, and let it go at that. After reluctantly disconnecting, she immediately wished she hadn't. Monroe's voice and the interruption caused by the arrival of his gift had made the empty house almost seem livable for a change.

She felt excited—for no reason at all.

The phone remained in her hand for several more seconds before she made an SOS call to Brenda.

"Help," she said when her friend answered. "He's at it again, and I'm afraid I might be weakening."

Twelve

"Just to be clear," Brenda said, "when you say you're weakening, are we talking about the jolly guy in the red suit, or our gorgeous, if rather nosy, new boss?"

"Both," Kim said, her skin prickling with a new kind of anxiousness.

"Shall I come over?"

"No."

"You know, it isn't always a bad thing to have temporary insanity, and for you that might mean letting go of preconceived notions about liking a man."

"He sent me a gift."

"Who did?"

"Monroe sent a package. Here. Tonight."

Brenda's pause amounted to a dead line. "Please tell me there were diamonds involved, as in a bracelet or necklace, because otherwise what would constitute a proper apology for behaving like a cad in your apartment last night, and leading you astray about the job?"

"Cookies. He sent a box of cookies," Kim said.

"Doesn't work for me, Kim. That's much too benign for a sincere apology. Do you want me to come over there and help you break those cookies into tiny pieces?"

"I'd like your idea on what to do about *him*."

"I'm honored by your confidence in my advice, Kim, but honestly, I'm not sure about this."

"Brenda!"

"Well, okay. In this case, I'd probably note that Monroe sent you his version of an earnest apology."

"He said he hoped they made me happy."

"You talked to him?"

"I thanked him on the phone."

"I see. Well, it's probably okay, I'm thinking. Cookies, though delicious, aren't truly personal. They're not like lingerie, so you can probably ignore this and move on if you choose to."

"Thing is..." Kim didn't finish the sentence. She really felt confused.

"Thing is, a box from Monroe might actually help you in this self-imposed crisis?" Brenda observed, picking up on Kim's thought pattern.

"Yes." Kim silently applauded Brenda for understanding the pros and pitfalls of the situation.

"Then it's a win-win, Kim," Brenda concluded. "He was being nice, and you've thanked him. Now you can eat those things and make more progress on your objective behind going home. Did you actually open the box?"

"I did."

"How did that make you feel?"

"Scared."

"I do kind of get that, but will ask this question, anyway. Why? Why were you scared?"

"It's my mother's house, Bren. Feeling good here seems strange. Holiday gifts were taboo, sacrilege."

"Were taboo, but not anymore. That stuff happened when your mom was alive, but she's gone, and you've gone home to change and rearrange your attitude about things. There's not one person on the planet to stop you from accomplishing that goal, except yourself."

"Right." Kim sighed. "Except for me."

After an audible breath, Brenda asked, "Are they from a decent bakery?"

"Becons, by the park."

"Well, you can be thankful he has good taste. Take them out of the box. Have some for dinner. Sweets always make us feel good, right?"

This was good advice and another necessary push along a new path. She wasn't a child in need of a lesson, though Kim felt like one every time she entered this house. In her own world, she took charge. In her own world, she was successful and happy enough…if there was such a thing as being happy *enough.*

"I'm flawed, Bren, and I don't want other people to find out. One in particular."

"Because you care what he thinks?"

"I think I do."

"So what's stopping you from dropping the *I think* part of that?"

Brenda spoke again over Kim's thoughtful pause. "I was heading to the bar with the art guys to catch up on gossip, but I can grab the next train if you need me. Say the word and I'll be on that train."

"No. I'm okay. Thanks for the pep talk."

"No problem. Sending you hugs over the ether. Good luck with the caloric fallout, Kimmy."

"Have an appletini for me, Bren."

"Heck, it has been a very long day, so I might have two."

Disconnecting, Kim glanced around, inwardly reciting the words Brenda had offered. There was no one to stop her from attaining her objective for coming here, but herself.

Time to get on with things.

The old bathroom in the hallway seemed big and drafty after the tiny one in her apartment, but the shower still worked, and she had brought along clean towels. She took her time under the spray of water, trying not to think about how Monroe had nearly succeeded in getting her naked.

She scrubbed her back hard, sloughing off the sensation of his hands on her skin, erasing the memory of his fingers exploring with a blistering heat…but not quite ridding herself of those sensations.

In her determination not to think of him, she was doing a

lousy job. In fact, she failed miserably. In Monroe's strong arms, and for a few brief, sizzling moments, she had been someone else. She had let him in. For the first time, she hadn't allowed her past to influence her actions.

She did like Chaz Monroe.

She'd been hot and bothered since that first glimpse of him in his office. Her body responded favorably each time he neared, as if her nervous system needed to bypass her damaged, overworked brain, and get to the good part.

Fact was, she had the hots for her boss and wished he was in the shower with her, working his magic right that minute. Heck, if she was that far gone, was she so severely damaged that she'd refuse to accept his offer of a truce?

Yes. Because liking him and pursuing a liaison would surely mean professional suicide eventually, as she had told him. And she had nothing without her job.

In her bedroom, she removed clothes from her bag and shook them out. She pulled on a pair of well-worn sweatpants and fingered a silky blue camisole as she drew it over her head, knowing Monroe would also have liked its texture and color. Covering that with a loose wool cardigan sweater, gathering her hair into a ponytail, she headed downstairs in her bare feet.

The house had warmed up considerably now that the old heater hummed. She turned on all the lights, hesitating at each switch to think about how Monroe seemed to like her, too. Not all had to be lost in this situation, if she looked on the bright side. He was willing to overlook the clause in her contract if she stayed in her cubicle. He just couldn't promote her or send her any more gifts if she remained an employee.

She might or might not be able to deal with that.

Circling back to the living room, she stared at the floor. *Step one: take the cookies out of the box. Eat one, or ten. It will be a good thing, a helpful thing.*

Kneeling next to the box, she lifted out the first smaller box, noting again that lightning did not strike. The walls did not fall down.

She lifted out another container and went back in memory to the times as a child when she had wished for a gift like this.

"It's okay. Therapy."

After she had unpacked all four-dozen cookies, she got to her feet. The first step was working. Some of her guilt had already fled, chased away by things that weren't really magical at all, but at the moment seemed magical to her.

She was smiling.

"What if I had invited him to dinner?" she said aloud. "Wouldn't that hurry things along?"

No reply came. No argument or lament from the house's ghosts. She was free now to make her own choices, and had been for some time. Suddenly, she understood that fully.

When her phone rang, Kim took the stairs two at a time, figuring that Brenda would be checking in. She plopped down on the bed. "Bren, guess what?"

A low-pitched masculine voice said, "Are you sure you won't change your mind and invite me over if I say please and categorically deny being a stalker, providing references upon request?"

Monroe. Her heart began to thud inside her chest. Her throat tightened. How persistent was he going to be? And why wasn't she displeased?

"I'm nowhere near where you are, as you already know, having sent the package," Kim said.

"You'd see me otherwise?"

"No," she lied again, ill-equipped to handle what he was suggesting. Admittedly, the house might have been brighter already, though it remained too quiet. More cleaning would only get her so far in terms of occupying her time. A whole night stretched in front of her, with far too many hours to fill.

She missed her cozy apartment.

Clearly, Monroe's gift had shocked her into some kind of middle ground where she might consider seeing him.

If she did, she'd find out what he really wanted from her. She could stand her ground and face him; she'd show him that she was taking charge of her life in all situations, and that she would make up her own mind about her future. In that light, seeing Monroe might be a good idea.

"Kim? You there?"

It was rotten how her pulse jumped after hearing his voice, and how the hand holding the phone trembled, especially when only five minutes before she'd made up her mind to stand firm against the potency of his allure.

"Well, maybe. If you were closer," she said, not really having to worry about that remark since she was no longer in the city.

There was a knock on the front door.

"You'll have to excuse me. Someone is at the door," Kim said. "I have to go."

"Take me with you, in case it's someone you don't want to see," Monroe said. "Be on the safe side."

Kim ran back downstairs, turned on the porch light and looked through the glass. She whirled with her back to the door and leaned against it, raising the phone.

"What is it?" he whispered in her ear.

But she could not speak.

Outside, on her porch, was a Christmas tree, its shape unmistakable.

"Did you send a tree?" she demanded, her voice faint, her heart hammering.

"I did not, in fact, send the tree," Monroe replied.

Do not open the door, Kim's inner lecturer told her.

It's too much, too soon.

Placing a hand on the knob, she waited out several racing heartbeats. An idea came to her, along with a sudden waft of familiar heat. She said into the phone, "I suppose if I open this door, someone will be holding that tree?"

"Someone who could possibly contract pneumonia from standing in the cold," Monroe said. "Plus, I did get an invitation, sort of. I am in the area, as it turns out."

Kim lowered the phone and opened the door. Monroe stood there, all right, holding the tree. The sight registered as surreal.

"Semantics," he clarified. "I didn't send the tree, I *brought* it."

Before Kim knew what was happening, she was up tight against him, listening to the muffled crash of the tree falling to the porch floorboards as she pressed her mouth to his.

Thirteen

Kim McKinley was a frigging enigma. But who had the time or inclination to put on the brakes?

The woman who occupied every waking thought was in his arms, at least for the next minute or two, until her sanity returned. And though he had planned on talking to her and keeping a discreet distance, his hunger came raging back from where logic had stored it, overpowering his struggle to comprehend the situation.

What else could he do except let himself go?

The meeting of their mouths was intense, and like food for the starving. She welcomed his touch, his tongue, his strength, seemingly determined to have a replay of the night before, and to see this through. Whatever *this* was to her.

She did not want the kiss to stop, and made that quite clear. But she was tense. When his arms tightened around her, she breathed out a sound of distress.

He loosened his grip, moving his hands to her rib cage, waiting to see if she'd repeat the sound. She didn't. Through the sweater, he caught a feel of something slick, like a silky second skin. The thought of Kim's body again sheathed in the filmy material was a deal breaker in terms of his vow to keep his distance.

A big-time vow breaker.

Deepening the feverish kiss, then easing up, he stroked her softly, almost tenderly, with a desire to discover every part of the body he had dreamed about. Her hips molded to his. Her back arched each time his hands moved. She clung to his shoulders. Her breasts pressed against his chest. She was going for this. There was nothing to impede the forward momentum of this reunion.

Well, okay.

Chaz backed her up, through the open doorway. As he turned her to the wall, the impact of their moving bodies slammed the door. The sound seemed to reverberate through Kim, as though she'd felt a chill wind. A shiver ran through her. Her mouth slackened. Her hands were suddenly motionless.

Hot and cold...

Seriously?

The dichotomy of those temperatures ran through his mind with the fury of a wildfire. Chaz drew back far enough to see Kim's face in the dim light of an overhead entryway lamp. As before, when Brenda Chang's voice had driven a wedge between them, her face paled. Did she regret her reaction to him already? Was she nothing but a tease? Damn it, what just happened? He was all fired up.

"What is it?" he asked. "What's going on?"

Her eyes were wide and unseeing. He cradled her face with both hands and spoke again. "Kim? Look at me."

The hazel eyes, more green than brown, refocused.

"It's okay," he said. "I didn't come here to do that. We don't have to do anything but talk. See?"

He dropped his hands and stepped back. "You sounded lonely on the phone. I'll go if you ask me to, though I'd like to stay."

She shook her head. "It's just that… It's just that there hasn't been any company in this house for as long as I can remember. Certainly never a man. I felt…"

"I can be good company when I put my mind to it," he said when she didn't finish. "So what do you say we make up for lost time?"

"Yes." She smiled, though she looked wary. "Okay."

He glanced past her at the living room and withheld a frown. This wasn't like any room he had imagined her in, and nothing like what he'd seen of her apartment. This room didn't reflect her personality at all…unless of course she actually had a split down the middle.

The place wasn't drab, really, but very close to it. There were faded floral curtains, a beige cushioned sofa, and hardwood floors covered by rugs. The musty smell hinted at the house having been closed up for some time, though he also caught a whiff of a cleaning product.

On the floor sat the box he had sent. Kim had looked at the contents, at least. She'd had her hands on that box.

He wanted her hands back on him, but had to play nice and see how far he got with that idea. His plan was to break the news no one else yet knew—about his intention to turn over the agency to a new owner in the near future. Once the finances were settled in the black zone, he'd be gone. If he told Kim about this, and she realized she would still have a shot at the job she coveted, they might have a chance to explore the heat building up each time they came into contact with each other.

It wasn't the first time he'd thought about that. He just had to wait for the right time to spring it on her.

"Shall we start by bringing in the tree?" he asked. "I feel sort of sorry for it out there."

He took her silence for a no. Maybe she wasn't ready for another surprise gift.

"Conversation would also be nice," he suggested. "How about if I start, and clear the air?"

Her eyes remained on him in such a way that he wanted to kiss her again and bypass the rest of what kept them apart. Even her serious expression was sexy. As for her killer body…well, that was the icing on the cake he couldn't yet have a bite of.

"I'm here because I didn't want to leave things the way they were," he said. "Our confessions in the elevator only whetted my appetite for truthfulness. I thought by coming here, we could patch things up and move forward at a faster pace. If you're game, that is."

"Is there a rush?" she asked, tilting her head, showing off more of her long, bare, graceful neck.

"I thought so," he replied, stunned at how that stretch of pale skin affected him. "And now that I see you here, in this place, I'm not so sure this is a good location for you to spend your vacation time."

She didn't argue with his assessment. "This is a sad house."

"Does that mean you have to be sad in it?"

"It's hard to change the past, but I'm here to try."

"Yes, I suppose change is difficult. You might start by inviting me in. We could liven up the place for an hour or two."

She raised an eyebrow. "Do you recognize the word *pushy?*"

Chaz raised his hands. "How about if we start over and I go outside and knock, and you don't accost me wickedly this time when you open the door?"

She made a face. He had to wonder how deep her inner pressures went for her to embrace so many different emotions in the span of a few minutes.

This was indeed a sad house, but houses were built of wood and plaster, and possessed no souls. Though the temperature was warm inside, the room had an empty, cool feel. Already, after a few hours here, Kim looked like a different person, a sadder version, and his protective hackles had gone up.

Was he back to being a fool for wanting what he might never have? Why would he desire her when she was so confusing most of the time?

"Or you could ask me to take off my coat and sit down." He gestured to the sofa. "And we could try to behave like civilized people."

"Be my guest," she said, stepping aside.

Chaz tossed his coat on a chair and sat down on the couch, relieved to have gotten this far and wondering how she could look as good in sweats as she did all dolled up for work. He liked the fact that Kim seemed less formidable in this kind of casual wear, and in her bare feet. He liked her hair swept back in a ponytail, and felt an urge to pull strands loose to run between his fingers.

"Would you like something to drink?" She remained by the door. "I've got wine in teacups. I'm thinking of starting a new fad at wine bars. Merlot in chipped china. Very snazzy."

Chaz smiled. "All right. I'll try that. Can I help?"

"Let's confine you to one room at a time," she replied with a slight smile.

Kim seemed to have thawed again, though he had a feeling she might run out the back door and leave him there. Relief came when he heard her closing cupboard doors in the next room.

He didn't bother to check out more of his surroundings, noting only that there were no pictures, either on the walls or in frames set on the end tables. Not one photo of Kim existed in this room, whereas in his parents' home, every surface held a snapshot or two chronicling the family through the years.

The lack of personal touches here bothered him. After seeing a small portion of her apartment in the city, albeit in the dark, Kim's taste ran to modern. No clutter. Sleek lines, with lots of leather. That kind of decor suited her much better. This was old stuff, and quite depressing.

Clinking sounds brought his gaze to the kitchen doorway. Kim hadn't been kidding about the cups. She appeared carrying two, and handed him one without allowing her fingers to touch his in the transfer. She moved his coat and sat in the chair opposite him with her legs curled under her.

Very much like a kid. Also like a seductive siren with no idea of how hot she really was.

Several deep breaths were necessary before Chaz's first sip of wine. He eyed her over the rim. "Hate to tell you this, Kim, but even our agency couldn't sell your new wine in china fad to the public."

She smiled earnestly, he thought, and the smile lit up her face. "Something about the textures being wrong," she agreed. "Porcelain adds a taste of its own."

"What's the wine?"

"I've no idea. It was recommended by the local grocer."

Chaz chuckled and took another sip before setting the cup on the coffee table. He folded his hands in his lap to keep himself from reaching for the woman who had the ability to drive him mad with desire.

"How long has it been since you lived here?" he asked.

"A couple years. I stayed as long as I could and until..." She let whatever she had been about to say go, and started over. "Nothing has changed in here since I was a kid. I'm going to fix it up to sell. There will be a lot of work to get it ready."

"That's why you're here?"

"Partially."

"The other part?"

"Confronting ghosts."

It was a reply Chaz hadn't anticipated. His smile faltered as he watched Kim slip a silky aqua-blue strap back over her shoulder, beneath the sweater, where it stayed for a few seconds before falling back down. *Treacherous little strap.* His eyes strayed to her breasts, their contour visible through the slinky blue-green silk. She wasn't dressed for ghost hunting, but for cuddling.

And he had to stop thinking about that.

Whether or not she noticed his appreciative gaze, Kim pulled the soft sweater around her, which was a good move, and helped him to avoid more thoughts about how smooth her skin was, and where touching it might lead.

Still, as he saw it now, they were faced with a quandary. He was, anyway. Perfume wafted in the air he had to breathe. Kim's body taunted him from behind its cloth barrier. His reaction to these things were proof positive that he couldn't work in the same building with her after this. Maybe not even in the same city.

But he had started this by asking for a night of sharing confidences, and by showing up on her doorstep. Confidences and sex didn't necessarily go together.

He wanted her, but so what?

"Are we past the tape recorder duel?" he asked.

"Are we still negotiating?" she countered. "Is that the reason for the gifts?"

He shook his head. "No. Since we're being honest, I'll admit again to feeling uneasy about the way things have gone down between us. As I mentioned, our chat in the elevator didn't ease my mind much as to what to do."

"Why?"

"I don't honestly know. I wish I did."

"Are you sorry about the kiss in my doorway?" she asked.

"No." He zeroed in on her eyes. "Are you?"

"Not really."

Chaz swiped at the prickle on the back of his neck that was a warning signal to either get out of there with his masculinity intact, or get on with things. Talking about emotions wasn't listed in his personal portfolio of things he liked to do best. He was pretty sure no guy excelled at this kind of thing.

"I do hope you don't welcome everybody like that, though," he said in a teasing tone.

Kim shrugged. "How do you suppose I've kept my clients so happy?"

Chaz grinned before remembering her comments about sleeping her way to the top.

"Shall we move on to something else?" he suggested.

"I don't think so. Part of my healing process is to deal. So I'm going to tell you what you've wanted to know, and fulfill your objective for showing up here tonight."

When she took a breath, the damn sweater fell open. He did not look there. Her serious expression held him, and also made him uncomfortable. All of a sudden, he felt like the bad guy, when he'd never, as far as he knew, hurt anyone on purpose.

"I kissed you because I wanted to," she said. "I find you extremely attractive and hard to resist on a physical level."

"Only physical?"

She waved his question away and let her gaze roam the room.

"My mother basically died of depression, as a direct result of a disappointment too terrible for her mind to accept."

Her gaze lingered on the door. "She had stopped eating, and wouldn't get out of bed. She didn't die here, at home. My mother isn't the ghost I came here to confront. Her ideas are what I need to address, ideas that were pounded into me since the time of the event that kicked her decline into gear."

Chaz swallowed. Should he stop her from digging deep into her secrets, when he had been pushing her for this explanation? Though it wasn't entirely what he had expected, it was also much more than he could have imagined.

"My father left us on Christmas Eve when I was very young," she went on. "He left presents under the tree, as if that would make up for the loss to follow. He walked out without explanation and never looked back, leaving his uneaten dinner on the table. We heard sometime later that he had chosen another family to spend that Christmas morning with, and the rest of his life with after that, which meant that he had cheated on us for some time."

Uncomfortable with her disclosure, Chaz carefully watched Kim readjust her position in the chair and take another long, slow breath.

"I don't do Christmas because my mother hated it, and hated the memory of the night my father left. She never got over the betrayal, and didn't speak to my father again. Neither of us did."

"I see," he said to fill the following pause.

"I've honored my mother's wishes about avoiding this holiday for a long time. So long, I can't remember what life was like before that promise. My mother died six months ago, and since then I've kept up the routine by refusing to celebrate Christmas either in my work or my personal life."

Chaz ran a hand through his hair, feeling like an idiot for pressuring her into admitting a thing like that, and for having almost convinced himself on the way over here that her issues might have derived from something as simple as never getting the gift she asked Santa Claus for. In retrospect, he had failed to give her full credit for having real and serious causes that required the special clause in her contract.

He felt like a heel, and deserved every name she might have called him. The cookies he sent were in a pile of boxes on the floor by his feet. He had brought a tree, planned a party and insisted she go—which made him no better than a goddamn bully.

It was too late for his lame excuses, though as her boss, this was something he had needed to understand. The question now was how much damage he had done to a potential relationship by applying all that pressure?

He kicked a box with his foot and sent it skidding in McKinley's direction. Her gaze moved from the box to him, where her focus stayed.

Chaz was certain the hunger he felt for her was mirrored in her eyes.

* * *

"Will you excuse me a minute?"

Kim got to her feet, fending off two urges at once. The first was to throw herself at Monroe again, no matter the consequences. He stared at her seriously, as if seeing her inner workings for the first time. Kissing him would break the tension in the room and release some of her pent-up emotions after a confession like that.

The second urge was to sprint for the kitchen, close the door and lock herself in.

The latter seemed the best option now that he knew her secrets. If he equated her frank announcement with her recent mental state, it might someday undermine their business relationship. He'd keep an eye out for signs of the same tendency for depression exhibited by her mother, or her threats to pack up and leave. But if that were the case, and he held this against her, Chaz Monroe wasn't worth the shirt on his back.

Laugh maniacally or cry? Run or break down?

She wavered among all of those options, having disclosed what haunted her. Her life had been laid bare, the darkness had taken wing, but elation didn't come right away. Some ghosts were clingy.

The way Monroe studied her was sensuously sober, and produced another flicker of heat deep inside her. She had all but begged for him to leave her alone, though she desired the exact opposite. She craved closeness and sharing and mind-bending sex. With Chaz Monroe.

She had bought into her mother's beliefs about men long after they had stopped making sense.

"Suffering isn't supposed to be prolonged, especially this time of year," she said. "Christmas is about joy and light, ideas that might have made a difference to my family if my mother had gritted her teeth and moved on."

Did things have to be so complex? Light…company…

happy times…cookies and a tree. A man beside her to love, and who would love her back unconditionally, loyally and forever. These were what she wanted so badly.

Sex with Monroe wasn't going to get her those things, and yet it somehow seemed a fitting end to the evening. He would hold her. He would be here and make her happy, if only temporarily and for tonight. The main result would be that with his ultramasculine presence in this house, her mother's dark spell over her daughter would be lost, once and for all. She felt that spell already beginning to crack.

To hell with work, her job and how she'd feel tomorrow.

"I'm sorry you had to go through that," he said, getting to his feet, moving to stand beside her.

He didn't touch her and didn't need to. His voice and his tone created a vibration that worked its way down her spine and keep on sliding, finding its way beneath the waistband of her sweatpants and along the curve of her hips to end in a place a vibration had no right to be.

Monroe was no longer the enemy, and she didn't want him to go away. Arguments aside, she felt good around him. She felt completely awake and alive, every nerve tingling, each neuron she possessed calling for her to get closer to him.

"I'm not sure what you'll do with all that," she said, feeling unsteady, unnaturally warm and slightly queasy with him beside her.

The touch came. Only a light one. He tilted her head back with a finger so that she had to look into his eyes. "I'd like to move on to another confidence, one of mine, putting yours aside for now, if you don't mind."

Kim tried to turn her head. He brought her back.

"You do like me, in spite of all this, and all that we've been through so far," he said. "I can feel this. Am I right?"

He went on when she didn't answer. "I want to be near

you. As a matter of fact, I can't seem to stay away. I believe we can make this work. You and me. We can try."

"How? It's already going to be bad when rumor of the scene in the bar spreads. I love my job, and it looks like I'll have to leave it."

"No. Trust me, Kim. Ride this out, and you'll see what can happen. Stick out your tongue at those rumors. I'll take the heat. While I'm in that building, I'll spread my own story about everything being my fault, and we'll make the other employees believe nothing bad happened."

"Nothing did happen."

"It's about to now, I think. Don't you?"

His mouth came close. Kim worked desperately to keep from closing her eyes, needing to see him before feeling the truth of his statement.

"There are more things to disclose in the future about the business that might positively impact your position in the agency. We will get to that, I promise. For now, for tonight, let's enjoy what this is."

His arms encircled her possessively, his warmth persuading her to give in to the rush of need coursing through her body.

She had spoken the magic words to free herself from her mother's tyranny, and she had let a man in. The difference here, between this situation and what happened to her mother, was that she didn't expect any future with Chaz Monroe. If he left that minute, she'd be no worse off because she wasn't fully invested in this liaison producing any kind of relationship and neither was he.

That's what she told herself, anyway, knowing it to be a lie and afraid to admit otherwise. Each minute in Monroe's presence was like one of those holiday gifts she had never received. Being with him brought her some long-awaited anticipation and joy.

"Bedroom," he whispered to her, a world of meaning in that one word.

"No. Not there." Her heart continued to pound. Adrenaline rushed through her to whip up the flames.

They were going to do this.

"Then it will have to be here," he said, swinging her into his arms, kneeling on the floor and placing her there, beside the pile of boxes and bows.

Kim looked up at him, realizing she'd really done it this time. She would soon see all of Chaz Monroe, test her theory on one-night stands being okay for the truly needy, besides being one hell of a spellbreaker…and trust him to take her mind off the rest of the world.

Just for tonight.

No one could stop what was about to take place. She craved heat and closeness and for the pain of her family's story to end here, now, completely.

"There's only one problem," she said, pulling him closer.

"What's that?" The mouth hovering over hers held promise in the way it curved up at the corners.

"We have too many clothes in the way," Kim replied with her hands on his chest.

Fourteen

The kiss was new and intense. Open mouths, damp, darting tongues, breathlessness. There was nothing patient about their need. This wasn't going to be a night of foreplay and tender exploration. They were too excited.

Kim savored the burn of Monroe's closeness, drank him in with each kiss, bite and scratch of her fingernails across the fabric of his shirt. The lid was off the pressure cooker, and she was savage, desirous, anxious for everything he had to give, anxious to find out if it would be enough to permanently keep the ghosts of Christmas past at bay.

In between deep kisses, he gave her time to breathe and searched her face. Their bodies were pressed tightly together, his stretched out on top of hers. His hands were in her hair, on her cheeks, feathering over her neck. Trails of kisses followed each touch of his fingers.

Kim thought she might go mad with her need for him. Her body molded to his, their hips meeting in all the right places as if their bodies were a perfect match. His lips inflicted a torture of the highest caliber, offering promises of what was to come.

When he pulled back, it was only to head south with his incendiary mouth—over her collarbones and over the blue silk covering her breasts. He kissed her there, and she moaned.

She tore at his buttons with impatience. The next sound was of fabric tearing. He had ripped apart the thin ribbon straps of her camisole, exposing her shoulders. Hungrily, he pulled her forward, kissed her again then eased the sweater off and away.

He paused to look at her, his gaze incredibly intimate.

Upright, and without the straps, the silk slid downward over her breasts in a sensuous rustle.

He pressed the palm of one hand against her right breast then cupped her. Kim shut her eyes and began to rock, first backward, then forward. He quickly replaced his hands with his mouth and drew on the pink exposed tip of her breast so deftly, she fought back a cry.

It was too much, and too little. She had never felt anything remotely like this, or wanted so much.

Finding the strength to withstand the pleasure Monroe's mouth gave her, she shoved him back, and with her hands on his buttons, looked at him pleadingly. *No more time. No distractions.*

He understood.

His shirt came off with a twitch and a shrug, baring a muscular chest with a slight dusting of brown hair. As if his magnificent nakedness were a magnet, Kim couldn't keep herself from touching him, running her fingers over him, getting to know every inch from his shoulders to his stomach. He was taut, in perfect shape, the epitome of masculine perfection. But then, she had guessed that from the start.

Aware of her silent approval, Monroe eased her back to the floor and removed her sweatpants in a graceful move that left her shuddering in anticipation. He didn't have time to get to his own pants. She had his belt off and was at his zipper with shaky fingers.

That sexy sound of a zipper opening filled the room. Kim saw only Monroe's face—his expression of lust, his own version of need. Mixed in with those things lay something else: something that she didn't dare put a name to, but knew was reflected in her own expression, and somewhere deep in her body. Deep in her soul.

Chaz Monroe hadn't been kidding. He liked her. He wanted her. His expression said he cared, and that he needed her, at least tonight, as much as she needed him. Knowing this changed things for her, and upped the ante.

He scooped her hips up in both hands and settled himself against her, still looking at her with his eyes wide open. She felt how his muscles tensed. He dipped into her gently at first, easing inside, eyeing her all the while for her reaction.

She had to close her eyes again. Had to. The pleasure of having him inside her was extreme. Suddenly, she wasn't sure if she could handle this, handle him. Already, she felt the rise of a distant rumbling deep inside her body.

He must have felt that rumbling. He used more force after that, entering her with a slick plunge that rocked her to her core. The cry she had withheld escaped.

"I know," he whispered in her ear. "I know."

With strong thighs, he urged her legs to open wider. This time when he entered her moist depths, it was with real purpose. The plunge went deep, forcing another cry to emerge from her swollen mouth.

The internal rumbling gained momentum quickly, hurtling toward where he lay buried inside her, threatening to end what she refused to have finished.

"Can't..." she gasped.

"Yes," he told her. "You can."

His hips began to move, building a rhythm that drove him into her again and again. Her hips matched his, thrust for thrust. Her hands grasped at his bare back, tearing at his flexing muscles with no intent to control his talented ministrations, but to encourage him to proceed, lock him to her, ensure that he wouldn't get away until this was finalized. Until it was over.

The claiming was mutual, necessary and too hot for either of them to prolong. Finally, as time became suspended and the world seemed about to crash down, he drove himself into her one last time...and their startled cries mingled loudly, shockingly, in the room's musty air.

They lay on the floor, quiet and trembling while they caught their breath. Moments later, they started the whole process over again.

Fifteen

Chaz spiraled in and out of dreams. He wasn't cold, exactly, yet he felt a distant discomfort that forced his eyes open.

He was on his back, on a hard surface. His shoulders ached. So did his knees. Something soft covered him. A blanket?

It took a minute to remember where he was. The room was dark, which meant that not much time had passed since he and Kim had gone at each other.

She wasn't beside him. He sat up, noticing right away that he was buck naked. Their clothes had been discarded completely after round two, in preparation for round three. The edge of a shaggy rug scratched at his thighs.

Kim was gone, but had covered him with a blanket, which was a nice touch. Maybe she preferred a soft mattress to cushion her spent body after a couple hours of sexual gymnastics, and had trotted off to find one. He couldn't really blame her. Then again, she hadn't offered to take him to bed with her, and this threatened to bring on a bout of concern.

Using the coffee table for leverage, Chaz got to his feet. He felt for a lamp on a table next to the sofa and clicked it on. Their clothes were there, strewn across the floor and the chair. Seeing those clothes, Chaz felt slightly better. Kim hadn't tidied up, gotten dressed or removed the outward evidence of their union.

He blew out a breath, unable to recall having spent a night like this in…well, ever. And, he reminded himself, this didn't have to mean love was involved. Great sex amounted to great sex, that's all. Problem was, he wanted her again right that minute. Stranger yet, he desired to hold her, nestle against her, sleep beside her, with Kim curled up in his arms.

This realization came as a shock. Usually the one to grab his clothes and hit the road to terminate a one-night stand, he had stayed, drifting off into a blissful slumber.

And Kim had left him on the floor.

Her absence didn't have to mean she had left him altogether, though. After all, this was her house. So, what did this incredible impulse to nuzzle her imply?

More trouble ahead.

The intensity of the sex they'd shared was rare, sure, but did the rest of his urges have to have anything to do with *love?*

Surely not. He was merely feeling satisfied and empathetic.

He looked around. The floor was a mess. Piles of cookies had been scattered. Crumbs were everywhere. They had left the tree on the porch. Nothing in this room reflected comfort, really. Kim needed to get out of here. She no longer belonged in this place, and how she felt mattered to him.

She mattered.

His gut tightened. "Kim?" he called out, daring to wake her, needing to disturb her to confirm the new sensations rippling through him.

Finding the stairs, he took them two at a time. Although the hallway at the top lay in darkness, light from below made it possible to see four closed doors and one open doorway. Chaz made for the latter with his heart in his throat.

The blinds in the room were partway open, and the curtains drawn back. By the light from a streetlight, he made out the outline of a bed, a dresser and a light switch, which he flipped on.

Though the bed looked rumpled, Kim wasn't in it.

"Kim?"

No reply came.

He found the bathroom in the hall filled with Kim's scent, but she wasn't there. Back in the hallway, he stopped to listen. The house lay in complete silence.

Bedroom number two was empty, as were the rest of the rooms on that floor. Kim McKinley simply wasn't there.

He'd been jilted. Left. Abandoned in somebody else's house.

And that left him with a very bad feeling about what this meant.

Kim waited by the curb after calling for a cab. Nearly out of breath from hustling to get her act together, she was sloppily dressed in a pair of old jeans, a turtleneck sweater and boots she had found in the closet.

Sore, tired and anxious, she limped back and forth along the sidewalk. The man of her dreams lay on the floor of her mother's living room, surrounded by the cookies he'd brought her. There should have been a law against leaving a man like that, but her first waking instinct had been to flee.

They had broken the house's spell, smashed it to smithereens. And she wanted to run right back inside and do it again, have Monroe again, feel his breath on her face and his naked body against hers.

Breaking old rules had never been so glorious, and at the same time confusing. She hadn't made love to him in order to plan for a future of bedrooms and kitchens. She looked for companionship and warmth on a chilly night, a temporary relationship worthy of blasting away the past. Well, she had found those things. Too much of those things.

She was doing the walking-away routine. As hard as that was and as bad as she felt about it, she had to leave. Monroe might be one hell of a guy, but leaving him now meant he wouldn't have the chance to leave her later or be afforded the opportunity to break her heart. Monroe would cause trouble in her future if she stuck around, because she really, really liked him. She wanted him badly. More than ever. She needed iron willpower in order to remain on the street.

What would he do when he woke up in a strange house, alone? Curse? Get angry?

She wasn't going to see that reaction now or in the future. In the aftermath of shared confidences, confessions and a night of raw animal sex, being in the same business, in the same building, would be out of the question. No way would she be able to hide her hunger for Chaz Monroe after tonight. If she caved on this point, she'd be setting herself up for a fall.

She felt as though she'd had a taste of the fall already. Her chest hurt. The inner fires still raged.

When the cab pulled up, Kim took one more glance at the dark house before giving the driver her destination and some special instructions. Then she climbed into the backseat. With Monroe off-limits from now on, she'd at least have a keepsake. A trophy to remember this night by...as if she could ever forget it.

It's okay. I'll be all right.

The hurt of leaving Monroe would stop eventually. With her mother's hold broken, she was free to sell this house and enjoy the things she had shunned. Acknowledgment of that gave her a sense of freedom.

Having made the decision to part company with Monroe and get on with her life, she'd be embracing the phrase *starting over.* Monroe had helped with that. "Thank you," Kim whispered as the cab headed for the city.

Halfway there, her tears began to pool.

Damn if she didn't miss him already.

Chaz didn't want to focus on the phrase that came to mind as he sat down on a step in Kim's mother's house.

The little vixen used me?

After years of dating, he'd been jilted after the best night of his life. By the only woman he wanted in his life.

How did that happen?

Could he have been wrong about her? Wrong about how fully she'd enjoyed the sex and his company? No one had that kind of ability to fake the pleasure of round after round of mind-blowing physical connection. No, Kim had thoroughly enjoyed what they'd done. She'd participated, wanting that union as much as he had. Tears had stained her cheeks once or twice, and that had damn near broken his heart.

What about the blanket she'd covered him with? Was that the action of someone who had faked her way through an entire evening, possibly with an ulterior motive or secret agenda?

Can't see that.

So, if she had gotten as much pleasure out of their evening together as he did, why had she gone, and where?

Chaz glanced at his watch. *Two o'clock in the morning.*

In a few hours, he had a meeting with some bankers to discuss the possibilities of a future sale, a meeting that had been set up before he stepped foot inside the agency, and before he'd first caught sight of Kim's enviable backside in the corridor. Her disappearance sidelined the opportunity to tell her about his plans for the future sale of the company. Likely she had left him believing it imperative for one of them to go. The way she left, without a word, presented only one scenario. Kim was saying goodbye to all of it—the job and him.

"Well, that sucks," he muttered, looking around the room where they had *merged.* An appropriate term for what they had done, as many times as they'd done it, since they hadn't taken the time or the precision necessary for it to have been called *making love.*

Making love would have meant something more than casual sex. The thing that came after all the lust had been explored, involving slow exploration and much softer kisses.

Tonight had been about casual sex between consenting adults. Right?

All of a sudden, he wasn't so sure.

His spirit took a dive.

He wanted her back.

Kim McKinley had one-upped him again in a game he had no longer planned to play. Regretting that, Chaz looked to the front door, then to his clothes on the floor.

So, okay, he had tried and lost. He had lost *her.* He'd live. Monroes were champion survivors. Buying and selling businesses hardened his anti-relationship stamina, and he had every intention of learning to deal with the consequences.

In need of air, he picked up his pants and dressed. Opening the front door, hoping Kim might be on the porch, his stomach took a tumble when she wasn't.

But he paused in the doorway, heat shooting up the back of his neck. He grinned. Something about that porch seemed different, and that difference told him this wasn't over.

The silky-skinned little siren might have fled, yes. But she'd taken the Christmas tree with her.

Kim woke exhausted and achingly sore in every muscle after two full days of recuperation time from her evening with Monroe. The sense of being perpetually on the edge of a state of anxiousness refused to leave her. Her heart continued to race. Her ears rang.

Not her ears. The cell phone on her table by the bed made the racket.

After rolling onto her side, she checked the caller ID, holding the phone aloft while it continued to screech. The screen said the call came from a private number. Letting it go to voice mail, she tossed the phone to the foot of the bed and stretched out on her back. She had nowhere special to be on day three of her plan to not only eradicate the sadness of the past, but to obliterate it, too.

Her fingers slid sideways to the empty spot next to her on the mattress, then recoiled. *He* wasn't there. No one was. Funny how real dreams could be.

Her project for today was to make another attempt at forgetting Chaz Monroe, which had so far proved difficult. She'd spent another mostly sleepless night thinking about what to do next and trying to erase all thoughts of him. Each time she closed her eyes, he was there, strong, handsome and tenacious. Last night, six cups of strong black tea had been necessary to keep her eyes open and the memory of him controlled.

Her body now paid for the lack of sleep, as well as the antics of her hours spent with Monroe on a hardwood floor, by offering up protests, bruises and stiffness whenever she moved. Monroe had deliciously involved every part of her body, over and over, until she thought she might perish in a state of pure, blissful pleasure. Being manhandled by him had been outrageously satisfying.

But that was in the past.

Today was all about new beginnings that didn't include Monroe or his advertising agency. This was about her, moving on.

And what was the best way to take a break from reality?

Shop.

She planned to pile on new sensations, spend some of her savings and revel in the freedom of a new mind-set.

Today was the first day of the rest of her…

She sat straight up.

Somebody knocked at the door.

Scrambling out of bed, wincing with each movement of her tender thighs, Kim limped to the door. The visitor had to be a neighbor, or Sam would have let her know. Maybe it was Brenda, who had her own key, and therefore didn't really have to knock, except out of politeness and to prevent Kim from having a heart attack.

Through the peephole she saw Brenda, chic and festive in a dark green suit.

Kim opened the door. "I don't actually want a gossip hour today, Bren, unless you've heard of a decent job opportunity through the grapevine *and* brought breakfast along. I'm starved."

Brenda gave her a pained look, pursed her mouth and stepped aside.

Traitorous Brenda wasn't alone.

Surprised, Kim stepped back with her heart hammering.

"I have a line of gossip I think will interest you," Monroe said in the husky voice that always made her knees weak and made them weak now.

Kim blinked, and looked to Brenda.

"It's news you truly might like," Brenda seconded. "You can kick me later for delivering it this way."

Though she tried hard not to look at Monroe, the strength of his presence drew her like a suicidal moth to an impenetrable flame.

Sixteen

Monroe stood on her doorstep, looking like every woman's idea of a prebreakfast treat.

Dressed to impress in soft gray pants, black leather jacket and another blue shirt that matched his eyes to perfection, he stared back, his expression a mixture of stoicism and worry.

After denying herself the luxury of purposefully giving in to her thoughts about him for the last couple days, Kim's first instinct was to jump his bones. From a distance of three feet, he smelled like heaven.

Her inner alarm system went to full alert. She said firmly, "You understand the meaning of the term *vacation?*"

"I'll explain if given the chance," he said.

"Do I actually have to be here?" Brenda interjected. "I have a meeting in twenty minutes. You two can work this out without me."

"You brought him here," Kim reminded her friend. "This one's on you."

"Wrong," Brenda argued with a shake of her head. "It's quite possibly all about *you,* and I'm merely the middleman *again.*"

"I'm in my pajamas, Bren."

"I didn't notice," Monroe said lightly, lying through his teeth. His eyes continued to roam over every inch of her anatomy, from her head to her bare feet.

She crossed her arms to cover herself, hoping to delay the quick-rising crave factor from reaching her breasts.

"I've been calling you for the past fifteen minutes, to warn you that we were on our way," Brenda said.

Kim glanced over her shoulder as if she could see her cell phone through the wall. "From another cell?"

Brenda nodded. "Mine's at the office. We left in a hurry."

"How was I supposed to know you were calling?"

Brenda threw up her hands. "I don't know. Psychically?"

Brenda was usually connected to her phone at the hip, so for her not to have it meant that Monroe had dragged her here. As what, a buffer or a mediator?

Kim confronted Monroe with narrowed eyes. "You can't come in."

"I'm having a déjà-vu moment in this hallway," he remarked, "when I thought we were beyond that."

His meaning wasn't lost on her. Yes, they were beyond it, if their recent nakedness and exchange of body fluids meant he had a free pass to bother her anytime he wanted to.

Kim felt the flush spread up her neck and into her cheeks. Her sore thighs were heating up, as if she were more than willing to go another round on any surface with the man across from her.

Managing to tear her gaze from him, Kim looked to her friend. "Go on. You wanted to tell me something important enough to bring him along?"

Brenda nodded. "His plans were to sell the agency after getting it up and running and more profitable. That's what his family does. They buy and sell businesses, and they've made a fortune doing so."

Brenda tossed a glance Monroe's way before continuing. He remained mute.

"If he sells the agency, you'll still have the opportunity to be promoted, and he will be gone, so no worries there about pesky rumors or anything else. It looks like all this is in your favor," Brenda said. "I trespassed on your vacation time to tell you this so you won't plan on leaving the agency, or town. You don't have to. Not now. Plus, I wasn't supposed to tell anyone, so the boss decided to come along when I did."

Kim's gaze bounced back to Monroe. "Is this true?"

He nodded. "Yes, it is."

"You never planned on owning the agency for long, or being there long-term?"

"That was the initial plan," he replied. "I was going to tell you about this the other night, but we got distracted."

Distracted? Seriously? That's what he called it?

"This is the news you said you'd postpone until later?" Kim asked.

"Yes," he said.

"You didn't think it was important enough to bring up right away?"

"There were other issues to deal with first."

Admittedly, the news should have made her feel better. She should have jumped for joy. She didn't have to leave the job she loved. She just had to make it work, or prolong the vacation until Monroe sold the place. Instead of feeling relief, though, her stomach churned.

Chaz Monroe would be gone.

The last few days of her life passed before her eyes. Monroe hadn't really taken the VP spot but had simply gone undercover in his own business to help it along on the road to full financial recovery. She didn't have to worry about him in the future, as far as work went, because he wasn't going to be there to give her hot flashes each time they passed in the corridors.

And the part of this situation that had bitten her in the backside—the contractual issue—was ebbing away due to having confronted her mother's ghosts.

She was nothing like her mother. Not even a bit. She had a lot to look forward to.

Monroe's news was good, all right, though it also left them both on uneven ground. If he left the agency and wanted to see her, there'd be no more excuses to stay away from him. In truly shedding her mother's fears, there'd be no need to stay away from him. If he left the agency, she might *want* to see him, often, and would be free to do so, if that one small fear didn't remain about being left behind after giving her love to a man.

"Kim?" Brenda said.

Does that meet with your approval?" he asked. "I'll soon be out of your hair, and you can pursue the promotion any way you'd like to."

Out of her hair?

Her stomach constricted. The words were like a blow.

His comment didn't sound as though it came from a man ready to pursue a relationship with her.

She'd been fantasizing about him for nothing?

Kim closed her eyes. *Fool.*

Maybe he'd already gotten what he wanted from her, with no plans for furthering their connection. A male victory. A conquest.

His expression had become guarded. He hadn't made the slightest move in her direction, or agreed with Brenda's suggestion that she leave them alone to work this out.

Because there was nothing to work out?

Kim staggered back a few inches, struck by the pathetic degree of her own vulnerability. *I haven't learned anything.*

"Fine," she said softly. "Good."

Then she closed the door in Monroe's face.

She leaned against the frame, gathering her wits, bolstering her courage to be the new Kim McKinley she had only three days ago set out to be, while sensing Monroe's presence through the closed door.

"I take it she wasn't happy with the news," he said in the hallway.

"She was in her pajamas," Brenda remarked, as if that fact explained everything.

"Well, I'm done here. I've given up trying to determine what might make her happy," Monroe said. "I went out of my way to reconcile, with every intention of helping her out, but I'm no idiot. She's on her own. Come on. I'll walk back to the office with you. Sorry you came along without a coat. It's cold outside, so you can use mine."

"Hell, Monroe," Brenda said. "You can be downright chivalrous when you want to. If you weren't in love with my best friend, I might want to date you."

"Love?" Monroe said. "I think you must be a true romantic, Brenda."

"Your eyes lingered."

"I'm a man, and she was in her pajamas."

"You can't fool anybody, Monroe, except maybe yourself."

Their voices faded, but the comments rang in Kim's ears like an echo. *Love?* How little Brenda knew about what had happened, and about Monroe's subsequent victory.

He had given up, thrown in the towel. Why did his proclamation send icy chills through her overheated system?

The other night, everything she dared to want had been within her grasp, yet she hadn't reached for it, needing to be strong on her own terms. Now some of those happy endings were no longer viable, and only the stuff of dreams.

She was sick to death of what-ifs and games and hypothetical problem solving. Monroe had given up without a word to her about their night together and how he felt about it, personally. He'd needed to accompany Brenda here; there was a chance he wouldn't have come on his own.

He hadn't agreed with Brenda about loving her, or mentioned anything other than wanting to help her to get the promotion she deserved.

A professional visit, then.

Not personal at all.

Nothing remotely resembling love.

All right. She'd have to make that work, and for now occupy her time elsewhere. Keep busy, and on the right path. Back to shopping. She'd indulge every other whim to its maximum potential. This would make her feel better and blur the emptiness deep inside that Chaz Monroe had temporarily filled.

Pondering how many times in the last seventy-two hours she'd arrived at the same conclusion, Kim headed for her closet to dump the pajamas. There was some serious *forget-him* therapy to do, and no time to waste.

"Who am I kidding?" she whispered, dropping to her bed with her head in her hands. "What we had felt like love to me."

It was insane. Possibly the worst idea she'd ever come up with. Nevertheless, it was what a mature grown-up would do.

Her dress was black, short, sleeveless, with a moderately cut neckline and a perfectly fitted waist. She covered it with a fur-trimmed sweater and added a string of crystal beads at her throat. Her shoes were black Louboutin knockoffs with tall, gold heels that significantly increased her height and lent her an air of confidence that came with overspending.

She sat in the cab, eyeing the big house with determination, and took a few deep breaths before emerging on a cobbled driveway bordered by a knee-high hedge. The mansion was aglow with bright golden light. Windows and doors glittered handsomely, welcomingly. Garlands of evergreen and holly swooped in perfect loops, tied with red velvet bows and dripping with colored glass balls. Rows of cars lined the driveway, as well as part of the street.

What would growing up in a house like this have been like? She hadn't thought to ask Monroe where he lived now, and it no longer mattered, anyway. Ten days had passed since he last stood in her hallway, declaring his decision to give up on helping her further. Ten miserable days. She hadn't been back to the office yet, since her projects had been completed before she'd taken a break. Time and distance away from Monroe had been necessary in order to contemplate her future.

So, here she was, at Monroe's parents' home, about to attend a Christmas party she was supposed to have helped design. It was Christmas Eve, and she was here as she'd promised Monroe she would be, before the rift with him widened. Coming here was a big step, but doable, now that she was getting used to the idea of going it alone.

She would smile at Monroe, and maybe shake hands. They'd share a laugh over how silly they both had been. She'd wish him well with the sale of the agency.

The front door of the house stood wide open, manned by a greeter in a black suit holding a silver tray of sparkling champagne flutes. Kim took a glass as she entered the expansive foyer with its warmly aged wood floors, mirrors and framed oil paintings of lush landscapes.

People of all ages were everywhere. Children raced through the foyer, and back and forth into adjoining rooms, laughing, teasing, having a good time. She envied them. Christmas was magical for children, and this party exemplified that magic to perfection.

If the exterior radiated glow and welcome, the interior of the Monroe house magnified that. Kim knew what the living room would look like before entering, and found it exactly like the rendering she'd seen. Ice sculptures towered over plates of food on center tables. Foam snow whitened windowsills. There was gilt tableware and crystal. Best of all, the largest tree she'd ever seen took up one full corner, at least ten feet of greenery loaded with decorations, twinkling lights and dangling candy canes.

Though she expected this kind of sensory wonderland, the sight stopped her. Her eyes filled, and she choked back a sob. The room was unbearably beautiful. For a holiday-starved woman only now overcoming the past, the magic seemed overwhelming.

Her hands began to tremble. Champagne sloshed from her glass. Would Monroe find her? Welcome her? Save her from all this beauty by snapping her back to reality?

A subtle movement, singled out from the comings and goings of the people around her, caught her eye. A man stood in the opposite doorway, leaning casually against the jamb. He was dressed in a tasteful black sweater and pants and wore a look of casual unconcern. Kim's heart skidded inside her rib cage. She almost spilled more of her drink.

But it wasn't Monroe who raised his glass at her. It wasn't Monroe who smiled, or Monroe's eyes that took her in. Similar in height and weight, and nearly as handsome, with the same dark hair and fair face, whoever this was pushed off the wall and headed in her direction when their gazes connected.

The lights suddenly seemed too bright, too real, too magical. In the middle of the wonderful holiday glitter she'd only began to wrap her mind around, dealing with another man who looked like Monroe, but wasn't, became too much for Kim to handle.

She should not have come. She wasn't ready.

Setting her glass on the table, she turned. Before the man could reach her, she'd reached the foyer, and with just one more look over her shoulder at the luxurious wonderland that was Monroe's life, she exited quickly, and as silently as she had arrived.

"Rory?" Chaz said, finding his brother in the foyer looking perplexed.

"You missed it, bro," Rory said, staring at the door.

"What did I miss?"

"Only the most gorgeous creature on the planet."

Chaz grinned. "There are a lot of beautiful women here tonight."

"Not like this one."

"By the way, how much champagne have you chugged? Have we run out yet?"

"I'm serious," Rory said. "She was a vision."

Chaz looked past his brother. "So, where is this goddess?"

"She left."

"The party just started," Chaz pointed out.

"That's what makes her exit so dramatic."

"Sorry you lost her so soon, bro."

"I didn't imagine her, Chaz."

"Sorry," Chaz repeated, ready to get another drink in order to catch up with Rory, and intending to drown his sorrows.

Rory's laugh was self-deprecating. "Well, I suppose there is another blonde here somewhere with an alluring hazel-eyed gaze and a body like sin. If so, I plan to find her."

Chaz experienced a slight bump in his drinking plan, but couldn't have explained why. "Hazel eyes?" he echoed.

"Yeah. Aren't we all suckers for eyes like that?"

Chaz had to ask, knowing the question to be ridiculous, but unable to beat off the strange feeling in his gut. "Did she wear a red dress?"

Rory shook his head. "A little black number that fit like a glove. But hey, this isn't all about women. Tonight's for celebrating. You've found potential buyers for the agency, I hear, and they'll wait six months to decide to move forward on a sale if you get the place running smoothly."

"Yes. I suppose that's good news."

"Suppose? Chaz, it's your first big deal. Shall we have a toast?"

That bit of odd intuition returned and clung. Chaz couldn't seem to shake it off.

"Did she have hair about to here?" He touched his shoulder. "And long legs?"

"You did see her, then?" Rory replied teasingly. "I didn't imagine her in some Christmas-related state of hopefulness?"

"Was she alone?" Chaz pressed.

"I wouldn't be pining if she'd had a guy by her side."

Chaz barely heard Rory. He was already out the front door and thinking that if it could have been McKinley…

If there was any way it might have been Kim, and she had made the effort to show up here after all…

Did that mean she was interested? Had she hoped to find him?

He didn't see her on the portico or in the yard.

Hell... Wasn't there an old fairy tale about finding a shoe on the steps that would fit only one person on the planet? Which would help to narrow things down a bit for a poor, lovesick guy tired of pretending he didn't give a fig about the woman who owned that shoe, when he cared a whole frigging lot?

When he, Chaz Monroe, cared about Kim McKinley so much, he felt empty without her?

His keys were in his pocket. His car was parked in front of the garage. Waving people out of the way, uttering quick words of greeting and something vague about an emergency, he got in, started the engine and stepped on the gas.

Seventeen

Chaz couldn't get past Sam, no matter how hard he tried.

"No, sir. Not tonight. Strict orders to let no one in, on the threat of ending my life as I know it."

Kim wouldn't answer her phone. At first Chaz thought that she might not have come home, but at last, Sam, sensing a desperate man's weakness and caught up in the holiday spirit, confirmed she was indeed up there.

"Hate to see her alone on a fine night like this," Sam said.

All Chaz thought about was seeing her. She had come to the party, showed up on his parents' doorstep, and he'd somehow missed her. Rotten luck. But she hadn't stayed long enough for him to find her. According to Rory, she'd dashed out the door. So here he was, with his heart thundering way above the norm, determined to see Kim tonight. And as he paced in front of her building, looking up, there seemed only one way to accomplish that…if he didn't get arrested first.

The fire escape.

Floor six. Several windows down ought to be hers, but it was possible he'd gotten turned around. That window virtually beamed with flashes of red and green light emulating the wattage of an alien spaceship trapped in a tunnel.

Could that be her window?

The only thing left now was to scoot over, ledge by ledge, until he reached that one. Briefly, he wondered if Santa had a fear of heights.

He slipped twice, caught himself and began to sweat, despite the chill factor. Glancing down, he swore beneath his breath and continued, placing one foot on the ledge outside where he thought he needed to go.

The light in that window was blinding, so it couldn't be hers. If it was, she'd had a major turnaround, and he was going to need sunglasses.

He got his second foot on the ledge and reached the window unscathed. Maintaining a fairly tight hold on the brick, he craned his neck and peeked around the corner.

The light came from a tree, lit up and glowing. There had to be twenty strings of lights on that tree. Tinsel dangled like silver icicles. Gold and silver baubles gleamed.

But that wasn't all.

Candles lit other surfaces, one of them on the sill not twelve inches away from where he clung. The wonderful scent of cinnamon wafted to him through the closed window.

This can't be hers.

All this?

Yet somehow he knew it was, and that if she had progressed to this degree on the serious issues, where did that leave him?

The truth hit him like a blow to the gut as he looked inside that window. He loved Kim McKinley for this.

He loved her for showing up at the party, and for that room full of lights. He loved her beautiful face, the graceful slope of her shoulders, her bare feet, berry-colored toenails, and her slightly haughty attitude when she got angry. He loved the big eyes that held the power to make a grown man, a confirmed bachelor, climb a fire escape in the middle of winter.

Come to think of it, he didn't need a tally of all the things he loved about her. There were just too many things to list.

His heart ached to be inside of that apartment with her, and to know everything else about her, down to the smallest detail—all the stuff, bad and good, sickness and health.

He put a hand to his head to make sure it was still screwed on tight, sure he'd never felt like this, or considered the *M* word before. Yet he was seeing a future with Kim McKinley that included a ring.

He grinned. Rory was going to have a heart attack.

The only thing now was to convince Kim to take him back, and to remain by his side. *Forever* seemed like a good place to start.

Though elated over this decision, Chaz did not raise a victory fist to the moon, which would have been a dangerous move for a man stuck to a ledge six floors above pavement, wearing entirely unacceptable clothes for the weather. And it was time to go before someone called the cops. He'd bribe Sam to plead on his behalf for Kim to let him in. He would take Sam with him to her front door if necessary. Just one more look in this window, then, he swore to God, he'd go.

He pressed his face close to the pane…

And nearly fell backward when Kim peered back.

Kim stepped away, stifling the urge to scream. There was a man outside her window, and she had to call the cops.

But the face looking in was familiar.

"Monroe?" she said in disbelief.

He grinned. "Just trying this fire escape out to see if it will hold Santa, and wondering why cops never go after him."

The sight of Monroe on the other side of her window made her blink slowly. "What do you want?"

"You left the party without saying hello."

"I made a mistake thinking I could handle the party."

"The mistake was to flee before I could stop you."

Kim shook her head. "Why are you out there?"

"Why did you give Sam orders to shoot me on sight?"

"I wanted to suffer alone."

He took a beat to reply to that. "Suffer?"

"Go away, Chaz."

"I have a better idea. Why don't you let me in?"

"For one thing, I haven't been able to open this window since I moved in."

He stared at her thoughtfully. "How about if I knock on your door?"

"You haven't answered my first question about what you want," Kim said. Her heart was leaping frantically. Monroe was on the fire escape. He had left the party and come here to see her. This had to mean he wanted to see her pretty badly.

When he didn't answer, she repeated the question. "What do you want, Chaz?"

He shrugged without losing his balance and said, "You. I want you. And you just called me Chaz."

And then he was gone, and Kim didn't think she could move from the spot. He hadn't given up. If this was some particularly nasty joke, and the business needed her for something…

Would he do that?

She couldn't have read his expression incorrectly—that look of longing in his eyes that probably looked exactly like her own.

She'd been halfway out of her dress, and yanked it back over her shoulders. She pressed the hair back from her face and looked at the tree and the trimmings that had set her bank account back more than the dress and shoes combined.

What would Chaz do now that he had seen how she embraced Christmas? That the tree he brought her had made her happy, despite the thought of losing him.

The call came. Her hand shook when she told Sam to let Chaz come up. She waited by the door, planning what to say first. Maybe she'd start by asking him to repeat what he said about wanting her, just to be sure he meant it.

She opened the door before he knocked, unable to wait or keep calm. Chaz stood there with his hand raised. He reached for her instead.

He held her tightly for several seconds before pushing her back through the door. The momentum carried them to her kitchen, where he paused long enough to look at her and smile.

"This isn't what you think it is," he said.

"Damn." Heat flooded Kim's face as she smiled back.

"You want it to be what you think it is?" he asked.

"Yes," she answered breathlessly.

He closed his eyes briefly. Then he kissed her, long, deep and thoroughly, with his body tight to hers. After that, he kissed her again and again, as if he had saved up longing and had to get it out.

When he drew back to allow her a breath, he said, "You have a tree."

"Yes."

"You came to the party."

"I did."

"You were looking for me?"

"Yes."

"Because you wanted to be with me? Had to be with me? Could no longer picture a life without me in it?"

"Yes. Yes. And yes."

When Chaz smiled again, his eyes lit up with emotion. She saw relief, joy and the finality of having found something he was sure he'd lost. Genuine feelings. Very personal stuff.

"What do you think of the word *love?*" he asked quietly.

"Highly overrated," she said with a voice that quavered.

"Unless it covers us?" he suggested.

"Does it cover us?"

"I believe so."

"When will you know for sure?"

"As soon as you take me to that bedroom. The one all lit up like the North Pole."

"That's sex, not love."

"To my way of thinking, the two are mutually beneficial. Am I wrong?"

She shook her head. "Isn't there some kind of law against naked bodies under a Christmas tree?"

"Oh, I don't think so. Definitely not. So let's make love, Kim, beside that tree and under the lights. Let's slow down and create a path to the future that will suit us both."

It was the defining moment, and Kim knew it. The future Chaz spoke of had to be built on trust and understanding. She must believe he would make good on those things. In return, she'd have to do the same. She'd have to believe him, and believe in a future with him.

He pressed a kiss on her forehead and another on her cheek. His hands wrapped around her, warm through her dress, as he pulled her to him possessively.

Her world spun off into blissful chaos. Goose bumps trickled down her spine. A rush of delight closed her eyes tight.

Each glorious inch his lips traveled over hers left a trail of fire, the same raging flames she'd felt before, though this time, he also ran a hand down her bare arm, to her wrist. He clasped her fingers in his and held her hand.

Something so simple. So defining and rich. Better than anything. Two promises in one. She wasn't alone. Together, they would get through this, and be better for it.

Kim's shoulders twitched. Her hips ground to his hips as she kissed him back, matching his hunger with hers and forgetting everything else but the desire to have this man inside her, and with her always.

She was going to take this chance. She was going to trust Chaz Monroe because she loved him.

She moaned into his waiting mouth. With a tight hold on her hand, he turned and led her toward the lights.

"The best Christmas ever," he said over his shoulder.

Eighteen

"Kim?" Brenda called out from her cubicle, standing up quickly. "What happened? I haven't seen you for days. I haven't heard from you."

"I didn't get fired," Kim said with a straight face.

"He left a message on your desk about wanting to see you the minute you came in."

"Yes. I have to sign a new contract."

"He convinced you?"

"He's one hell of a negotiator, Bren."

"You'll fill me in, won't you? There's something strange in your expression. Not at all like a woman having lost a battle of wills. It's going to be okay, isn't it? You're going to stay?"

Kim nodded. "I'm staying."

"I knew you could work it out," Brenda said, showing major relief.

Kim took the longest strides her tight skirt allowed, stopping in her cubicle just long enough to open a drawer and retrieve something she had stored there, before heading down the corridor to Chaz's office.

Alice didn't stop her or offer up a protest. Instead, Alice smiled, and nodded her head.

Kim didn't bother to make a pretense of knocking or waiting to be asked to come in. This was her déjà-vu moment, and she intended to experience it to the fullest. Things had changed. She had changed, and felt downright hopeful about the future.

Her heart beat thunderously, tellingly, as she opened the door. The anticipation of seeing Chaz was always like that, and had grown worse over the last few days of spending nearly every waking minute with him. She'd been wearing a smile since his daring use of her fire escape.

He wasn't at his desk. She waited, pulse soaring, body anticipating the onslaught of sensation.

She didn't have to wait long.

All of a sudden he grabbed her by the wrist and swung her around. The door closed. The lock clicked.

His warm mouth covered hers immediately, and her lips opened in a ravenous response. Warm tongues danced. His hands explored possessively, already knowing what they would find. She had lost count of the number of times they had made love lately, but the vast number was a dizzying indication of shared feelings. They had talked, too, and laughed. Together, they had banished the dark and let in the light.

His incredibly steamy kiss was indicative of his new need for her. She wanted to protest when the treacherous bastard peeled his lips from hers way too soon and began to hum a tune that turned out to be a slightly off-key rendition of "Jingle Bells."

Several seconds passed before Kim said, "See? I'm cured. And that's behind us now." Then she began to laugh. All the emotion of the past had just melted away. They had made Christmas wonderful; a time never to forget.

Chaz laughed with her as he began to raise her skirt. She loved that he never had enough of her. That's the way she liked it. She loved everything about him, too. This was love at its most exhilarating.

But she placed her hands on his hands to stop his progress.

"We won't do this kind of thing in my future office," she said.

"Luckily, it's still mine," he countered. "And I have no such rules."

"We already did it this morning."

"Are you tired of me already?"

"What if they still say I slept my way to the top?"

"I'll agree."

Kim cuffed his shoulder then ran her hand along the seam of his perfectly ironed shirt, looking for a way inside. There was something hard in his shirt pocket. A tiny box.

She glanced up at him.

"I'm pretty sure I can't show this to you yet," he said, his grin firmly in place. "Seems too pushy. Too desperate. And after all, as the owner of this agency, I have a reputation to maintain."

Kim waited this out, anticipating a punch line.

"But I have another present for you today, one that you might not have noticed."

She raised an eyebrow, nervous and excited about the contents of the box in his pocket.

"To see the other surprise, you'll have to open that door again," Chaz said. "The one you just waltzed through."

"I'm kind of content right here," she protested.

"Well, then… Have you ever made love on a desk?" he asked teasingly.

Faking a fluster, Kim smoothed her skirt down and turned to open the door. She saw right away what she had missed on her way in, and her heart again began to thump. In black paint, outlined in gold, was her name, printed on the glass. *Kim McKinley, Vice President.*

It took her a full minute to realize this was going to be true.

"I've decided to hang on to the place for a while," Chaz said. "So I'll need someone I can trust in this office while I pursue other interests."

Kim stared at the name on the door. After that, she looked to Alice, who was smiling. She looked to Chaz, also smiling. Heat began to drift over her. Way down deep in her body, in a place reserved for his touch, a drum beat started up.

Chaz Monroe was going to trust her with this promotion in a company he had decided to keep, at least for now, and hopefully long enough for her to prove herself. Waves of happiness washed over her. She squeezed her eyes shut to contain her joy.

"I won't be around much, so rumors about us won't matter," he said.

Kim didn't open her eyes. This Christmas, her wishes had come true. She had the job, and a relationship with the man beside her. That was all she needed. She could do this. Mutual trust was a beautiful thing.

"Will you say yes?" Chaz asked.

Her eyes again met his.

"About the office," he clarified, his voice dropping to a whisper that told her he meant something else entirely.

She nodded.

He smiled.

"You're an asset to the company, Kim Monroe," he said. "Come on, let's take a good look at your future desk, and see if there might be anything else you'll need to put on it."

It wasn't until he pressed her across that desk with his arms around her that Kim dropped her stranglehold on the golden plaque she'd fished from her drawer. She'd soon be able to use the plaque that announced her new position in the agency.

Vice President.

She didn't have to toss it away or wave it in his face.

Only then did she realize what he'd said. The name he had spoken. *Kim Monroe?*

He placed a finger over her lips to stop her from commenting. His eyes shone a merry, vivid blue. "Good. Great. Terrific," he said. "More on that later, and plenty of time for that conversation. Just now, I find that I can't let you waste another good, overheated breath."

The kiss, probably the hundredth like it since she had met Chaz, each of them better than the first, told her all she needed to know. He was not only going to trust her with the business, he was going to trust that she'd stay with him forever, too.

And the desk she had coveted for so long was as fitting a place as any to seal that new bargain.

"Happy New Year, my love," Chaz said in a scintillating whisper before he proceeded to make good on the meaning of the sentiment.

* * * * *